Thrice to Thine

Once & Future Book 3

Meredith R. Stoddard

Erkita Press

Fredericksburg, Virginia

Erkita Press
P.O. Box 41053
Fredericksburg, VA 22404
www.meredithstoddard.com

Publisher's Note: This is a work of fiction. Names, characters, places, and incidents are a product of the author's imagination. Locales and public names are sometimes used for atmospheric purposes. Any resemblance to actual people, living or dead, or to businesses, companies, events, institutions, or locales is completely coincidental.

Book Layout © 2014 BookDesignTemplates.com

Thrice to Thine/ Meredith R. Stoddard. -- 1st ed.
ISBN 978-0-9904333-7-8

For Eric, my careful steward

CHAPTER ONE

Every folktale no matter how ancient or fantastic it sounds, begins with a few threads of truth. That factual warp and weft hold together the cloak of legend. It becomes embroidered with symbols and metaphor, embellished with poetic license and draped around the collective shoulders of a people. It's handed down through generations and each time it's told, it changes. The fabric is worn and patched and worn again. It is altered, appropriated and obscured.

Sometimes, those threads of truth that hold it together are easily visible, brightly colored cloth that can't be missed. Sometimes they're faded and plain, hidden under patches or hard to find among the added decorations. Sometimes the cloth is worn to wisp thin threads barely clinging to each other. But without that bit of truth, the part that endures, everything else would fall away and be replaced by a new tale, a new mythology.

Like the storytellers that bring legends to us festooned with drama and romance, there are some whose art it is to find those original threads among the ruffles and lace of later generations. They peel back the layers of the storyteller's art and distill what is left. They seek the threads of truth, and in the process, they find other truths behind the choices and changes made to a legend from the first generation to theirs. As society evolves so does our perception of a legend. Our grandparents and their grandparents may find different meaning in a story than we do. What is true is not absolute. Meaning is in the mind of the beholder.

***

December 28, 1995

Sarah tapped her fingers on the handle of her suitcase as she watched each floor tick slowly by in bright red numbers. She was only going to the sixth floor, but this was possibly the longest elevator ride of her life. She had hoped that leaving Raleigh before dawn would let her sleep on the flight over, but no such luck. Nerves, her seat, and the loud talker in the row in front of her had kept her up most of the way.

Now, she practically swayed on her feet while the elevator crept higher. Finally, the six appeared with a soft ding and the door slid open on a long gray hallway dotted with closed doors. She couldn't help a twinge of disappointment. She had expected the University of Edinburgh to look more old world, but this building was 1960's modern. With a sigh, she stepped out of the elevator dragging her suitcase. As she made her way down the hall she noticed small signs next to some doors stating what offices housed. Most of them were university administration offices.

She could see one door near the end of the hall that was flung wide open. On the floor outside was a cardboard box. A sheet of white paper with 'Scots Preservation Field Team' scrawled in black marker was taped over the little plaque beside the door.

The large room behind it was in disarray. Several desks were pushed into one corner while a few chairs were shoved into another and a long table stretched against the wall next to the window. Boxes were stacked on almost every available surface and a petite dark-haired woman with her back to the door was rummaging in one of them.

Sarah cleared her throat, "Pardon me. I'm looking for Dermot Sinclair."

The woman turned around and arched an eyebrow at Sarah. She looked to be in her mid-twenties, pretty, and annoyed at having been interrupted. She rolled her eyes before walking toward a narrow hall that Sarah hadn't noticed and leaned into the hallway. *"A'Dhiarmad. Tha an bean an seo."* [Dermot, there's a woman here.]

Sarah heard Dermot's muffled voice from the office say something, but she couldn't make out the words. Her nerves jumped at the prospect of seeing him.

The woman cast Sarah a withering glance. *"Ma thogair! S'ise Aimeireaganach."* [Who cares! She's American.]

The last bit was said with a decided sneer, and Sarah wondered how jarring her accent must be to folks here. After a sound that must have been a wheeled chair running into a wall, Dermot came barreling out of the office and into the larger room his blue eyes aflame.

He made straight for Sarah. She thought for a second that he would grab her, but he caught himself abruptly a few feet away. His eyes scanned her from head to toe. His face looked thunderous. "I don't know whether to kiss ye or throttle ye."

His body was rigid with tension, but he was the best thing she'd seen in weeks. At over six feet and powerfully built he was an imposing figure. His short dark hair was mussed as if he'd been running his fingers through it, and he looked like he hadn't shaved that morning. If she hadn't known him better, she might have been intimidated. As it was she drank in the sight of him and grinned. "I know which I'd prefer."

"D'ye have any idea how worried we've been?" She could tell he was upset when his worried sounded like wuhrrit. She felt the tiniest bit of satisfaction that her stunt had gotten under his skin.

Sarah cut her eyes over to the young woman who was avidly watching their exchange. "And here I thought you'd be glad to see me."

Dermot pulled his shoulders back making an effort to calm down. "I am glad. I only wish ye would have told me ye were coming today."

"That's better," Smiling, she turned to the dark-haired woman and extended her hand. "I'm Sarah MacAlpin. I'm going to be helping with the field work."

The woman looked at Sarah's outstretched hand then at Dermot. *"Aimeireaganach? Bheil gu dearbh?"* [An American? Really?]

Dermot looked sharply at the young woman. "Kirstie, don't be rude. This American…"

Sarah stopped him before he could say more. "It's no problem," She smiled sweetly before addressing the young woman in flawless Gaelic. "I may be American, but I've spoken Gaelic all my life. I learned it from my Grandmother who emigrated before The War. I'm please to meet you, Kirstie."

The other woman's face turned crimson and she grunted before turning back to the box that she had been digging in.

Dermot eyed her back and Sarah had a feeling Kirstie would be getting a little talk about teamwork and professionalism in the near future. He looked back at Sarah and held out an arm indicating the direction of the interior hallway.

Sarah walked ahead of him and found her way to the first door on the right. She glanced over her shoulder in question and he nodded. The tiny office could barely fit a desk and two chairs. Dermot came in behind her.

As soon as the door was closed he turned her around and pulled her into a rib cracking bear hug. Sarah buried her face in his sweater and inhaled filling her lungs with the scent of wool and soap and him. She felt a small easing of the tension she'd been carrying around for the last three weeks.

"I thought ye'd run away." He whispered into her hair without loosening his grip.

She'd thought about it many times, wondered if she'd have made it, if she'd have been successful where her mother had failed. "And leave you here to have to explain why," She pressed her cheek to his chest not caring that the wool was scratchy. "Would I do that to you?"

***

She tore his heart out almost daily without even trying. Who knew what she would do if she set out to hurt him? He'd been holding his breath since getting the call from Fleming that Sarah hadn't been in her apartment this morning. Now, with the solid shape of her in his arms and her curls tickling his nose, he could breathe again.

He forced himself to release her and moved around his desk putting the barrier between them before he did more than hug her. She stood in the same spot as if she was waiting for him to come back and put his arms around her again. When he didn't she sat in the other chair. Her eyes burned with that quiet, determination that he'd seen before. She may be here, but she had her own agenda and Dermot was sure it probably ran contrary to his.

"Ye're a week early."

"Well, there wasn't much to stay for. I packed everything up and Amy needed to pick up her things. I thought I would get out of the way before she got back." He didn't miss the note of sadness at the mention of Sarah's friend and roommate.

"How is Amy?"

She took several seconds to answer, her eyes drifting down to examine a scuff on the toe of her brown clog. "Probably no more interested in talking to me than she was the last time you saw her. There are a lot of different emotions going on there. I think she understands intellectually that Ryan was playing her, but part of her still blames me."

"That's ballocks." He hated that there was a rift between the two girls. They'd been like sisters when he met them.

"Like I said, a lot of emotions. Besides she doesn't have all the background information that we do. She just thinks a psycho pretended to be her boyfriend to get close to me, so he could kill me." A ghost of a smile floated across her face. "I can cut her some slack, but that doesn't mean that I'm going to hang around there feeling guilty and awkward while she works it all out. I'd rather get a head start here."

"And here ye are." He watched her carefully as he asked the next question. "What exactly does that mean?"

She lifted her eyes to his. They were again full of the same tenacity as when she'd told him how she would get over being held hostage by her roommate's boyfriend only three weeks ago. "It means that I have a dissertation to finish and that's what I'm going to do."

"And James?"

The scuff on her shoe became suddenly fascinating again. "James is a big boy. And no matter how much his family has spoiled him, at some point he's going to have to learn that he doesn't get everything he wants."

If anyone could challenge James Stuart, it would be Sarah. Dermot hoped that there would be something left of her after she tried.

***

"Now this is more like it." Sarah said as she stared up at the stone façade of the row house that Dermot had led her to. A couple of blocks from the university it had all the old-world charm that Sarah had expected. Four stories of buff colored stone with broad bay windows and an ornate brick chimney. "This'll do."

"Hmm?" Dermot came up behind her having insisted on pulling her bag for her. She jerked her head toward the building. "Oh, aye. No one fancies those university buildings."

"Which one is yours?" She asked without taking her eyes off the building.

"First floor. You're on the second, and I believe that when he gets back to town, Fleming is taking the third."

"Wow. Are all my neighbors James's guard dogs?" So much for privacy.

He gave her a warning look. "No, and ye'd do well to remember that we're here for your protection. There's no telling what kind of hell Fleming is going to catch for losing track of ye."

"Shit!" She winced.

"Didna think about that, did ye? And there's naught ye can do to help him without letting James know that ye knew the real reason he was there, which would open a whole other sack of cats."

Sarah let out a slow breath. Suddenly her plan to slip away and show up here early didn't seem like such a good idea. "What do you think James will do?"

"It's not James he has to worry about, it's Walter Stuart, and Mark Shaw, the head of security."

Sarah felt a little chill creep up her spine at the thought of James Stuart's uncle and chief adviser. "I didn't mean for anything to happen to Fleming. Now I feel awful."

"Don't worry. Fleming can handle it. But don't be surprised if he doesna feel so neighborly when he gets here." He rubbed a hand across her shoulders as if he could brush off the guilt that was now weighing them down. "Come on. Won't do us any good standing out here fretting."

He unlocked the weather worn but sturdy front door. It must have been solid hardwood. When Sarah caught up to him and tried to hold the door as he pulled her bag inside she had to lean on it with all her weight. As she followed Dermot toward the stairs the great door slammed back into its frame with a bang that made her jump.

The stairs creaked enough to show their age as they made their way up. Otherwise the hall appeared to be well kept. The plaster was clean and bright, not crumbling. The carpet runner on the stairs was only slightly worn. Sarah admired the banister as they climbed. At least a century's worth of hands running up and down had polished it to a shine and the wood felt smooth as silk under her fingers.

She was happy to see that the door to her apartment wasn't nearly as imposing as the front door. Still, like any good city apartment it sported two locks, a chain and a peep hole. Dermot unlocked it and ushered her into the main room. The bay window let in plenty of light and gave the room an open feel. The furniture was comfortable looking in neutral colors. Sarah made a mental note that she was going to have to get some colorful pillows or throws to spice the room up.

Dermot wordlessly slid her backpack from her shoulders and carried both bags back to the bedroom. Sarah glanced around to find an open kitchen separated from the main room by a small island. Past the kitchen ran the hall where Dermot had disappeared. Sarah followed slowly checking a utility closet and bathroom as she went.

She found him in the bedroom. He had left her backpack on a chair and was hoisting her giant suitcase onto the bed. Sarah wandered past Dermot and the bed to the window that overlooked the courtyard garden behind the house. There were a couple of small trees and some potted plants around a brick patio. Sarah thought it must be heaven in the morning with a hot cup of coffee and a Scottish mist descending.

"What d'ye reckon?" he asked behind her.

Sarah looked over her shoulder, smiling. "I think it's perfect."

He smiled. She wasn't sure how long they stood there smiling at each other, content breathing the same air and thinking of good things, simple things they could do for each other like making coffee and carrying bags.

"Right, then." Dermot gave his head a shake breaking the spell. "I'll leave ye to yer unpacking."

He started for the door and Sarah had to follow quickly to see him out. "Thanks."

"It's no bother. I'll see ye later then." And he was gone before she could say anything more. Leaving Sarah standing at the door of her empty apartment listening for the creak of the stairs under him.

An hour later Sarah was in the little kitchen foraging for food. The sun had gone down and the television was on. She found the local news incredibly interesting but realized that the last time she'd eaten she had been somewhere over the Atlantic.

She opened the strangely thin and tall refrigerator for maybe the third time, but it was still empty. There wasn't so much as a tea bag in the small pantry either. She was on the point of rummaging in her backpack for a probably smashed up granola bar, when there was a knock at the door.

She checked the peep hole before opening the door. Dermot stood there with a brown take out bag. "I've got curry and beer."

Sarah followed him to the kitchen and reached for the bag. She immediately began unpacking and opening containers. Sarah drew in a long breath filled with spices and felt instantly better without having to take a bite. "You read my mind."

He chuckled as he searched the cabinets for plates. "More like I heard yer stomach growling all the way downstairs."

"Oh, very funny. I know how you eat. If you were this hungry you'd be gnawing on the furniture by now."

"No," he handed her the plates and checked the drawers for silverware. "I'd have walked down the stairs and asked my friend if he had any food."

Sarah waved a dismissive hand as she unwrapped foil from a steaming hot serving of naan. "Too many steps. I'm exhausted."

She tore off a piece of the hot buttery bread and popped it in her mouth chewing with relish. "I feel like I haven't eaten in a month."

Dermot reached around her with a large spoon and began filling a plate with different dishes. He topped it with a piece of naan and handed it to Sarah. "Grab a beer and go sit. I'll be there in a tic."

He joined her on the couch and they quietly ate their dinner watching television. Sarah told him about the loud talker on the plane. He told her about getting the office established for the research team. They laughed and talked with an ease that Sarah relished. He always made her feel safe. Even when she had pushed him away and suspected him of stalking her, his physical presence had always been comforting. Tonight, it also gave her hope.

No matter how he denied it, Sarah knew that everything was possible as long as he was with her. When she'd finished she laid her plate on the coffee table. "Did you really think I had run away?"

He leaned back on the couch, one arm resting on the back cushions. He looked at his beer in his hand, at a worn spot on the knee of his jeans, at the wall behind her before he finally met her eyes. "A verra small part of me wishes that ye had."

She nodded. "I don't think I would have gotten very far."

"It's not going to be easy, Sarah. I told ye, they're verra persuasive."

She leaned back on the couch and gave him an arch look. "So am I."

She thought she felt his fingers tangling in the ends of her curls. "Ye know that would be putting us both in danger."

She shifted to lay down on the couch resting her head on his lap and turned her attention back to the TV. "I thought I was already in danger."

***

He couldn't argue with that. But then he could barely think with her so close. He waited until her breathing evened out and he could tell she was asleep before he laid his hand on her hair feeling the soft honey-colored curls slip between his fingers and tickle the back of his hand. He gently brushed her hair back revealing the shell of her ear. With soft fingers he traced the line of her neck to where it met her shoulder remembering the mewling sound she made when he bit her just there.

God, he'd missed her; the sight of her, the energy that sparked between them with nothing more than a look. He tried every day to forget the taste of her, the weight of her in his hands, that slick glide of his skin against hers.

Had it only been three weeks since they'd made love, three weeks since he'd broken her heart? He knew what he'd taken from her that day when he told her that they couldn't be together. But here she was, sleeping with her head resting on his thigh. He'd finally given her a real reason not to trust him, to hate him, but she didn't.

Keeping his hands from her was going to be near impossible, and he knew she meant to be more than he could resist. He'd have to, though. Too much depended on it.

He used his free leg to push the coffee table away to make room. He slid his hand under her head and held it in place as he slid out from under her. Then he slid his arm down around her shoulders and the other under her knees. He carried her down the hall and laid her on the bed. She shifted and rolled again onto her side sliding a hand under the pillow. He thought she might wake, but she settled down and slept on.

Dermot found a chair against the wall beside the wardrobe and sat watching her sleep. He wondered if she'd had any problems sleeping or sleep walking over these past weeks. Sitting there watching her reminded him of her summary of a steward's role when he'd explained it. *Like a husband without the benefits.* He settled himself more comfortably.

***

...white and pink swirled around in a bright kaleidoscope. And Sarah heard her mother cooing in her ear.

...They won't have you. Keep yourself...

Mama's arms cradled her as she floated in the warm water.

...Not my baby...loved your father...

...Mama, what if it's a trap...

...won't do it to you...I'll protect...

"Stay with me, Mama." she said in her dream.

"I'm always here."

Sarah's eyes popped open, she sat up startled by the unfamiliar room. It was a minute before she remembered where she was. But a soft snoring sound beside the bed caught her attention. Dermot was sound asleep in the chair with his head leaning on one arm and legs stretched out in front of him. Her heart swelled. She'd made it. She had missed him so much. As the fog of sleep lifted she remembered falling asleep on the couch with her head resting on his lap. He must have carried her to bed.

Jetlag must have knocked her for a loop, which explained why she'd had the bathtub dream. They had been happening less often over the last few weeks. Maybe reading Molly's journal and getting a better understanding of her mother's circumstances had made Molly less terrifying. Maybe the dreams had been a subconscious warning about the danger that had been stalking her, or a symptom of Sarah's own anxiety. Either way, something was different. The dreams didn't scare her the way they used to. What scared her now was the possibility of the same thing happening to her. To prevent that, she needed to understand more about what went wrong with Molly's time in Scotland. She could start with finding *Làrachd an Fhamhair*, which should lead her to its people. Sarah glanced over at Dermot where he slept in the chair. His chest moved easily, and his breathing was steady. She would rather not tell anyone about her gift especially anyone who might work for the Stuarts, and as much as she loved him, Dermot did still technically work for them.

Assynt was on the northwest coast a couple hundred miles away. She wasn't even sure her gift worked that far. She had never used it to find something that was more than a few miles away. But it was worth a try. As long as Dermot was asleep. She wasn't sure what he would see if he woke up while she was *casting out* as Molly called it. With one more glance at his sleeping form, Sarah settled down on her back and looked up at the ceiling. After a couple of deep breaths, she closed her eyes.

She focused on her breath and with each exhale felt herself get lighter. Eventually, she slowly lifted off the bed. She looked down to see her body lying there serenely. Another exhale and she could see the roof of their building, then the street and the neighborhood around their house. She continued expanding out until she could see the lights of the city and the streets below her like veins on the back of a hand. Focusing on the name *Làrachd an Fhamhair* she continued her ascent until she was soaring in the clouds.

Minutes later she descended to find herself surrounded by the dark outlines of mountains against the sky. She looked to the ground, but there was nothing but grass and scrub and the occasional pool or stream. She lifted her gaze, renewing her focus on the village hoping to see something. But there was no sign of it. Her heart sank. She was still learning this gift. Maybe there was something she was doing wrong. Sarah focused on her breathing, which had quickened as her search proved fruitless. In a few minutes she was back in her room staring at the ceiling.

She would have to try again in the daylight or try again thinking of a person rather than a place where she'd never actually been. But who would she think of? She'd never met those people, and apart from her desire for answers that only they could give, she wasn't sure she wanted to meet them. No doubt they had very different opinions about what had happened than Molly did. If Duff hadn't corroborated parts of

Molly's story, Sarah might still doubt all of it. A secret tribe of people that lived in a secret village that wasn't on any maps and practiced some ancient rites sounded like a fairy tale.

A snort to her left pulled her attention back to Dermot who was shifting positions in his chair. He was still asleep and having trouble getting settled. Sarah slid out of bed quietly, and started to pull him up, slipping an arm under his. "Come on. That chair is not doing your back any good."

He grumbled something incoherent, but she thought she heard 'Mum'. He let her half guide, half drag him to the foot of the bed before falling onto it. He crawled his way to the pillow and sank back into sound sleep. Sarah laid down beside him resting a hand on his back before sliding into sleep herself.

CHAPTER TWO

"It's a good thing I'm not so addicted to American food." Sarah said lightly as they strolled back from the grocery store. She had enjoyed the warmly domestic feel of shopping with Dermot. It had also been very educational. You could learn a lot about a place by seeing what people ate. Having grown up without large grocery stores, she didn't think the lack of common American manufactured foods would be a difficult adjustment. "Still, I have a feeling the coffee situation might become a problem."

"You yanks drink too much of the stuff anyway." He winked at her knowing how much the term *yank* grated on her nerves.

She was about to give him what for until she saw what was in front of their building. Parked there, in complete disregard for the no parking sign was a sleek black limousine. Sarah stopped in her tracks. "Is that who I think it is?"

Dermot made a throaty sound somewhere between a groan and a growl. "Very likely."

By unspoken agreement their steps slowed. She had known that they couldn't keep to themselves forever, but she had hoped to be able to pretend at least for a little while longer. "I suppose there's no avoiding him."

The limousine door opened, and James Stuart stepped onto the curb. Whatever her feelings about his designs on her, Sarah had to admit that he was a sight to behold. In the gray

December afternoon, he seemed to bring his own sunlight. To call James handsome would be a gross understatement. He was tall and straight with dark brown hair, and piercing blue eyes, and a jaw that could cut glass. He had the kind of dazzling good looks that distracted people in mid-sentence. On top of that he had more money than Sarah could even imagine. His family's fortune in oil and countless other investments gave him the easy confidence of a man who was never denied anything.

He turned, buttoning the jacket of his perfectly tailored suit with the practiced motion of a man who wore such things daily. When his eyes met Sarah's, he broke into a wide grin. It was like a magnet drawing her closer whether she liked it or not.

Dermot wordlessly took the grocery bags from her loose fingers.

"Sarah, you look lovely as ever." James's smooth patrician accented voice washed over her as he bent to kiss her cheek. "Scotland seems to agree with you."

The blood rushed into Sarah's almost frozen cheeks. She couldn't help being charmed by him. He was everything normal little girls were taught to dream about. "James. It seems word gets around fast."

For half a second, he looked flummoxed, but then recovered with his usual smoothness. "Well, Dermot told me you had arrived."

"Really," She glanced over at Dermot who stood by the door with the groceries shifting awkwardly from foot to foot and trying not to look at them. "I had no idea you two were so close."

"Oh, we've been great friends since we were children." James said smoothly following her gaze. He turned back toward the car and nodded smoothly at his driver before saying. "I've brought you a little housewarming gift. Shall we go inside?"

"Sure." Sarah turned to the house to find Dermot holding the heavy door open with a foot as he waited for them. Sarah began walking and fumbling in her purse for the key to her flat. When she reached the door, she went to take her bags from Dermot, but he stopped her with a silent shake of his head. She gave him a quick confused look but walked on up the stairs with James at her elbow.

As they approached her door, James gently covered her hand with his and slid the key from her fingers. He fit the key in the lock and opened the door, holding it for her. Sarah noted that Dermot frequently did the same thing, but she could never get used to those kinds of manners. Boys in the holler didn't open doors for girls, at least not for poor girls with crazy mamas, and neither did college guys in largely feminist Chapel Hill. She had always written Dermot's manners off as a product of his military service. She supposed James's were the result of some Swiss boarding school.

She walked into the flat and into the kitchen as James propped the door open. He strolled in, looking around him with a proprietary air. Sarah watched as he frowned contemplatively at the furnishings and fixtures.

"I love it." Sarah chatted a little nervously. "I've never really lived by myself before. It's a little drab now, but I mean to look in second-hand shops for some colorful pillows and things. I'll have it looking like a home in no time."

He lifted a brow at the bay windows with their sheer white curtains. "You'll probably want some heavier drapes as well."

She shook her head. "I actually like those drapes. They let in a lot of natural light, well as much as you can get in Scotland in December. I was thinking about getting some plants."

"What about privacy? People from the street can see right in." He looked mildly alarmed at the idea.

Sarah remembered James's problems with paparazzi and thought keeping the sheer curtains might be the best thing to keep James from invading her flat at every opportunity. She gave him an understanding smile. "Some of us don't have to worry about that quite so much. I'm really not that interesting."

He looked as if he might argue the point, but then his driver appeared in the doorway. He was an enormous man with blunt features and jagged scar through one eyebrow. In one arm he held a large gift-wrapped box and a beribboned gift basket gripped in his other meaty fist.

"On the island, Liam." James indicated the kitchen island with a wave of his hand and the bodyguard slid the box onto it and placed the basket behind it before disappearing out the door. James walked over to stand next to Sarah. He gave her that warm open smile and nodded at the box. "I thought you might appreciate this addition to your kitchen."

Sarah felt a little shy looking at the box with its large bright bow and paisley printed paper with gold accents. The paper alone was finer than most things she owned. She wasn't used to extravagant gifts, but that was James's M.O. For her birthday a couple of months ago he had sent her what her roommate had referred to as "half a flower shop".

She slid the ribbon off and tilted the box up to slice a finger nail through the tape. Not wanting to tear the paper she slowly lifted it off to reveal the nicest coffee maker she'd seen outside of a coffee shop. She sighed in awe. "Oh James, how thoughtful."

He beamed at her, obviously pleased with her reaction. "I thought you might like it."

"Now, I just need to find some coffee to brew in it."

"I've thought of that as well." James said pulling forward the basket that was behind the box.

Sarah untied the bow and pushed down the red plastic wrapping to find a pair of mugs, tins of cookies, and coffee from all over the world. Her eyes lit up as she scanned the variety. "Kona, Blue Mountain, Kenya. Goodness, James, I would have been happy with anything I found in the grocery store."

He made a face of mock horror. "Heaven forbid!"

Sarah laughed and again found herself charmed. She rose up on her toes to kiss his cheek. James placed a hand on her hip holding her in her spot. She retreated a little by dropping to her flat feet. His eyes fastened on her lips, and Sarah's nerves jumped.

"Ahem."

James stepped back, and her eyes darted to the door where Dermot was standing with her groceries looking grim.

***

So, it was beginning already, then. He could see his cousin's irritation at being interrupted. *Too bad, mate.* He thought. *You're not going to rush her like that. She's worth waiting for.* Sarah for her part wore a look of blended relief and guilt that stirred his temper and his jealousy. How on earth would he get through this?

"Look what James brought me. Wasn't that thoughtful?" Sarah asked too brightly.

"Aye. Verra thoughtful." Dermot glanced up and down at James's suit. "Headed back to the office today?"

James looked puzzled before saying. "Oh. Yes."

"Well, dinna let us keep ye." He stepped into the kitchen and maneuvered himself between James and Sarah and placed the groceries on the counter. He knew it was a bold move to get in James's way, but he didn't really care at the moment. The man couldn't swoop in and start romancing her when she'd already told him she wasn't interested. Never mind that Dermot wasn't ready to witness said romancing.

James for his part glared hard at Dermot before turning his eyes back to Sarah. "I do need to go, but I was wondering if you have plans tomorrow night."

She shook her head smiling. "I haven't been here long enough to make any."

"I was hoping that the two of you would come to the Torchlight Procession with me. It's a breathtaking event. I really think you'd enjoy it."

Sarah glanced at Dermot her eyes alight. "Sounds fun. I'd love to. Dermot?"

Dermot shrugged. "Yeah, alright."

They stood there in awkward silence for what felt like ages. James looked at Sarah as if he had something more to say. Dermot looked at James as if daring him to say the wrong thing, and Sarah glanced back and forth between the two of them as if one of them might explode at any moment.

James finally broke the silence. "I really should go."

Sarah stepped toward the door to walk him out. "Thank you again. It really is a thoughtful gift. I'll get a lot of use out of that."

At the door James turned smiling and bent to kiss her cheek. "I'm glad you like it. I'll see you tomorrow night." He shot a hard look at Dermot. "Dermot, a word?"

"Right." To Sarah, "Dinna forget to lock the door." He followed James out. They stopped at the bottom of the stairs and listened for the click of the lock on her door.

James waited a few more seconds before giving Dermot's arm an irritated slap. "What was that? Why did you interrupt us?"

Dermot took a deep breath and tried for patience. "Ye canna start pushing her as soon as her feet hit the ground. She's not even used to the time change yet and here ye are trying to make her forget her principles. She's already told ye she's worried about appearances. Ye've got to go slow about it if ye want her to forget that."

James rolled his eyes. "I think I know how to get a girl, cousin."

"Oh, aye. Ye wave your wallet in the air and they come running." Dermot stepped into James's space. "*She's* not like that."

James arched an eyebrow in warning. "And you're an expert on what she's like?"

Dermot didn't back away. "I know her well enough to know that extravagant gifts make her uncomfortable. I also know that she cares a lot about her career. She's not likely to change course for a man based on a few gifts and kisses."

He couldn't tell if he was reaching James, or merely pissing him off. The man stood there eyeing him. Suddenly Dermot felt like they were a couple of rams about to lock horns. Finally, James relaxed enough to grind out. "What do you recommend, then?"

This was the moment that Dermot had been dreading since the first time he'd met her. He was going to have to help James win Sarah, his Sarah. "For one thing, be yourself, not the executive, playboy, tabloid you, but really be James Stuart. None of the usual ways of getting a lass's attention will work for her. Ye have to be genuine and as honest about yerself as ye can."

James huffed. "That's a lot easier said than done. It's hard to show someone the real you when the tabloid version of you is everywhere."

"Trust her. She's perceptive enough to see through that. You need to show her what's real. She can smell a load of ballocks a mile away and it only makes her angry."

"Right. I'll try." He looked out the front window and gave his driver a nod. "I've got to go. Bring her to the start of the parade route tomorrow night. I'll meet you there."

"Aren't you doing some official thing?"

"That's not until the end." He reached for the doorknob and nodded to Dermot. "I'll see you then." He opened the door and strode out to the car in the fewest possible steps. In less than three seconds he was in the car with the door closed. If any photographers had followed him, they would hardly have had time to get a picture.

***

He didn't go back upstairs. He really ought to thank James for the reminder that she wasn't his. Who would have thought that doing the shopping would have been so romantic? Her eyes lit up as soon as she walked into the store. She'd spent half their time marveling at how different and yet the same the selection was. She greeted each new discovery with wonder and curiosity and Dermot found it intoxicating.

Their walk home had been so easy and relaxed that he found himself imagining what it would be like to go home with her every day. They'd unload their groceries and set about making tea. Sarah would sing and dance through the kitchen as he'd seen her do in her kitchen in Chapel Hill. He'd be right there beside her. He'd maybe even sing along. When the food was ready, they'd sit down at her little table each with a book or academic journal and quietly enjoy their tea. He could picture Sarah giving him a saucy look over the top of her book before stretching her foot across the space between them to rub up against his calf. He would try to ignore her because he had work to get back to, but he could never resist her. In his daydream, he didn't have to.

Then there was James in his limousine with his bloody coffee maker. It was like having a bucket of ice cold water or in this case coffee dumped on his head. She wasn't his, and while his daydream could easily happen, he couldn't give in to that kind of temptation not even for a minute.

Sometime later, there was a knock on his door. He trudged over to open it, knowing it was her. Her green eyes were full of uncertainty. "Want some dinner?"

Dinner and more. "No, thanks. I've got some work to do before the meeting tomorrow."

"I know, boss. But I made too much food as usual and I'd hate to see it go to waste." She gave him her flirtiest smile.

He tried to smile back and must have failed miserably.

She let her shoulders sag as she stepped into his flat and closed the door behind her. "Is this about James?"

"No," He drew the word out trying not to sound impatient. He walked to his work bag and reached in for his agenda for tomorrow's meeting. "It's about our first team meeting tomorrow, and me needing to be prepared."

"You still need to eat." She walked around in front of him.

"And I will, but not now." He gave her arm a squeeze before returning to shuffling his papers for the meeting.

Sarah would not be ignored. She didn't move, didn't back up. He waited through several heartbeats for her to move or speak. Her voice was quiet when she finally said, "You know I don't want him."

He closed his eyes. "I know neither of us can avoid him."

"There is a difference between needing his financial support for the research project and falling in line with all of his other plans." She bent lower to catch his eye. "You know his money doesn't matter to me, right? Not that way."

He nodded, afraid to look at her. Hadn't he just been telling James the same thing. "Aye. I know."

She laid her hand on his cheek. He couldn't avoid her eyes anymore, but he feared what she might do if she saw the naked longing in his. Her voice grew even softer and she leaned in close. "It would be so good. I know you think about it." Her lips were so close to his that he could feel her breath, "Fall with me."

Her lips grazed his and he fought every impulse to lean in and take her mouth. In the space of a breath, his mind calculated the centimeters between them, the steps to his bedroom, the number of seconds it would take for them both to be naked, and the exact cost of such a mistake.

He put his hand on her shoulder and gently pushed her away. His eyes were soft, but his voice was firm. "No."

She searched his eyes. He thought she might feel hurt or angry, but she didn't seem bothered at all. She leaned into his hand that was still on her shoulder.

"Alright." She said, but he could tell it was only a tactical retreat.

She turned and walked out closing the door behind her with a soft click. He closed his eyes again and spent a few moments trying to relax, willing his body to let go of the tension. When he thought he had himself under control he turned his attention to the papers he'd been shuffling to avoid her and began going over his meeting agenda.

He'd been sitting at the table for a few minutes when there was another knock on the door. He sat there in silence wondering if he could resist her a second time. The memory of her breath on his lips paralyzed him. There was no further sound from the other side of the door, but in his mind, he could feel her whisper, "Fall with me".

He leapt out of his chair and went for the door. Wrenching it open, he was prepared to drag her inside and finish what she had started. But the hallway was empty. He leaned out looking up and down, but there was no sign of Sarah. Then he looked down. On the floor in front of his door was a tray with a plate of grilled chicken, steamed vegetables and roasted potatoes and a cup of tea.

CHAPTER THREE

Sarah was glad that she had Dermot to lead her around Edinburgh, because she had no doubt that she'd never have made it anywhere without him. That wasn't because it was a difficult city to navigate, but because every time she left her flat she found herself gawking at this old building, or that restaurant she wanted to try, or a busker doing something amazing. A building at home was old when it had been standing for a hundred years. Here, that was practically new. And while Chapel Hill was fairly cosmopolitan, it had nothing on Edinburgh. There was every kind of culture food and art on display, and she was ready to soak it all up.

She had no idea where Dermot had taken her for lunch, or what type of food it had been other than delicious. They had been working all morning at the research team's office putting furniture to rights, assigning desks, and organizing equipment and supplies. Aside from the utterly drab environment of the white walled office, her mood had been dampened by having to endure the company of Kirstie Robinson. Sarah was sure that Kirstie was probably a nice person under normal circumstances, but she made it plain at every opportunity that Sarah was an interloper, a yank, and a nuisance.

When Dermot called lunch, Sarah jumped at the chance to get out of the confines of the office. She felt a little bad about how relieved she was when Kirstie declined to join them. It was obvious that the girl needed some kindness and maybe some help loosening up.

The restaurant had been small and dimly lit, between two other small shops on West Nicholson Street. The owner had been friendly and boisterous suggesting dishes most of which Sarah had never tried before. Now, as they made their way back to the office with the spicy aroma of the restaurant still clinging to them, Sarah felt nothing but excitement. She'd always dreamed of coming to Scotland. The reality of being there with him was beyond anything she had imagined. She glanced up at Dermot as he was walking beside her. The sun was behind him and burst in rays around his head. Suddenly, Sarah couldn't hear the bustling noise of the street and the traffic behind him blurred. She'd change his mind. She had to.

He glanced down at her and away again quickly, clearing his throat. "Are ye cold?"

"Not really," She smiled. "Still getting used to Scottish weather."

He made a throaty noise and they continued walking.

Around the corner, Sarah noticed a panhandler sitting on the cold sidewalk. He sat cross-legged close to the wall. He had wrapped his legs with a worn and filthy blanket. The edges of a folded newspaper peeked out from underneath him. His coat was also filthy and torn at the shoulder with batting spilling out in a little cloud of fluff. He wore a threadbare stocking cap that Sarah didn't think could be offering nearly enough warmth for the weather and several strands of matted gray hair trailed across his shoulders from under it. His salt and pepper beard was straggly, and his eyes stared vacantly across the street toward the campus.

As beautiful and exciting as Edinburgh was, it was still a big city. There would always be those who needed help. She was struck by the difference between the rural poverty that she had seen in the holler, and the urban poverty of a modern city. They had been poor, but at least they had been able to grow their own food. At least they'd had a home. Sarah fingered the change in her pocket where she had stuffed the few pounds she'd gotten after paying for lunch.

When she reached where he sat, Sarah knelt in front of him and put the money in the rusty can at his feet.

He turned his eyes her way giving her a gap-toothed smile. She gave his shoulder a friendly squeeze and stood. She was a couple of steps away when she heard the cracked, old voice whisper, *"Mòran taing, a'bhana-phrionnsa."* [Thank you very much, princess.]

Sarah stopped dead, and suddenly felt the mid-winter cold surge in her veins. The last man who called her princess had been holding a gun to her head. She turned back, but the man was gone. Sarah stepped back to where he'd been. There was no sign that he'd been there, not even a rust stain on the concrete where his filthy can had been. Sarah checked her pocket for the money, wondering if she had hallucinated the whole thing, but the money wasn't there, and it wasn't on the sidewalk.

She was about to go back around the corner to see if he had run that way when Dermot's voice cut through her confusion. He had walked on, not noticing that she had stopped. "Sarah? Where did you go?"

"Sorry." She said when he reached her. "I stopped to give the man some money."

"What man?" His forehead wrinkled in concern.

Sarah glanced up and down the street again hoping to see him. "The panhandler. He was right here. I gave him a few pounds and then he disappeared."

"I didn't see a man." He shook his head.

"You walked right by him. He was right here." She hoped she didn't sound too crazy.

"Alright. I wasna really looking." He took her elbow and leaned down to admonish her softly. "But you shouldna be stopping for people like that. I know you want to be kind, but anybody like that could be the next Ryan Cumberland in disguise."

"That's just it!" She hated the frightened tone in her voice. "He called me princess."

Dermot grabbed her wrist and scanned the street around them. "What was he wearing?"

"He was filthy. All his clothes were grimy. He had on a..." She thought, trying to remember something distinct through the dirt. "...A black stocking cap, grey beard...straggly gray hair."

Dermot scanned the crowd on either side of the street. Then walked to the corner to look back at the way they had come. He hadn't let go of Sarah's wrist and dragged her around the corner a few yards, scanning side to side. Sarah looked too, but there were no alleys or shops that he could have ducked into fast enough to completely disappear the way he had. "He was here, Dermot. I swear."

"Aye, well. We won't find him now. But ye'll let me know if you see him again. And do us both a favor and hold off on the in-person donations, yeah?"

She sighed, hating that she had to be afraid of showing a little kindness. "Yeah."

***

The lingering effects of her strange encounter on the street were soon replaced by the nervous tension of first impressions when they arrived at the team office. The dour mood of the morning had been replaced by the buzz of activity. A wiry young man with long blond hair pulled into a ponytail was setting up a camera in the corner where they had set up a long folding table to serve as a conference area. He was nervously giving instructions to a lovely red-haired woman. Kirstie was busying herself shuffling copies of information that Dermot had printed to handout. A tall thin man with wavy blue-black hair and warm brown skin was unpacking notebooks and setting up his desk.

Dermot went to discuss the camera setup with ponytail guy. Sarah moved to her desk which was in the far corner next to the one where the black-haired man was unpacking his things. On closer inspection he appeared to be Indian or Pakistani. When Sarah set her bag down he looked up and gave her a broad smile and his dark brown eyes lit with warmth. Sarah smiled back and felt her nervousness melt away. Somehow this man, without even uttering a word soothed her usual awkwardness. It was an odd sensation for someone as cautious as Sarah to feel an instant urge to trust someone. For his part the man merely nodded and went back to his unpacking.

Sarah pulled her planner and a notebook from her backpack and placed them in front of a chair in the middle of the conference table. She considered helping Kirstie with the handouts but decided that the woman would only see the offer as an intrusion. So, she offered her help to Dermot.

"Would ye fetch my agenda. It's on my desk." He said over his shoulder as he helped Ponytail find the right camera angle.

"Sure." Sarah went down the narrow hallway to Dermot's office. She found the agenda on his desk. She noticed a couple of things that she hadn't noticed before. For one, their illustrious team leader had a computer of his own. And right next to his computer was a framed photo. It was a beautiful woman sitting at a table next to a window in what appeared to be a library. Soft sunlight glinted off her strawberry blond hair. A book was open on the table in front of her and she looked as though she'd been interrupted while reading. Her blue eyes smiled at the camera with such love that it gave Sarah a hollow, homesick feeling. The colors looked slightly washed out like it was from the seventies. Sarah knew it must be Dermot's mother.

Her study of the photo was interrupted when she heard Dermot call the meeting to order from the other room. She grabbed his meeting agenda and planner and left the office. When she came back to the conference table she noticed that her own planner and notebook had been moved toward the head of the table to Dermot's right. She gave him his things and sat down only to find herself across from Kirstie who was staring daggers at her. Dermot was really going to have to have a talk with her about professionalism.

"It looks like we're all here, so let's get started." Dermot was standing at the head of the table appearing authoritative and only slightly uncomfortable about it. "I've spoken with all of you at some point already, but many of you don't know each other, so let's start by introducing ourselves and telling what you are hoping to get out of the project." He looked to his left. "We'll start with you, Kirstie."

The smile Kirstie gave him was so sweet it made Sarah's teeth hurt. Then she turned that smile on Sarah like a challenge. "I'm Kirstie Robinson. I'm from Dumfries, and my focus is on handcrafts like knitting, weaving, carving, and the like. I hope to create a geographic catalog of handcrafts of the Highlands."

Next to Kirstie was the red-haired young woman whose peaches and cream skin was flawless with a dusting of freckles across the bridge of her nose and cheeks. She had striking green eyes that showed a sharp intelligence. "My name is Isla Reid. I'm from Fort William. I guess I'm the resident music expert. I play fiddle, tin whistle, and bodhran among other things. I'll be collecting as much traditional music as I can. Next?"

Ponytail guy zoned out on Isla's lips as she talked. He jumped when she turned to him with one ruddy eyebrow cocked. "Oh. Yeah. I'm Ewan Crawford from Glasgow. Filmmaker. I'm making a documentary on the state of Gaelic preservation in the Highlands and Islands, which reminds me, I have releases for everyone to sign."

He began shuffling through a backpack beside his chair. Dermot chimed in, "Why don't you tell the group what audience you think you'll get for the film?"

Ewan's head popped up. "Oh! Yeah, it's very exciting. I've gotten some interest from BBC and maybe even some cable channels in the States."

Everyone looked around the table in excitement. Dermot put in, "Although our main focus is studying the oral traditions of the Highlands and Islands, we have the added opportunity of raising awareness of the value of the language and traditions. Ewan is going to help us do that."

Dermot nodded to the man next to Sarah. When he spoke, his voice was warm and smooth with a soft English accent. "I am Jujhar Gurudatt. I'm a linguist. I'm studying the similarities between Celtic languages and the languages of the Indus Valley. I am not a fluent Gaelic speaker, so I am excited to get out and hear it in a nonacademic context."

"I think that's true for a lot of us." Dermot said. "I think Isla and Sarah are the only two of us who actually spoke Gaelic at home. They should be able to give you some help." Jujhar turned a friendly smile on Sarah and Isla.

Sarah took a deep breath and gave her short bio. "I'm Sarah MacAlpin. You probably noticed from my accent that I'm from the States. North Carolina to be specific, but as Dermot said I grew up speaking Gaelic at home with my grandmother. I am here to study folksongs."

"Sarah is also an outstanding Gaelic singer. I'm hoping she and Isla can help us with some of our fund raising and publicity efforts." Dermot beamed with pride, and Sarah could feel her cheeks flushing under everyone's collective gaze.

"Right, that's done. Now, let's discuss our schedule for the next few weeks." Dermot leaned forward sliding a stack of calendar pages down the table. Everyone reached forward to take one. "I think we have most of the office set up done. Thanks to Kirstie for coming in early to help with that. We're targeting mid-March for the start of our trip. We'll be heading to Inverness, then across to Skye, up through the islands and back across the north coast. But hauling ourselves and our equipment all over the country won't be cheap, so we're going to have to do a bit of fund raising. Our current grant covers the basics of equipment and some travel costs, but we're going to need more unless we want to be sleeping in our cars.

"To that end our first official fundraiser is going to be a gala Burns Night dinner on the 20th hosted by James Stuart. He has graciously offered his home for the event. We are expected to provide the readings as well as a program of traditional music. We can discuss the specifics of the program later, but Isla and Sarah I'd like the two of you to work together on that." He looked between the two of them.

Sarah glanced at Isla before answering. "I'm game, but we shouldn't let music get all the attention. What if we also had a silent auction? Maybe Kirstie can round up some hand-crafted goodies. If they're donated, then all the proceeds can go to the project."

Sarah looked across the table to see Kirstie's cheeks turning pink. She sat forward getting excited about the idea. "I'm sure I could find something."

"Great. Good thinking, Sarah." Dermot put in. "Now, I will handle all media interviews, so send any media inquiries my way. In the meantime, we need to setup some regular mechanisms for meeting and communication…"

The meeting continued with everyone agreeing to a weekly planning meeting for the research trip and established a few deadlines. Isla and Sarah agreed to meet the next day to brainstorm the Burns Night program. Sarah had to admire how easily Dermot stepped into the leadership role and effectively delegated tasks. Sarah was sure her biggest challenge on the team would be not staring doe-eyed at Dermot during every meeting they had. Unfortunately, Kirstie didn't seem to share that sense of propriety. Sarah noticed her openly goggling at him more than once.

As the meeting broke up. Ewan went about breaking down his camera, and everyone else went to their desks to finish settling in. Dermot went back to his office. Sarah found herself once again facing Jujhar across their desks. "Jujhar? Is that Hindu or Sikh?"

He gave her a quick flash of his startlingly white teeth. "It's common to both actually. Though my family is Hindu."

"From Punjab, right?" She thought she remembered that from her undergrad days. She'd taken a class on world religions and had been particularly fascinated by the variety of religions in south Asia.

He nodded, and his smile grew. "That's right. My grandfather was a student at Oxford when the Partition happened in 1947. His family had to flee Pakistan. He's never made it back for more than a visit."

Sarah remembered when her grandmother would look out over the Blue Ridge Mountains and get a far-off look as if she was looking at an entirely different set of mountains. "But probably missed it every day."

"Yes." He studied her for a moment, his nearly black eyes showing a kinship that Sarah now thought she understood. They both lived between worlds. "Your grandmother?"

She nodded. "Fled to the Nova Scotia and then the States right before World War II and spent the rest of her life looking homeward. Let me guess, you grew up with a mix of English and Punjabi at home."

He chuckled. "My sisters were determined to speak English and my parents let them but would only speak

Punjabi. And my grandfather always refused to speak English at home, even though his English was perfect."

Sarah laughed. "My Granny was the same way. Although my mother refused to speak Gaelic. Bilingual conversations were the norm until my mother died."

Jujhar's smile disappeared, but the warmth didn't leave his eyes. "I'm sorry. When was that?"

Sarah waved off his sympathy. "Oh, I was only six. It's been ages. I do miss speaking Gaelic at home."

"That sounds like you learned in a vacuum. Are you sure you learned it right?" Kirstie's voice came from behind Jujhar. He turned to the side to reveal the woman giving a decidedly disingenuous smile.

Isla on the other side of Kirstie's desk stopped what she was doing and glanced back and forth from Sarah to Kirstie. Sarah was determined not to rise to the bait. She tried to keep her tone friendly, "Well, I haven't run into any trouble so far, but if I need any help, Kirstie, you'll be the first person I ask."

Kirstie eyed her stone-faced, then turned back to shuffling things on her desk. Isla caught Sarah's eye and gave her a look that said she didn't get what Kirstie's problem was. She looked like she might say something, but then Ewan stumbled up to her desk, several pages clutched in his hand. "I found those releases."

"Right," Isla gave him a brief smile and took one of the pages he held. She began reading it, while Ewan stood there obviously staring at the elegant curve of her neck.

Sarah almost felt embarrassed for him. "Do you have one of those for me?"

Ewan jumped as if she'd poked him with a pin. He shook his head to clear it and reached out a release form to Sarah taking a couple of steps toward her desk. "Oh! Yeah, hen. Here ye go."

He handed forms to Jujhar and Kirstie as well, then like the needle on a compass his attention swung back to Isla. *Bless his heart,* Sarah thought, *wonder if he has a chance?*

Sarah caught Jujhar's eye and could tell he was thinking something similar. It was his turn to try to distract Ewan, before he made a complete fool of himself. "Any big Hogmanay plans tonight, Ewan?"

"Ah, no. Reckon I'll head down for the Torchlight, but not much else planned." He cut his eyes over to Isla. "What about you, Isla? Any plans?"

Isla looked up from the release form she was still reading. "Some mates and I are playing at a ceilidh at The Three Sisters. You should all come down if you're around Cowgate."

"How about you, Jujhar, any plans?" Sarah asked.

"I think The Three Sisters sounds great, though I've never seen the Torchlight Procession. Might be good as well."

Isla spoke up. "No reason you can't do both. The procession will pass right by."

"Well then, that sounds like a plan," Jujhar looked at Ewan. "Are you with me?"

Ewan looked so relieved to have a friend to go with him Sarah thought he might hug Jujhar right there. "Aye. Sounds good then."

"Sarah?" Jujhar invited.

"Sounds good, but I'm afraid Dermot and I are meeting a friend for the procession. So, I'll be out in the cold."

Before Sarah could finish her statement, Kirstie shoved the release form into Ewan's chest, shouldered her bag and stomped out. The rest of them looked at each other eyebrows raised.

Isla rolled her eyes, "Look like someone's not used to being the last one picked on the playground."

CHAPTER FOUR

Sarah could barely feel her nose and cheeks within thirty seconds of leaving the house. It didn't even get this cold high in the mountains at home. She wasn't sure how her Southern girl blood was going to adjust to the Scottish brand of damp cold. She was bundled up in a sweater, wool coat, scarf, hat and mittens. Still, tiny tendrils of midwinter air snuck through the layers and touched her like icy fingers on her ankles, wrists, and the back of her neck.

They were nearing the National Museum and the sound of pipes and drums warming up for the parade grew louder. According to Dermot, the Torchlight Procession was parade meets bonfire ending with fireworks and a massive party. The two of them blended into the crowd near the start of the parade route. Dermot had sensibly chosen to wear jeans for this event, although Sarah saw many men in kilts. She couldn't help thinking about what Scotsmen wore or didn't wear under their kilts and wondering how the Scots ever managed to reproduce with weather like this.

When they turned onto Chambers Street, the sight took Sarah's breath away. Thousands of people crowded the pavement and sidewalks. Most of the electric lights had been turned off and the street was ablaze with firelight. Nearly every person she could see held a torch. They clustered around and behind the pipe bands assembled up and down the street from the museum toward the George IV bridge.

Dermot took Sarah's hand in a firm grip and pulled her through the crowd toward a low retaining wall in front of the museum. "James should be here. I'm going to take a look."

He stepped up onto the wall and began scanning the crowd looking for James. Sarah imagined it wouldn't be hard to find him, since he usually came with a bodyguard in tow. Dermot hung onto her hand as he stood on the wall, which made her feel a little like a child. Still, it was better than getting pushed along by the crowd and lost.

Sarah felt a tap on her shoulder and turned to find a tall man in a nondescript knit hat and dark gray scarf covering the lower half of his face. He was standing too close for her comfort and she squeezed Dermot's hand in alarm. Then the man leaned down and pulled the scarf from his face. James Stuart gave her a rakish smile.

He held a finger to his pursed lips before leaning close to her ear and saying. "I've escaped."

Sarah looked around for his usual bodyguard, but there was no one. She turned back to James who was wearing a dark gray pea coat and kilt with some scuffed and worn hiking boots. Sarah let go of Dermot's hand and stretched up to get closer to James's ear. "Do you think that's safe?"

"It's fine." He said looking confident.

Sarah could feel Dermot standing at her back, ready to pounce on whoever was talking to her until James looked up at him.

"What are you doing?" Dermot's voice showed a hint of alarm.

James gave him a sly smile. "Well, I was trying to chat up this woman here. Do ye think she's taken?"

"Ha." Dermot deadpanned.

James shook his head. "No sense of humor. The security team wanted me to wait at the end, but I would rather walk with the crowd."

"Right, then. Shall we." Dermot waved a hand toward the street where the pipe bands were forming up behind a group of costumed "Vikings" with large torches.

James handed Dermot some slips of paper that looked like tickets. "Let's get some torches."

Nearby some volunteers were exchanging the tickets for torches made of rolled and waxed burlap. There were burning barrels for people to light their torches. Once the three of them had lit theirs, they made their way into the street.

"Where to?" Sarah looked to James for direction. He took her free hand and pulled her into the crowd of torch bearers behind the first pipe band. The drummers were warming up and the pipes had gone quiet. Instantly, Sarah flashed back to the last time she'd been in a crowd like this. Halloween, when Ryan Cumberland had pushed her in front of a bus. She stopped walking, her eyes scanning the crowd. They were all pedestrians, no buses, no cars. Still she knew how easy it was to be anonymous and hidden in a crowd like this. James obviously knew too. He was using the crowd to hide right now.

Ryan was dead. She had watched him die. But she had seen his face dozens of times since then; in nightmares, in dark corners, in crowds. Sarah's chest tightened, unable to get enough air. She tried to act normal but couldn't help the rising panic. Her eyes searched the crowd looking for danger. She hadn't known about Ryan then, and there was no way to know now if any of these people meant her harm. She could still hear his cocky voice, *"There will always be more."*

"Sarah?" James was watching her, confused.

She looked back at him but couldn't speak past the panic bubbling up from her chest.

***

Bloody crowd, bloody James. How was he supposed to protect both of them in this mob? He'd nearly gotten his eyebrows singed already by a wayward torch. This was NOT what he'd meant when he'd told James to be himself or that Sarah wasn't impressed with the trappings of wealth. A bit of security never hurt.

Dermot pushed past some people who'd gotten in front of him, blocking him for a moment from Sarah and James. When he reached them one look at James's face told him something was wrong. His cousin was gripping Sarah's arm, his brows creased with worry.

"What's wrong?"

"I don't know she just stopped." James shook his head. "She hasn't been able to tell me."

Dermot pulled Sarah's arm gently until she looked up at him. Her eyes were wide, frantic. He glanced around and saw exactly what she must have seen. Halloween in Chapel Hill a few months ago. He remembered his own panic at seeing her fall into the path of an oncoming bus, her curls silhouetted in its headlights. He cursed himself for not thinking of it sooner.

He pulled Sarah into his arms and bent his head to her ear. "Hey. I'm here. It's all right. I won't let anything happen."

"What is it?" James stepped closer to them.

"The last time she was in a crowd this large, the same bloke who broke into her apartment pushed her in front of a bus. Her friends saved her from getting hit, but I think the crowd and the drums put her right back there."

"Oh God, Sarah. I didn't realize." James laid a firm hand on her back and stood close trying to give her some sense of safety.

The pipe and drums went silent, ending their warm up. In seconds they struck up "Scotland the Brave" all together. After a few beats they began marching and the crowd of torchbearers followed.

Sarah, James and Dermot held their place as the crowd flowed around them.

***

Sarah had no idea how long they'd been standing there. One minute she was alone and frozen watching a sea of faces swirl around her, searching for Ryan Cumberland's among them. Then everything melted together into a blur. The next thing she knew she was wrapped in warmth.

Dermot was in front of her, saying every reassuring thing possible in her ear. "I won't leave ye. We're here. We won't let anything happen to ye…"

She vaguely wondered who *we* was. Then she realized that the large warm form at her back was James. He was standing close protecting her back as people jostled by with their torches. He left Dermot to do the talking, but he remained a stalwart presence behind her.

Her breathing eased as their warmth seeped into her. The panic that had gripped her began to recede, and the noise around them filtered back in. She realized that the bands were playing music now. Warm up was over. She peered around

Dermot's shoulder to see people marching away from them. "Has the parade started?"

Dermot leaned back to look at her but didn't let go. A smile of relief spread across his face. "There ye are."

She tried to smile, but it still felt a little weak.

"Sarah, I had no idea…" James said behind her. She could hear the guilt in his voice.

She looked at him over her shoulder. "It's okay, neither did I."

"Do you want me to take you home? I can have a car pick us up in a moment." James offered.

Sarah straightened her shoulders beneath his hands. "No." Her voice was firmer now. "You have a role to play here, and I want to see the procession."

"Are ye sure?" Dermot asked, his blue eyes searching hers.

She gritted her teeth and took another reassuring breath. "Keep breathing, right? If I let this kind of thing slow me down, then he's won." Another breath and a shaky smile. "I can't let that happen."

Dermot smiled back, remembering her determination to put the events of three weeks ago behind her. "That's my girl."

James cleared his throat behind her, and Sarah turned. He ran a comforting hand down her back. "You're sure, you'll be all right?"

Her smile grew along with her confidence. "I'll be fine. Now, what happened to my torch?"

They found it a few feet away. Fortunately, it had gone out when she dropped it. They re-lit her torch and joined the procession. Once the lingering effects of her panic attack faded, Sarah began to have a good time. How could a girl not when she was closely flanked by two tall, handsome guys who only seemed to care about her state of wellbeing. Between the walking, the crowd, and the fire, she didn't even feel the cold anymore.

James took her free hand, and Dermot stayed close behind. By the time they reached The Royal Mile, the only thing taking her breath away was the river of torchlight stretching as far as she could see. The event itself was a sort of mishmash of various Celtic and Norse traditions. It was intoxicating to be a part of the many thousands all marching toward the same end.

The pipe bands ran through every traditional song they could and some not so traditional ones. As it always did the *ceol mòr* of the pipes gave Sarah that stirring sensation from the bones out. She found her steps growing stronger the further they went.

They picked up the pace skirting around a couple of pipe bands and wove back into the crowd behind the Vikings at the front of the line. They reached Calton Hill and the crowd gathered in front of a high stage equipped with a microphone. Behind the stage was a huge effigy of a stag built out of twigs. As they neared the stage there were barrels of water for putting out their torches, although many people kept theirs lit. The bands continued playing as the crowd gathered and the noise was nearly deafening.

There were some organizers moving around the stage and watching the mass of people below. When they judged that enough of the procession had gathered an emcee stepped up to the microphone and raised an arm. The bands stopped playing and the buzz quieted.

"Back to business." James leaned over to Sarah and kissed her cheek. He nodded to Dermot who stepped up closer behind her.

James went a few feet away from them and waited watching the stage. The emcee began to speak.

"Welcome! To the Edinburgh Torchlight Procession kicking off our annual Hogmanay celebration." Cheers and applause rose from the crowd.

"Let's thank the Up Helly 'A Vikings for leading the procession…" The Vikings gave a battle cry and the mob cheered again.

"…And all the massed bands for piping us along our way…" Another cheer.

"Now, to light this effigy of the old year and ring in the new. This year the honor of lighting the fire goes to James Stuart, Lord Caledon." Cheers.

"Unfortunately, Lord Caledon, doesn't appear to be…"

"Here!" James shouted from where he was waiting in the crowd. He pulled off his hat and scarf. A daring move Sarah thought, given his security concerns. Still, it was a crowd pleaser as they erupted in their loudest cheer yet. James made his way through the crowd shaking hands and receiving pats on the back. As he climbed the steps to the stage he shed his coat to reveal an Aran sweater that worked beautifully with his green Stuart Hunting kilt.

The result was dazzling. He was the epitome of the modern Scottish laird, and Sarah noticed stars in the eyes of more than a few women standing around them. James took the microphone from the stand. "Good evening."

Cheers, even louder than before erupted.

"You probably expect me to get up here and give a speech about politics or independence, but tonight is not the night for that. All that stuff can wait for the new year, and it will be a great year. But tonight, is about celebration. And I hope that's what you'll do."

He turned to the back of the stage and was handed a long torch with which to light the stag. He lifted the torch high. "To a fantastic 1996!"

With that James touched the stag with the torch. In seconds the sculpture was ablaze, its black outline engulfed in bright flames and against that background James cast his own stark figure with his torch held high. Behind them fireworks shot to the sky, and the crowd went wild.

As ridiculous as James's ambitions sounded when Dermot had told her about them, tonight James was every bit the king that he wanted to be. She had come here determined to take what she could from the situation, learn what she could about her people and convince Dermot that the Stuart ambition didn't have to be his destiny. But here in the cheering crowd with the fire blazing behind him, Sarah could see how James and the Stuart engine could steamroll their way through almost anything.

CHAPTER FIVE

Over the next week Sarah and Dermot developed a rhythm of going to work in the morning on the research team projects. After lunch he would drop her off at the School of Scottish Studies, so she could prowl through the collections looking for songs to support her thesis, and sometimes fruitlessly looking for information on *Làrachd an Fhamhair*, the village where her grandmother had grown up. Then he would walk her home and they would grab a bite on the way or she would cook. It felt natural and comfortable.

Sarah had been looking forward to sleeping in Saturday morning after a late night spent trying to plot locations for different versions of "The Two Sisters" on a map. A loud bang like a shot woke her. She popped up in bed her heart racing, the fog of sleep instantly gone. She sat frozen listening for any other sounds of danger. When she had decided that the building wasn't full of crazed murderers, she threw on some sweats and went looking for Dermot.

She had started down the stairs when she heard the bang again, louder. A blast of cold air coming up the stairs told her it had been the sound of the heavy front door closing. She'd heard it dozens of times before, but she had usually been standing near it. The bang of the great door back into its frame sounded a lot less like a gunshot when you were the one who had opened it.

The front hall was filled with boxes, suitcases and a gargantuan man in a royal blue tracksuit. As she reached the bottom step, he straightened and turned her way. He had the look of a man who had been hit in the face a few too many times. His ruddy skin sported a smattering of scars as did the huge blunt-fingered hands that were gripping the box he was carrying. His hair was so short that it was little more than a brownish haze above his scalp. He looked stone-faced out of deep-set eyes at Sarah and gave a silent nod as he started up the stairs.

She pulled her sweatshirt closed at the top and knocked nervously on Dermot's door. She looked over her shoulder up the stairs where the giant had gone carrying his box. His legs, as thick as tree trunks, took the steps two at a time with ease. She was lifting her hand to knock again when Dermot opened the door. She didn't wait for an invitation but went right into his apartment. "Please tell me you knew that...person was coming."

"Who, Calum?" Dermot waved back toward the hallway.

She turned and shut his door before going to the kitchen. Despite her best efforts her nerves were still frayed. She busied herself with the French press he used to make coffee hoping the movement would hide her shaking hands. "If Calum is the heavyweight champ out there, then yeah, that's who I'm talking about. Is he James's new guard dog?"

He followed her, watching closely as she flipped on the electric kettle and got cups down from the cabinet. "Ye knew someone was coming. I warned ye, you might not like who James sent."

She opened and closed a cabinet in search of sugar. "Where's Fleming?"

He retrieved the sugar from the counter behind her and slid it into place next to the cups. "He's working security at the Alba Petroleum offices."

"Is that some kind of demotion?" She looked at him for the first time. He looked like he'd dressed in a rush with a flannel shirt unbuttoned over a white T-shirt that left little to the imagination. He was barefoot, and his hair stuck up around his head in wet spikes. He looked so damned good she wanted nothing more than to curl up in his arms. Instead she turned back to the kettle and willed it to boil faster.

He gave her a look that said she already knew the answer to her question, "He lost track of the person who means the most in the world to his boss. He's lucky he still has a job."

She sighed heavily. She knew that would be his answer, but it didn't make it any easier to hear. "I don't mean anything to James. What he thinks I can give him, whatever the hell that is, means something to him. Not to *me*. He barely knows me."

The kettle started boiling and she picked it up and went to pour the water into the French press only to realize that there was no coffee in it. He didn't comment on what she'd said but slid over the canister where he kept the coffee and gave her a gentle smile.

She laughed, short and breathy and shook her head scooping coffee into the press. She poured water over the grounds and put the lid on. With nothing left to do she let her hands rest on the counter. The little spike of adrenaline from waking up suddenly to find a stranger in the hallway was gone. When she spoke again her voice was tight with frustration. "This week has been so nice and peaceful. It was us and the work and," To her horror her voice cracked. "I almost forgot."

He let the words hang there between them. She wished he would say something, put his arms around her, tell her not to worry about it. She wished it would all go away and leave the two of them there in the flat with their coffee. When they finished they would crawl back into bed together or go to the store or work or a movie. They would have a future. Of course, he didn't do that. "We can't afford to forget, love."

She closed her eyes tight. "Don't call me that. Even if it's just an expression, just... don't."

Another tense silence spun out for what felt like minutes. Eventually, Sarah heard Calum's footsteps coming down the stairs. "Well, I might as well meet the new neighbor properly."

"Right," Dermot seized the chance to do something. "Back in a tic."

In a few quick steps he was out in the hallway intercepting Calum on his way back out the door. Sarah heard masculine voices rumbling from the hallway. In a few more seconds Dermot returned followed by the hulk that Sarah had seen in the hallway. "Sarah MacAlpin, this is our new neighbor Calum Ridland. Calum, my friend and colleague, Sarah."

"Nice to meet you, Calum." She showed him her friendliest smile.

"Aye, alright." Sarah took that to mean something in the neighborhood of 'likewise'. His voice was as deep as she had expected. Sarah could see why he worked in security. His size alone was intimidating, but he didn't seem inclined to either talking or smiling.

"We were about to have some coffee. Would you like some?" It might be wise to be on good terms with your bodyguards even if they didn't know that you knew that was their job.

Calum looked as if the offer made him uncomfortable. Maybe he'd been warned not to get friendly with her after what happened to Fleming. He glanced over his shoulder back at the hallway. "Uh. No, thanks. I'd best finish moving my things."

"Okay. Well, let me know if you need anything." Smiling again, "I'm on the second floor."

"Right, cheers." He said over his shoulder as he walked back to the door.

Sarah and Dermot exchanged a look that said, *Well, that was friendly.*

"Oh!" Dermot stepped quickly back into the hallway. This time he left the door open and Sarah heard his brief conversation with Calum.

"Hey, mate. Can ye mind the door when it closes? It bangs like a gunshot." His voice lowered into a confidential tone. "Put me a bit too much in mind of my army days."

There was a pause, and she could almost imagine the look of understanding transforming Calum's stern face. "Oh yeah, mate. No worries."

"Cheers," A second later, Dermot came back into the apartment and set about fixing his cup of coffee.

"That was for my benefit wasn't it?"

"I have no idea what ye mean." He took a sip of coffee and winked at her over the top of his mug.

***

Dermot spit the mouthwash into the sink and rinsed his mouth with water. He checked his teeth, then his hair in the mirror. He buttoned his shirt collar nearly to the top. A date had seemed like a good idea when she'd invited him. Now that he was on the verge of walking out the door, he was absolutely certain that it was not.

When she had asked him to dinner, his first instinct was to kindly refuse. He should know better than to get involved with someone on the team. Under normal circumstances he would not have even considered it. But there was nothing normal about his current circumstances.

Whatever his feelings for Sarah were, they both needed to move on. It was increasingly clear to him that Sarah would never give James a chance if she thought she still had one with him. So, when Kirstie had invited him to dinner, it was the perfect way to send Sarah the message that he wanted. He was moving on and so should she.

He told himself that it couldn't hurt Sarah any more than he already had. If this last week had shown him anything, it was that they could too easily slip back into their comfortable friendship and more if he wasn't careful. He had convinced himself that getting involved with someone else close at hand would serve as a barrier to that.

He should have picked someone else, not someone on the team. He would tell Kirstie at dinner, that this was a bad idea. No, he would call her now and call it off. He found the number in his agenda book and dialed. Of course, there was no answer. He checked his watch. She was probably already on her way to the pub where they'd agreed to meet.

Then the intercom by the door buzzed. He pushed the button. "Yeah?"

"It's me, Kirstie. I was in the neighborhood and thought we could walk together."

He thumped his head against the wall next to the intercom. It was just his luck she had come to fetch him. "I'll be right out."

"Can I come in?" She pleaded. "It's freezing out here."

"Yeah, sure." He really would rather she didn't, but he couldn't very well leave her outside in the January cold.

When he opened the front door for her, Kirstie smiled broadly at him and followed him to his apartment. "Cheers."

"Let me grab my coat and we can be on our way." Hopefully before anyone saw them.

"Oh, don't rush on my account." She said over her shoulder as she perused his bookshelves.

He picked up the coat that he had slung across the back of a chair and turned back to find her looking around his apartment with avid curiosity. Her eyes ate up every detail, and the scrutiny made him feel distinctly uncomfortable. He settled his coat on his shoulders. "Shall we go?"

"Sure." She rushed to follow him to the door.

He locked his flat with one ear listening for Sarah's footsteps on the stairs. He was convinced now that this was a bad idea. He only hoped he could get Kirstie out of the building and let her down easy, before Sarah saw them. She would get the message, but he no longer thought this was a good way to send it. He turned to open the front door for Kirstie who insisted on standing closer than he liked, only to find Isla on the stoop with a grocery bag.

"Oh! You're not Sarah." She stepped into the hall laughing and he heard the clink of bottles from the bag she held. Her eyes took in Dermot and Kirstie. "Going out?

"Ah…" He froze, like a kid caught doing something he knew he shouldn't. He didn't want to linger there in case Sarah was coming down to let Isla in, but he couldn't be rude either.

"Yes, we're off to dinner." Kirstie looped a possessive arm through his. Dermot squirmed, and then the worst happened. A door closed on the second floor and Sarah's footsteps came hurrying down the hall. She got to the stairs in time to hear Kirstie saying, "Then maybe we'll go and see the band at the Bannerman's Bar."

That was news to him, but it didn't matter. All his attention was on the woman coming down the stairs. She stopped a couple of stairs from the bottom looking at the three of them. Her eyes went to where Kirstie's arm was linked with his. She blinked twice, then met his eyes with a look that said, *you'll regret this.*

Then she smiled and looked at Isla. "Guess you didn't need me to open the door after all."

"Yeah, these two were on their way out." She arched one auburn eyebrow at Dermot and Kirstie, making him even less comfortable. Definitely should not have done this with someone on the team.

"We're going to dinner." Kirstie piped in, tightening her grip on Dermot's arm. Her eyes were a little too bright for his taste. "What are you girls up to?"

Sarah grinned back at her as if they were great friends. "Oh, just a night in. Dinner, a bit of planning for Burns Night."

"Sarah's cooked something called Brunswick stew. She said it was perfect for a cold night." Isla put in, making Brunswick stew sound like something exotic. Dermot hadn't had it, but he was sure it would taste better than anything he might manage to choke down tonight.

"Then I'm sure you're in for a treat." He looked back at Sarah who cocked her head to one side. A secret smile tipped the corners of her mouth up. "Sarah's a fine cook."

They stood there in the hall for several awkward seconds unable to think of any more small talk and not wanting to seem rude. Finally, Kirstie broke the silence, and pulled on his arm. "Well, we'd better go."

"Right. Calum is upstairs if ye need anything." He told Sarah as he let Kirstie pull him to the door. Isla passed them on her way to the stairs.

He glanced back over his shoulder. Sarah held his eyes with hers as the heavy door slammed back into the frame.

***

"Well that was a surprise." Isla put the bag of groceries on the island in Sarah's kitchen.

"Yeah," Sarah still couldn't quite believe what she had seen. "I don't think that's the best idea."

Isla pulled a bottle of wine out of the bag and held it up in question. "Certainly, won't be fun when it starts to go wrong."

"And you can bet it'll go wrong." Sarah retrieved the corkscrew from a drawer and handed it to Isla.

Isla gave her a wry look while she opened the wine. "Whatever makes you say that?"

Sarah snorted and rolled her eyes. Instead of answering she reached in to the cabinet for some bowls for the stew.

Isla poured the wine while Sarah busied herself dishing out stew. She handed Sarah a glass, they clinked and took sips. "Actually, I thought you and Dermot had something going."

Sarah nearly choked on the wine. "Why would you think that?"

"Oh, you're always in each other's pockets, you have a history, the telepathy…" She ticked off a list on her fingers.

"Telepathy?"

"Please, the two of you have whole conversations just by looking at each other." She took a sip of wine. "It's like you've known each other forever."

Sarah let out a short laugh as she handed Isla a spoon. "Believe it or not, we only met about six months ago."

"You're kidding. Then why on earth don't you have a thing going?" They made their way to the living room and settled comfortably on the couch. "I'd love to find a man who looked at me like that."

Sarah arched an eyebrow at her. "Ewan does, or haven't you noticed."

Isla rolled her eyes. "I've been trying hard not to notice. I feel a bit embarrassed for him."

"I think it's sweet," Sarah chided. "Besides he's not bad looking. Why not give him a chance?"

Isla took a spoonful of stew and her face lit up. "Mmm…this is good."

Sarah tasted it herself. It was good, loaded with vegetables and chicken. She had been craving a little home cooking. After a couple more bites, Isla picked up the conversation. "Well, with Ewan it's hard to tell. You're right, he's not bad to look at, and he seems nice enough, but," She sighed. "A girl likes to be approached with some…confidence, a bit of swagger."

"And poor Ewan is so nervous whenever he sees you that he can't seem to do that." Sarah filled in.

"Poor lad." Isla tipped her wine glass in confirmation and giggled. "The other day I went to help him move some equipment and he nearly dropped his camera."

Sarah felt bad for laughing, but poor Ewan was unable to be within ten feet of Isla without making a fool of himself. "He's definitely smitten."

"Aye, but then anyone who saw the way Dermot looks at you would think he fancies you. He hangs on your every word."

Sarah barked a laugh. "Ugh. Life might be a lot easicr if that were true. No, he only feels protective of me. We haven't known each other long, but we've been through a lot."

She had meant to leave it at that, but she should have known better. Isla didn't have to say anything. She merely looked pointedly at Sarah over the top of her wine glass and waited.

Sarah stalled by taking a spoonful of stew and a sip of wine, formulating exactly how much truth to tell. "We worked together last semester, did some field work, became friends. Then a little over a month ago…Dermot saved my life."

Isla gasped before settling in to hear the story with a curious look. "My roommate, my best friend, met this guy. She really liked him, and he made her happy. But he and I never really got along. There was something about him that felt wrong. I wasn't happy about her giving him free access to our apartment, but I let it go because she thought she was in love. I even caught him in a big lie, but when I told her about it she got mad at me."

"Kill the messenger." Isla put in.

Sarah nodded and swirled the wine in her glass. "Then, right at the end of the semester, she had to leave town. Her grandfather had a stroke. That was when he came for me. He had made his own key and got into the apartment. He was going to kill me and make it look like a suicide. Dermot showed up and almost got himself killed trying to help me get away." She stopped overcome by the memory of Dermot and Ryan Cumberland wrestling for the gun on the floor. Leaving him there as she ran barefoot and half-naked from her apartment had been the hardest thing she had ever done.

"And?" Isla sat forward in her chair.

"Ryan, the bad guy, knocked Dermot out and caught up with me. By then I was in the street. There was a standoff with the police that went on forever. We were all focused on each other; me, Ryan, the police. None of us saw Dermot stumble out of the apartment building. When he saw us, he shouted. It startled Ryan enough for me to slip out of his arms. When he didn't have me anymore, he pointed his gun at the police and they shot him."

"That's the maddest thing I've ever heard." Isla stared wide-eyed, her wine and stew forgotten. "And that was last month?"

Sarah nodded.

"And you're alright?" She was incredulous.

"I'm fine, aside from the occasional panic attack. But Dermot never wants to let me go anywhere by myself. I'm tougher than I look." Sarah gestured to Isla's bowl. "I didn't mean to put you off your dinner."

"No, you didn't. It's delicious." Isla shook her head and exchanged her wine glass for her bowl. They ate for a few minutes in silence. It had been good to tell someone, even if she couldn't tell the whole story. Telling the bare facts to someone else made it a bit less scary. "But did you ever learn why he did it?"

Yes, but Isla would never believe it. "Not really. When he was holding me, he said a bunch of different confusing things. None of it made any sense."

"What about your friend? What did she say?"

Sarah released a slow breath. "She's still processing it all. It's definitely been a strain."

"I can imagine." Her auburn eyebrows drew together in sympathy.

"It was actually, kind of a relief to come here. I was alone in the apartment where I was attacked for three weeks after that and I hated it. Everything there reminded me of that night."

Isla gave Sarah's arm a friendly squeeze. "You are tougher than you look."

***

"So, what's the story with you and Sarah?" Kirstie asked over dinner when they'd run through polite small talk. So far, he'd heard about where she was from, her family and interests. She had asked him about his family, army days, and interests outside of work all of which he had answered as vaguely as possible. Up to this point dinner had been pleasant, even diverting. He couldn't understand why she would want to spoil that.

Dermot took a sip of his pint to give himself time to think of the best way to answer that. "We worked together last term. She came highly recommended by a professor there."

"That's all?" She looked skeptical.

"That's all." He didn't need rumors flying around the team about their relationship, but of course there was little other way to explain the amount of time they spent together.

"You don't think it seems odd to have an American on the team as the expert in Gaelic songs? Weren't there any Scottish scholars available?" She used her fork to toy with what was left of the mash on her plate.

"I'm sure there are. But none of the other applicants had her qualifications." That part at least was true. Sarah might be American and maybe she hadn't finished her dissertation yet, but she had already published articles and had a more impressive CV than any of the other applicants. She'd have gotten the position even without James Stuart's intervention.

"And what are those qualifications?" Kirstie pinned him with a sharp look though she tried to soften it with a smile.

His hackles went up. He bit his tongue against the urge to tell her that Sarah's accomplishments were far more impressive than hers. He leaned back in the booth and straightened his fork on the table thinking about the best way to handle this. He'd had enough of Kirstie's animosity toward Sarah. He had noticed that she didn't have the same objection to Jujhar, a Hindu who grew up in England. If he hadn't noticed before, he was sure after this evening that Kirstie's objection to Sarah had more to do with her closeness to him than her country of origin.

He took a slow breath and let it out marshaling his temper. When he spoke, he hoped his voice didn't show his frustration. "I hope you will take this as the friendly advice it's intended to be. Your performance on this team can create connections for you that will benefit you for your whole career. But if you develop a reputation for unprofessional behavior, it will haunt you for years. You should be focused on your own work, rather than asking inappropriate questions about someone else's qualifications. I don't know what your problem is with Sarah, but you have to get over it. I've seen how it is. She's been nothing but kind and professional. The only one who will be tarnished by any conflict is you."

Red hot embarrassment crept up her neck and flamed across Kirstie's cheeks. She looked down at her hands on the table blinking rapidly. Dermot felt awful for making her feel so bad, but she needed to hear it. She gave a short nod. "Of course, you're right. I'll try to remember that."

He took another swig of his pint and looked away to give her a moment to collect herself.

"I suppose it's my competitive nature." She laughed softly. "I've always had to be the best at anything I did. It's gotten me pretty far, but it can get in the way."

He smiled in what he hoped was brotherly reassurance, "You are the best at what you do. Sarah is the best at what she does. That's why you're both on the team. We all have our own goals, but we're on the team to help each other. If you work with her you'll both benefit."

"I'll keep that in mind." Her smile didn't quite reach her eyes. She pushed her almost empty plate away from her. "Do you want to go to the Bannerman's?"

"I'd really better not. I have somewhere I need to be early in the morning." That wasn't strictly true, but he did mean to visit Mum now that Calum was around.

"Oh. Right then." She tried unsuccessfully to hide her disappointment.

"Come on." He jerked his head toward the door. "I'll walk you home."

CHAPTER SIX

Sarah's feet tapped in time with Isla and a couple of her musician friends as they burned their way through a rousing rendition of *"Bog A Lochan"*. The driving rhythm, and the rise and fall of the fiddle was enough to make Sarah forget that she was standing in the cavernous dining room of James Stuart's "town house". When James said 'townhouse', he merely meant the house in town as opposed to the estate in the country. James's town house was actually both halves of a duplex on Polwarth Terrace. It looked unassuming enough from the street with its small front garden and simple brick facade. But once you got past the front door, there was nothing plain about it.

They had been led from the front through a foyer fit for any palace down a dramatic rounded staircase to a giant open room with a glass wall that offered a sweeping view down the sloping back garden to the Union Canal. It was a room that was obviously made for entertaining with a small stage at one end and swinging doors into what Sarah imagined was a commercial sized kitchen on the other. There were also three pairs of wide French doors in the glass wall that led to a patio where staff was busy strategically placing gas heaters.

Isla didn't play with a band exactly but had a loose network of musician friends who would cobble together a group to play at the drop of a hat. For the dinner however, she had planned with a little more forethought. They were all outstanding, and within minutes of unpacking their equipment, they had begun rehearsing and planning their set. Sarah and Isla had outlined the songs that they would play but hadn't been too specific about when. Sarah figured that could be left up to the musicians. The dinner would be punctuated by readings of Robert Burns between courses followed by a traditional music set. Finally, after the program ended, a DJ would take over and play popular music for dancing.

Sarah and Ewan setting up the sound equipment and cameras, but she found herself getting easily distracted by the music. She didn't feel too bad about it. Ewan was easily distracted by Isla playing the fiddle, or the tin whistle, or walking around the stage, or breathing. The poor guy tended to flounder like a nervous twelve-year-old whenever she was around. When the song ended Sarah glanced over at him and caught him staring moon-eyed at the stage. One elbow leaned on a nearby speaker, and a loop of cable dangled from his other hand. She took a few steps closer to him and said sotto voce. "Have you asked her out yet?"

"Wha… och, nah. You've seen me. I turn into a numpty anytime I get near her." He shook his head and went back to connecting the speakers to the soundboard. "I'd probably trip over my own shoes and knock us both on our arse's."

Sarah followed him having finished the last task he gave her. "Nonsense. You just need a little confidence. Maybe tonight's the night."

Ewan plugged in the cable he'd been running and looked back at the stage. The musicians were debating the order of songs they would play, and Isla was making notes on a set list. He sighed heavily. "Maybe."

"That's the spirit."

"Meantime let's get these wireless mics setup and tested." He handed her a handful of small boxes with clip-on microphones dangling from thin wires.

Sarah worked her way through the room from table to table testing and labeling each microphone and transmitter combination. She was near the back of the room when the transmitter box she was testing was plucked from her hand. She spun around to find James Stuart standing behind her with that dazzling smile of his. He glanced down to where the microphone was clipped to the V-neck of her sweater. She hadn't thought her sweater revealing when she put it on that morning, but when James's deft fingers slid down the collar to unclip the microphone, it seemed almost indecent.

Without taking his eyes from hers, he lifted the microphone a few inches from his chin. "I need to borrow Miss MacAlpin for a few moments."

He laid the microphone and transmitter on the table and took Sarah's hand. As he pulled her toward the stairs, Sarah looked back to find Ewan, Isla and everyone else staring in stunned silence. "I'll be right back."

James pulled her up the stairs and through the hallway. They passed Dermot, Kirstie and Jujhar setting up the handcrafted items for the auction. Dermot watched stone-faced as James drew Sarah down a side hallway. He let her hand go when they were in a cozy wood paneled office dominated by an enormous mahogany desk. Between the desk and fireplace was a sitting area with a burgundy leather love seat and wingback chair.

James made straight for the desk and lifted a wrapped box. He turned to her and held it out, his blue eyes sparkling. "I have something for you, for tonight."

Sarah stopped in front of the love seat. She was still reeling from being pulled through the house. It was hard to be mad at him, when he looked so excited. She didn't take the box from him. Smiling, "You know you don't have to bring me gifts."

"I know." He looked slightly embarrassed but wasn't deterred. He lifted the box a little between them. "I like to give gifts. Think of it as one of the perks of being my friend."

If he thought he could buy her affections, then she had to shut him down before things got out of hand. She kept her hands at her sides, not accepting the box. "That may be, but it makes me uncomfortable. I can't ever give you anything like the things you've given me. Besides, can't I like you for you, and not for what you can give me or do for me?"

"I'm sorry." The excitement drained right out of him. Crestfallen, he let the box drop to the coffee table and sank onto the love seat. "I suppose, I'm not used to being seen as a person rather than a means to an end."

He looked pitiful. He usually appeared supremely confident. This kind of vulnerability wasn't something she expected. It touched her, and for a minute she forgot that he was anything other than a man, a lonely one. She knew what it was like to be alone even when you were surrounded by people. She sat next to him and put a hand on his knee. "I have a feeling we're both short on true friends."

He covered her hand with his. "You have no idea."

She turned her hand up and wrapped her fingers around his. "Then that's what I'll give you, true friendship no strings attached, and that's all I ask in return."

He looked at their joined hands before giving hers a squeeze. Sarah held her breath hoping that he wouldn't ask for more, or worse confess some attraction that he had for her. He looked up into her eyes. "Now that sounds like a fair trade."

They smiled at each other, and Sarah felt like she was seeing the real James Stuart for the first time, not the prince, the mogul, or the tabloid playboy. He was only a man, and not a bad one at heart.

There was a short knock on the door and Dermot poked his head in looking concerned. "Everything alright in here?"

James and Sarah looked at him over the back of the love seat. She answered first, "Fine."

"I've been trying to convince Sarah to take this gift. It would be perfect for tonight." James lifted the box as Dermot stepped into the room and closed the door behind him.

Sarah looked back at James, head shaking. "You're incorrigible."

"Yes, I am." He gave the box a shake. "Come on. Last gift, I promise. And it's nothing compared to what you've offered me."

She eyed him wondering if the conversation they'd just had had been an act or if he was putting on a show for Dermot. With an exasperated sigh, she took the box and slid the ribbon off. She set pretty gold wrapping paper on the table and pulled the top off the box. She pushed aside the tissue paper to reveal the blue and green under check of the MacAlpin Ancient tartan. "Oh…James."

She pulled the bundle from its wrapping and stretched out a luxurious shawl of her family's tartan. She couldn't resist rubbing a corner of it against her cheek. "It's so soft."

"It's cashmere." James beamed at her. "It should be soft and very warm. I hope it will match whatever you were planning to wear tonight."

"It will, actually." She had found a wonderful green gown at a second-hand shop near the university. This shawl would be the perfect addition.

"That's great. Now Sarah has work to do." Dermot cut in.

James looked at him sharply and looked like he might say something. Sarah stood and spoke first, "I'm afraid he's right, but this is beautiful. Can you have someone keep it for me until I leave?"

"Of course." James stood too and followed her to the door.

Sarah stopped at the door. She turned to James and gave him a kiss on the cheek and a sweet smile. "Thank you. That's the last one, right?"

"Last one." He assured her.

Sarah stepped into the hallway and was quickly followed by Dermot. When she heard the door to the study close again, he stopped her by grabbing her arm. "What was that about?"

"About giving me a gift." She shrugged his hand off.

He was obviously unsatisfied by that answer. "What did he mean by, 'what you offered' him?"

Sarah watched him. The last couple of weeks since his date with Kirstie had been a little strained, but she didn't want to have an argument here in the hallway before their big event. "Friendship, Dermot, only friendship."

"It didn't look like friendship when you were practically running down the hall with him." He grumbled continuing down the hall slowly.

"You mean when he dragged me down the hall? I'm afraid you'll have to take that up with his highness." She walked along.

"Aye, well, thanks to that little show people are starting to talk."

"Well, I'm sure that was part of why he did it." She hissed. Sarah had no doubt that James had intended to make his interest clear. She only hoped that their talk had put the brakes on any further displays of favoritism. "You can't be jealous."

"Of course not!" He snapped, "You're walking a fine line here Sarah. Remember that."

She stopped in her tracks and looked at him. For an instant she dropped the wall that she had put up between them over the last couple of weeks, the one that kept her from showing him how much he was hurting her by denying what they could have. "As if I could ever forget."

CHAPTER SEVEN

Sarah fidgeted with the fringe at the end of her shawl and studiously avoided looking at Dermot beside her. It had been easy enough to ignore him as they made their way through the streets, but the traffic ground to a halt as soon as the car turned onto Polwarth Terrace. They inched down the street as cars pulled in and out of James's circular drive.

It wasn't that she was angry with Dermot. She didn't know what to say after their argument that afternoon. He'd spent the last couple of weeks keeping her at arm's length, which was fine because she'd spent the last couple of weeks quietly fuming over his date with Kirstie. Then as soon as James showed up, Dermot acted like a jealous boyfriend, which of course he claimed he wasn't. Part of her wanted to hope that this afternoon's confrontation was a sign that he still cared more than he wanted to admit. Another part was worn out from the constant push and pull.

"I'm sorry I snapped at ye this afternoon." He didn't look at her when he said it and his voice was so low that for a second, she thought she'd imagined it.

She blew out a long breath, "It's fine. James was a bit high handed. I wasn't happy about being dragged away either."

They went back to looking out the windows and fidgeting. The car moved another length or two down the street. After several more minutes of tense silence, the car stopped in front of the house and Dermot opened his door. A blast of frigid air rushed in and under Sarah's skirt. She slid across the seat and took the hand that he extended to her. Once she was on her feet she surveyed the front garden and street. Security had been dramatically stepped up from what she had seen that afternoon. Now there were black suited guards stationed at entrances and exits of the semi-circular driveway, each corner of the garden and across the street. She guessed that this concentration of wealth, power and fame required that kind of display.

"Shall we?" Dermot stood waiting arm extended to escort her to the door.

Sarah squared her shoulders and slid her arm through his. "Here goes nothing."

The sight that greeted her at the door was like something from a movie. James's house was stunning to begin with. Its front hallway was a classic display of Victorian grandeur, with ornate molding and rich dramatic colors, but Sarah had seen all of that earlier. At night, buzzing with people, and lamplight reflecting off the brass hardware and glittering guests it was breathtaking.

The door closed behind them while she was gaping at the people mingling around the hall and parlor. She barely noticed when Dermot slid her coat off. He handed their coats to the coat clerk and draped Sarah's shawl around her shoulders.

"Let's have a look at the auction." He showed her to a parlor where people were milling about exclaiming over certain pieces. Kirstie had done a great job rounding up donations for the auction. She had barely said a word about it since Sarah brought up the idea, but Sarah could see that she had worked hard. There were handwoven shawls and scarves from Harris, carved stones and wood carvings. They were all stationed at various tables in the room. An attendant stood by each table with a clipboard for recording bids while Kirstie and Jujhar mingled with the crowd answering questions about the items. Dermot and Sarah separated to browse the tables.

"This looks fantastic, Kirstie." Sarah told her when they met near a handmade spinning wheel that was on auction.

Kirstie looked around the room with a satisfied smile. "It has turned out well, hasn't it? Better than you thought?"

Sarah didn't know what to make of that question, so she took it at face value. "I was sure you would make it a success."

A woman in a burgundy dress and gold lamé scarf stopped to ask Kirstie about an item that was stationed in the hall and they walked off together. Jujhar stepped in to the spot where Kirstie had been standing in time to hear Sarah mutter, "I don't know what I did to that girl."

"You are talented, and you are here." He answered in his smooth voice and careful accent. "I fear Kirstie spends a lot of energy comparing herself to others."

"Imagine what she could do if she refocused that energy." She patted his arm and gave him a knowing smile before moving off to continue looking at the items on the tables. She paused by a set of antique carved wooden animals. They were arrayed on a piece of white satin that had been draped over various blocks and pillows to show the animals at different heights. The display would have fit nicely in any museum, and the light fabric made every detail of the pieces easily visible. Still, Sarah couldn't help thinking that they looked out of place, like animals in a zoo, taken from their home and placed on satin pillows to be gawked at when all they wanted to be was played with.

The wood was worn smooth on their sides, one sheep appeared to have had his leg repaired, and a dog was missing an ear. They had clearly been played with often and for a long time. Sarah could picture generations of little hands wearing away the edges.

"Like them?" Dermot's voice rumbled from behind her.

"They remind me of some that Duff made for me back home." She could still see Duff sitting on a log by the still, his rough calloused hands shaping the animals. She had always loved watching his blunt tipped fingers working the knife as he whittled the wood away curl by curl, and the joy in his eyes when he'd given her each one.

"Do ye still have yours?"

"Mmhmm. In storage back in Chapel Hill." Her voice was wistful. "I even still have the pasteboard box that I kept them in."

"Ye treasure them."

She blinked back the sting of tears. "I do."

"Treasure what?" James joined them in front of the display. Looking up, Sarah felt swamped by that same breathless awe that struck her dumb the first time she met him. He was stunning in his kilt and jacket, and his eyes were all for her.

She felt like a butterfly wriggling on a pin when he looked at her like that, like something he was about to add to his already considerable collection. She waved a hand at the wood carvings. "Just some toys from my childhood. They were a lot like these."

"Were they from Scotland?" James asked.

"No, a family friend carved them for me."

"Ah." James waited the appropriate time to be polite. "Do you have a moment, Sarah? There are some people I would like to introduce you to."

Sarah spent the next half hour being squired around the room by James. He introduced her to a dizzying number of people, few of whom she thought she was likely to remember. Still she tried to be as pleasant and personable as she could.

Finally, the doors to the ballroom were opened and everyone descended the stairs for the main event. The room looked fantastic, even better in the low evening light. The tables were all set with elegant centerpieces of Royal Stuart tartan draped between vases of evergreens and hurricane lamps with thick pillar candles. The band was warming up, and the wait staff was staging water pitchers and ice buckets at a long table near the kitchen.

***

The program went off without a hitch. Dermot's team wove their recitations in between the courses of the dinner. He gave the "Address to a Haggis" himself. After the meal, Isla and the band took the stage with a rousing set of reels. The crowd began buzzing, enjoying their sweets and whisky and lively music. When the first set was done, Sarah got up to sing. He had seen the song on the program. He knew she'd been planning to sing it. But nothing had prepared him for hearing it. The crowd was already half in love with her after the recitations, but she was singing "Ae Fond Kiss" for him.

No matter how he might tell himself that he needed to move on, or that he couldn't have her, the love song gutted him. His chest ached with longing.

Had we never lov'd sae kindly,
Had we never lov'd sae blindly,
Never met - or never parted,
We had ne'er been broken hearted.

Not for the first time he wished they'd never met, that he had never left the Army, that Walter Stuart had never been able to extort his help in this whole ridiculous business. Of course, they hadn't really parted. He was joined at the hip to a woman he loved but couldn't have. And when the song ended, it was James Stuart who helped her from the stage. It was James that drew her onto the dance floor, and James's arms that were around her as they danced.

Seething and cursing the whole damned situation, Dermot made a bee line for doors to the patio. Maybe the cold air would help clear his head. He let the glass door close behind him and went straight for the edge of the patio past the range of the heaters. He welcomed the burn of the icy air in his nose and lungs. Eyes closed, he took several deep breaths enjoying the quiet.

"It is a bit close in there." A smooth voice cooed to his left. He opened his eyes to find a woman with perfectly swept back brown hair and a red dress that hugged every curve. A man would have to be a monk not to notice.

"Aye, well. Now the program is done, I could use the air."

"It was a nice program. Not as racy as some Burns suppers I've been to. Perfect for this crowd." She looked thoughtful then smiled.

"Thanks. I think the team did a good job."

"They struck the right tone, and this looks good for the boss. I should know. I'm a professional." She took a step closer and extended a hand to him. "I'm Felicia Banks, public relations for Alba Petroleum."

"Ah. Dermot Sinclair. I lead the research team that we're raising funds for." Her handshake was firm and business like, but she leaned his way and twisted toward him in obvious interest.

She eyed him up and down before purring, "I never would have pegged you for a professor."

He had to laugh at that. He'd heard it before. "I did a stint in the army before going back to university."

"Yes. That sort of thing leaves its mark." She watched him closely. He sensed that not much got by Miss Banks.

A patrol walked past the patio in the yard, a stark reminder of the need for security. He looked back through the glass doors at the party. The dance had ended, and Sarah and James were talking with some guests. James hung on her every word.

"The boss has his eye on that one. She's certainly good with a crowd. She has a rare blend of charisma and approachability." Miss Banks said, following his gaze.

He made what Sarah would call one of his mumbly grunts. "I was just thinking something similar." He glanced at the woman beside him. "And by boss you mean…"

"Oh, James Stuart of course. Who else?" She arched an eyebrow.

"No one, of course." If she didn't already know about Walter Stuart's faction within the company, he wasn't going to tell her. There were more than a few executives and board members who only supported James as the public face of the company while remaining completely loyal to Walter behind closed doors. Walter may have been the brains behind the young CEO at first, but Dermot knew James wanted more control. He had been taking charge and pushing his own agendas more in the last year. Of course, Walter still managed to be the puppet master that kept much of the company moving. "Sorry, Miss Banks, I'm trying to figure out whose creature you are."

It was a bald statement and she could have easily been offended. He didn't have the patience this evening for subtlety. He was surprised when she threw back her head and laughed. "I'm no one's creature but my own. I can tell you understand a lot about the dynamics at AP."

He shifted awkwardly. He didn't really like claiming the relationship with James. It tended to make people look at him differently. "I've been around this crowd for a while."

"Then you do know how this game is played."

He let out a low growl. "I'm not much for games. I'd rather everyone were up front about things."

She considered him, her eyes sweeping down his body and back up. "Then I'll be up front. Would you care to dance, Mr. Sinclair? You look like you might be a very good dancer."

He glanced back through the doors to see Sarah deep in conversation with James. He offered her his arm, "I would love to dance, Miss Banks."

Her eyes lit with anticipation as she took his arm. "Felicia, please. I have a feeling we're going to be friends."

CHAPTER EIGHT

Sarah politely accepted another glass of champagne from James after leaving the dance floor. She would take a couple of sips while he was looking and then most likely leave it on a table when his back was turned. She had no idea how these other women managed to stay on their sky-high heels while drinking as much as she had seen tonight. Her little kitten heels were already pinching her toes as he led her to a cluster of older men near a bar, Walter Stuart among them. Sarah pegged them as the Scottish equivalent of what in Carolina she would call the Good Ole Boy Network. Walter and two other men were talking politics and easily made room for James to join their group. The man talking when they arrived had a prodigious mustache and a snifter full of brandy. The other man wore his hair unusually long for a man of his age. He stood a little apart listening while enjoying his own brandy. Sarah was sure that they allowed her in only because she was on James's arm and to exclude her would have been rude. They nodded to her politely and continued their conversation.

"Devolution is a foregone conclusion. The commission will support it. After the Thatcher years, a referendum campaign would be a cakewalk. It's merely a matter of time." The mustached man waved his brandy and looked pointedly at James. "I hope you're ready to take the reins."

James straightened his shoulders. "I assure you, I am ready."

The man eyed James skeptically, "You may want to put a stop to some of the tabloid attention, if you expect to go into politics."

"We're working on that." Walter put in. He spoke quietly, but James's uncle had a way of being forceful even when he was nearly silent. He reminded Sarah of a predator hiding barely out of sight waiting to strike. "It's more a matter of the right tabloid attention. We simply must control the narrative. With James's cachet, the right story can carry him straight to the throne. People will be clamoring for a new king."

Sarah felt her eyebrows go up. These men had obviously had a few too many drinks, or they would never have been talking about this kind of thing around her. James put his champagne glass on the bar and covered the hand that she was still resting on his arm. Sarah looked around their little circle. The only one looking at her was Walter Stuart. He was watching her closely, no doubt gaging her reaction to that last statement.

She knew she probably should keep her mouth shut and stay under their radar. Then James gave her hand a proprietary squeeze and smiled down at her. Everything in her rebelled. "I think you're all assuming a lot. What if people don't want a monarchy?"

"I'm sorry, what?" The mustached man looked at her as if he had only just realized she was there.

"Well, it's 1996. There aren't any monarchs in the developed world that are anything but figureheads." She looked up at James. "Is there really any point to that?"

"Of course, there is. It's about national identity, morale, patriotism." James turned to address her more directly.

"You need a monarchy for that?" She looked sideways at James. "I'm American, we don't have a figurehead and believe me there is no shortage of patriotism or national identity. What makes you think an independent Scotland would need or want one, or for that matter recognize one other than the one it has right now?

Mustache man shifted uncomfortably and gave her a piercing look. "But what about those who still bemoan the fate of the Stuart monarchs?"

Sarah couldn't miss that his *bon vivant* veneer was thinning, but she wasn't about to be cowed. "I'm sure there are some people like that. We have some in America who still complain about the result of our Civil War, but we don't usually make public policy based on that small chunk of the population. Those people might claim to miss the Stuart monarchy, but how much are they willing to pay to reestablish it. I think you'll find that when you ask people to financially support a figurehead, they won't want to open their pockets."

"But it would be privately funded, like the Windsors are now." James put in.

"They didn't start that way. And they don't make public policy." Sarah turned toward James. "If you are interested in a monarchy that has anything more than a nominal role in the government, it would have to be publicly funded. Anything else would be loaded with conflicts of interest. No one would be able to trust the monarch not to advocate for policies that would line his or her own pockets rather than benefiting their subjects. That's not monarchy, it's fascism. You might find that people would rather spend their tax dollars on the National Health Service, schools and pensions than pomp and palaces."

"Spoken like true Labor voter." The dark eyed man, who had been silently listening to the conversation said, his focus on Sarah.

"I probably would be, if I voted here. In America I'm considered pretty liberal." That wasn't something she was going to apologize for. Walter and the other man exchanged a dismissive look that had Sarah bristling.

James patted her hand and leaned closer. "I would love to discuss this further. Will you join me?" He waved a hand toward the door to the terrace outside.

"Alright," Sarah followed him to the door and went out when he held it open. The terrace was gleaming marble and kept warm by a row of gas patio heaters. James let the door close behind them.

In a flash his arms were around her and he found her lips with his. He walked her back into the shadows between the potted pines not stopping until her back touched the cold brick wall. Sarah was so shocked that she didn't even resist at first, but within seconds pushed against him. He lifted his head but did not let her go.

"I think we have a misunderstanding here." She pushed at his arms until he released her.

He turned to the side and blew out a long breath but didn't move. "I'm sorry. I couldn't help myself. Matching wits with you is so…exciting."

"We talked about this. I thought we were going to be friends." She wanted to move from where she was in the shadows, but he had effectively boxed her in. "I can't have a romantic relationship with you."

"I know you say that, and I do understand why…I do," He slid a hand along her waist. "I wish you would reconsider."

"And I," She pushed him away gently with a hand on his chest. "Wish that you would take no for an answer."

He let out a short huffing laugh. "It's not a word I'm used to hearing."

Dermot had been right about one thing. James was certainly persistent. "I noticed. You might have to get used to it, especially if you're going into politics."

"Mmm. That seems more and more likely. Perhaps you would consider advising me." He leaned against the wall next to her but sprang away from it immediately. "God, that's cold. Come away from there you must be freezing."

He pulled her away from the wall and ushered her to a spot next to one of the heaters. Sarah adjusted her shawl to cover her shoulders. "Thanks. I was cold."

"I'm sorry I did that. It was terribly inconsiderate of me." He pulled the end of her shawl higher, closer to her neck.

Sarah shrugged. "I'm sorry too. I like debate. I forget sometimes that not everyone is interested in an opposing view."

"I like it, but I don't think Aberdeen cared for it much." He smiled slyly.

"Who?"

"The Earl of Aberdeen, the man who was talking with my uncle."

"That mustache is an earl?" Of course, he was. Sarah had lectured an earl on politics. "Who was the other guy?"

"Oh, that's Greene. He's on the board of Alba Petroleum." James waved the thought of Greene away.

"You have to warn me about these things before I stick my foot in my mouth."

James chuckled. "Would you have said anything different?"

"No, but I might have phrased things less harshly. Is he a donor? Should I go apologize?" She took a step back toward the door.

James caught her wrist laughing, "I will never forgive you if you do. You made some valid points and both my uncle and Gordon needed to hear them. They live in their own bubble and don't often consider what the average person is going to think. What you said might do them some good. Although, I don't think they expected to hear it from you."

"Alright. If you say so," She let him pull her closer to the warmth of the heater. They stood there in silence for a few minutes. Sarah looked through the garden toward the canal. In the moonlight she could make out the shape of a small dock and boat house. James watched the goings on inside over her shoulder.

"You do know that I'm an earl too." His voice was quiet, contemplative. "Is that what bothers you about me?"

"You weren't introduced to me as Lord Caledon. I had no idea who you were. I had time to get a little used to you before learning about all of this," She waved a hand toward the house. "And there's nothing about you that bothers me. I just don't want to date you."

He exhaled slowly. "You're not still pining over that anthropologist, are you?"

"Jon? How do you know about that?"

"Dermot told me."

"Of course," She hoped he didn't hear her grinding her teeth. "I don't much like being gossiped about, even by people who are supposed to be my friends."

"He was concerned, and he shared those concerns with me. We are old friends you know."

"So, I've heard." She looked out toward the canal again. "And no, I am definitely not pining for Jon. I honestly can't believe how much time I wasted on him."

"You deserve better." He stepped closer.

She gave him a chilling look. "Jon used me to smooth the way with his colleagues because he lacked social skills. I deserve someone who is interested in me, and not only what I can do for him."

That stopped James in his tracks. She couldn't help feeling a little satisfaction at the way his face fell before he looked away. That was exactly why he was pursuing her. It wasn't because he lacked social skills. He was prince charming if there ever was one. He wanted her for her genes. Despite what he said, he didn't care about Sarah. Of course, he didn't realize that she knew exactly what he was up to.

James looked at his feet. "Indeed. You deserve better."

"I think I'd like to go back inside now. What do you think my chances are of getting a cup of coffee?" She smiled at him. She had made her point.

He smiled back, though it wasn't the movie star grin that he often used on her. This smile was not calculated. She saw a vulnerability that he hid most of the time. "Oh, I'm sure we can arrange that."

He stepped away from the heater and offered her his arm. She had to admit she could get used to his manners. She glanced over her shoulder at the canal one more time and happened to see a familiar face walk by on the security patrol.

"Fleming!" She called to him walking to the edge of the terrace.

He looked wary but met her there. Sarah wasn't sure how he would receive her. Dermot said she had gotten him into trouble by sneaking away from Chapel Hill. "Sarah, it's good to see you."

"I hope you mean that." She whispered before James came close enough to hear.

"You know Mr. Sinclair?" James asked when he arrived at her side.

"Of course, I do. He saved my life." Sarah grinned. She might have gotten him into trouble, but maybe she could help him out a little now.

"I did what anyone would do." Fleming rumbled in that deep voice of his.

"Don't downplay it." She turned to James. "When I was being held hostage a few weeks ago, Fleming is the one who called the police. Then when I almost got away and that madman caught me in the street, it was Fleming who talked to him. He distracted him long enough for the police to arrive. I don't think I would be here without this man who I'd never even met before."

Even in the low light she could see his cheeks turning red. "It was nothing, really."

Sarah gave a skeptical laugh. "Most people would have hidden in the house and hoped for the best. He could have easily turned that gun on you. What you did was very brave."

"Very brave indeed," James was appraising Fleming.

Sarah decided a more direct hint wouldn't go amiss. "Well, I'm freezing. So, we're going inside." She stretched up to give Fleming a quick kiss on the cheek. "I hope they don't keep you out in the cold too long."

"Good night, Miss MacAlpin, sir." Fleming nodded to them both and cleared his throat before returning stiffly to his patrol.

James was thoughtful as he escorted her inside. Sarah felt like she was batting a thousand tonight. The program had gone well. They had raised a lot of funds for the project. She thought she had made her point with James and maybe even reversed some of the damage she had done to Fleming.

"Let's see about that coffee." James turned toward the kitchen.

"Actually, can you ask about that? I need to use the ladies' room."

"Certainly, it's down that hall there." He pointed to a hallway that ran under the stairs toward the front of the house.

"Great. Thanks." She followed his directions and made her way to the bathroom. For all the ballroom and kitchen looked like they belonged in a hotel, the powder room was grand, but still a powder room. Sarah noticed though that the small room next to it had been setup up with mirrors and chairs as a sort of retiring room.

She was freshening up her lipstick in a large mirror, when two young women came in behind her. "...don't think he's serious, do you?"

"Of course not, you should have seen him in Ibiza last November. We were inseparable." A blonde who looked like she had recently walked out of the pages of Vogue said as she leaned toward another mirror to blot at her eye liner.

"I wouldn't be too sure of that. He certainly seems occupied tonight." The only slightly shorter woman with warm brown hair with chunky blonde highlights leaned a hip on the counter beside her. Their easy interaction made her miss how it used to be between herself and Amy.

"I'm not worried about that," The blonde rolled her eyes and gave her head a shake that sent her hair flying. It fell back into place looking slightly tousled and incredibly sexy. "She's only someone his parents..."

"...find a new captain for the yacht. I'm certain the last one fed information..." A perfectly put together middle-aged woman walked in drowning out the younger women. She was with two friends, one of whom wore white fox stole across her shoulders that Sarah was sure was as real as the diamonds around her neck.

A woman who had been sitting quietly rubbing her feet in the corner perked up. "Katherine! I haven't seen you since the..."

All the women were talking now, their voices swirling in to what felt like a wall of noise at Sarah's back. She felt suddenly very tired. Their voices swam in her head. Her limbs grew heavy. She leaned forward and braced her hands on the table in front of her. She closed her eyes and focused on breathing evenly and slowly.

"*Cuimhnich.*" [Remember] Her granny's voice whispered in her ear. Sarah could almost feel Granny's breath on her skin. "*Arbirainn I finaidh banaon chann ur afoinn,*" Sarah opened her eyes and stared hard into the mirror. There was no one there, but her and the crowd of clucking hens behind her. Granny wasn't beside her, but the voice went on, "*Ach ur pham chann ur n fawur breanain.*"

"No, Granny," Sarah muttered through her teeth. "Not now." The wave of tiredness abated, leaving only a slight headache and a patch of goosebumps on the back of her neck.

Sarah looked around to see if the other women had heard her, but they were all wrapped up in their own conversations. Conversations about yacht captains, trips to Spain and fashion shows. Sarah left shaking her head and stepped into the hallway. It was blessedly empty giving her a moment to straighten her shoulders and take a deep breath before diving back into the crowded ballroom.

"Sarah," Jujhar's smooth honeyed voice came from her left.

She turned and smiled. There was a calmness about Jujhar that she always found soothing. He smiled and took her elbow. "You look tired."

"I am a bit," She admitted. "I'm not a big fan of crowds. Hopefully we've raised a lot of money."

"The auction went well. We'll be announcing the winners shortly." He pulled her in the direction of her table. "Why don't you have a seat?"

She let him steer her to a chair. "Thanks, James went to get me a cup of coffee. I could use the caffeine."

She craned her neck looking for James, but it was Dermot that she spotted. He was pressed chest to knees against a brown-haired woman in a red dress that fit like sausage casing. They were entirely focused on each other and smiling. Sarah couldn't help noticing the obvious connection.

The song ended, and the woman stepped out of his arms, but kept her grip on his hand. He followed her out to the patio. A curtain blocked her view of Dermot as the door closed behind them, but Sarah couldn't miss the light of anticipation in the woman's eyes as she turned to him. The budding pain in the back of her head blossomed into a full-blown ache, and her skin prickled along her shoulders. *Oh,* she thought. *This must be what jealousy feels like.*

"On second thought, Jujhar, I am really tired, and my head is aching. Can you find Dermot for me and tell him that I'm ready to go home now?"

Jujhar gave her a sympathetic look before setting off to find Dermot with a murmured. "Of course."

The ride home was a whole different kind of tense. Sarah sat quietly seething, her face turned to the outside window. She had no interest in airing their differences where the driver could hear, but she definitely had some things to say. She folded her arms across her chest, keeping a firm grip on her temper.

CHAPTER NINE

When the car pulled up in front of their house, Dermot stepped out and checked the street with characteristic military efficiency. He held out his hand to help her out. She bypassed his hand and gripped the top of the door to pull herself up from the seat before walking straight to the front steps. She began fishing in her evening bag for her keys, but he stepped around her to unlock the door with his.

His calm politeness made her want to hurl herself upstairs and slam the door in his face. She nearly did, but of course he had to check her apartment first. Calum, like much of the AP security force was at the party on guard duty. The house had been left unattended and they couldn't have her walking into an apartment that wasn't secure. This was what her life had become. She was starting to wonder if she had made the right choice coming to Scotland. Were Dermot and the answers about her mother worth the risk?

She followed him into her flat without a word and waited by the door while he cleared every room and closet.

"All clear." He said as he walked toward the door.

"Who is she?" She asked through her teeth. Her voice shook with fury.

He stopped and turned her way, "Who?"

"Who? The woman in red that was draped all over you, that's who." She hated how she sounded; strident, shrewish. They'd done this to her. He'd done this to her.

He took a careful step back raising his hands as if she were armed. "Her name is Felicia Banks. She does public relations for James."

"Oh, I can imagine what that involves." She muttered.

His eyes sharpened on her. "Ye know, this particular shade of green doesna suit you."

"Yeah? Well you picked it out." She tore off the ridiculously expensive cashmere shawl and flung it over the back of the couch. Unbuttoning her coat helped her cool off. Each button she undid let her breathe a little more.

She was surprised that he didn't leave. Now that her initial burst of rage was gone, maybe they could have a reasonable conversation. She took a deep breath before turning back to him and leaning against the back of the couch. "What are you doing Dermot? First Kirstie and now this Felicia person?"

"Come on. Do ye really not know?" He gave her the same look that Amy used to when she was being especially dense. "I'm moving on."

She raised a skeptical eyebrow, fighting not to show how much that stung. "When we're together every day, when it's your job to protect me, you're moving on?"

"I'm trying to." He barked. "Do you expect me to spend my life waiting on your every move? Don't I get a life of my own?"

She stepped toward him and raised her hands to him, pleading. "That's exactly what I want. For you to choose what will make you happy, but that woman isn't it."

He stepped back avoiding her touch. His voice was firm, unequivocal when he said, "Neither are you."

His words were so unexpected, it was like walking into a wall. "What are you saying?"

He rolled his eyes, as if he couldn't believe he had to explain it to her. "I'm saying that I did what I thought I had to do to get you here. Nothing more."

"No." Tears stung her eyes, and an ache tightened her throat. She shook her head as if that would keep the words from sinking in. "No, I'm not so pathetic that I fell for some line and followed you across an ocean."

"Why not?" He smirked, actually smirked, looking like a frat house Lothario. "It was a pretty good line. And after ye told me about your mother, I knew it was exactly what would work."

It would have been better if he'd hit her. She let out a huff of air and bent forward, disgust making her gut churn. Her mind ran back through that early morning in his apartment in Chapel Hill trying to find some clue, some indicator that he was deceiving her. They'd been through one of the worst nights of her life, and he'd held her and listened to her. I love ye. I'm here. We're alive. I'll always be here. Those words had not been a lie. They couldn't have been. She refused to believe it.

She inhaled long and deep and let the breath out slowly, breathing through pain. When she looked back at him she was smiling and shaking her head. "That's not going to work on me, Dermot. I'm not some dog you can drive away by talkin' hateful."

"Sarah," His voice held a note of warning, but she wasn't going to hear it. If she had to get through his resistance, she would have to lay everything on the table.

"Wait here." She practically ran to her bedroom. The journal was in her top drawer right where she'd left it. She took it back to the kitchen and dropped it with a thump on the island.

"What's this?" He looked wary.

"Open it."

He eyed the book like it was a bomb. After she sighed with impatience, he finally picked it up. His strong fingers curled around the spine as he opened the cover.

She had read and reread her mother's final message over the last few weeks. She knew the first lines by heart. *You'll learn that this story goes back a long, long time, but my part of it started in the spring of 1968. I was seventeen...*

"It's my mother's journal, really more of a memoir." She said softly. "It's all about her time here in Scotland." She cleared her throat around the lump that had formed. "How she met my father."

"That's great." He looked up, eyes seeking hers.

"It's given me a whole new understanding of her." Sarah took a step closer to him. "Something went wrong while she was here. It broke something inside her. I think I might have an idea what it was, but I can't be sure."

"It was in Assynt?" He asked after skimming a few pages. His eyes were bright, eager. "We could be there tomorrow."

"Not so fast. I'm not running off to the Highlands with nothing but my suicidal mother's word to go on. Also, those people were awful to her. I don't think they'll be exactly excited for me to show up on their doorstep. I've been researching the village. I want to be prepared when I go." The tears were back in her eyes. She walked around the counter to stand close to him. He stood his ground not moving back when she stepped into his space. "I knew you were lying."

"What?"

"A man doesn't jump at the chance to fix something like this for a woman he doesn't care about." He stilled. Hope surged in her chest. She'd been right. He did love her. "I came to Scotland for two reasons. I have to find out what happened to my mother."

"And?"

"I came here for you." She bit her bottom lip and her pulse ticked up. His eyes zeroed in on her lips and she could see the hunger there. She pressed closer keeping her voice whisper soft. "I love you Dermot. I know you love me. I'm not going to give that up, and you, and James…and Walter, and your Miss Banks can't make me."

His blue gaze shifted from her lips to meet her eyes. There was a flash of pain there, before he shuttered his emotions. His look turned cold, hard. That same smirk returned, and his tone took on a derisive sneer. "I did what I had to do to get you to come here. I won't say I didna enjoy it. But after what yer mother did to ye, ye are so hungry for it, that ye canna recognize when it's not real."

She hated the hot tears that rolled down her cheeks, hated that he knew all the right buttons to push. Her voice was hushed but hot with fury. "That's the second time you've used my mother's illness to hurt me tonight. It won't happen again."

"Or what? Ye'll hate me? I'll regret it? Ye'll tell James?" His voice was like a schoolyard bully; ugly, hateful. Ronnie Sue Corbett flashed through Sarah's memory, and her fingers clenched into a fist. "He'd probably be impressed that I would go so far for him. All in the line of duty, aye?"

Like she done to Ronnie Sue, Sarah punched him. She might be a little on the petite side, but she knew she had a good right cross. He didn't even attempt to block it before it connected with his jaw. His face was a lot harder than Ronnie's had been almost twenty years ago, but she wasn't about to show how bad the pain in her hand was. Her cheeks were red with rage. Tears streamed from her eyes. "Get out!"

He didn't have to be told twice. He whirled around and stalked to the door. She followed and slammed it behind him shooting the deadbolt home with a loud thunk.

She ran to the ice box in the kitchen and thrust her right hand inside. She rested her forehead against the side of the refrigerator hoping the cold steel would help cool her rage. She caught sight of the stupidly ostentatious coffee maker that James had given her. In one last burst of rage she sent the glass carafe flying at the door. It shattered with a satisfying crash.

Sarah grabbed a bag of frozen peas to wrap around her bruised knuckles as she slid to the floor, finally letting the tears take over.

***

Dermot spent the better part of the night sitting on the stairs in the hallway at the house. Partly because he was expecting Sarah to try to run and partly to punish himself for being such an ass. He had waited on the stairs for Calum to come home from the Burns supper. When he had filled his partner in on the situation, he had gone into his flat to lie down. He spent the rest of the night flat on his back staring at the ceiling and wishing he could see through it.

Sarah's bedroom was right above his. After that first crash of breaking glass, he hadn't heard anything else. He'd had to force himself not to go back into her apartment. He was sure she wouldn't harm herself, and he convinced himself that it hadn't been a window he heard shatter. What was she doing now? Was she still angry?

His feet felt like lead, but it was Sunday morning. He was sure that if she'd been able to sleep at all, she'd be sleeping late today. It was the perfect time to visit his mother. He needed a reminder of why he'd done what he'd done last night.

He made his way across the city through the chilly morning to his mother's care home and trudged up to the reception desk. "Morning, Rachel."

"Morning," The nurse smiled at him, but her brows creased in concern. "You look like you've had a rough night."

"Mmph. You're not wrong." He grumbled.

"Well, you're in luck. She seems pretty sharp today." She nodded to the lounge area where his mother liked to spend much of her time. It was still early in the day, and she was alone in front of the one windowed wall that overlooked the street. She had her knitting in her lap and was shaking her head at it.

He approached her slowly. He was never sure what he was going to get on his weekly visits. Hopefully, Rachel was right, and it was a good day.

"Mum?"

"Dermot, love!" She dropped her knitting and opened her arms. Relief swamped him as he hugged her and kissed her cheeks. "You look tired."

"I was working late last night. Had a fundraiser for our field work project." He pulled a chair up next to hers and sat down beside her.

"Really? Tell me about it." She picked up her knitting again and settled in to listen to him. That was how she listened best. *Busy hands mean open ears.* She'd always told him, even before she got sick. She said the knitting kept her mind from wandering.

"In the spring we're going to be going through the Highlands and islands recording songs and stories, learning traditions. We've got a filmmaker who's making a documentary about it..." He went on telling her about the project. He didn't know how many times he had told her about it before, but it didn't matter. He'd tell her a thousand times as long as she was listening the way she was today.

They chatted about field work and the university for a while before he noticed that she wasn't knitting, she was undoing the stitches. "Why are you undoing your knitting?"

"Och, I don't know what I thought I was doing with this, but it's all wrong. This color wants some prettier stitches to show it off." The color was a light brown that he'd spotted through the window of a yarn shop a couple of weeks before. It had reminded him of an old tweed coat she'd worn when he was a boy. "I think maybe some cables."

"I'm sure it'll be great." His throat almost closed on the words. He knew there wouldn't be any cables. Most days her mind wasn't sharp enough to remember the complex stitches. But he wasn't going to remind her of that. He was going to enjoy every lucid minute that he had with her.

He stayed with her almost the whole day. He didn't mean to, but she'd been so engaged. They had talked about everything, and nothing of consequence. They had done a crossword together and she'd known many of the answers. Taken on its own, that day made it seem as if there was nothing wrong with her. That was the way the disease worked. It blew through her mind like winds in the desert. One day, hour, minute she would be herself, mind intact. The next the sands would shift, and the landscape changed. Giant dunes would block her from his view, block her reasoning from her memory.

But not that day. It was as if she knew that was exactly what he needed. They'd had a pleasant lunch together, then returned to her room. She liked to take a nap in the afternoon. They turned on the television with the volume down low. He settled into a chair beside her bed.

"It's been a good visit today, Dermot." She gave his hand a squeeze.

It was several seconds before he found his voice. "Aye, Mum. It has."

Within minutes, her hand went slack in his. Her breathing slowed to a soft steady snore. Even though he'd been there longer than he planned, he found that he didn't want to leave. He looked around the room. It was mostly sterile, institutional. There were a few personal touches. She kept an old photo of the two of them on the nightstand. She'd brought some pillows from their old home to make the place cozier. Of course, there was a knitted throw from home as well, like one that she'd made in better days when she could follow a pattern.

She had started some cable stitches today after all. The patchwork piece of knitting that she continuously worked on now sported a few rows of braided stitches right at the top. It was a good day. She had been his Mum today, right when he'd needed her.

"I've met someone, Mum." He said softly. He wasn't sure what made him start talking. He hadn't told her about it when she was awake and could offer advice. Maybe because he knew what she would say. She would tell him that his happiness was the only thing that mattered. She would tell him that she was lost, and he should leave her. But she'd never left him.

She'd kept him with her when she was young and alone and could have given him up. She'd endured whispers and sly looks from people who knew she wasn't married, that his father wasn't a part of their lives. She'd never made him feel like a burden, and he knew it had been hard to build a career and be a single mother. He couldn't leave her. So, he'd tell her now, when she was sleeping.

"She's smart, and kind, and brave." Tears pricked his eyes and he heard his voice crack. "She's so brave, Mum."

"And fierce, and stubborn," A laugh bubbled up inside him. "Ye'd say she was a good match for me…And she is. I love her, and…" a sob broke free from his chest. "…and she loves me too."

A hot tear slid down his cheek. "But there's someone else who wants her, someone I can't compete with. He can give her so much more. He can protect her; and she needs…deserves protecting. But so do you. And I can't protect you both."

CHAPTER TEN

Sarah shut the ancient map book with care and slid off the cotton gloves they'd asked her to put on. It was the oldest map the university had of Sutherland and it hadn't offered her any more information than the maps that were made yesterday. She'd been through every atlas and property record that she could get her hands on from modern ordnance surveys to ancient hand sketched maps in journals. None of them showed a village that fit the location or description of *Làrachd an Fhamhair.*

She nodded to the attendant that she was done and left the collection room, gripping the gloves tight in one hand. She signed out of the collection, retrieved her bag and made her way from the unassuming stone buildings that housed the Scottish Studies Library around the corner to the main library where she could spread out on a work table.

She found a table in the main hall and pulled out her notebook. She ought to be listening to folk recordings trying to find a new song to pin her thesis on, but since telling Dermot about the journal she hadn't been able to get it off her mind. She tried to tell herself that this could be a whole new avenue of research, but the truth was she just wanted to find the place. If nothing else, it would prove that her mother's story was at least in some part true.

It had also provided a nice distraction from the tension between them over the last few weeks. It had been almost a month since she'd kicked Dermot out of her flat, a month full of strained, awkward conversations and pretending not to be alternately heartbroken and furious. In the meantime, James continued to pursue their "friendship" with almost nightly calls. He would inquire about her day, and how the research was going. He asked how she was liking Edinburgh. It was nice to have someone to talk to. She was sure that when he met someone he genuinely loved, he would make that person very happy. A few times he had asked her out to dinner, but she had kindly turned him down pleading the need to study.

She and Dermot had continued going to work together in the mornings and working on the preservation project in as professional a manner as possible. More often than not, Dermot had left the afternoon bodyguard duties to Calum, who stayed close enough that if something went wrong he could be there in seconds. Of course, Sarah wasn't supposed to know he was following her, but she knew what to look for. At that very moment he was about thirty feet to her left pretending to peruse a rack of information sheets about the university's library system.

The library was full of people on a Thursday afternoon near the middle of the term. Their whispered conversations were a pleasant, breathy hum through the quiet building. It was a relief to have the near anonymity of being there with nothing but her research.

If *Làrachd an Fhamhair* wasn't on any maps, then she would have to switch to plan B, tracing the people. The geographic location might be vague, but she had names and approximate ages in 1968. It was a place to start. She opened her notebook and listed the people who might still be around in Scotland.

- Robert Ballantyne
- Sheila MacLeod
- Eilidh MacLeod
- Jock MacLeod

How far out of the system could these people live? There was no record of the village, but if the people wanted any kind of state services, they would have to have records. She could start with the census, then anything from the registry office. There should be a record of Willie Cross's death somewhere. She hoped she could get access to some of these records here in Edinburgh. Once they hit the road she would be working and living with the team. She wasn't likely to get much opportunity to search local records.

She sat back staring at the list. She would have to try her gift on one of these people. The trouble was, she wasn't sure she wanted to find some of them. Eilidh and Sheila had been cruel, and Rab had been a coward. Would they have changed in the last twenty-six years? Only Jock had been kind. She remembered her mother's description of the jolly man who kept the village running while she'd lived there. He had been a good source of information for Molly. Maybe he could help Sarah too. She would look for Jock.

In the meantime, Sarah tried to think of any other concrete things that she knew about the village. There wasn't much information in Molly's journal beyond basic geography, which hadn't been any help so far. She doodled in her notebook, letting her mind wander through the verifiable things that Molly had written. She remembered something Jock said. There had been prisoner of war camps in the

Highlands during World War II. He had even mentioned some escapes. There should definitely be records of that.

Sarah grabbed her notebook and went for the information desk to ask where she might find information on POW camps. Within half an hour she had a list of the three closest to Loch Assynt. There were camps at Loch Watten, Dornoch and Dingwall. Details on whether the prisoners were "high level" as the journal had said were sketchy, but there should be records of any escapes. It would be tedious work, but newspapers of the nearby towns during the war looked like the next step. That's precisely where she would start tomorrow. She went back to the table where she'd left her backpack feeling energized.

Rounding the table, she stopped dead. Sitting on top of her bag was a book that she had not left there. Calum was two rows away in the card catalogs pretending to look something up. Seriously. Did he think she wouldn't recognize her own neighbor following her? She hoped he was better at the protection part of his job than he was at the stealth part.

The book on her bag was one of those cheap paperbacks of Macbeth, not unlike the one she had bought in Chapel Hill when she started researching the three witches. The cover showed a man obviously meant to be Macbeth but dressed like a Roman warrior. He looked on as three crones meant to be the witches bent over a steaming cauldron. There was a torn piece of paper sticking out of from between two pages.

Holding her breath, Sarah picked up the book. She opened it to the page marked by the paper. The top of the crude bookmark was straight with a bold line drawn right below the edge and placed precisely under a single line.

I'll give thee wind.

On the paper a note was scrawled in Gaelic.

Find the answers in your own field, princess.

The book slipped from her nerveless fingers and landed on the table with a whack. Sarah took a step back fighting to control her panic. She looked around for the culprit. No one was snickering behind their hands or a bookcase. No one was even looking at her. Everyone she could see was going about their own business. No one appeared to notice her. She pulled out a chair from the table and dropped into it eying the book as if it might explode. Her hands gripped the seat on either side of her and she took several deep breaths trying to get her panic under control.

Three months out and she still hadn't forgotten the last thing Ryan Cumberland had said to her, right before his suicide by cop. *I'm not the only one, princess. There will always be more.* Was that it? Had someone else been sent by whoever sent him? But, if someone was trying to kill her, why would they warn her? Delaying the job to cover his own tracks had been Ryan's downfall.

She had to get out of there, had to tell Dermot, but she felt glued to her chair. Dermot. The last time they'd been at odds for this long, he'd left her flowers in the library. What are the chances he would try something like that again? After all, he'd been with her when she'd purchased the copy of

Macbeth before. The more she thought about it, the icy fear she was feeling, transformed in to burning fury.

***

Sarah stalked into the office to find Dermot by the conference table talking to Ewan looking like he didn't have a care in the world. He certainly didn't look like a man suffering from a broken heart. In her current state, that only made Sarah angrier.

She flung the little book at his head. "Is this your idea of a joke?"

He ducked and picked up the book. "What?"

"I read the note." She practically shouted. "You don't get to call me that, God damn it!"

"Right. My office." Gritting his teeth, Dermot came around the conference table and took her by the arm. He hurried her into the hallway and pushed her into his office. Shutting the door, he set himself in front of the door knob. "Tell me and keep yer voice down. These walls are thin."

His calm demeanor grated. She nodded to the book that was still in his hand. "Your little gift is what I'm talking about. It didn't work before and it's not going to work now."

"I've never seen this before." He examined the book. "Where did you find it?"

"You didn't leave that for me?" She felt her rage deflating and giving way to the same panic that she'd felt before. She swallowed hard, as her breathing sped up.

Dermot shook his head and she swore his tiny office started to tilt. She couldn't quite fill her lungs.

"Some..." She waved a shaking hand at the book. "Left for...library." Talking wasn't working, hell her lungs weren't working right. She grabbed the book and opened it to the note. She held it up for him to read.

His face went dead calm, and he quietly took the book from her. He wrapped his arms around her. "Listen to me, love. I need ye to breathe with me. Feel when I breathe, and you breathe too." Her knees sagged, but he held on. "No, stay with me, and just breathe. I won't let ye go."

She nodded. She felt his chest expand and fought to make hers do the same. He exhaled, and she blew out a shaky breath. They did it again. Each breath got stronger. His arms warmed her, thawing the ice that had frozen her nerves. After several minutes, she felt strong enough to push away from him.

He watched her closely as she sank into the visitor's chair in front of his desk. He squatted in front of her and looked up into her eyes. "Better?" She nodded, "We're going to keep you safe. Do you believe that?" Another nod, "To do that, I'm going to have to get James's help. He'll put every resource he has on finding out who this is and why. We're not going to let what happened in Chapel Hill happen here."

She didn't want to feel any more indebted to James than she already did. *There will always be more.* She took a steadying breath and nodded again.

"Can you tell me how you got the book?" His voice was a patient rumble.

Sarah blew out a long shaky breath. When she could speak again her voice was quiet, but steady. "I was in the library doing research. I left my bag at a worktable and when I came back, that was sitting on top of it."

His eyebrows drew together. "Where was Calum?"

"I guess he followed me. He tries not the let me see him, but I usually do."

He made throaty noise of disapproval. "Alright. Let me see your bag."

She looked around, not remembering where she had dropped it. It was lying on its side against the back wall of the office. Dermot picked it up and unzipped each of the compartments examining the contents. Gripping it by the top, he opened the door and stepped into the hall. "Ewan. Can you hand me one of those bin liners?"

He returned with a plastic bag in his other hand. "Is there anything in here that you can't live without?"

"The whole thing?" She asked, surprised. "All my research is in there."

"And ye'll get it all back tonight. I need to take the bag to get checked out. We have to make sure there's nothing on it or in it that we don't want."

"Like what?"

"Like a bug or a tracking device." His voice was stern, and it chilled her. When had this become her life?

She ran through a mental list of items in her bag, thankful that she'd decided to leave Molly's journal at home. She wasn't sure it would mean anything to James nor Walter, but she would rather it stayed with her all the same. "No, nothing that I can't do without for the next few hours."

"Keys? Wallet?"

She shook her head. "In my pockets."

"Good." His lips tipped up at the corners. "I'm going to have someone escort you home and stay with you until I come back. Calum will still follow you, but you shouldna be alone."

She didn't bother to protest. At this point the fear and rage had drained out of her. She found that she was so exhausted that all she could do was nod and let Dermot take the lead.

"Come on, love." He held out an arm to her, and she slid under it. He steered her out the office door and into the main room. Ewan, Jujhar, and Kirstie were there whispering among themselves. She hated being gossiped about. It made her feel suddenly like the little girl from Kettle Holler that people whispered about behind their hands.

"Lads, will ye make sure Sarah gets home safely, and keep her company until I can get there?" He looked between the guys.

"Sure," Ewan hopped off the desk where he'd been sitting.

"Of course," Jujhar picked up his satchel from beside his desk.

"Can I help?" Kirstie offered, making doe-eyes at Dermot.

"That's alright, thanks," said Dermot. As tired as she was, Sarah caught Kirstie's stiff reaction to his easy dismissal. Dermot on the other hand was oblivious.

When the guys had collected their bags, Dermot turned to her. His eyes sought hers and for a second, she forgot the trouble between them. He wasn't the man who claimed he didn't care, or that he'd used her loneliness to manipulate her. For that instant, he was the man she loved, the one who was always there when she needed him. Whenever she thought she'd managed to start moving on, she felt her heart slipping again. "Go on home. I'll be there in a tic."

CHAPTER ELEVEN

"Can I get you anything while you wait, Mr. Sinclair?" A pleasant voice asked from his right.

Dermot turned from the window. He wasn't sure how long he'd been staring out at...well, nothing really. He found the sweet-faced receptionist whose desk was the gateway to James's suite of offices smiling at him. "Eh, no. Cheers."

"I'm sure Mr. Stuart will be out of his meeting soon, and then he'll be glad to see you." She smiled and returned to her desk.

Doubt that, Dermot thought as he turned back to the window. James's office commanded quite a view from a high floor of an ornate Georgian building on The Mound. He trained his eyes on the people walking through the Princes Street Gardens, but watching the crowded, bustling city below did nothing to ease the tension that knotted his shoulders. Any one of those people down there could have been the one who left the note on Sarah's bag. Any one of them could be stalking her, like Cumberland had. He couldn't let himself fail like that again. The man had stalked her right under his nose for months and he hadn't figured it out until it was nearly too late. For all she probably hated him now, it was still his job to keep her safe.

He stood with his arms crossed over his chest. The bin liner containing Sarah's backpack, the book and note dangled from his white knuckled grip. He'd clung to it so hard on the interminable taxi ride over from the university that his fingers ached. Time had slowed to a crawl the moment she'd flung that book at his head. His shoulders bunched, and a roaring filled his ears. He couldn't be sure if it was fury, or fear, or a mix of the two. He cursed himself a hundred times over. He'd been so worried about pushing her away, pushing her toward James, that his focus had slipped. He shouldn't have left things up to Calum. At the very least James would have to give him more manpower.

He started when he heard a door open. Turning quickly from the window he found the double wooden doors to the office suite were open. Standing between them was a primly dressed woman with dark hair pulled back from her face in a tidy twist. Her shoes clicked smartly on the parquet floor as she strode over to him, "Mr. Sinclair?"

"Miss Lennox."

"Mr. Stuart is wrapping up his meeting. If you'll follow me…"

She led the way into the suite of offices. There was a sitting room that acted as a central hub with several rooms branching off it. Unlike, the sitting area outside the suite, this one had no windows, but its paneled walls were hung with portraits of previous Alba Petroleum executives, including the largest central portrait of Henry Stuart, James's father. Henry had run Alba Petroleum through the oil boom of the nineteen eighties. When James had come of age, however Henry had retired and left the company to his son under the watchful eye of his younger brother, Walter. Dermot studied the painting from several feet away. Ironic, he thought, to give such pride of place to a man who had retired at such a young age. But then, James had been training to run the company for his whole life.

The door beside the portrait opened and James came out accompanied by a gray-haired man in a sharp suit with a neatly trimmed goatee and piercing green eyes that reminded him more than a little of Sarah's. James made his goodbyes with the gentleman's club joviality that he had been perfecting since birth, and the older man made his way to the door. The man did look sharply at the bag in Dermot's hand as he passed by, and Dermot felt suddenly ridiculous holding a bin liner in his hand in the middle of what he was sure was one of the finest offices in the city.

He awkwardly passed the bag from one hand to another as the older man walked to the door. James turned to Dermot and held a hand to usher him into his personal office. When he had closed the door behind them James leaned back against it and sighed. "Save me from nervous board members," He pushed away from the door and walked around to his desk. Behind him was a grand view of the gardens below, but James didn't even glance at it. He sank into his burgundy leather chair. "I'd like to say it's good to see you, but I have a feeling you didn't come over here to brighten my afternoon."

"Someone left a book and a note for Sarah on her bag in the library," He lifted the bag he was holding. When this didn't seem to catch James's attention he gave him a significant look. "It calls her 'princess'."

James eyes widened, and he stood, reaching for the phone on his desk and pressed the intercom button, "Miss Lennox, I need Mark Shaw in my office immediately, and if my uncle is in the building, he might want to attend as well."

He hung up the phone and returned his attention to Dermot. "Where was her guard?"

"With her. She left her bag at a table while she was researching something. I doubt she'll be leaving it unattended again."

He nodded to the bag that Dermot still held. "This is the bag?"

"The bag, book and the note that was left in it." He held up the bag. "I thought Shaw might want to check the bag for devices."

"He'll be checking it for devices, fingerprints and anything else he's got equipment for." James said with definite steel in his voice. "How is she?"

"Spooked," He huffed. "And furious. She's no fainting flower."

"Indeed, she isn't." The corners of James's mouth tilted up hinting at a smile, and he looked off to the side as if examining some memory. Dermot waited patiently. "What do you need to make sure this doesn't happen again?"

"At least one more man. I'm busy maintaining the cover of the research group. I can only cover her when she's in the office or her flat. Calum is only one man. If she catches him, she'll think he's a stalker." Of course, she already knew what Calum was, but James didn't know that. And he would use anything he could to get James to give him what he needed.

There was a scratch at the door followed by Miss Lennox leaning in. "Mr. Shaw is here."

James waved a hand in an invitation, and the door swung open to admit Mark Shaw, his head of security. Gray haired, though undeniably fit, Shaw's military experience showed in his bearing; shoulders back, spine straight, walking with confidence. He took in the room with one quick scan and zeroed in on James. Were it not for the muscles flexing in his jaw, Dermot would never have known how nervous the man really was. "What can I help with, sir?"

James eyed him like a bug. "You can explain to me how your man let someone get close enough to plant a book and threatening note on Sarah MacAlpin's bag."

Shaw looked uncomfortable, but when he spoke his voice was steady, "Yes, Mr. Ridland informed me of the incident."

"Did Mr. Ridland have an explanation?" James snapped.

"He was following Miss MacAlpin. She left her bag at a table and walked away from it. He thought it more important to follow her than worry about her things."

Dermot had to speak up at this. He'd said as much. "That was the right choice. That also makes my point. One man is not enough."

"Sir," Shaw picked up the thread. "Ridland has expressed the same thing. He also feels hamstrung by the need to stay hidden."

The door behind Shaw swung open, and Walter Stuart strode into the room as if he owned it. "We shouldn't have to stay hidden from her. It's time Miss MacAlpin learned the truth. We can't keep her safe with this ruse about studying folk nonsense. She'll be much easier to guard when she's under our control."

Dermot felt the cold burn of rage start to heat the back of his neck. His fingers clenched even tighter on the bin liner. A small part of him wished they were wrapped around Walter Stuart's throat. He addressed James and tried to keep his tone level. "If you tell her now, she will run at the first possible opportunity."

"Then we don't give her an opportunity." Walter passed Shaw approaching James's desk.

"And make her a prisoner? That'll definitely win her over." Dermot sneered as he took a step closer and tried to block Walter. "James, ye don't want her like that. She will hate ye, and ye will hate yourself. Ye want a queen, not a prisoner."

Walter waved a dismissive hand. "She'll come around."

"No, she won't. I've spent a lot more time with her than he has. She's stubborn as a mule, and she would hate you for the rest of her days."

"Have you forgotten that we are on a timetable here?" This time Walter addressed Dermot.

"We've waited more than three hundred years. I think we can take a few more months to get it right." Dermot kept his focus on James.

"Has anyone ever told you you're impertinent?" Walter's voice was tight.

Dermot shifted his attention to the old man. "Has anyone ever told ye no?"

"Enough!" James cut through their building fury. He looked past them to where Shaw was still waiting, wisely staying out of the line of fire. "Can you put someone else to work with Ridland?"

Shaw nodded, "I can see who is available."

"You're only delaying the inevitable." Walter muttered shaking his head.

James cut off any further protest with a sharp hand motion. "Sarah's value is more than simple genetics. We *need* her cooperation."

The tension in Dermot's shoulders eased. "I have an idea. Tell her ye're giving her a bodyguard while she's in the city. When we go out to do field work she'll have me, until then let Fleming Sinclair protect her."

"He already lost her once." James started to object.

"And he will not likely do it again. She's terrified. She'll be far more likely to cooperate now."

"Can't we do that with someone who hasn't already failed?" Walter complained.

"He's a familiar face. She'll feel less threatened and she believes he already saved her life once." Dermot argued.

James sat at his desk considering. His gaze shifted among the three of them before settling again on Shaw. "Is Fleming Sinclair available?"

Shaw nodded. "He's downstairs."

"Talk with him. Make sure he understands the assignment and that I will not tolerate further lapses."

"Of course, sir."

"Have him report to Dermot at the house on Bernard Terrace at…" James looked to Dermot in question.

"Seven tomorrow morning."

James turned back to Shaw to make sure he'd gotten the time. He waved a hand at the bag that Dermot still held. "Go through this bag and the book and note. Make sure there are no devices in them. I'm sure she would like to have the bag back."

Dermot held out the bag, "I'll pick it up from yer office shortly."

Shaw took the bag. With a nod he spun about, making a beeline for the door. Dermot couldn't blame him for wanting to make a quick escape.

"You're going to regret this." Walter continued to grouse.

James gave him a quelling look. "Uncle, you are going to have to allow that Dermot and I know Sarah MacAlpin better than you do. She has a strong will, and we want that working with us, not against us."

The old man seethed. James chose to ignore him, turning his attention back to Dermot. "Do you think that will be enough?"

"We can always reassess, but I think it's a start. I'll also remind her not to leave her bag unattended."

"I doubt she'll forget that soon." James muttered.

Dermot made his retreat, hoping he didn't look quite as eager as Shaw had. If he weren't fretting about Sarah so much, he might feel chuffed about winning that round with Walter Stuart. It was a rare thing for James to second guess his uncle's guidance, rarer still for him to openly disagree in front of others. Dermot made his way to the lift. It wasn't until he'd pressed the button and the doors had closed on him that he let himself relax.

He leaned back against the wall and closed his eyes feeling the vibration of the metal against the back of his head. A couple of floors down, the bell dinged, and the doors opened. He glanced up at the display to see that he'd only gone down one floor.

"Well, this is a surprise." Felicia Banks purred as she stepped into the lift. Smartly dressed in a trim suit, much like that of Miss Lennox, Felicia's was punctuated by a bright paisley pashmina that swept across her shoulders and brought out the color in her cheeks. She carried a leather business case that was a perfect match for her pumps. She was always so well put together, he imagined she coordinated everything down to her knickers.

"Afternoon, Felicia." He straightened, standing away from the wall and tugged down his jacket as she pressed the button for the ground floor.

Even with her heels she was almost a head shorter than him and used it to her advantage smiling up at him through her thick curling lashes. "Been to see the boss?"

"Mmph. Had a bit of urgent business."

She cocked her head and looked skeptical. "Urgent folklore business?"

He leaned down as if sharing a confidence, "In my business, funding is almost always urgent."

"No doubt." She lifted her case a few inches. "Well, I'm off to the Scotsman to face down the lions in their own den. Seems James has an ex who's peddling a story to the gossip pages."

"What kind of story?"

She waved a hand. "Oh, some rubbish about how he took her to Spain and said he loved her, but then threw her over. Honestly, quashing tales from these models keeps me in Louboutins. My department would be half the size it is if James would settle down."

"Well, I'd hate to see us lose jobs over James's love life."

"Oh, he may surprise us all one of these days." The bell dinged, and the door began to slide open sunlight from the building's front windows flooded in. Dermot waited to allow Felicia out first. She stepped forward but turned and braced her hand on the open door. "Listen, Dermot, I don't suppose I could tempt you to have dinner with me some time."

Gobsmacked, he opened his mouth to refuse, but he thought of Sarah's face when she'd slapped him a few weeks ago, or the fury he'd seen when she threw the book at him earlier. He may have effectively burned that bridge already. "Aye, sure."

Her glossy pink lips curved into a satisfied smile. "Excellent. Are you free Friday?"

He nodded, still stunned.

She opened one of the front pockets of her briefcase and slid out a card. "You can pick me up at this address at seven."

He took the card and glanced at it. Her address was printed on the back. He nodded slipping the card into his pocket.

She stepped back, and he had to jump to keep the lift door from closing. He watched her back as she sashayed her way to the door, her shape silhouetted against the sun.

***

Sarah glanced at the clock on the microwave. It had been three hours since she'd left Dermot at the office, and here she was quietly making tea in her little kitchen waiting for him to come back and trying not to think about all the things that could have been planted in or on her backpack; listening devices, tracking devices, contaminants of all varieties. Not for the first time, she wondered how her life had gone from that of a slightly obsessive academic to a magnet for crazies in only few short months. Was it knowing James that had put this target on her back, or had it been there all along?

If it wasn't for the calming presence of Jujhar, she would probably be climbing the walls. Ewan had left for a meeting, but Jujhar stayed with her distracting her with stories about the antics of his four younger siblings. He could tell that she wasn't ready to be alone.

She produced a box of cookies, she supposed she should call them biscuits around here. That was one British term that she still couldn't get used to. Biscuits were soft fluffy buttery things that were best when smothered in sausage gravy or surrounding a good salty piece of ham. Cookies were cookies.

"I've told you all about growing up in London. I'm interested to hear what it was like where you grew up." Jujhar asked, as if he could tell she was thinking of home.

"Well," Sarah poured the boiling water into the two cups that were waiting with tea bags. She blew out a long breath. "Imagine the complete opposite of growing up in a cosmopolitan city like London, and you're about halfway there. Tack on that my grandmother was a foreigner and a moonshiner and my mother was unwed and chronically depressed. That's the perfect recipe for a small-town pariah, and really calling where I grew up a town is generous."

"It can't have been all bad." He picked up his tea and motioned toward the couch. "Tell me something good about your childhood."

Sarah followed him, tea in hand. She curled up in the chair next to the couch. "I would love to say no one left threatening notes on my book bags, but that wouldn't exactly be true. I took a lot of flak from people calling my mother crazy on top of not having a father. I didn't really see much reason to make friends with people who were judging me for things I didn't have any control over."

She looked up from her tea to find him watching her. He gave her a look that said he could wait all day for her to find something positive.

"Okay, okay. Good things." She took another sip of her tea. "I mean, I wasn't completely miserable all the time. I knew my grandmother loved me. Duff loved me; he was a friend of my mother's. But I think the best part was the mountain. Once I got old enough, Granny pretty much let me run wild. Now, by old enough I mean old enough to know not to play with snakes or eat the bad mushrooms. I guess I was about eight."

"Our life was like something from another time. We got most of what we needed from the mountain and the forest. I knew how to hunt and fish and forage. When I was a little girl, the forest was where my friends lived. At least, the ones I made up for myself; fairies and brownies. I always liked the stories of knights, and kings, and princesses that my Granny used to sing about. I know," She felt her cheeks heating. She hadn't admitted this to many, but she had a feeling Jujhar wouldn't judge. "Fairy tales, but they were real then, and they were all around me."

Her gaze drifted away from his, unfocused. "As I got older, it was my solace. I could just *be*, in the forest. I didn't have to worry about anyone's expectations or prejudices. There were parts of that forest that had probably never been touched by people. Year after year, I watched the seasons change. Trees fell; others grew; everything changed. But the mountain and the forest? They always stayed the same. They were..." She felt the unexpected sting of tears in her eyes. "...eternal. And it made me realize that all those things that were making my life hard, were only temporary."

She was brought back to the present, by his hand on her wrist where her hand was gripping the mug. His smile was gentle, and his voice was smooth like creek water over round rocks, "What about those trials is different from now?"

Warmth swept through her as she laid her hand on top of his. Tears threatened to overflow, but this time they were tears of relief. She smiled back into his dark eyes. "Thank you."

"It's why I'm here."

She squeezed his hand and grinned, "I knew we were going to be friends."

"Indeed. Sarah…" He stopped at the sound of a key in the door.

Both of them turned as Dermot came in, her backpack in his hand. He held the bag out to her. "It's clean."

Sarah rose and took the bag. She carried it to the counter and checked the contents. She could feel Dermot's eyes on her, but he didn't say anything.

"I don't suppose you know yet who left the book." Jujhar said to Dermot as she accounted for the things in her bag. Everything was there.

"Not yet. James Stuart's security people are going to look into it." He answered flatly.

Having verified that nothing was missing from the bag, Sarah turned back to them. There was an awkward silence during which Dermot watched her closely. Jujhar set his mug on the coffee table and retrieved his coat from where It was draped over a chair. "I should be going."

"Oh, stay and finish your tea." Sarah pleaded.

He shook his head with a little smile. "I really should be going, and I'm sure you two have things to talk about."

Within seconds he was out the door, leaving them in silence. Sarah never knew which Dermot she would get these days; the strong reassuring Dermot who liked to take care of her, or the sharp-tongued stranger determined to alienate her. From the way he was shifting back and forth on his feet, he didn't seem to know any better than she did. "Are ye alright?"

"Yeah." She nodded and busied herself with collecting the mugs and returning them to the kitchen.

"James's security chief has people working to find out who left the note. We're hoping the library had a camera on that table." He waved at where she'd left the backpack on the counter. "In the meantime, we're assigning you a body guard, one that can stay right beside you when I can't."

Or won't, she thought.

"I got Fleming assigned that duty. I thought ye'd prefer him."

"Yeah. I do. Thanks."

"Stick with him, only until we go out into the field." He bent to catch her eye. "And ye shouldna leave yer bag unattended anymore."

She went back to rinsing the mugs, "I'll remember that."

Tense silence stretched out while Sarah put the mugs in the dishwasher and the tea back in the cabinet. "It was nice of Jujhar to stay with ye."

"Mmm. He's a good friend." She looked over to the couch remembering their conversation and again feeling that warm peace that being near Jujhar brought. "He's good company, very relaxing."

He looked thoughtful. "Well, if ye're alright then."

"Yep." Nodding stiffly, "Fine."

"Well then," He opened the door and stepped into the hall. "Cheers."

Sarah went back to fidgeting in the kitchen until she heard the door close with a soft click. She blew out a long breath trying and failing to relax. She was back to being under constant guard. She hated being watched, hated feeling helpless. There was one thing she could do, that they wouldn't see. She could cast out. If she could manage to relax enough, she could look for Jock MacLeod as she had decided to do earlier.

She went to the living room and sat on the couch, putting her feet up on the coffee table. She leaned her head back and focused on breathing. With each exhale she felt her body get heavier, and her mind get lighter. Then she thought of Jock; kind, dedicated, jolly Jock MacLeod who looked like Santa Claus and kept *Làrachd an Fhamhair* running.

She didn't know how long she stayed on the couch thinking of Jock MacLeod, but at some point, she fell asleep. Maybe she relaxed too much, or maybe Jock wasn't around to be found anymore. He had been old when Molly met him. She would probably be better off looking for someone from Molly's generation like Sheila or Rab.

She tried to cast out again this time focusing on her mother's description of Rab Ballantyne. Her father was handsome, green-eyed and charismatic. The trouble was that every time she tried to think of Rab, she was swamped with emotion and anxiety and her ability to relax and use her gift went out the window. The same thing happened when she focused on Sheila, and on Eilidh. She was still learning her way around this gift, but she thought it was safe to say that relaxation was one of the key components. She couldn't help laughing at that. With her childhood, she thought it was a miracle she was ever able to relax at all.

CHAPTER TWELVE

This is a terrible idea." Fleming grumbled in Sarah's ear, so she could hear him over the crowd and music. Other patrons jostled them as they went to the bar to get drinks and Fleming maneuvered himself between Sarah and as much of the crowd as he could.

"Well, there are plenty of terrible ideas floating around lately." She muttered.

"What's that?" He leaned close again.

"Nothing." She shook her head. No sense in dragging him into her foul mood. To the barman she said, "Cider, please."

Rather than shout to be heard over the music, the man nodded holding up two fingers to indicate the price. He reached for a glass and started to pour from the tap. Sarah dug into her pocket for the coins to pay for her drink. She was still getting used to being able to pay for more than a candy bar with coins. Of course, the two coins she slid across the bar were worth about four dollars, which was close to what she would have paid in an American bar. The barman took the coins and slid over a cider before looking at Fleming. "Club soda."

The barman shook his head and slid a club soda across the counter waving off payment. Fleming took the drink and turned looking around the bar. There was a band playing on stage. A crowd of people down front bounced with the loud music. Back near the bar there was room to move, but still a good crowd. Sarah spotted a tall table with a perfect view of the stage. She got Fleming's attention and nodded toward it.

He shook his head and nodded toward another that was closer to a wall. Sarah followed him to the table he chose.

"The other table had a better view." She had to crane her neck to see the whole stage, not that there was much to see over the roiling audience.

"Aye, but it was out in the open. Here I can watch the room without having to worry about what's behind me."

That threw a cold bucket of water on any excitement Sarah felt about the evening. She had hoped for a fun night out with friends. Of course, the need for a bodyguard had a way of spoiling a girl's good time. Still, she needed something to get her mind off the fact that Dermot was out on his *third* date with that Felicia Banks person. She had so far resisted the temptation to spy on his dates using her gift. She was sure that it wasn't something she wanted to see.

She couldn't hold it against Fleming. He was the nicest guy and he'd been great at making her feel safe without intruding. But nothing else had happened since she got the note and she was getting restless. Thank goodness they'd be hitting the road in another week.

"Hey!" Isla shouted to be heard over the music as she arrived at the table. She nodded to the stage as she slid her jacket off. "They're not bad, eh?"

Sarah looked over to where a fiddle player was playing a reel at center stage to the very loud accompaniment of guitar and drums. "No, they're pretty good."

"I think Alan's band is next." Isla said, leaning close.

Ewan joined them at the table and slid a black and tan in front of Isla. She leaned back and said something to him that looked like more than a simple thanks. The kiss she delivered by his ear was so quick that Sarah almost missed it. There was no missing the furious blush that bloomed across Ewan's cheeks as he focused his attention on the stage.

When Isla turned back to the table, Sarah gave her a questioning look. Isla returned a shrug as if to say, 'Maybe we are.'

It looked like Ewan had finally found that confidence Isla was looking for or at least some of it. Isla could still make him blush easily, and by the twinkle in her eye appeared to enjoy doing it. Sarah hoped she wouldn't be too hard on the guy. He was awfully sweet.

Shortly, Jujhar and a flat mate of his joined them. They rearranged themselves around the small bar table. Fleming stepped back and leaned against the wall behind Sarah and was so unobtrusive that she nearly forgot he was there. Sarah found herself between Isla and Jujhar. When the band finished their set, Sarah asked Jujhar. "Is Kirstie not coming?"

He shrugged, "I told her about it, but she didn't say either way."

"She's probably still pouting over Dermot and his new lady love." Isla interrupted, eyes on the stage as her friend Alan's band began to set up. Sarah wondered if that was what she was doing, pouting. Dermot had been so closed off from her since January. Maybe he'd been telling the truth that night when she'd slapped him and thrown him out. Was it really nothing more than a ploy to get her to come to Scotland? With his mission accomplished, he was free to move on to the perfectly polished Miss Banks.

Sarah watched cider bubbles sliding down her nearly empty glass and hoped her mood didn't show. She felt an arm wrap around her waist in a surreptitious one-armed hug and looked up into Jujhar's kind black eyes. She leaned into him and hugged him back.

They all got another round of drinks and settled in to hear the next band. But when the band took the stage the guitarist, a wiry man with a wild shock of bright red hair, stepped up to the microphone, "Right. We're ready to play for yez, but I was talking to Pete backstage and he said he reckons he's the best fiddle player in this room." The crowd erupted in cheers.

"That's Alan." Isla shouted in Sarah's ear over the din.

The leader bobbed a hand the air. "Settle down. Now I says to him, that can't be right. Because I know for a fact that Isla Reid is in the audience tonight. Are ye out there, Isla?"

Isla gave a whoop and raised her drink in the air above her head. Some in the crowd who had heard her before cheered. Sarah felt Fleming push away from the wall and step up closer behind her but tried not to let it ruin the fun.

"And he says, 'Isla who?'" This prompted jeers from the crowd as Pete, the offending fiddle player, stepped up to the front of the stage. Holding not one, but two fiddles. At the microphone Alan said, "That's mighty big talk,' I says. And he says, 'I'll prove it!'"

"Now, as I see it, the only way to prove that is to get our Isla to come up here and give us a taste of what she can do. What do yez think?"

The crowd roared. Isla wasn't going to let the challenge go unanswered. She leaned back and bussed Ewan on the cheek before making her way through the crowd.

Once on stage, Isla began tuning the extra fiddle while exchanging some good-natured trash talk with Pete, the fiddle player. Isla was from a long line of musicians, and this sort of friendly competition and banter was second nature to her.

Sarah imagined she'd been doing this since she was old enough to hold a fiddle.

When she was ready, she played a quick reel. Pete followed in with the same tune but added some flourishes. Isla started another more complicated tune, and the crowd began clapping along. Pete followed with a more complex tune. Isla picked up his tune and added to it. Together they moved into a song that the rest of the band could accompany them on and the energy ramped up even more. By the end, the fiddles were working in unison and the crowd was hopping. Isla and Pete wrapped arms around each other laughing.

Alan, returned to the mic, "Isla Reid everybody!"

The crowd went wild. Isla stayed on stage for a few more songs continuing her new musical rivalry. Eventually, Isla stepped up to the microphone. "This is great fun, lads, but I think there's something missing."

Alan answered, "What's that?"

"I think we need another lass up here." She looked around at the all-male band. "It's a bit of a sausage fest."

"D'ye have someone in mind?" Alan scanned the crowd.

"Well, I have this friend, she's back there." Isla waved at Sarah, then made a come-hither motion. "She's really quite good."

"Well, come on up, then." Alan waved as well.

Sarah was more than ready for the chance to perform. It had been too long, and Burns Night had only been a taste of the kind of fun she used to have. She started into the crowd, but someone grabbed her wrist. She turned to find Fleming shaking his head, with a determined look in his eye. Sarah twisted her arm from his grip and spun toward the front. She skirted around the crowd to the side of the stage. She could feel Fleming at her back. He wouldn't make a scene, but he would stay close.

Sarah climbed the steps to the stage. Alan gave her a rakish smile before stepping back to give her his microphone. Sarah looked over to Isla. "How about a little *puirt à beul*?"

"I like the way ye're thinking." Isla grinned.

Sarah took a breath and waited for a lull in the noise from the crowd. When she was satisfied that she had their attention she sang a verse of the song slowly first. Her voice was clear and steady. When she finished the verse, she launched into a round of fast rhythmic Gaelic singing. Isla picked up the accompanying fiddle tune. Together they whipped the crowd up into a foot stomping frenzy. When the song was over, Sarah felt breathless and more relaxed than she'd been in weeks. It felt so good to lose herself in singing for an audience.

They returned to their table cheeks flushed, out of breath and feeling like they owned the room. Isla threw her arms around Ewan and kissed him with gusto. They reminded Sarah of her friend Amy and Andy MacAffrey after playing a ceilidh. Not for the first time, she missed her old singing partner. She wondered what Amy was doing now, and if she'd forgiven her.

Alan, Pete and the rest of the band joined them when their set was over. They all moved to a quieter table at the back of the pub and began talking and having a grand time. Isla bought them all a round to toast the band's performance. Then Pete bought a round to thank everyone for coming out. Then Alan bought a round just because, and before she knew it Sarah was starting to feel quite a bit tipsy. Her frustration with Dermot and James and her nervousness about being stalked were no competition for four glasses of cider and a whisky, or maybe two.

After a while, Alan sat down next to Sarah on the bench, his shoulder pressing against hers. "Sarah, my love, tell me where on earth ye've been hiding."

Sarah smiled at him and blushed a little. "America. I used to do festivals with a friend of mine."

"Is she as good as you?" He gave her a flirty smile.

Sarah giggled, "Better."

He grinned and pretended to search the crowd, "Where is she?"

Sarah looked down at her glass, "Back home. We had a falling out."

He sobered and placed a comforting hand on her knee, "Now that is a shame. Still, if you're looking for a band…"

"I'll keep that in mind. Right now, I'm about to hit the road with Isla to preserve some traditions."

"I keep trying to tell her there's no money in that academic business." Sarah didn't miss that his hand was still on her knee. He jerked his head to where Fleming was standing almost behind them like a raptor waiting to swoop down at the first sign of trouble, "Is that your boyfriend?"

She shook her head, "Bodyguard."

Alan leaned closer to her ear, "Why, are ye famous?"

"God no!" She couldn't help laughing, "I have a stalker."

"Seriously?" He gave Fleming an appraising look.

"Unfortunately." She took a swig of cider. Her head was starting to swim, and she noted that this, would have to be her last drink.

"Ex-boyfriend?" Alan asked.

"Ha! That would require me to have had a boyfriend with enough passion to generate that kind of madness. I assure you I have not." She might have leaned a little too close, and maybe slurred a bit. She didn't miss Alan's hand slide further up her thigh.

"Listen my flat's around the corner. Why don't we take this conversation somewhere a bit more private?"

Sarah looked at him for a few beats. Was he leering at her? Yes, that was definitely a leer on his lips. They weren't bad lips. Alan really wasn't a bad looking guy, but this wasn't her game. She plucked his hand up by the wrist and gently set it back in his lap. She focused on not slurring as she told him, "First, I'm not that kind of girl. Second, even if I was..."

"That'll be enough of that, mate." A firm voice cut over what she was about to say. And Sarah felt a hand wrap around her upper arm. "I think it's time to go home."

"You might be right," She said as Fleming pulled her off the bench. Sarah stumbled a step before waving to the group "Night, y'all."

Fleming steered them toward the stairs without delay. Sarah heard a chorus of goodbye's behind her. He was irritated, even in her state she could tell. Ignoring her requests to slow down, he pulled her down the street to a taxi stand in front of a hotel and shuffled her into the next cab.

Sarah slumped back and closed her eyes hoping the world would stop spinning. "You could have given my head time to catch up with us."

"Not likely," he muttered looking away from her.

After several minutes of tense silence, he asked, "Do ye ever talk to her?"

"Who?"

"Amy." He said as if it were obvious.

Sarah almost laughed, "Why on earth would you ask me about her now?"

"Because it looks like ye could use a friend." He gave her a hard look.

"Yeah, well last time I checked, she wasn't too interested in being my friend," She mumbled bitterly. "Doesn't matter. I don't even have her new phone number."

They rode on, with Sarah trying not to be sick as the taxi zipped through the narrow streets. When they arrived back home, she let Fleming help her out of the car, but shook off his hand as she made her way up the stairs. In her drunken state Sarah forgot their routine of Fleming opening the door and checking the apartment before she went in. She pulled her keys from her pocket and made for the door.

He took the keys easily from her fumbling fingers. Sarah didn't bother to wait for him to clear the place. She trudged over to the couch and laid down taking care not to jostle her head too much. Closing her eyes, she waited for the room to stop spinning.

She heard some paper shuffling followed by what sounded like pencil scratching. "I'm going to leave this here in case ye change yer mind."

Sarah stared at the plaster ceiling cursing herself for drinking so much. After several minutes, she rolled off the couch and used it and the coffee table to push to her feet. She made her way carefully to the bedroom.

As she passed the kitchen island she noticed the piece of paper that Fleming had left. It said, "Amy" in bold block letters and had a phone number on it. She didn't recognize it, but the 919 area code told her it was a North Carolina number.

CHAPTER THIRTEEN

The scent of freshly brewed coffee tickled her nose, but that didn't mean she was about to open her eyes. For one thing, her eyelids weighed a ton. For another she was afraid that if she lifted her head, what was left of her brain would flop out of her skull and stay there on the pillow. What had she been thinking?

The coffee smell got suddenly stronger and with it came a gentle but firm voice saying, "Time to wake up, Sleeping Beauty."

"Don't think this makes you Prince Charming." She burrowed her face in to the pillow wondering if it was all some kind of hangover induced hallucination.

"Well, I am technically a prince," Said the smooth voice.

Sarah cracked an eyelid and spotted the cup of coffee that was being held next to her pillow. Wrapped around the handle were long elegant fingers, one of which wore a signet ring with the Clan Stuart crest on it. Sarah stared at the image of the pelican in her nest regurgitating food into the mouths of her young and her stomach lurched. She sprang up almost knocking the cup out of his hand. "Shit, James!"

A slow grin spread across his face as he took her in. She was sure she looked absolutely horrifying, until she glanced down to find that she was wearing only a camisole and panties. She dove back under the duvet. "How the hell did you get in here?"

"Dermot let me in." He said as if it were the most natural thing in the world.

"Of course, he did." She muttered through her teeth.

"I had to use the French press to make the coffee. The carafe to your coffee maker seems to be missing." He set the coffee cup on the night stand.

"It broke." No need to mention that it broke when she threw it at his number one henchman.

"Ah. You should have said. We'll get you another."

"James," She wasn't in any shape to chat about coffee pots or anything else. "Did you seriously come uninvited into my flat to talk about my coffee maker?"

He shook his head. "Quite right. You have fifteen minutes to shower and dress; something comfortable and trainers. We're going for a long walk."

"Um, I don't know if you've noticed, but I'm not really up for a long walk."

His expression grew serious. Suddenly, he looked like the man who ran the largest oil company in Europe. When he spoke again, it was clear that this was an order. "I have noticed, and I do wish you would take better care of yourself. I'm not going to take no for an answer today. Kitchen. Fifteen minutes."

He strode back to the kitchen without a backward glance; sure that she would obey. Sarah dragged herself to the bathroom and stood under the hot spray. She wasn't sure how long she was in the shower, but since James hadn't come in after her she supposed it was within his fifteen-minute time frame. After towel drying her hair, she threw on some sweats and her sneakers. She was wrangling her damp curls into a pony tail, when she walked into the kitchen.

James Stuart, billionaire and would-be King of Scots was spooning porridge into a bowl. When he saw her, he nodded to a stool at the island. "Sit down."

He topped the porridge with berries and a drizzle of honey. Caught off guard by this new side of James, Sarah didn't know what to say.

"Eat. You'll feel so much better once you've had some porridge, and you need fuel."

Sarah propped an elbow on the counter and supported her forehead with her hand. She ate her porridge in silence. She wouldn't have thought she could stomach anything that morning, but it was creamy and warm. The berries and honey made it sweet, and before she knew it she was scraping the bottom of the bowl and feeling mildly better.

When she looked up, James had put the pan in the sink and was wiping down the counter.

Sarah still couldn't figure out why he was there or what was going on, "Who are you?"

His smile was indulgent, "I'm your friend, James. Remember?"

She nodded. This was in fact something she could imagine Amy or Barrett or Dermot for that matter doing for her. She wondered if this was James's idea, or if Dermot had told him she would need this. No, not Dermot. He was too busy with Felicia. He probably had no idea about what she'd been up to last night.

"Better?" James asked.

She nodded again, not knowing what to say to him. He understood that talking wasn't something she was ready for. "Good." He smiled. "Let's get going."

He held out a light jacket for her to slip into. He picked up his own jacket and ushered her out the door locking it behind them. He slipped the keys into her jacket pocket. When they got downstairs, Fleming was waiting for them, also dressed for a hike. He obviously felt better than Sarah did, but he still looked tired. She felt a twinge of guilt for keeping him out so late.

Fleming opened the heavy door and she stepped outside. She was thankful for the shade offered by the crag to the east that shaded the street. She hadn't looked at a clock, but if the sun hadn't risen above the top of the crags then it was still relatively early in the morning. A car door opened in front of them, and Sarah looked over to see Dermot holding it. His face was grim, and he avoided her eyes. He probably disapproved of her evening out too. Wasn't a girl entitled to cut loose every once in a while? It's not like she made this a regular thing.

She got into the car and scooted over to the opposite side. She propped her elbow on the door, shielding her eyes with her hand. The porridge may have restored her stomach, but the changing light as the car moved was murder on her head.

Sarah didn't look up until the car stopped, and even then, she was reluctant. They had driven out of the shade and into the morning sunlight. She felt James get out of the car and slid across the seat to follow. The sun hit her like a nail through her temples. She stood in front of the open car door blinking the world into focus. When she could finally see what was in front of her, she wished she hadn't.

The grey-brown rock face of the Salisbury Crags shot straight up out of the green hillside before it curved back toward Arthur's Seat. It suddenly dawned on Sarah exactly which long walk James meant for them to go on.

"Aw, hell no." She turned directly around and was halfway back in the car when an arm came around her waist.

"Not so fast."

She stood and turned to him. "James, I can't do this right now. I'm a mess. I feel awful. I can barely keep my balance on flat ground."

James pulled her close effectively pinning her between himself and the car. He leaned close to her ear and she could feel his breath as he whispered. "That's precisely why you should do it. Right now, when you're feeling weak. You've done far more difficult things in your life than climb this little hill. I'll be right there beside you. I won't let you fall."

She lifted her eyes again to the hill, and found Dermot standing near the start of the trail. He was turned in their direction, but sunglasses hid his eyes. Sarah couldn't tell if he was looking at them, if it bothered him. She gritted her teeth, "Fine, then. I don't want to."

A laughed rumbled through his chest so close to hers. "Consider it a challenge. I doubt you've ever backed down from a challenge."

She didn't have much to say to that. He pulled back to look at her and gave her his best Prince Charming smile. Ignoring the daggers shooting from her eyes, he pulled a pair of sunglasses from a pocket and slid them onto her face.

***

By the time Sarah stopped at the halfway mark roughly an hour later, her lungs were heaving, and her sinuses burned. On the other hand, her head felt much clearer and she had lost that walking through soup feeling that she'd had when they started. She was stepping with purpose now, rather than dragging one foot in front of the other.

"Come on. I thought you grew up in the mountains. This should be no trouble at all for you." James goaded from twenty feet up the trail.

"I haven't lived in the mountains in a long time." Sarah huffed, as she followed along. He was right though, and the incline at least reminded her of home. Her body certainly remembered. Despite her hangover, she was managing to keep up with James.

She followed James up countless stone steps that didn't seem to give him any trouble at all. Still, a little off balance, she was thankful for the chain railing in some parts that gave her something to hang on to as the trail got steeper. Near the top, the stairs gave way to packed dirt and stone.

"Almost there," James called back to her before disappearing around a rock face. Sarah stopped and rested her hands on her hips. Looking back, she saw Dermot down the trail. He glanced up and stopped mid stride. He still wore his sunglasses, so she couldn't tell what he was thinking. He didn't come any closer but waited for her to walk on.

She turned and followed James around the peak. A few steps up and there they were at the top of Arthur's Seat. A broad area of uneven stone topped the iconic hill that overlooks Edinburgh. On a slight rise in the rock stood a concrete plinth. It looked as if it were waiting for a statue or flag to be installed. Instead there was graffiti defacing the sides. Sarah leaned back against it to catch her breath thinking how ridiculous it was to make that climb only to vandalize something at the top.

James produced two water bottles from the pockets of his jacket. He held one out to her, "Drink."

They stayed there in silence drinking water until their breathing evened out. When Sarah had caught her breath, she pushed away from the plinth and walked around the summit. Every direction offered a view that went on for miles. She could see the firth stretching out to the sea, the monuments on Calton Hill, the castle and the hills beyond.

James came to stand next to her where she looked out at the water. "Breathtaking, isn't it?"

"Even without the climb." Sarah chuckled. She pointed to an island out in the firth. "Which island is that?"

James squinted at the blue horizon in the direction that she indicated. "I think that's Inchkeith. There's an interesting story about that island. During the Renaissance, James IV sent a woman and two babies out there to live alone. The woman was mute. They had their basic needs taken care of, but no contact with the outside world. You see, James wanted to see what language the children spoke when there was no one to teach them. He thought he would discover some primal language."

"And, instead he discovered that they didn't need language."

"Have you heard the story before?" He glanced at her.

"No, but I lived in an isolated place. Half the time I only had my grandmother for company. When I got older, sometimes we would go days without saying a word. In a group that small, you develop an understanding that doesn't need language. Still, I can't imagine growing up without stories or songs. That's how we learn when we're children. I wonder how they adjusted to society once the experiment was over."

"I've never heard anything about them after the experiment."

"No surprise there. History isn't written by test subjects."

"You've done very well though."

"Sure, but I wasn't completely isolated. Granny told me stories about our history and the community. She taught me how to get along in the world. I learned some lessons the hard way, but I had a chance to learn them. Those poor kids didn't."

They stood silent for several minutes listening to the wind.

James lifted a hand and pointed to the right of Inchkeith. "Further out, is the Isle of May. Some say it was the home of nine pagan priestesses."

"Thrice to thine and thrice to mine, And thrice again to make up nine." She quoted Macbeth while following the direction that he'd indicated. "Another case of witches in multiples of three. I seem to hear that a lot in Scotland."

"Witches, waterhorses, or King Arthur." He nodded toward the water again. "These priestesses are said to have rescued the mother of Saint Mungo after her father set her adrift while pregnant in an oarless coracle."

"Hmm, saved by pagans and went on to persecute them. That's gratitude for you."

He let out a little laugh. "Yes, well by most accounts, Mungo wasn't the nicest character. Still, he ushered in a new era."

They continued looking out at the view. James asked, "Glad you made the climb, now?"

She gave him a grudging smile. "Yeah, alright."

"I like to come up here on clear days and take it all in." He said gazing out toward the firth.

"King of all you survey?" She smirked.

"Not like that." He rolled his eyes, "This is one of the greatest cities in the world. Its universities have produced some of the finest minds of the last three centuries. Scots have been responsible for many of the inventions that make modern life what it is and a lot of that started right here. It's an exciting place to be."

She turned surveying the city below. "It is a remarkable place."

"And yet you don't seem to be enjoying it."

She took a deep breath feeling the bite of the early spring air. "Oh, I don't know. I think I might have enjoyed it a little too much last night."

"Hmph. That's not quite what I mean." He stood close beside her watching the city. He seemed to consider his next words. "You've been here for three months now, and you've worked nonstop. I know you're driven, but…" He turned her to face him. There was worry in his eyes. "You barely smile. You don't socialize outside of your team. You have exactly what you wanted six months ago, but you don't seem happy."

Sarah looked down at his jacket unable to meet his eyes. He was right, she wasn't happy, though she couldn't exactly tell him why. "A lot has happened since then."

"I know," He turned back to the vista, and put his arm around her shoulders. "But I know you're tougher than this. I also know that working as hard as you do without finding some kind of balance, is a good way to burn yourself out."

"You're not the first person to tell me that."

"Did it work before?"

She sighed, "Sometimes. It usually takes a friend dragging me out of the library."

He gave her shoulders a friendly squeeze. "Well, I'm glad to hear this was the right tactic."

"Definitely," She laughed and wrapped her arm around his waist, resting her head on his shoulder. "You know you're not so bad at this friend thing after all."

He kissed the top of her head, "You know I would like to be more."

Sarah closed her eyes. Every time she thought she was making progress with James. She pulled away from him in frustration and started walking back toward the trail. "We've already talked about that."

He stepped in front of her, "Please, hear me out."

She took a step back and watched him, waiting.

James held up a placating hand. "I know what you've said, and I do understand why. I wouldn't press you on this, if I didn't feel strongly about you, about us."

Sarah shook her head and turned away. She looked back down the trail and saw Dermot looking up at them from the rock ledge. James took her elbow and pulled her back to face him. His look was earnest. "All my life, I've been treated like a prince. Everyone around me knew where I was going in life and what I would be. I haven't been denied anything that I've wanted. But it all feels hollow. I've never had to earn anything."

"Then you came along, and you don't care who I am, or who my parents are. You are the first person outside my family who has challenged me, told me no, made me earn your friendship." He stepped closer placing his hands on her arms. His blue eyes captured hers. "That would be enough to get my attention, but you're also incredibly smart, and strong and beautiful. I know you don't want to risk your professional reputation and I want to respect that. But," He paused and took a deep breath his eyes pleading. "I'm falling in love with you. Will you give me a chance? Please."

Whatever reasons he had for pursuing her to begin with, he believed what he was telling her. He believed that he was falling in love with her. Maybe he was. That didn't mean she was falling in love with him. She was already in love, not that it mattered. "I'll have to think about it."

One corner of his perfect mouth curved up, "I'll take that as an improvement. Could we try a date? Maybe before you leave town?"

"I'll think about it." She repeated more firmly.

He stepped back, letting go of her arms. "Fair enough."

"Can we go down now?" She looked pointedly at the path behind him.

"Oh," He stepped aside for her to pass. "Of course."

She started down the trail, James following on her heels. When they reached Dermot, his expression was stony behind his sunglasses.

In the car home, Sarah and James sat in the back seat and Fleming rode shotgun, while Dermot drove them back to the house on Bernard Terrace. Their bodyguards reversed their roles from when they'd left with Dermot opening the door to the house. His sunglasses were gone. Sarah tried to catch his eye as James escorted her upstairs, but he kept his eyes trained elsewhere. Dermot followed them up the stairs and went around them to unlock and check the apartment. She was so tired of being guarded all the time, but then she imagined James had been putting up with it for much longer.

"It's clear." Dermot told them as he came back into the hallway. Sarah and James went inside. Sarah slid her coat from her shoulders. As she hung it on the coatrack by the door, she looked out into the hall to find Dermot watching her, his expression inscrutable. Their eyes met, and he looked as if he might say something, but James closed the door between them.

CHAPTER FOURTEEN

Sarah checked the clock and calculated the time difference. Afternoon in Edinburgh would make it Sunday morning at home. Before her doubts about how they had left things had time to creep in, Sarah had dialed the phone.

The voice that answered was masculine, but familiar. "Hello?"

"Barrett?" Sarah's throat ached with emotion. She hadn't realized how homesick she was until hearing a friendly voice.

"Sweetmeat! Oh, honey, how are you?" At least someone was happy to hear from her. She had forgotten that Amy and Barrett planned to live together this semester.

"I'm good now that I'm talking to you." Sarah sank down to sit cross legged on the floor and leaned back against the island. Her head felt somewhat clearer.

"We miss you so much. But I know you didn't call to talk to me." He put the phone down to call Amy. Sarah could hear voices and rustling.

"Sarah?" Amy's voice was soft and tentative.

Sarah had to fight to keep her voice from cracking. "Yeah."

"Oh god, Sarah! I've been so worried about you. I'm so sorry." There were tears in Amy's voice and Sarah felt tears of relief sliding down her own cheeks.

"No, I'm sorry…"

"I was the worst friend ever…"

"No, you were hurt…"

"So were you! God I was horrid. Can you forgive me?"

"Of course! Can you forgive me?"

"Already done." Amy sniffed and sighed. "I'm so glad you called."

"Me too." Sarah couldn't put into words the relief that she felt. "So, do you want to tell me how Fleming Sinclair knows your new number by heart?"

"What?" Amy was clearly puzzled, but she also sounded curious.

"Yeah, he wrote it on a piece of paper for me. From memory. That's how I called you."

"Huh…I mean I gave it to him, but it's not what you think. I told him to give it to you if you needed a friend."

"Well, it worked. He gave it to me last night while he was lecturing me about how I need a friend and I should call you."

"I'm so glad you did. Now, spill it. What's bugging you?" Good old Amy, getting straight to the point.

"Forget about me. How are y'all doing? What's happening there?"

"Oh, Barrett's trying to leave me for some artist he met in New York, and I'm chugging along. Mr. Bynum finally showed me around his woodshed and I wrote an article about it."

"Oh! Any woodshed revelations?" Amy had been trying to view the folk artist's workshop for months.

"Only that Bynum will salvage anything and make art out of it. He had everything from old porch trim to taxidermy disasters, and he knows exactly what project he's going to use every item for. The man is amazing."

"How's your granddad?" Amy's grandfather had had a stroke at the end of the previous semester.

Amy turned serious. "He's getting along. There's a little bit of paralysis in his face. He's more cantankerous than ever, but he's still with us. He asked about you last time I was there. He said, 'Where's that hillbilly friend o' yours? She ain't out makin' moonshine, is she?'" Amy said in a spot-on impression of her gruff and boisterous grandfather.

Sarah felt the tears pool in her eyes. If anyone doubted Amy Monroe's Scottish heritage, they only had to meet Tom Gregory to know the truth. Large, ginger and opinionated, the old man had treated Sarah like one of their own from the first time that Amy brought her home. "Aw. Give him a kiss for me next time you're over there."

"You got it. Now, back to you. What's going on?"

"I can't fool you, huh?" Sarah asked with a wry smile.

"Never could."

Sarah took a deep breath. "It's kind of a long story, but I guess it starts with me being in love with Dermot…"

"I knew it! Barrett, pick up the other phone. She needs both of us." They waited for Barrett to pick up, "Okay, Sarah finally admitted that she's in love with Dermot."

"Duh," Barrett groaned.

"Well, don't get too excited. The story goes downhill from there." She told them about their one night together in Chapel Hill, and about Dermot changing his mind the next day. She left out his real reason though. They'd never believe it if she told them. "So, he's been doing nothing but pushing me away since I got here. Now he's started dating this PR executive from Alba Petroleum. And next week we're leaving for the

Highlands to do field work. We're going to be stuck together for weeks and I don't know how I'm going to deal with it."

"Just like anything else, sweetie. One day at a time." Barrett put in.

"And then there's James."

"James, as in Hottie MacMoneybags?" Amy interjected.

"Yeah. He's convinced himself that he's in love with me and wants me to go out on a date with him. I don't know if I should."

"You do realize that you are probably the only single woman in the world who balks at the idea of going out with James Stuart, right?" Sarah could almost see Amy shaking her head in exasperation.

"Sure, but what about professional ethics?"

"You've already got the fellowship, and they know you're amazing without his input. No one will care now." Sarah could practically see the dismissive wave of Amy's hand through the phone.

"Geez, this guy must really be something?" Barrett muttered.

Amy answered without missing a beat. "Imagine Brad Pitt but with dark hair, and more money than God."

"Honey, I'm a waiter. As far as I'm concerned Brad Pitt has more money than God."

"Well, he doesn't have more money than James Stuart. I'm talking billions."

"Guys!" Sarah interrupted.

"Sorry." Amy said, "Although, I still don't see what the problem is. Is he really awful to be around?"

"No, he's actually very nice. One of the things that worries me is that he only thinks he wants me because I've told him no so many times. No one tells him no, and that makes me different. If I do start going out with him that he'll get bored fast and dump me as soon as the next shiny new supermodel comes along. Also, it seems kind of dishonest to go out with him, when I'm in love with someone else."

"Mmm...that's fair." Barrett said. "I still don't get why Dermot changed his mind."

"I don't entirely get it either. He just said it would never work. I think part of that has to do with him knowing that James was interested. Which makes me feel so stupid for loving someone who could throw me over so easily. I really thought he felt the same way."

"So did I." Said both of her friends.

"So, wait a minute." Amy said. "James says you should go out with him. Dermot says you should go out with James, and Fleming told you to call us because you needed a friend."

"That about sums it up."

"It sounds like Scotland is full of men who want to tell you what to do." Barrett's tone was gentle. "What do you want to do?"

Sarah took a deep breath and searched for the first impulse that struck her. "I want Dermot. I love him."

"Have you told him?" Amy asked.

Sarah groaned. "It's downright embarrassing how many times I've told him. We ended up having a big argument over it. He said some really ugly things and I threw him out of my flat."

"And now he's seeing someone." Barrett finished.

"Yeah." Stated that plainly, it did sound pathetic. Dermot had done everything he could to push her away.

"It might be time to cut your losses." He said.

"What's wrong with James again?" Amy sounded puzzled.

"Plenty. He's mostly nice, but kind of spoiled. His personal life is so much tabloid fodder that he practically lives in a fish bowl. He has to travel with security everywhere. And I'm enough of a hippie to be bothered by the whole oil company thing."

"And he's not Dermot." Barrett added.

"And that."

"Okay, that's big." Amy conceded, "But what have you got to lose? It sounds like the HMS Sinclair has set sail without you. He's got a thing with this PR chick. Continuing to pine over him is only going to make you miserable. James is crazy handsome, filthy rich, mostly nice and really into you. At best, you might find you're really into him. At worst, you'll have an interesting story to tell your grandkids about how you broke a billionaire playboy's heart."

"Okay. Y'all have given me something to think about. It's good to get an outside perspective."

"Hey, what were you doing hanging out with Fleming?" Amy asked.

"Oh, nothing really. A bunch of us went out for a drink last night. He's a good guy."

"Yeah, he kind of is." Amy sounded thoughtful.

"So, I guess you've talked to him since the last time I talked to you."

"Yeah, I stopped by the old apartment after you left. He was kind of pissed that you took off without word to anybody."

"Sorry about that." Sarah still felt bad about leaving, but she had needed to do something if only to feel like she had a little bit of control over things. Leaving for Scotland early was the best thing, all things considered. "I miss y'all. You're my family."

"We miss you too." They said in unison.

"When you come home, we're going to cook a massive dinner and invite the whole gang over." Amy said.

CHAPTER FIFTEEN

When Sarah opened the door to James the following Thursday night, her jaw nearly hit the floor. She had expected him to pull out all the stops with a limousine and fine dining in a romantic setting. How else does a billionaire catch a girl's fancy?

What she got, by all outward appearance, was a regular guy. He wore blue jeans that looked like he'd had them for years, sneakers and a flannel shirt under a dark brown leather jacket. Unlike the enormous spray of flowers, he'd sent her for her birthday last fall, this time he held a modest bouquet of spring flowers. He lifted his eyes to hers and looked a little less than his perfectly confident self.

"I'm going to have to start calling you Jim. James seems way too formal when you're dressed like that." Sarah said giving him a once over.

He held out the flowers to her. "Jamie, then?"

She took the flowers shaking her head. "Nope, where I'm from Jim is more common, or Jimmy."

"No, I don't care for that at all. Though a nickname isn't a bad idea." He wrinkled his nose before leaning toward her with a comically conspiratorial look. "I am incognito."

"Don't most celebrities use aliases when they travel? Do you use one?" She asked running some water into a jar.

"Promise it's only between us?" He asked. When she nodded. "I use Alan Young. Don't you have a vase?"

She cocked her head and gave him a look that said, 'I'm a student who just moved here.'

He cocked his head to the side. "I should have thought of that."

"It's no big deal. A jar works fine. So, does this mean I can call you Al?" She arched an eyebrow and giggled thinking of the Paul Simon song.

"Erm…Alan would be better." He said stiffly, but a corner of his mouth ticked up in a hint of a smile.

"Whenever I think you're loosening up." She shook her head in mock disappointment. Standing back, she called his attention to her A-line skirt and sweater. "I hope I'm not overdressed."

He gave her a once over and his eyes sparkled. "You look lovely. Make sure your shoes are comfortable. We'll be walking quite a bit."

Sarah glanced down at her clogs. "These should be fine. So where are we off to?"

"The Royal Mile." He held out his hand to her. "We'll have dinner, then I've arranged something special."

"That sounds awfully public. Are you sure that's a good idea?"

"Are you afraid to be seen with me?" He lifted an eyebrow in challenge.

She gave him a side-eyed look as she took his hand. "Of course not, but you're usually so concerned about safety and privacy. I'm surprised."

He drew her out in to the hall and waited while she locked her door. "There is privacy in anonymity. As long as I don't look the part, no one will recognize me. As for safety, Fleming will never be far away."

"How romantic." She said with a laugh.

"Trust me?" He flashed an irresistible smile, his blue eyes sparkling.

About as far as I can throw you, she thought. She trusted him to do whatever it took to achieve his goals, even though they didn't align with hers.

***

James's manners were impeccable, and his attitude was proprietary. He offered Sarah his arm as they got out of the car and walked down the Mile, then down one of the steep closes off the High Street. He held the door of the cozy restaurant and waited for her to sit. His manners alone would be enough to turn a girl's head, but paired with that face, voice and physique...Sarah had to admit, Amy was right. He had been right about anonymity. No one had bothered them on the street. They appeared to be any typical couple on a date.

Like most couples on a first date, once they found themselves seated across the table from each other, they were at a loss as to what to talk about. Unlike the dinner in Chapel Hill when they been accompanied by Dermot and Walter, Sarah found that James on his own was a little less self-assured than he was when surrounded by the trappings of his status. He seemed nervous, which she thought endearing in spite of her determination not to.

"When are you leaving for your trip?" He asked, once they had ordered. It could only have been for the sake of making conversation. Sarah was sure he knew exactly what her schedule was.

"Tuesday. Our first stop is at the Folklife Museum in the Cairngorms. Then we'll work our way across to Skye, up through the Western Isles, and back along the north coast."

"You'll be gone for a while." He looked down and fidgeted, straightening the flatware beside his plate.

"Six weeks." She wasn't sure where he was going with the question.

He let the subject drop. They sat for several minutes in awkward silence, broken only by the waiter delivering the wine. Sarah was about to excuse herself to the ladies' room for a breather when James said with a pained smile, "I'm really not very good at this."

"Neither am I." She laughed. "I'm much better at teasing stories and songs out of elderly people than I am at making small talk."

He lifted an eyebrow. "That's an interesting skill set to have. Could be useful around the board room or golf club."

"Only if you're looking for fish stories or tales of holes in one."

He laughed. "Come to think of it, I have heard a few of those. Do you record those, too?"

"Only if they're especially fantastic." She said. "The thing about fish stories, is that they're a dime a dozen. Almost everyone has a story like that. Something that happened or that they did that was cool to begin with. Then with every telling it gets, bigger and more outlandish. They're a prime example of folklore that we encounter every day. They're also a good way to see how stories change over time. It might start with an actual event. But after many tellings it's sometimes hard to remember what that event was. People even convince themselves that the newer, more fantastic version is true."

"Isn't it?" He smiled. "I mean it's true for them, at least."

"Sure. As long as their truth doesn't run up against someone else's. Let's say we're talking about an actual fish story." A memory struck her. "Here's an example. Dermot told me a story about when you were boys and were tickling trout."

"Ah. I think I know the story you mean." He nodded.

"You tossed a trout out of the burn and it landed on your mother's Chanel suit."

He leaned forward. "First, that was Dermot that tossed the fish and I think my mother's suit was Versace."

"My point exactly." She held out a hand as if her argument were an object sitting on her palm. "You both tell it differently. And I'm sure that your mother tells an entirely different story about the incident."

James laughed out loud at that thought. His brilliant white teeth flashing. "Doubtless."

"You see? It had me in stitches when Dermot told it, but if we were all at the dinner table and one of you tried to tell the story, I'm sure the other two would have something to say about it. By the time everyone had their say the story would be hopelessly muddled and not nearly as entertaining."

He nodded sipping his wine. "I see what you mean."

"The only difference between a fish story and the stories that I collect is that there's usually no one around to fact check legends."

"Is that where you come in?" He tipped his glass at her before setting it on the table.

"I mostly record stories and songs. Sometimes, when I have more than one version of a story, I can look for the truth." She pressed her lips together and tilted her head to the side. "I think you'll find that facts and truth are not always the same thing."

***

An hour later James was pouring the last of the wine into Sarah's glass. With the ice broken, they had been laughing and talking about everything from folklore to oil wells and corporate acquisitions. Sarah had to admit that James was good company. They didn't have the easy rapport that she had with Dermot, but she was enjoying the evening in spite of her apprehension. "Tell me something about Sarah McAlpin that I don't know."

Sarah took a sip of her wine thinking before she said without heat. "Is there anything about me you don't know? I mean your people read my master's thesis. You've probably seen my grade school transcripts."

James squirmed in his seat looking guilty. "I will be the first to admit that was a bit invasive. In my defense, I should tell you that it wasn't my idea."

"You can't be too careful, right?" She surprised herself with the directness of the question.

"Something like that." He looked guilty.

Wanting to return to their easy rapport, she decided to answer honestly. "I like to cook when I need to think about something."

James propped his chin on his hand and elbow on the table looking rapt. "What do you like to cook?"

"Oh, anything. I have my favorite recipes, but I really enjoy improvising." He motioned with his hand for her to say more. "When I was growing up, we mostly lived off the land.

We had a vegetable garden, and we would hunt and fish. When you're bound to whatever is in season and whatever you have on hand, you get pretty good at making things up as you go along."

"Did it bother you, growing up that way?" He asked. Sarah looked for the pity that people often showed when they heard about her life in the holler. He didn't seem anything but genuinely curious.

"No. It didn't bother me. It wasn't that unusual. A lot of families where we lived were subsistence farmers. " James looked down at the table in thought. The idea of that kind of poverty must have left him feeling like they were worlds apart, at least she hoped it did. "What about you? What do you do to clear your head?"

He thought for a moment. "I exercise, I suppose."

"Any particular kind of exercise?"

"I rather like running and swimming." His brows knit together as if he were examining for the first time why he liked those things. "It's so rare that I'm alone. Running or swimming at least allow me to be alone inside my own head."

"And hiking?" Sarah asked thinking of his enthusiasm on their hike the other day.

He gave her his best movie star smile. "And hiking."

She smiled back. "Well, I'm afraid you are on your own in the running department. I don't generally run unless I'm being chased by a wild animal."

"Does that happen where you're from?" He asked his eyes growing wide.

Without missing a beat Sarah said, "Only in the winter when they're hungry."

James stared at her. "You're having me on."

Sarah couldn't help smiling and giving the joke away. "Yes I am."

The waiter had delivered Sarah's after dinner coffee when James gave her a wicked look over the rim of his wine glass. "For a woman who grew up in the woods, you seem to fit into city life quite nicely."

Sarah laughed. "Were you expecting Elly May Clampett?"

"Who?" James looked puzzled.

Sarah cocked her head in disbelief. "You've never seen the Beverly Hillbillies?"

"Is that a musical group?" He asked innocently.

Sarah tried to gauge whether he was serious. "No, it was an American television show back in the 60s about a family from the Ozarks who found oil on their land, and after cashing in on it, moved to Beverly Hills. Sort of a fish-out-of-water story at its most ridiculous."

"Ah," He said before taking a sip of wine. "We didn't get a lot of American television shows at my boarding school. Still, you seem to be adapting well. I seem more like a fish out of water than you do."

"That could be the pedestal that everyone puts you on." She took a sip of her coffee. "I wasn't feral. I did have a home. I went to school like any other child, and I've had years of living in civilization since then to polish my rougher edges."

"Sorry," He conceded. "I grew up with everything regimented, curated and mapped out years, sometimes decades in advance. I suppose it seems so exotic to have been so…normal."

She laughed at that. "Wearing second-hand clothes and foraging for your dinner is only exotic if you don't have to do it. As for the rest of it, I became good at observing and adapting. It was so liberating when I went off to college. No one there knew my family, or history. I could be anything that I wanted."

He set his wine glass down on the table and adjusted its position studying the tablecloth. His blue eyes avoided hers. His voice was low, wistful. "I can't even imagine that kind of freedom."

"Really?" Sarah asked. "You're the boss, right? All that Alba Petroleum money doesn't buy a lot of freedom?"

He sighed heavily, "I'm afraid it can't hire someone else to carry the weight of my family's expectations."

"You can say no." He laughed, but she went on. "Let's say you aren't...who you are. You're Alan Young, free agent. Your life can be anything you want. What do you choose to do?"

A smile flitted across his mouth, but he didn't look up. He paused and straightened his knife beside his plate while the silence stretched between them. Finally, he said, "It's not that simple."

"It could be. Your father left it behind when he turned things over to you. You could turn the company over to Walter. He seems to want to run things anyway." She wondered if this could be her way out of the Stuart's plan. She could talk James out of it. Maybe like her, he wanted to steer his own fate. "What would you do, without those expectations?"

He cocked his head and looked at her. She could see the wheels turning in his mind. "I have never lived without that pressure. I honestly don't know what I would do if it weren't for that."

Sarah felt sorry for him. All his money and privilege and he was as trapped as she was maybe more. "You should think about it. One day, those pressures will diminish, and you'll be able to choose. Who do you want to be; James Stuart playboy oil baron, or Alan Young regular guy, free to be whatever he wants?"

He was silent for several seconds, deep in thought. Eventually, he raised his hand to summon the waiter and quietly asked for the check. "I think we should go for a walk. I'd like to show you something."

CHAPTER SIXTEEN

Sarah stared in awe at the stone walls that appeared to grow out of the crag in front of them. Lights shone on the outer walls of the castle. When they left the restaurant, James had laced his fingers with hers. He drew her up Castle Hill and across the wide Esplanade and stone bridge to the great wood and iron doors. There were a few people on the Esplanade, but not many that late at night, and no one that close to the castle door. It had closed to tourists hours ago.

James had pounded on the door and within a few minutes a uniformed security guard opened the door enough for the two of them to slip in. Sarah felt like a kid sneaking into a movie theater without paying. It felt wicked to get access when no one else could. James flashed her a satisfied smile as they got into the guard's car. He chatted with the guard like a friendly acquaintance while Sarah gaped at the castle complex around them. They drove up the winding lane through the Portcullis Gate and past the battery and various buildings. The castle complex was a town unto itself. Museums, restaurants, shops and management offices filled buildings that crowded every corner and alley up the hill. They went through another gate into the upper level of the complex and around a curve lined on one side with a battery of cannons until the guard parked in front of a stone building decorated with gold flourishes over the doors and the date of 1615 in gold on a plaque midway up.

Sarah was still reeling from the unexpected access they were getting when James opened her door and offered her a hand out of the car. "How?"

He smiled nodding to the guard who had also gotten out of the car and was unlocking the door in front of them, "It helps to know someone on the security staff."

James introduced the guard. "Sarah this is Graham. Graham, Sarah. When he's not minding the castle, Graham works security for Alba Petroleum."

Graham was in his forties, slim and fatherly with salty hair and a kind face. Sarah smiled at him. "It's nice to meet you, Graham."

He nodded, his hand on the doorknob. "I'm please to meet ye as well, miss."

"Graham will be accompanying us, so that we don't get into any mischief while I give you the tour." James said with a twinkle in his eyes.

"I can't wait."

Graham opened the door and ushered them inside. The castle was dark and silent except for a few safety lights along the hallways. Graham and James led her through a maze of hallways and anterooms until he ushered her into larger space. Sarah couldn't see much in the faint glow of the city lights coming through the windows, but she heard the echo of their shoes on the tile floor. Graham disappeared into the shadows while James pulled her into the center of the room.

James stood in front of her, and Sarah could barely make out his silhouette. He said, "Now."

Somewhere behind them, Sarah heard the soft click of light switches, and in a second, they were bathed in a warm glow from the chandeliers. Sarah gasped when she took in the room around them. Dark wood paneling stretched up crimson walls to an open beam ceiling. Pikes, swords and pieces of armor decorated the edges of the room. She breathed a soft "Wow. This is amazing."

"This is the Great Hall." James stepped back spreading his arms wide to encompass the enormous space.

Sarah walked from one end of the room to another, her eyes darting over the ornate millwork and artifacts. She was eager to see every detail.

"I don't even know what to say." She turned back to him to find that he was watching her. "It's breathtaking."

He smiled warmly. "It's most likely from the early 16th century probably before the Battle of Flodden. Cromwell used it as barracks."

"Of course, he would." Sarah said thinking of the puritanical revolutionary.

"It's hard to imagine all of the things these walls have seen." He said casting his eyes around the room.

Sarah continued studying the room. She was looking up at the ceiling when she heard James's voice close behind her. "The roof is very special. There are only a few hammerbeam roofs like that surviving, and only a couple in Scotland."

"The beams look like ribs." She said turning to him.

James took her hand and began to pull her toward the door. "Actually, that's not too far off. The roof was built like a ship's hull, then flipped over and lifted into place."

Sarah looked back at the roof as they left. She couldn't help thinking of the legend of her people sailing away from the New Folk in their boats made from the roofs of their homes.

"Let me show you the Royal Apartment." He pulled on her hand with an excited smile.

They made their way through the rooms where the royal family had lived. Sarah listened as James described some of the more famous incidents and royal peccadilloes that had occurred there. All the while, Graham the guard accompanied them, turning lights on and off, and unlocking and locking doors. Sarah had to admit she was enjoying the private tour. What girl wouldn't like being shown around a real-life castle by Prince Charming?

"And now, the thing that I really want you to see." James turned serious as they entered another set of rooms. Like the Royal Apartments the furniture in these rooms was spare, but mannequins were staged in tableaux of moments in the history of the Honors. In the dimly lit rooms, Sarah found the mannequins creepy, like groups of shadow people watching them. She walked closer to James until they reached a vault door. It blended into the decor of the castle, but Sarah could tell as Graham opened it that it took more effort and a combination rather than a key.

Wood paneling lined the barreled ceiling of the vault, giving the room a warm glow. At its center, was a case of thick glass that housed the Honors. Sarah walked to the railing that surrounded the case to get a closer look. James stood beside her, his eyes on the case. Inside, presented on a dark blue cloth and red pillow were the sword, scepter and crown of Scotland.

"They're the oldest crown jewels in Britain." His tone was hushed and reverent.

Sarah's breath caught. Was this the moment that James told her the part he believed she would play. She suddenly wanted to be anywhere but there. She walked around the case to the opposite side, putting what little distance she could between herself and James without running from the room.

He looked at her from across the display. His eyes looked bleak. "I have been told all my life that they're meant to be mine."

Sarah's heart beat faster. "I thought the Windsors traced themselves back to the Stuarts."

He shook his head dismissively and began to walk slowly around the display case. "Their link is tenuous at best. Ours is more direct, though the history books won't tell you that."

He came around the end of the case and approached her. His eyes were fixed on hers. The look in them was full of longing. Gone was the confident, dashing billionaire, and in his place was a man that Sarah didn't recognize. She stood rooted to the spot. Her hand gripped the rail like a lifeline. Suddenly, she wanted to be anywhere else in the world.

"You talk about freedom, about living without the history and the pressures of family and expectations." He stood in front of her and rested his hand on hers on the railing. His fingers curled around her wrist. "I have lived every minute of my life with centuries of it pressing down on me. It's been crushing me for as long as I can remember."

Sarah breathed his name to stop him. Tears stung her eyes. She wanted to tell him he was worth more than someone else's expectations. She didn't want to feel sympathy for this man. No matter how she tried to see him as an obstacle or even an enemy, she couldn't close herself off completely, not when he was begging for a friend.

"I never knew what freedom felt like, until I clapped eyes on you." She could feel his breath hot on her lips. She should move away, should put a stop to this, but she was caught in the pull of his blue gaze. "Sarah, you must know by now that I can't stay away from you."

His free hand slid into the hair behind her ear. He pulled her closer and his lips skimmed hers. "James, I…"

His kiss stole the next words right out of her mind. This was nothing like the last time James had tried to kiss her. Then it had felt practiced, planned, almost textbook. This kiss was hungry, drugging, and for longer than she wanted to admit, Sarah enjoyed it.

He pulled away, and his eyes fixed on hers. They were so like Dermot's that for an instant Sarah caught herself leaning closer. She stopped, horrified. She couldn't catch her breath. Her hand drifted up to touch her lips that still tingled. Her eyes darted around the vault room desperate for a way out.

She turned and bolted for the door, coming up short in the anteroom. There were two doorways leading out, but the rooms beyond were dark as caves. Sarah thought she knew which one led back to the way they had come. She glanced around. James stood in the doorway to the vault. His eyes held a mix of shock and hurt. "Sarah."

Sarah could only shake her head before turning to plunge into the darkness. She ran with one hand brushing along the wall and another extended in front of her. She had no idea where she was going. All she knew was that she needed to get away from James Stuart, and the feelings that he had stirred up. She should have known she wouldn't get far.

Before she made it out of that hallway, James was there, his hand grasped hers where it touched the wall. Her own momentum pulled her around to face him. His voice was soft, pleading. "Please don't run. I won't kiss you again."

Sarah stood there in the dark trying to catch her breath. She shook her head struggling to find something to say.

"Not here," He whispered. "We have an audience."

Sarah looked up to see the silhouette of Graham, the security guard, standing in the doorway. There was no telling what his imagination was doing with the scene she had just made. Her stomach lurched. "Oh, God!"

"No worries." James reassured her. "He's paid for discretion."

Sarah nodded, still trying to catch her breath. She was sure her face was red as a beet. She drew in a deep breath, but it turned into a guttural sound that was half groan, half sob.

James carefully slid an arm around her back, turning toward the door. "I'll drive you home."

***

The drive back to her house was beyond tense. James had offered his support until they got to the car that awaited them on the esplanade in front of the castle, but in the car, he had put as much distance as possible between them. That was fine by her but glancing over at his clenched jaw and arms folded tight across his chest she felt almost as guilty for her reaction as she did for enjoying his kiss. He had opened himself up to her in a way that she doubted he ever had with anyone else, and she had reacted with horror. It wasn't his fault. Then again it was. If his speech at the castle had told her anything, it was that he didn't feel very in control of the situation either. They were all trapped.

The car came to a stop in front of her house. By habit she glanced at Dermot's window, noticing that it was dark. No doubt he was still out with Felicia. Maybe there weren't three of them trapped after all.

"I'll walk you to your door." James said, leaping from the car.

He turned back and offered her his hand. She took it and allowed him to help her out of the car. Inside she gave him her key and followed him up the stairs. He opened her door and handed her the key without looking at her. He hadn't looked directly at her since the vault.

Sarah stood on the threshold of her apartment. She should be happy. She might have succeeded in driving him away, but it felt hollow. James didn't deserve this. She wanted to apologize, explain, find some way to bridge the widening gulf between them. She turned to him, and asked, "Will you come inside?"

"I think not." He said through clenched teeth, his eyes on the doorknob.

Sarah put her hand on his sleeve. "I owe you an explanation."

His eyes shot to meet hers flashing blue fury. "You owe me nothing."

Sarah looked behind her into her apartment, and then back at him. "We both know that's not true, but that's not what I mean. I'd like to explain my reaction at the castle."

"Think nothing of it. It was my mistake." He started to back away shaking his head.

"No." She took a step toward him. "I don't want you to go away thinking that was your fault. Please."

He sighed heavily but allowed her to pull him into the apartment. She drew him to sit on the couch. Now that she had his agreement, she was struggling to find the right words.

"I'm sure I don't have to tell you that you are everything that most girls dream of."

"But you are not most girls." He said sounding defeated.

"Oh, I'm girly enough to be tempted." She smiled. "But, before I came to Scotland, really before I met you, I fell in love with someone else."

She saw the news settle on him, like a weight. She didn't like the idea of adding to the weight he already carried. "If you don't mind my asking, who is he?"

"That's not important anymore." She shook her head and lowered her eyes hoping that no tears would fall. "He's not the man I thought he was."

James sat forward resting his elbows on his knees and folding his hands together between them in thought. "I am sorry that he hurt you, but I can't say I'm sorry that you were disappointed."

She let out a sharp soft laugh. "At least you're honest." She sighed. "Whatever my disappointment with him, I still haven't…let go. I thought I had. I don't want to hurt you. I heard what you said in the vault. I don't want to make things harder for you. But when you kissed me, and I enjoyed it." Her voice cracked, and she stopped to get it under control. James didn't look at her. He kept his eyes on the floor. "It felt like a betrayal."

He tilted his head to the side and nodded, thoughtful. "I see."

"James, I want you to be happy. I don't think I'm the person for you."

James took several deep breaths. Sarah hoped he was coming to terms with what she had told him, hoped he would accept that she wasn't interested.

He turned to her picking up her hand and holding it between both of his. "I accepted a long time ago, that happiness wasn't something that I could expect. But I would very much like to be trusted with yours."

Sarah started to protest, but he held up a hand and she fell silent.

"I understand that you aren't ready now, and that you feel as if you may never be." He kissed her hand. "I believe that one day your hope will return. When you are over this man, when you are ready, I'll be here. And I will dedicate myself to your happiness."

Sarah shouldn't have been surprised by his declaration, but she couldn't think of a single thing to say. He had made his interest clear almost since they met, but it had always been about him and what he wanted. He had never focused so clearly on her wishes before. His feelings seemed genuine at the moment, but who knew how that would change once outside influences pushed at him again.

James turned to her for the first time since they had sat down. He lifted a hand to her cheek and turned her to face him, placing a chaste kiss on her forehead. "Think about it." He let himself out.

CHAPTER SEVENTEEN

"Hey Dermot, can you give us a few words about the plan?" Sarah heard Ewan ask as she and Isla were setting up tables and recording equipment in the hall.

"Get Sarah to do it." Dermot grumbled before stalking out into the chilly morning.

Isla shot a concerned glance after him. "He's grouchy."

"Yeah. The ride up here yesterday was a barrel of laughs." Sarah muttered remembering the nearly silent drive from Edinburgh. The day before when they had been packing up to leave, James Stuart had stopped by to see them off; more specifically, to see Sarah off.

"The truth is I needed to see your face once more before you left." James had said, when he caught her alone in the team office. "I don't know how I'm going to survive so many weeks without you. Can I meet you somewhere along the way?"

"Absolutely not." She'd said swiftly. "I need to be focused, and the team doesn't need that kind of distraction. Please, promise me that you will leave me to do this on my own."

He hadn't liked it but had eventually agreed that he wouldn't interrupt her trip. He leaned closer and whispered, "I hope you'll think about what I said last night."

"James," She'd lifted a hand to push him away when she heard a throat cleared in the room behind him. She looked around his shoulder to see Dermot standing near the hallway that led to his office. His face was red with fury.

James had turned to face him but kept his hold on Sarah's hand. He hadn't been at all bothered by Dermot's apparent ill temper. He grinned with his usual bonhomie. "Ah, Dermot. It looks like everything is in order for your trip."

Dermot seethed. "Aye, it is as long as ye can manage to let go of my most experienced field worker long enough for us to get the van packed."

"Then I had better leave you to it." He nodded to Dermot before giving Sarah a quick buss on the cheek. "Have a safe trip. I look forward to seeing what you collect."

Sarah and Dermot had stood there for several seconds after James had closed the door behind himself. The silence and space between them stretched further by the second. She took a breath trying to think of something to say that would wipe the look of judgment off his face, anything that would tell him that he hadn't walked in on them in some kind of romantic embrace. But that was exactly what he'd done, even if the romance was one sided. "I…"

"Save it." He'd snarled bending down and picked up the largest of the boxes. He propped the box on his knee and opened the door.

"Dermot," She wasn't sure why she'd felt the need to explain but she had.

"You don't need to say anything." He'd said on his way out. "It's your business."

And with that, the hollow feeling in her chest returned, the same feeling she'd had weeks ago after kicking him out of her apartment. She had tried her best to fill it since then with work, with research, with anger. It wasn't as easy as she thought. Her mother hadn't been wrong about a broken heart. It felt like dragging your heart behind you, catching every rock and splinter in your path. It left you raw, susceptible to every little hurt. At least, Molly had been able to turn her back and try to forget. Sarah had to see her heartbreak every day.

So, she hadn't minded a bit when Kirstie had volunteered to navigate, leaving Sarah to ride in the back seat. She should have loved driving through the Cairngorms, but she had spent most of the ride staring at the back of Dermot's head, wondering what he was thinking. Meanwhile, Kirstie had relished the role of navigator and droned on at Sarah about everything she knew about the area. If Sarah were the rube that Kirstie thought she was, she would have appreciated the narration, but Sarah was sure the girl's tour guide mode was meant to make her feel foreign. It had been a thoroughly unpleasant couple of hours.

"Hey, Sarah." Ewan approached them as they moved out of the way of Jujhar who carried in another crate for the van. "Do you have a few minutes to talk to the camera?"

"Sure." She smiled. She was going to have to get used to Ewan and his camera. He had filmed a few meetings so far, but when they were in the field he would be filming a lot more.

"Great. Do ye mind if we go outside. I'd like to get the shot in front of one of the older style buildings." She followed him outside. The morning was gray and chilly, but Sarah liked it. Unlike the city, she could smell the earth here and it reminded her of home.

The Scottish Folklife Museum was a living history museum that included buildings showing the various types of historic construction in Scotland. It reminded Sarah a little of a folklife museum she had visited in Virginia once. You could walk from a typical Hebridean blackhouse to a Highland croft house and several other examples of vernacular construction. Ewan led her in front of the croft house and positioned her where he could get the best shot before hefting the camera to his shoulder.

Sarah checked her hair and straightened her shirt. "Let me know when you're ready."

"Ready when you are." He gave her a thumbs up.

"Great. Where should I start?" She asked awkwardly.

"Just give us an overview of how this works."

Sarah cleared her throat and smiled looking into the camera. "Well, we've divided up the Highlands and Islands into various parts where we'll be setting up shop. We've spent the last couple of months arranging events at village halls in these areas. Then we put the word out through local newspapers, councils, grapevines that we'll be in the area and hope that people will come and share their stories, songs, and crafts. Sort of like an Antiques Roadshow of folklore. We will also be going to visit people nearby who we have been told have things to share but might not be able to make it to the gatherings. Like any good folklorist, we'll mix in the communities keeping our ears to the ground for any leads on good material."

"We're starting here at the Scottish Folklife Museum and will be here for a few days. Then we'll move on to Inverness, before heading west toward the isles. We plan to stop in small communities, and towns as we go to capture as much local culture as we can."

"You seem excited." He said without stopping the camera.

"I am very excited. I grew up listening to stories of life in the Highlands from my grandmother. It's why I became a folklorist. I feel like a kid going to Disneyland."

"What are you looking forward to the most?"

That required some thought. Of course, she was looking most forward to Assynt, and exploring the area where the hidden glen should be. But there was a lot of traveling and work to do between here and there. She would rather not call attention to her interest in the area. If the village had been kept secret for longer than anyone remembered, she wasn't about to expose it. "I'm very excited to go to Skye. I think I'm most excited to hear people speaking Gaelic. I grew up speaking it, but it was only me and Granny. It was like our secret language. I can't wait to get to meet more Gaelic speakers and hear their songs and stories."

"That's great." Ewan lowered the camera. "Can ye send one of the others out? I think I'd like to ask them the same question.

"Sure," Sarah walked back to the hall where they would be receiving people.

***

"He turned 'round, but there was naught behind him but a gray mist passing over the trail." Seumas Menzies leaned forward in his chair resting his hands-on top of his cane. He was well into his eighties, and every year could be counted on his face like tree rings, but his steel gray eyes flashed. "But when he started walking again, he heard them again. Footsteps, behind him. Couldnae be more than ten feet or so."

Sarah smiled and leaned toward him. Seumas was a storyteller at heart, and a folklorist's goldmine. He lowered his voice to tell the next part, as if it were a secret. "So, he stopped again, but this time he crept off the path and hid behind a rock. He watched the trail as the mist overtook where he had been, and through that mist he saw him, the Grey Man. He must have been eight feet tall wi' lang arms and hands that reached doon to his knees. And he walked slowly doon the trail, all the time surrounded by a gray mist. My cousin, he was sore afraid and stayed there behind that stone 'til it was near dark. Then he reckoned he should get home before the Grey Man came back. And that was the last time he ever climbed Ben Macdhui."

Sarah sat up straight. "And that was your cousin?"

"Aye. Aye, it was. He loved munro bagging until that day, he did. Since then, he's kept to the low walking trails."

"I believe I would too." Sarah said.

Seumas took a sip of the cup of tea that Sarah had brought for him when they sat down. She did the same and leaned back in her chair. She had been listening to Seumas and a few others who had come to talk with them. Seumas had said that he lived near Corgarff, and his grandson had brought him into town and dropped him off at the museum for the afternoon. Sarah made a note to check her map for Corgarff. She'd had fun talking with the old man, who was still a bit of a flirt.

"Do you not climb the mountains like your cousin?" Sarah asked.

"Och! On these auld legs? Feh!" He waved a hand in dismissal, but he was laughing. "Ah couldnae get to the post box on these pegs."

"Is there a spot that you miss walking too?"

He sat back and thought. "Aye, *Tobar Fuar Mòr*."

"Not a terribly romantic name, the Big Cold Well." Sarah prompted. "Is that a holy well?"

"It is indeed." He looked surprised that she would know about holy wells. "But it's not like some others. It's not fed by one spring, but three. They all come up near to each other and feed into a pool. And they each have their ain magic. A drink from one well cures the blindness, another cures lameness, and the other deafness. But the cure comes wi' a price. Ye mun leave gold for the spirit of the well. There's a stone there called the Kettle Stone and a wee hole under it. Ye slip the gold under the stone and there's a kettle there tae catch it."

Sarah slid forward to the edge of her chair. "Can you see the kettle under the stone?"

"Och, no. It's like a wee cave, aye?" He said. "I heard that many years ago, some lads tried to dig it up, but they never found the kettle, nor any gold though folk hae been leaving gold there as long as anyone remembers." He arched an eyebrow at her. "When those lads came away with naught, they ran into an auld woman on the road. She saw what they'd been up tae and told them they would all meet a bad end."

"Did they?" She asked.

"I dinnae ken, but I wouldna want to risk it myself." He nodded in affirmation before sighing. "It's a bonny spot though."

"Do you think it would help you?" Sarah asked nodding to his cane.

He looked at the cane himself and shifted in his chair as if his hip hurt. "I think I'm past any help that well might give. Who kens if any of those auld wells does what they say. Mind ye, I never knew anyone who was hurt by drinking from a holy well."

"Not even liars or cheats? I heard *Tobar na Glas a Coille* would make a person die of thirst if he drank without dropping a pin in the well." Sarah said thinking of another local holy well.

"Aye, I heard that too. But I dinna ken anyone who has died, or maybe I dinna ken anyone who has tested it." His laugh was a raspy rattle that made Sarah worry for old Seumas's health, but it was a contagious laugh nonetheless.

"Have you ever heard of a well that would tell the future or a matchmaking well?" She had spent some time looking for wells like the one in Molly's journal, but she hadn't found one yet. She hoped someone more steeped in the lore of the Highlands might have heard something. She still had a difficult time believing that a secret like that had been kept for so long.

He pursed his lips and rubbed a knotted hand over the white stubble on his chin. After some contemplation, he leaned forward and lowered his voice as if he was telling something that shouldn't be common knowledge. Sarah leaned forward too, hoping that the microphone was sensitive enough to catch what he said. "I havena heard of a well for divining, but some say the well spirits are really fairies. My grandfather had a brother who went to work as a fisherman. Before I was ever born, my great grandmother took ill."

"The doctor told my grandfather that it was the last. And my grandfather was sore fashed that he couldnae get word to his brother, who he thought was at sea. He thought their mum was gonnae die without seeing her son again. But that evening, his brother came walking in the door."

"When the funeral was over, and their mother was safe in the ground, my grandfather asked his brother how he knew to come home. And his brother said, "It was the strangest thing. But my boat docked to unload. I was in town walking doon the High Street and a wee lass appeared in front of me. She laid a hand on my arm and said, "Ye mun go home to Corgarff. Yer mum is dying. She needs ye." He asked her how she knew that. And she said, "I saw it in the well." He looked around, but there was no well nearby." Seumas shook his head and shrugged. "When he looked back to ask her what well, the wee lass had disappeared."

Sarah felt the hairs on her arm stand up. "Did he say where his boat was docked?"

Seumas tapped his fingers on the handle of his cane and looked up trying to remember. "It wasnae Ullapool, but somewhere around there, north of the Minch."

Assynt was north of the Minch, the stretch of sea that separated the mainland from the Isles of Lewis and Harris. A few months ago, she would have treated this like a strange coincidence blown out of proportion. Now she wasn't so sure. The area was right. The remote knowledge or future knowledge sounded like something her people could do. She'd done it herself, though never with a stranger. The little girl, if she was real, could have been one of her ancestors. "When did this happen?"

"Oh, it would have to be a hundred years ago at least."

"Did your great uncle ever see the girl again? Did he ever go back to that port?"

"You know, he never went back to the sea at all after that. He always said that he reckoned if God wanted him home so much that he sent a fairy lass to tell him to go, he shouldnae ever leave again."

Sarah hmm'd in understanding. "That's an interesting way of looking at it."

"Truth be told, I think he was tired of being rootless. He'd left home young and sailed from Thurso to Gibraltar, but didnae have much in the way of savings and possessions to show for it. I think he was ready to settle down."

"Then it sounds like he got the message he needed to hear." Sarah patted his hand.

"Aye. He did that." Seumas smiled wistfully.

After his grandson had returned to collect him, Sarah couldn't stop thinking of the stories he had told, both the fairy girl and the well fed by three springs each with their own gift. *Tobar Fuar Mòr* couldn't be the well that Molly had written about. The geography was all wrong. There was no way the auld folk could have walked from a glen near Inchnadamph to the Cairngorms. But this was another instance of three being associated with a well and fairies, and the fairy girl's mysterious message. It reminded her a little bit of Macbeth, and the weird sisters telling him the future.

She cleaned up her table and made her notes that would go with the cassette that she had used. She noted the date and names of the people she had spoken with. Then she wrote the number of the cassette in her own research notebook, so that she would be able to find it again easily. It was amazing how much of their time was spent cataloging and organizing things.

Seumas had been the last subject of the day. Everyone else had packed up and loaded their equipment except for Dermot, who was waiting to add her cassette to the box with the others. She approached the table where he waited, and he gave her a tired smile. "Always the last one working."

It had been so long since he'd smiled at her, that it caught her off guard. She smiled back and handed him the tape. "Granny didn't raise no shirker."

He took the tape, his fingers brushing hers. He added her cassette to the others and cleared his throat not looking at her. "That she did not."

CHAPTER EIGHTEEN

"Is it almost ready?" Isla poked her head into the kitchen of their hostel.

Sarah shot a dirty look over her shoulder, then nodded to a large bowl on the counter. "It would be ready faster if you gave us a hand. You can be in charge of the salad."

Isla took the bowl to a nearby table and came back for the lettuce and vegetables. "That's what I get for poking my head in."

Her words might have sounded grouchy, but Sarah knew she was only kidding. Over the last week spent working and living together, they had all grown into a cohesive team. Even Kirstie had managed to soften the worst of her competitive tendencies. They had been in Inverness for four long days working out of the Inverness Town House. The city had kept them hopping, with people telling stories, traditional musicians, and crafts. When they hadn't been collecting in the gothic Town House on the High Street, team members had been venturing out to pubs, churches and workshops documenting every tradition they could find. They were all exhausted.

Sarah had been packing up her recording equipment that afternoon when Dermot had pulled her aside and handed her some cash. "Everyone's been working so hard, I think we should take the night off. Would ye mind making a team dinner?"

She sighed with relief. "I would love a quiet night, even if it's at the hostel. I can definitely do that."

He gave her elbow a gentle squeeze. Sarah had to steel herself not to mistake it for affection. They had come to a professional détente if not friendship, over their time on the road. They had to work together after all and raging at each other in front of the team wasn't an option. No matter how frustrated they might be, they were both good at what they did and that managed to engender some mutual respect at least while they were doing it.

She had headed for the door, when he called her back. "Sarah! Take one of the lads with ye. Don't go alone."

And like that he reminded her of everything that she'd forgotten during the week and a half they had been on the road. Dermot had decided that traveling with the group, meant that she didn't need a constant bodyguard like she did in the city. Sarah had almost felt normal. She gritted her teeth and said. "Right, boss."

Sarah had tapped Jujhar to help her. They decided pasta was the best option for feeding the team on a budget and walked across the river to the grocery store. They'd been walking back across the bridge when Sarah's attention was caught by the castle on the hill above the bustle of the town around it. The late afternoon sun reflected off the windows. Sarah stopped and looked at the bank below the castle with its trees and bushes, a bright swath of green across the landscape sweeping down to the river's edge. "Is there a statue of Flora MacDonald there?"

Jujhar stopped beside her and repositioned the grocery bags that he had refused to let her help carry. "I don't know. I've never been."

"Hmm," She wondered if the spot was still there. The bench where her mother had kept her weekly vigil waiting for Rab Ballantyne to join her. She had been so busy since arriving in town that she hadn't had a chance to explore any of the locations her mother had talked about in her journal. They were leaving in the morning, so she doubted that she would get much of a chance to either. She shrugged and glanced at Jujhar who was peeking over the top of what she was sure was a heavy brown grocery bag. "Please let me help carry that?"

"Absolutely not." He said in a clipped way that said he would not hear any further argument.

"And I thought Southern boys were gentlemen." She said walking on.

As always, the act of cooking helped her clear her mind, even in a hostel full of young people. Isla had been entertaining them and the others staying there, by playing the fiddle in the next room. While Sarah and Jujhar had puttered around in the kitchen, toes tapping in time, it had reminded Sarah of Chapel Hill and her friends there. She glanced over at Jujhar who bent to pull the garlic bread from the oven, and Isla at the table now making the salad. She'd rarely had friends as a child, not true friends. So, the ones she made now were that much more precious to her. And these two weren't part of James's circle. They had no agenda besides the obvious one.

Sarah sniffed back tears and positioned potholders on the handles of the pot, so she could carry it to the sink to drain. "These noodles are ready. Can somebody get the others?"

"I've got it." Isla said putting a couple of serving spoons in the salad bowl.

In minutes they were all around the table in the dining room. Sarah set the pot of sauce and ladle on a folded towel in the center of the table. "It's still bubbling a little, so you might want to have some salad while it cools down."

"This looks great! Thanks, Sarah," Kirstie gave Sarah a saccharine smile. Since, they'd all been living in each other's pockets on the road, Kirstie had been cordial to Sarah if not quite friendly.

"My pleasure. I love cooking for people." Sarah returned her smile before taking her seat next to Jujhar.

Dermot came in and took the seat next to hers without meeting her eyes. "This looks great. Thanks."

"It was your idea, and a good one." She said accepting the salad bowl as it was passed around the table.

"I have them occasionally," He muttered just loud enough for her to hear.

"To Sarah and Jujhar, for this lovely dinner." Isla lifted her glass, passing the bottle of wine they had bought to Ewan beside her.

"To Sarah and Jujhar," Kirstie lifted her glass as well, and once everyone had wine, they all lifted their glasses and toasted.

Sarah amended. "To Dermot for the idea and the funds to feed us all."

Everyone agreed and drank before digging in. Conversation swirled about people they had spoken with and the more outrageous traditions they had collected. There were more than a few fish stories from the Moray Firth. Sarah noted the difference in the material they had collected in the Cairngorms and in town. There were more stories about the supernatural in the country. The city was full of musicians and even artisans more than storytellers. They laughed and talked long after they had finished dinner and Ewan couldn't resist getting out his camera to capture some of the camaraderie.

"Come on Isla," Kirstie said good-naturedly when the conversation dwindled. "We've got clean up duty."

Isla shot Sarah a look, surprised how much a part of the team Kirstie was becoming. She stood and took her plate and Ewan's. "Right there with ye."

"Well, we can at least clean up the table." Sarah said giving the lads a significant look rising to take her plate and the nearest serving dish to the kitchen. Dermot and Ewan followed her lead and soon they had the table cleared.

Sarah went off to take a shower, since she never knew if it would be available in the morning. Cleaned up and dressed for bed twenty minutes later, she came into the empty common room. Something had occurred to her while she was in the shower, and she couldn't believe she hadn't thought about it before.

She went to the hostel's single house phone which sat in the common room on a narrow table. She pulled out the drawer and picked up the phone book and flipped through the pages until she came to the B's. There were Ballantynes, but no Robert or Rab, nor was there a Sheila Ballantyne. Sarah flipped to the M's and looked for a Sheila MacLeod, but she was disappointed there too. She doubted that anyone else from the village would be in Inverness, and even if they were she didn't have a name.

The only other name she had was Green, the man who had helped her mother and Duff get home. But she didn't have any idea what Mr. Green's first name was, nor what kind of business he might have been in that allowed him to give two near strangers fare back to the States. It looked like the Inverness phone book was a dead end. Sarah was putting it back in the drawer when Dermot strolled in. Her disappointment must have shown on her face, because he asked. "Everything alright?"

"Yeah…yeah, I was looking something up, but it wasn't there."

She was about to leave when Isla came through with Ewan. To Sarah's surprise they were holding hands. Ewan looked blissful.

"We're going for a walk," Isla announced. "Anyone interested?"

Sarah was certain that they didn't want any company on their walk but were only being polite. "No, I'm fixing to turn in."

"Suit yerself. Don't wait up." Isla grinned turning to go.

"Hey, Isla," Sarah stepped a little closer to her friend and said quietly. "Among the musicians that you've talked to, have you come across one named Rab Ballantyne?"

Isla thought. "Can't say I have."

Sarah nodded. She figured it was a longshot. She wasn't sure what she would say to him if she saw him. What does a girl say to the father who turned his back on her and her mother before she was even born? Still, she was curious. "Can you let me know if you do?"

Isla nodded. "Any reason in particular?"

Sarah shook her head. "I came across his name while researching. He's a fiddle player from what I read."

"Yeah, I'll keep an eye out."

"Thanks." Sarah said. "Have fun."

"Come on, Ewan." Isla pulled a grinning Ewan toward the door.

Sarah laughed. She hoped Isla wasn't playing with him.

"I hope they know what they're doing." Dermot said looking after the pair.

"Oh, that's been brewing since day one." Sarah said.

"I know. I hope she gives him a chance to be more than a hookup."

Sarah shook her head, wondering again if he was telling the truth about their night together being nothing more than a hookup. "Yeah, I don't know Ewan that well, but his affection seems pretty genuine. But then I've been fooled before."

Dermot didn't say anything for a moment, not taking the bait. "Who is Rab Ballantyne?"

Sarah met his gaze, thinking he had no right to answers about her personal life after he effectively threw her away. She straightened her shoulders and lifted her chin. "He's my father."

She enjoyed watching his face take in the bitterness that was rolling off her. He looked like he might say something, but Sarah was sure that he didn't have any words that would change things between them. She turned on her heel and stalked out of the room.

***

Sarah watched a rabbit nibbling on the grass on the other side of the fence. She was delighted to find that the green side of the hill was teeming with rabbits. She lifted her gaze to the River Ness as it rushed by. In the States, rivers even at the fall line were slow lumbering muddy things. But the Ness was deep blue and rushing, like it couldn't wait to reach the firth. All around her the city was waking up. Soon the stillness of the morning would give way to the frenetic buzz of modern life.

But for now, she heard a lullaby that her mother used to sing to her. It was one of the few Gaelic songs that she remembered her mother singing. The singer told their darling child to go to sleep, because her man would steal goats and sheep to feed them. Knowing now how Molly and Rab had been forced to sneak around, Sarah thought it fitting.

Someone sat down on the bench next to her. She glanced over to find Jujhar. So, they had found her. He spoke softly. "Dermot is nearly apoplectic."

"I can imagine." She said picturing Dermot; red-faced and pacing.

"I managed to keep him from calling the police by telling him I knew where you were." He said. "I'm glad my theory was right."

"This is the last place…" She cleared her throat, tamping down tears and swirling anxiety. "The last place where my mother was happy, the last place that she had hope. When she was pregnant with me, she used to wait here every week for my father to join her like he promised."

"Ah." He said, understanding.

"He never did." Tears clogged her throat and spilled from her eyes. "Whew. That's the first time I've ever said that out loud."

Without a word, Jujhar reached over and took her hand where it rested in her lap. He held it, as if that connection could keep her from melting completely in grief and flowing downhill into the rushing waters of the Ness. In a way it did.

Sarah didn't think she had cried over Molly since she was a little girl. She hadn't understood then the kind of grief that never loosened its grip, the kind that came from a broken heart and shattered dreams. Now, the tears came, and she couldn't stop them. Now she knew what she couldn't have known when Molly had left her; what she'd been too bitter to recognize. It was like losing her mother all over again.

A sob escaped her, and she clapped a hand over her mouth feeling hot tears run down over her fingers.

Jujhar moved closer and wrapped his arm around her shoulders. Sarah couldn't stop herself from falling apart. She let herself feel the bone deep grief for her mother that she had denied herself for years. She had been wrapped up in bitterness over Molly's suicide and her own troubles. She was only now coming to understand what Molly had been through. Only now, understanding what that could do to a person. Only now, did she realize who the person she had lost really was. She wept for Molly, the girl full of expectations that she had been, for Molly's heartbreak and for her own.

Jujhar held her until her sobs faded. He didn't ask what was wrong. He simply accepted that that was what she needed and provided it. When she had cried herself out, Sarah pulled away, wiping her face with the sleeve of her sweater. Jujhar produced a handkerchief from his pocket.

"I'm sorry," she said taking the handkerchief. "I didn't mean to do that."

"I think you needed it." His warm brown eyes sought hers.

Sarah took a deep breath. "I think I did too. I never mourned her properly."

"Do you feel you have now?"

"I think I've made a start." She said, folding the handkerchief and thinking of the reason she had come to Scotland, the only one that mattered now. "There's more to do."

"And I'm sure you will do it." He said firmly.

Sarah nodded. "I will."

"That's the best way to honor her." He said, patting her hand.

After a few more minutes collecting herself, she and Jujhar walked back to the hostel. Dermot was pacing the common room waiting for her, as red-faced as she had imagined. Her face must have been red too from wiping tears away, because he took one look at her and the ill-temper went right out of him. His shoulders sagged, and he bit back whatever reprimand he'd been about to deliver.

CHAPTER NINETEEN

"You've…um," Dermot trailed off, not sure what to say next. He spent a few seconds focusing on the next stretch of road that he could see through the morning fog. "You've been a bit…pensive since we left Inverness. Are ye alright?"

Sarah didn't turn away from the car window. She rarely looked at him anymore, unless it was in a professional capacity. They couldn't explain to the team why they couldn't bear to be around each other. They couldn't explain it to anyone. So, they played at being friends, played at working together, pretended that they didn't both have holes in their hearts. He'd done that. For all he'd thought he had to, he hated the way they were now. When she spoke, her voice was soft in the close quarters of the car. "Are you James's *Thought Police* now too?"

That got him right between the ribs, but he deserved it. "I worry about you."

She gave a short, sharp laugh full of bitterness and never took her eyes from the rocky hills outside. "You don't need to anymore."

He gritted his teeth and drove on. It was nearing nine o'clock, but the fog lingered between the hills. They were driving from Portree to a couple of crofts along the coast of Loch Dunvegan. "This Davey MacLeod is supposed to have a lot of songs. His nephew told me the other day that he even has one about a fairy bride. Could be similar to The River Maiden."

She glanced his way for the first time since they'd pulled away from their hostel in Portree. That got her attention. "Really?" She was surprised. "We're not exactly in the right territory for that."

"We're not in Assynt, but if the story is as old as ye think it is, it could be all over Scotland, at least in some form." He said, relieved that they could at least talk about work.

"True, or it could be completely unrelated." She took a sardonic tone. "Seems like there was a time that every unhappy wife who ran off on her husband was explained away as a fairy, or a selkie, or a mermaid. Couldn't possibly be that she was tired of her situation."

"Mermaids?" He said. "I don't think I've heard that one."

"Oh, yeah. She lives in the caves under Loch Assynt. She jumped from the castle into the loch rather than marry the Devil because of a bargain her father made." Sarah told him.

"I don't think I've heard that one before." He said puzzled. "Where did ye find it?"

Her expression soured, and she turned back to the window. "In my mother's journal. My father told it to her."

"Ah." Clearly her father was a touchy subject.

He drove on, navigating through the hills to the other side of the island. They'd been on Skye for a week now conducting open sessions in halls in Kyleakin, Sleat, and Portree. Now they were branching out to visit those who couldn't make it to the larger towns. The others were crisscrossing the Trotternish peninsula while he and Sarah went to Dunvegan. He probably should have brought Jujhar along. She was always calmer when he was around.

Sarah brooded all the way to the other side of the island and after he made the turn at Dunvegan. After a few miles though, the gardens of the castle came into view. She leaned forward craning to see the lush beautiful gardens. This early in the year, there weren't many blooms, but the new growth was a brilliant green, almost garish against the natural landscape.

"Wow." Sarah breathed. "It's so stark, the line between the natural wildness and the carefully tended gardens."

"Aye, it reminds me of a golf course." He said wrinkling his nose in disdain.

"Mmm," She grunted agreement. "This island is so beautiful on its own. Why on earth would they want to conquer it like that?"

"That's one way to look at it."

"It's awful." She settled back into her seat as if put off the more she saw of the gardens.

He found her reaction reassuring, but for entirely the wrong reasons. Of course, Sarah preferred the wild and natural to the carefully manicured gardens. The magnificence of the castle and its renowned gardens was nothing to her. Like James and all of his carefully managed trappings were or had been. He had been afraid to ask her about their date. He had given up the right to ask her things like that.

Still a very small part of him that he preferred not to examine too closely, itched to know. Could she be happy with James? Could she know that already? He was sure James would have confided in him, but there hadn't been time in the few days between their date and leaving for their trip. He hoped for all their sakes that it would work out between Sarah and James, or at least that was what he told himself in his more rational moments.

***

Davey MacLeod's house was down a winding track near Loch Suardal. Small and whitewashed with a thatched roof, it was postcard perfect on the outside. Dermot knocked on the weathered door.

Sarah was heartened when the old man who answered the door grinned. He was missing a few teeth, but his smile was one of welcome. When Dermot had introduced them, Davey MacLeod sprang back from the door waving them in. "Come in, come in. Young Angus said ye'd be coming. I'm that glad ye're here. I just put the kettle on."

Dermot had to duck his head to get through the door. Sarah followed. Inside, the air was close and smelled of peat smoke, sweat and liniment. The furnishings were sparse and ancient, but the place was clean.

Davey shuffled to the tiny kitchen where the electric tea kettle that was standard for every Scottish kitchen Sarah had been in, was beginning to boil. Davey pulled two more cups from the cabinet and draped a teabag into each of them.

"Can I help with that?" Sarah asked.

"That'd be grand, lass." Davey said stepping aside. He shuffled out to the parlor. Before he settled himself on the couch, he turned to Dermot. "Would ye put another brick on the fire there, laddie?"

Dermot went to the basket of peat bricks next to the fireplace and added one to the smoldering fire. "What did Angus tell ye, then?"

Sarah brought a steaming cup of tea and set it on the small table next to where Davey was sitting. She went back to the kitchen for sugar and cream, and again for cups for Dermot and herself. As she took a seat in a chair next to the couch, the old man said. "He said ye were looking for songs and stories about the island."

"That's right." Sarah said. "We collect old songs and stories to preserve them."

Davey cocked his head to the side. "Ye're American?"

"Tha, ach bha mo sheanmhair as a h-Asaint." [I am, but my grandmother was from Assynt.] Sarah answered. They hadn't met many Gaelic speakers on the mainland, but since coming to Skye, she had found many more. She also noticed that folks were readier to speak it with her after they'd heard some Gaelic words roll naturally off her tongue. Most people in the Gaeltachd spoke the language only with each other, but rarely with outsiders. And if you ask someone of Davey's or even his children's generation if they spoke Gaelic, most of them would tell you they didn't. Generations of English managed schools had done their work in suppressing the language, even turning it into something to be ashamed of. Gaelic was for the uneducated, the unsophisticated. For too long, it was viewed by people in most of Scotland as a sign of ignorance, much the way folks in Chapel Hill viewed Sarah's mountain accent as the mark of a hillbilly.

Davey answered her bona fides as a Gaelic speaker with a wide grin. *"Bheil gu dearbh?"* [Is that so?]

He looked at Dermot in question, and Dermot confirmed in Gaelic that they both spoke the language. They all agreed to speak Gaelic. Sarah asked permission to record their conversation and pulled the recorder they'd brought out of her bag.

In the end, Davey's fairy bride song had not been similar to "The River Maiden". Sarah knew she would be filing it along with the other stories of disappearing wives. Still, they had a long conversation about the declining Gaelic on the island, and Davey's despair of the island's young people finding more opportunity in the cities.

The conversation swung back around to folklore. "If there are fairies still around," The old man said with a look that suggested he might believe there were. "They're here on Skye."

"What makes you say that?" Sarah asked.

"Och, it's the souterrains."

"Souterrains?" This was a new term for Sarah.

"Underground chambers made of stone." Dermot explained.

"Aye. I know that some people say they're old houses, and maybe they are. But they're fairy houses. I'm sure of it."

"Do you know any stories about fairies and the souterrains?" Dermot asked, leaning forward in his chair resting his elbows on his knees.

"Of course." Davey said. He took a sip of his tea in preparation for the story to come. "A cousin of mine was working up near the caravan park in Claigan. It was in the late fall, and there was almost no one staying there. He was sitting outside his caravan one night when he thought he saw something off in the trees. He was afraid it was a tourist, about to get hurt walking around in the dark. So, he followed. But it wasn't a tourist. It was a mist in the shape of a woman."

"A mist?" Sarah asked.

"Aye, like smoke, but like it was lit from the inside. And he followed it as it walked down the dark trail. It stopped by a wee rise and stayed still for a moment. Then it sank, like it was being sucked down." He lifted a hand and slowly lowered it, demonstrating the sinking mist. "The lad was terrified and ran back to his caravan and locked the door. But the next day, he walked the same trail back the way that the mist lady had gone. And in the spot where it had disappeared was the opening for the souterrain. He was sure that what he saw was a fairy returning home."

"Did he know that the souterrain was there before that day?" Dermot asked.

"Och, everyone knows it's there. It's ancient, and there are souterrains all over the island."

"Are they all fairy houses?" Sarah prompted.

"Don't know." He shook his head. "But there are so many other fairy legends on Skye. Have ye been to the Fairy Pools?"

They had in fact, taken the day off to visit one of Skye's main attractions, a series of eerily clear pools that could inspire belief in fairy magic. Sarah thought, if there was ever a site for a king to have fallen in love with a fairy maiden, it would have been in crystal pools like those. But she had learned from talking to locals, that although the pools were beautiful, there wasn't much in the way of fairy lore about them. "Do you know any legends about the Fairy Pools?"

Davey shook his head. "But there's also the Fairy Glen in Uig. Surely, there must be fairies living in those wee duns. And of course, the Fairy Flag of the MacLeod's. We've got more connection to fairies than anywhere else in Scotland." He held his arm out straight and pushed his sleeve up to show the white inside of his elbow, blue veins snaking close to the surface. "There's fairy blood in these veins."

Sarah was a little startled by his vehemence. He was sure of what he was saying. "Are there any other clans with fairy blood?"

Davey shook his head slowly. "It's a sad tale. The MacLeod clan split many generations ago. The sons of Tormod stayed here on Skye and on Harris. The sons of Torquil settled on Lewis and in the mainland in Assynt." He stopped lifting his eyes to Sarah's. "Was your grandmother a MacLeod?"

Sarah shook her head. "She was a MacAlpin, but we do have some MacLeod kin."

He smiled. "I kent it when I first saw ye. Ye have a fey air about ye."

Sarah felt the hairs on the back of her neck stand up, and a chill raced down her back. She glanced up at Dermot who was watching her. It likely meant nothing. He was probably commenting on her curls or green eyes, or shortness. "Are you flirting with me Davey MacLeod?"

The old man laughed heartily. "Och, it's been an age since I even thought to flirt with anyone, but if I were young as this lad," He jerked a knobby thumb at Dermot. "I'd not let a lass like you get away without stealing a kiss or two."

Dermot who had been taking a sip of tea, choked and set his cup down with a thunk. "Does the MacLeod family have any traditions that still call on that fairy connection?"

Davey blew out a long breath in thought. "Och, it's only the flag now. Most folk don't believe in fairies anymore. The young ones don't believe in things they can't touch, aye. But the flag sits up there in the castle waiting for the next time we need its blessing. We've already used it twice. Once against the MacDonalds, after they burned the church with MacLeods inside. Awful business that." He said shaking his head as if he'd witnessed the massacre himself rather than heard about it hundreds of years later. Memories were long in places like this. "When they attacked again, we raised the flag and beat them back at the shore, even though we were outnumbered."

"The other time we needed it to save the clan's cattle from a pestilence. It worked too. But we can only use it once more. So, they keep it locked away behind a glass. I don't think they'll ever take it out again. There isn't a need for such things today. Clans don't raid anymore, and we have science to cure what ails us."

"But science can't explain what it did before." Sarah said.

He shook his head then gave her a long look. "No, it can't. Maybe the fairies knew things we didn't at the time."

***

"Tell me the story." Sarah said so quietly that he wasn't sure he'd heard it. They were standing in the gallery at Dunvegan Castle looking at the ancient yellowed fabric behind the glass. When they left Davey MacLeod's, she had wanted to see the famed fairy flag.

There were many stories about the flag's origin, but he knew the one she meant. He stood close behind her to avoid attracting the attention of the other tourists milling about the hall. "The MacLeod fell in love with a beautiful woman, and she with him. But she was a princess of the fairies. She begged her father to let them marry. Eventually, the fairy king agreed to the match, but she could only live among men for…" Her nearness swamped him with emotion.

"A year and a day." Sarah finished, softly.

"Aye," He breathed stirring some of the curls near her ear. He closed his eyes and cleared his throat, glad that she couldn't see his face. "The MacLeod decided that he would rather have his bride for so short a time than no time at all. So, he agreed. For a year and a day, they were happy. They had a son. But when the baby was still a newborn, it came time for the princess to return to the fairies."

Sarah shifted to turn her ear toward him, and he lifted a hand and rested it on her waist. He didn't want her to turn around. He was already testing the limits of his self-control. "So, they walked out to the Fairy Bridge that would take her back to her people. Before she went, she told her husband not to let the babe cry. You see, fairies can hear the cries of babies above anything else. And she knew that if she heard it, she would have to answer and risk war between the fairies and her husband's people."

He looked down to see her breasts rising and falling rapidly. He was glad and sad to see that she wasn't unaffected by his nearness. "But some months later, the MacLeod's were having a great feast. And the wee lad's nurse left him alone in his cradle. When he woke, he cried like most babies do. But the nurse didna hear him for all the noise in the hall."

"When she went up to check on the babe, there was a woman there in a fine silk shawl leaning over the cradle. She started when she saw the nurse, who recognized her for the boy's mother. The princess wrapped the baby in the shawl and said. 'I must go, but I am always watching. This shawl will protect you all. If you need my help, wave it and help will come. But you can only use it three times. Then it will disappear."

Sarah drew in a deep breath and he swore her head tilted ever so slightly closer to his. He would only have to lean forward a couple of inches to plant a kiss on her temple. "And they've used it twice already."

"Mmm..." He couldn't find the words, so grunted his assent.

Sarah stood for a few minutes looking at the cloth. With a brief shake of her head, she stepped away from him to view the plaque listing the legends. "It says here that the cloth is probably fourth century from the Middle East and was likely brought back by Harald Hardrada as an early Christian relic, maybe the shirt of a saint."

Dermot slid his hands into his pockets resisting the urge to touch her again. "Yeah, He was an ancestor of Leod, the clan founder. Scientifically, that answer makes a lot more sense."

Sarah cocked her head to the side and looked back at the cloth. "But the people around here believe it came from the fairies."

"Ye know all too well, how facts get lost in time, and stories are made up to fill in the gaps."

She laughed, low and husky, and cast a glance at him over her shoulder. The mischief in it went straight to his gut. "It's funny though. For thousands of years, Christians have been co-opting older traditions to fit each colonized culture's preexisting ethos." She turned and walked toward him. "But here, the Christian narrative is rejected in favor of the pre-existing belief. Here, it's not a saint's shirt. It's a fairy flag."

He gave her an easy smile. It felt almost like it used to. "Memories are long, and Scots are stubborn."

"Mmm," She agreed. They stood there looking at the supposedly magical cloth for a few minutes longer. He was surprised when she said. "I went to the castle...in Inverness. That's where I was."

"If ye wanted to go to the castle, ye could have told me. I would have gone with you."

She gave him a look that without words reminded him that they had been at odds with each other for months. "It was something I needed to do alone. It was a spot that was special to my mother, and me before I even knew it. I read about it in her journal, and I needed to see it." She stopped and pressed her lips together. "I'm sorry if I worried you."

CHAPTER TWENTY

Stornoway and Lewis in general was Sarah's favorite place that they had been so far. The town was exactly the right size to her mind, big enough to have some culture, but small enough to still be friendly. Lewis had the largest population of Gaelic speakers in Scotland, and that increase had kept Sarah hopping throughout the week since they had arrived. Much as they had done on Skye, they were meeting subjects in town during publicized open houses. Then they would branch out to some of the other communities on the island. Tomorrow Sarah was scheduled to go to Barvas with Dermot and Jujhar to talk to a sheep farmer named Shaw, who she'd heard knew a lot of songs. Kirstie, and Ewan were going to see a weaver while Isla was staying in town to visit a local music studio. It felt like the team hadn't stopped since they'd arrived.

Sarah had popped into the newsagent's to pick up some drinks and snacks for later. When she saw the tabloid rack by the counter, she froze in her tracks, her blood going ice cold.

There she was, her blurry curtain of curls hiding her face as she got into James Stuart's car in front of Edinburgh Castle. The headline in bright garish yellow read "James Stuart Tamed by Mystery Woman" The light was low, and she was looking down, so there was no way to identify her. Still, anyone who knew her including everyone on their team would know that it was her.

Sarah snatched up a copy and put it face down on the counter. Isla saw the tabloid on the counter with the rest of their things and gave Sarah a questioning look.

Without a word, Sarah nodded toward the rack where additional copies waited, like a nest of snakes waiting to bite her. Isla followed Sarah's gaze and her eyes widened. She looked up at Sarah and opened her mouth as if she might say something. Sarah shook her head, the last thing she wanted to do was acknowledge that it was her in a public place.

The clerk stepped behind the counter and rang their things up. Sarah tried to smile at him as if she weren't terrified that he would recognize her.

To her relief, he didn't look up. She quickly paid and left the shop, Isla in tow.

"Och, ye're in it now." Isla said to her once they were out on the street and sure no one was listening.

Sarah gritted her teeth and walked as fast as she could without attracting undue attention. "I can't believe this."

"I can't believe it either. He took ye to the castle?" Isla said breathlessly trying to keep up.

"It didn't go well." Sarah said.

It was still early and there were only a few people at the hall other than their group. Sarah stopped inside the door and scanned for Dermot. When she spotted him near the kitchen door, she made a beeline for him. He was talking to one of their hosts, so she was forced to wait or make a scene. Their conversation finished in less than a minute, but it might have been the longest minute of her life.

She grabbed Dermot's arm and pulled him to the hallway that held restrooms and other small rooms. She went to the first door she found that wasn't a restroom and pulled him inside. It turned out to be a long narrow storage closet lined with utility shelves full of napkins, toilet paper and a rack of folding chairs.

"What is it?" He asked, face full of concern.

Sarah pulled the newspaper from the bag and spread it on top of the chairs. He took one look at the front page, snatched the tabloid up and opened it to the article. "Have ye read this?"

"I didn't take the time." She told him.

He read it out loud, but quietly so they wouldn't be overheard.

"It's been weeks since international playboy, James Stuart was spotted out and about town after dark. An avid partaker of nightlife all over Britain and the Continent, Stuart has been notably absent from night clubs and parties these last two months. Can a mystery woman have captured his heart?"

"These pictures of Stuart in Edinburgh with an unidentified woman were taken a month ago. At the time our editors thought nothing of it. In the past Stuart has been pictured with a different woman nearly every week. However, he has been living quietly now for weeks. After returning from a business trip in Dubai, Stuart has been spotted at his office, Edinburgh home and his country house. A survey of Edinburgh night clubs that he has frequented in the past has turned up no information. Is Lord Caledon ready to settle down?"

"You may recall last spring when he was linked with model Charlotte Mycroft after spending two weeks together in Ibiza. There was much speculation at the time that they were involved. However, the two seem to have cooled things off since then. These photos mark the first time he has been seen with this woman. However, our research has not turned up a name for her. Who can she be?"

"Ugh. What crap?" Sarah groaned. "They make it sound so salacious. For all they know I could be his secretary?"

Dermot shook his head looking at the picture on the front page of her getting in the car. There were other images accompanying the article, but none of them clearly showed Sarah's face. The closest was one in profile of her turning back to say something to James. James's eyes were fixed on her. "No. They know what she looks like, and I'm quite sure they've never seen him look at her like that."

"Great." She muttered. "How long do you think it'll be before someone tells them who I am?"

"That's hard to tell." He blew out a long breath. "Until someone has a reason to."

"What do you mean by that?"

He shifted uncomfortably. "The only people who know of James's interest in you are a handful of people who work for him, me, and possibly someone who was at the Burns Supper. No one who knows ye well would have reason to give ye up, and no one who works for James would."

"So, that leaves any one of the hundred people who saw me on stage at that fundraiser and then later on his arm." She sighed. "Well, I supposed it should comfort me that most of those people weren't paying enough attention to really learn my name. I got the feeling I was beneath their notice."

"Unless…" He trailed off not finishing his thought.

"Unless?" Sarah prompted after a minute passed.

"Unless this was done by Walter to move things along quicker." Dermot sounded defeated.

"You have got to be kidding me." Sarah said through her teeth.

Dermot shook his head. "I wish I was. I've seen them do more devious things than this, and the last time I saw Walter Stuart he was getting very impatient."

"Awesome." Sarah said sounding as if it was the farthest thing from awesome. "So, they leak the pictures and that James shows signs of settling down to build buzz and speculation. Then they out me publicly so I have nowhere to go, at least nowhere in the UK."

"That's about the size of it."

Sarah closed her eyes and pressed her fingers to her temples as if they hurt. After a moment she said. "Well, I can't say you didn't warn me."

***

When they had exhausted speculation on who might betray Sarah, they left the storage room and tried to go about their work as if nothing had happened. Dermot had shoved the tabloid deep in the rubbish bin, but he couldn't wipe the image of Sarah with James from his mind. Somehow, knowing that they had been on a date without him rankled more than seeing her on his arm at the Burns Supper. At least then, she'd been under his ever-watchful eye. Knowing that she'd been on that date and he had no idea what had happened was driving him mad.

He looked over to where she was talking with a woman in her fifties who had been singing. He loved watching her work. She knew how to draw stories and songs out of people. She welcomed them and listened to them in such a way that they never realized she was picking their brains. She made every source that she talked with feel as though their help was essential to preserving their traditions. No matter what was going on in her personal life, she greeted every person who sat down with an open smile.

It wasn't fair to her. She wasn't his. But he couldn't stand the idea of her going about her life without him. He'd never been jealous before about any other woman he'd been with. He knew that Felicia hadn't stopped seeing other men, and it didn't bother him at all. But then Felicia wasn't Sarah. He liked Felicia, enjoyed her company, but he didn't fancy himself in love with her.

He was in love with Sarah, and no matter how much he pushed her away that wasn't going to change. She stood as the woman she'd been talking to took her leave. The woman said something to her and Sarah bent her head to listen. The angle called to his mind the image of her from the photo, head bent getting into the car. He could feel his temper on slow boil. How could James have let this happen?

Then a chilling thought occurred to him. What if James had made this happen. He knew some celebrities would tip off paparazzi that they would be at a certain location. He had never seen James do it before, but in this case, he wouldn't put it past his cousin to manufacture news to move things along. Dermot thought that his advice to be patient had reached James. But then he had Walter on a daily basis pushing him to move faster. James could only withstand so much pressure.

He wouldn't have even had to do the dirty work. Felicia or some other lackey could have whispered to a photographer where they would be on their date. The rest could easily follow the timeline that Sarah had laid out. Release the photos with some strategic rumors to build the buzz, then when interest was high, feed her name to the press.

If it was James, Dermot expected that he would wait until their research trip was over or nearly so to release her name. That would mean the end of Sarah's role on the team. They wouldn't be able to work with photographers following them, or every other subject saying, "Hey, aren't you that lass?"

***

The team was packing things up for the day, when Dermot approached Sarah's table. He'd been thinking of contingency plans for how they would handle things if her name became public before they got back to Edinburgh. He was on the point of telling her that they needed to talk when Kirstie bounced up to the table. "The pub on Francis Street is having some musicians tonight. Sounds like it should be good craic. Maybe we should all go."

A couple of months ago, Kirstie would have been making eyes at him and suggesting that the two of them go without the others. He was pleased with her change in attitude. That talk he'd had with her and traveling together seemed to have helped her integrate with the rest of the team. She was treating Sarah with professional courtesy at least. It was a relief. They couldn't have gotten this far with her sniping at Sarah the way she had been. "Uh, I'm knackered, and I have something that I need to talk to Sarah about. But you and the others should go."

Her face fell with disappointment before she walked away, "Alright. We'll see you later then."

Sarah finished packing up her things and handed him the cassette that she had finished labeling. She gave him a questioning look. "Did you think of something else?"

He considered telling her about his thoughts on James's possible involvement in their current problem. But he wasn't sure that he wanted to poison whatever progress she had made with James. God, he hated this constant bloody push-pull between the three of them. "I'd like to ask ye a few questions about that night. Maybe we can figure out who or what we're dealing with here."

"Alright, talk over dinner?" She asked.

"Aye, there's a café on the way back to the hostel. We can stop there for a bite."

***

They followed the others out and said their goodbyes on the street leaving their equipment locked up in the storage closet at the hall. Although, Sarah noticed that Ewan had a small camera with him as always.

She tried not to feel awkward going to dinner with Dermot. They'd been inseparable once, and today when she had come to him with the tabloid, it had almost felt like old times. But the rift between them had gone on for months now. She knew he hadn't meant the things he'd said that night in her flat. Still, he'd felt the need to say them, to try to push her away from him. She tried to understand why, but she still couldn't. She also found it hard to forgive him for going about it the way he had.

They sat down with their dinner in the small café. There were only a handful of people there, but he still felt the need to speak softly when he asked. "What were ye doing at the castle?"

"I'm not sure how that's relevant, but he had arranged access for us so that he could give me a private tour." She said avoiding saying James's name for fear that someone might overhear.

"Did...he plan that ahead of time?" He asked. The "he" was little more than a hiss between his teeth.

Sarah thought back to that night. "I thought it was spontaneous at the time; like he got the idea while we were talking over dinner. But the guard who escorted us through the castle seemed to expect us."

"Right." Dermot took a bite of his food and chewed thinking about what to ask next. Sarah ate some of her own dinner and watched as the thoughts scrolled by behind his eyes. "Were those photos taken when ye left the castle or when ye arrived?"

"When we left." A thought occurred to her. "It's a good thing they weren't there before. We walked up the Mile arm in arm from the restaurant. If they had pictures of that, they'd probably print that we were secretly married already."

"Right, well thank heaven for small mercies." He said acidly. They ate for a few more minutes. Dermot leaned back and took a sip of his drink. "When ye came out to get into the car, did ye notice anyone else on the esplanade?"

That was tricky. She hadn't noticed anyone, because she had been upset. But she didn't want to explain to Dermot that she'd been upset because she felt like she had betrayed him. "No, but I wasn't really looking for photographers. It's Edinburgh Castle. Anyone with a camera could have easily been a tourist. There were probably people there. That part of

The Mile seems to never sleep, but I didn't notice anything unusual."

He made one of his speaking grunts and tilted his head to the side to show she had a point. "What did ye do in the castle?"

She sighed and dropped the chip she was about to eat. "He gave me a tour?"

"Of?" He prompted.

"Of the Royal Apartments, not that that's relevant to our tabloid problem." She snapped. She really didn't feel comfortable talking about her date with another man with him. He'd practically shoved her into James's arms, but she still felt like she'd betrayed him.

He arched an eyebrow at her. "What else?"

She sent him a look that said she did not want to talk about it.

He lifted a hand to show he understood. "I'm trying to figure out who we're up against. It will tell us what to expect next, or when to expect it."

"That's fine, but I don't see why what went on inside the castle is relevant."

"Was James with ye the whole time?" He asked ignoring her protest.

Except for the moment when I ran away from him like a cornered animal. She thought. But Dermot didn't need to know that. "Yes, he was."

"Mmmph." He grunted again, thinking.

"Wait." A thought occurred to her. "Do you think he did this?"

"I don't know." He bit out. "I didna think he was that Machiavellian, but he would have the same motive as Walter."

"Ugh." If James was behind this he had played her like a fiddle. He appealed to her sympathy by suggesting that he was trapped by his family; made her want to like him even if she didn't want to get involved with him romantically. She pushed her food away. "I'm not hungry anymore."

"Ye look green." He said with concern.

"Thanks." She balled up the trash from her meal. She was going to throw the rest of it away, but as she rose Dermot grabbed her wrist.

"Did something happen in the castle?" His blue eyes sought hers.

Sarah shook her head and pulled her wrist from his grip. She was done talking. He didn't get to ask her questions about her personal life. James or no James, he had given up that right. "Nothing that concerns you."

She found a trash can and dropped the remnants of her dinner inside. Without looking back at Dermot, she pushed through the door and out onto the street.

He followed hard behind her cursing under his breath. She had known he would follow, but that didn't mean she had to make it easy for him. She picked up her pace counting the steps to the hostel where she could shut herself in the room and he wouldn't be able to see how much what had happened at the castle bothered her.

She was striding past an alleyway when he finally caught up with her. He pulled her by the arm into the alley and positioned himself between her and the street. "What happened in the castle?"

"I'm not going to discuss that with you." She tried to walk past him, but he stepped in front of her.

"D' ye think I don't know where ye were, who ye were with?" He asked lowering his head to find her eyes.

"I've lived the better part of the last year in your pocket. I'm sure you know exactly where I was. That doesn't mean I'm going to tell you all the juicy details." She spat fury at him. "Besides, isn't that right where you wanted me to be?"

She watched his shoulders rise and fall as he breathed. Every muscle in his neck was tense, his jaw clenched. "How can ye think that?"

"Are you saying you didn't want me to go out with James?" She thought again of everything he had done to push her away knowing that James would pursue her. "I don't know how I could possibly have mixed up your signals. What with you practically ignoring me."

"When was I ignoring ye? I've been watching ye for…"

"And of course, there's your new girlfriend." She hated the shrill tone that crept into her voice. "Clearly you've moved on."

"It's not like that." He said raising a pleading hand.

She gave him a look that said she knew how it was. "And I think you were pretty clear when you mentioned how desperate I was to be loved because of my own mother."

"I know what I said." He barked.

"No! You don't!" She snapped. Her eyes bored into his as she crowded him stepping close enough that she had to tilt her head up to meet his eyes. "You said the very thing that the small, broken voice in my head has been telling me for the last twenty years. I thought I had learned something different, but you rem…"

This time he cut her off with his lips on hers, in a possessing kiss. His fingers threaded through her hair and gripped tight as he whirled her around and pushed her against the wall. His mouth pressed hers until her lips stung and his tongue invaded. His hips ground against hers. The suddenness of it all stole her breath, but after a minute she remembered where they were and what he had done. She began pushing against his shoulders and tore her mouth from his. He only backed off far enough to meet her eyes, which was probably for the best. No doubt she would have broken her hand hitting him if she could have gotten a good enough swing.

"Of course, I didna want ye to go out with him. The very idea of his hands on ye is like a snake in my gut eating me from the inside out. I love ye. You know that. I tried to make ye forget it, but it's tearing me apart." He ground out through his teeth.

"You bastard." She hissed through her still tingling lips. "You pushed him on me."

"I'm a bastard alright," she hadn't known that she was crying until he wiped a tear from her cheek. "But I'm yours. I always have been."

"And Felicia?"

"She's only a friend."

"You broke my heart." Her voice cracked, and she felt the tears now running down her cheeks.

"I know." Answering tears pooled in his own eyes. "I had to."

"Why?"

"Because as long as ye were focused on me, ye wouldna give him a chance." His sigh blew against her lips. "I can't protect ye like he can."

"Protect me from who?" Her eyes peered up into his, searching for some clue about who Dermot was afraid of.

"The Ryan Cumberlands and Walter Stuarts of the world."

She closed her eyes and breathed, trying to calm herself. All she got was a lung-full of his scent. "Who's going to protect me from James?"

"He won't hurt you." He whispered brushing curls away from her face. His hand came to rest like a comfortable weight on her shoulder, his thumb teasing the sensitive spot where her neck and shoulder met.

"Yes, he will." She nodded emphatically. "If I say yes to all he's offering, there won't be anything left that's mine. If he did this like you think he did, how far is he willing to go to get what he wants?"

He closed his eyes resting his forehead against hers. Then he looked into her eyes. "I'm yours. He canna change that."

Sarah felt defeated as she leaned forward and brushed his lips with hers, whispering. "Who's going to protect me from you?"

"Tell me to go, and I will." He gritted his teeth. His voice cracked when he said, "It may kill me, but I'll leave you alone. Just say the word."

She tried but the words caught in her throat. He had broken her heart, and she knew he probably would again. She should tell him to go away. "I can't. I love you."

His lips crashed into hers and he pressed her closer to the wall. Sarah almost cried with relief. After weeks and weeks of the constant push-pull and the awkwardness of having to work together, she could feel the tension drain away. She had begun to doubt everything he had ever told her, and her own judgment of who and what was true. But this felt right. This was true and pure, and she wasn't going to let him deny it anymore.

His hands slid from her shoulders to her waist as he pulled her closer to him. He lifted her, and she wrapped her legs around his hips. She couldn't get close enough to him. Her arms wrapped around his shoulders and she angled her mouth to deepen the kiss. The squeal of brakes sounded in the street and they froze. Dermot looked over his shoulder, to see a car turning the corner nearby.

"It's nothing, a car." Sarah told him, but at least part of the spell was broken.

Dermot turned back to her and stole a quick hard kiss before saying. "Not here. Come on."

CHAPTER TWENTY-ONE

His back was freezing with nothing but his jumper between it and the cold metal floor of the van. It was a stark contrast to the warmth against his side where Sarah was stretched out asleep her arm draped across him. Her curls tickled his chin and her hot breath blew across his chest stirring feelings that he had tried hard to bury. He could not believe they had made love like a couple of bloody teenagers in the back of the team van. He couldn't believe they'd made love at all.

He had told himself that he could stay away from her, that he would find someone else and she would be better off with James. That was before he thought James had been the one to feed the pictures to the press. He couldn't be sure it had been James, but it was something so underhanded that the very idea made his blood boil.

One of Sarah's biggest reasons for resisting James's charms was her own professional integrity. She didn't want even a whiff of scandal around any achievements that she made. He supposed that was a result of growing up being judged by everyone in her community for things that were out of her control. When she built her own life and career elsewhere, she was very careful not to give people reasons to discount her accomplishments.

"I can't believe we did that." She whispered sleepily. He could feel a smile swelling the cheek that pressed against him.

"I was thinking that same thing." He said.

"What are we going to do?" She asked. He was relieved that she didn't sound regretful or frightened.

"Well, we're going to have to go inside soon, or everyone is going to wonder where we are." He said. It was easier to focus on the immediate issue in front of them than the larger issues.

She sighed. "I figured that much. You know what I meant."

He made a throaty noise of acknowledgment. "I don't know. It's only a matter of time before the media learns your name."

"And then learns what I do, and where I came from, and what happened in Chapel Hill, and…" She trailed off leaving him to fill in the rest of the chain reaction that would occur when the media started looking into Sarah.

"Ruins everything for you." He tightened his arm around her.

She rubbed her cheek on his shoulder and said the thing that he had been thinking. "We could run away. Right here in Stornoway, we could catch a boat to the continent and be lost before anyone knew it."

He kissed the top of her head. "And be free for all of a week, maybe a month before they find us."

"You seem very sure about that." She said sounding as skeptical as ever.

He gritted his teeth. He didn't like talking about it, but he had to get her to understand how far the Stuarts would go. "I've never told ye the details of what happened to me in the Army."

"No, you haven't." She turned, resting on his chest with her chin propped on her hands so that she could look at him.

"I went into the Army after university. There were a lot of reasons for that, some of them I'm not terribly proud of. One of the reasons, though was to get away from Walter Stuart. Not long after I graduated, Walter contacted me to tell me what was expected of me by the family. It was all about duty and how I owed it to them after they had been so welcoming to my mother and me all those years. I was to join the company in whatever capacity Walter saw fit and be there to support James in all things. Even though James had gone off to school years before, Walter wanted to use our childhood friendship to manipulate James. He's always looking to control things."

She nodded, and he went on. "Walter's been pulling James's strings since his father retired. He wanted me to be his cat's paw, I was the same age and could follow James and observe things about his life that Walter couldn't. I could keep James out of trouble."

"Except that you didn't want to." Sarah prompted.

"No. I had seen how Walter had always looked down on my mother and couldn't reconcile myself with doing his bidding. So, I took myself to one of the few places that I thought Walter with all of his connections couldn't touch me. I figured that even if he knew where I was, he couldn't get in the way of Army service without creating problems for himself. So, I joined the Army. I wasna expecting to go to war. I don't reckon many of us were. But it was the fog of war that gave Walter the chance to pull me back into his web without any repercussions. I was in Saudi Arabia with my unit waiting for our orders to invade Kuwait when the Americans started the invasion, and Iraq started launching SCUD missiles at us. During one of the nights when the missiles were falling, and soldiers were running everywhere, I was attacked. I don't even remember what I was doing."

He shook his head. "In the scramble in camp, I was pulled by someone into a sort of alley between tents. There were three of them. I never saw their faces. They beat me, and one of them stomped on my leg. Even with all the noise of the missiles and hustle, I heard the bone crack. One of them got carried away. He was about to kick me in the head, but another one pulled him back. And I heard him say. 'We're not supposed to kill him, break something."

He took a breath and licked his lips. He could almost taste the mix of sand and blood in his mouth from that night. "They never said who sent them. They didna have to. I don't know who he paid, or how he managed it. But I do know Walter Stuart came to see me almost as soon as I landed back in the country with a cast on my leg and bruises that were just turning yellow. I think he actually smiled and said that he expected me in his office when my discharge was complete."

"And you're sure that he sent them?" She asked.

"Either Walter or his proxy. I canna prove it, of course." He shrugged.

"But you didn't go to work for James. You went back to school, right?" Sarah said. He could see her trying to puzzle through his timeline.

"For a time, I did work for James. Once I had military training, I became more useful as security staff. I went to school part-time and worked part-time. Eventually Walter decided that my work researching Scottish traditions could be used as part of their nationalist agenda, and he arranged for my security work to become only occasional. I could study full time. Which is what I was doing when they sent me to you."

"Would you have come to North Carolina if they hadn't sent you?" She asked.

"Eventually, I would have spent some time studying in the States, or Canada. But I wasna ready to do it last summer."

"So, what, they keep you on retainer until they need your work or your muscle?" She arched an eyebrow at him.

He would have to tread lightly. She had been suspicious of his motives since they met, and this line of inquiry was only confirming some of her worst suspicions. He pursed his lips trying to think of a way to explain the complex connections of family, patronage and duty. "It's not quite as...transactional as all that. The Stuarts did set up a trust for me when I was a boy. To hear them tell it, my mother is the poor relation. Well, poor by their standards anyway. The Stuarts always claimed it was their duty to include us, act as patrons if you will. If my mother needed a grant for a project, or an introduction at a university or publisher, she got it. If I needed a recommendation for a school, I got it. And in return, we were expected to support the Stuarts in whatever ways they asked."

She watched him for a few heartbeats. He held his breath hoping she would understand that kind of relationship. "That sounds positively feudal."

He nodded. "In a way it is. Some people still take that sort of clan loyalty very seriously."

"Some people..." She narrowed her eyes at him pushing herself up to her knees, holding her shirt to her bare chest. "Not you."

"Sarah," He warned sitting up.

"No," She shook her head, her eyes determined. "There's something here you're not telling me. Some leverage that they have over you."

"You're not wrong." He sighed and hooked a hand behind her head and pulled her close. He hoped that his eyes could tell her what his words could not. He had been caught in his own internal tug of war between her and his mother for months. Part of him wanted desperately to confide in her, but another part of him worried that if he did it would affect her choices. It was his job to protect her, and that included keeping additional worries from her. She had enough to deal with without him adding his troubles. "I can't talk about that, now. If I thought it would make things easier for you, I would. It's my burden, not yours."

He saw his own worries reflected in her eyes. She lifted a hand to his cheek. "It's ours. That's the beauty of being in love, I can take on some of your burden. Goodness knows you've taken on mine."

"That's what I'm afraid of." He closed his eyes and leaned into her hand. "I'll tell you one day, but not tonight." He leaned forward and kissed her slowly, deliberately. "Now, if we don't go inside, we are going to have four very curious graduate students wondering what we're doing naked in their equipment van."

***

"We can't keep sneaking around like this." She told him ensconced in the same storage closet they had hidden in to discuss the tabloid story. They had made frenzied love against the sliver of wall space not covered by shelves. They'd had to move a mop and bucket out of the way, and carefully avoid causing a deafening racket by bumping the rack full of metal folding chairs. When they were finished, Dermot held her caressing her cheek in that way he had that made her feel as if there was no one else in the world.

His lips hardened into a grim line. "Aye, I know. But I haven't thought of a way out yet."

She bit her lip and made a decision. "I have papers, another identity. If we can get one for you, then we could leave. No one would know until it was too late."

"Where did ye get papers like that?" He pulled back in surprise.

"I don't think people with fake identities are supposed to tell how they got them." She was not going to bring Duff into their mess if she didn't have to. He was her safety net. "But I got it in the States, so I don't think my friend could help you here."

"Certainly not in the time that we would need it." He grumbled. "That also doesn't solve the issue of transportation, or what we'd be leaving behind."

"Your mom."

His eyes sharpened on hers, and he searched them as if he was trying to determine what she knew about his mother. Of course, she didn't know anything, except that Seonag lived in Edinburgh. Dermot had gone to see his mother, but never invited Sarah along. "Mmmph...yes, my mother. And our careers."

"And figuring out what happened to my mother." She let her shoulders slump. "I'm not sure any of that matters now. My career, or even learning my history. The closer I get to losing it all to James's idea of what I'm supposed to be the less

I seem to care. Molly's life was hers. She made her choices, and I should make mine."

"But you're not." He brushed her hair back from her face. "You're letting them push you into choosing the lesser of two evils."

She placed her hand over his heart. "No, I'm ready to choose you over those other things."

***

He took in a deep breath and let it out trying to relax the tension in his shoulders. His eyes never left Sarah's. The last time he had visited his mother before they'd left Edinburgh, she hadn't known who he was. He'd found her in her usual spot by the window with her knitting in her lap. But she was rocking quickly, and her movements were sharp. Her nerves rattled. She had rambled on in her incoherent way about some memory that had popped up and caught her attention. Her memories often blended with current events until she couldn't tell the difference.

"I should have gone off somewhere, America or Canada. Should have left him behind."

"Left who?" He asked, always concerned that the staff was treating her well. He wanted to make sure this was a past problem and not a present one.

"Och. That man. That ridiculous, puffed up man, always flaunting." She'd stabbed her knitting needle through a loop and hooked the thread drawing it through and flicking it off the opposite needle. Her movements sharp and angry. "That bloody man, and his bloody wife. I should have turned my back on the lot of them. Taken my wee boy off, prophecy or no. They canna be trusted I tell ye."

It sounded like she was talking about the Stuarts. "Do you mean the Stuarts?"

His mother made a low guttural sound in her throat. "Henry bloody Stuart. And they've got him now." She rocked back and forth in her chair, knitting angrily. "They've got my boy. That's why he hasna been to see me."

I'm right here, mum, he thought afraid to say it. *But aye, they've got me alright.* Instead he thought to change the subject, "Ah now, Mrs. Sinclair. What's that yer knitting?"

"Och. It's a scarf for my Dermot. Much good it'll do him." She grumbled turning the work to start a new row. "The bloody Stuarts will probably steal this too."

He decided to ignore the latest jab. Instead he pulled the skein of yarn that he'd picked up out of its bag and held it up for her to see.

It was a deep green with flecks of bright color "I've brought ye some new yarn."

Her eyes lit up. She took the yarn from him. He watched as her thin fingers stroked the wool feeling its softness. "Well. That's kind of ye, lad. It's lovely. My Dermot will like that, or did ye want a scarf for yerself?"

He cleared his throat, trying to choke down the painful lump that formed there. "No, you use it however ye like."

"Such a nice lad. I'm sure yer mother must be proud." she patted his hand before stowing the yarn in her knitting bag and picking up her needles again.

She hadn't known him. In truth, it had been weeks since she had recognized him. Her doctors had told him that it was only a matter of time before she forgot simple tasks, things like brushing her hair and teeth, or knitting which was one of the few things she enjoyed doing anymore. A very small, scared part of him didn't want to watch her mind deteriorate any further. Looking into Sarah's hopeful eyes, that small, scared part of him found support with the pragmatic part of him. Would his mother, if her faculties were intact really want him to sacrifice his own happiness for her sake? Would she want him to be cowed by the likes of Walter Stuart?

He brought Sarah's hand to his lips. "Aye. I'm ready."

Tears swam in Sarah's eyes making them glitter like cut peridot. All her love and hope shined out of them, bathing him in their light.

She had a way of looking at him that could make him feel twelve feet tall; brave, smart, and capable of tackling any problem. Still, that small, scared part of him grew in proportion as his mind sped through the logistics of what they had decided.

"How will we do it?" She breathed.

"Well, I'll need a new identity. We could get transportation right now, but we'd be too easily tracked." He mentally ticked through a list of documents needed to accomplish that. "And we definitely canna stay in the UK."

"America? It's big. Lots of places to hide."

"Aye, it's a start." He agreed. There were plenty of places to hide in America. "The trouble right now is timing. The Highlands aren't exactly crawling with forgers selling fake passports. I might know someone in Edinburgh, but I don't think he can get it before we get back to the city. Who knows what'll happen in the meantime."

Sarah thought for a few minutes, leaning back against a set of shelves full of banquet supplies. "And we couldn't leave now to get that process started without attracting James's attention."

"I'd be more worried about Walter's attention, but ye're right. Any change in our schedule will cause questions. James would believe whatever answer you gave him, but Walter is dangerous and trusts no one."

"It's too bad. All these fishing ports we've stopped in." She sighed. "Any of them would have been a perfect under the radar escape hatch."

Dermot agreed with a grunt. Sarah thought for a couple more minutes. "So, we go on as we have been, I guess, waiting for the other shoe to drop."

"Or an opportunity." He smoothed a stray curl away from her face. Sarah had started wearing her hair smoothed back into a tight curl-taming bun to look as different as possible from the photos in the tabloid. She had also purchased some weak reading glasses from the nearby chemists and wore them as much as she could stand. He hoped the effect was different enough that no one would recognize her.

Dermot pushed away from the wall where he'd been leaning. Stepping close he kissed her forehead and straightened her shirt. "On the bright side, we're almost to yer family's territory. If we're not running yet, you may have a chance to get some of those questions answered after all."

Sarah straightened the collar of his shirt. "I'm not sure I want those answers anymore. I think I'd be happier if we let sleeping giants lie."

"And I'm sure that you would regret it later if ye don't learn what went wrong." He said kissing her one more time before opening the closet door.

***

The Ullapool Village Hall was to be their base of operations for the week that they spent in the port town. The trip from Stornoway to Ullapool was only a matter of getting the team from the hostel to ferry dock and ferry dock to hostel. The challenge, for Sarah at least, was in not behaving differently around Dermot. Now that they weren't at odds with each other, it would have been nothing to slip back into the natural ease with which they worked together. But the trip had been marked with tension between the two of them from the beginning. To act chummy now would only draw further attention. They spent their remaining days on Lewis pretending that little had changed between them, while stealing every moment alone that they could. Still, breathless kisses in closets and alleys was no way to conduct a relationship.

So, here she was standing on the ferry crossing Loch Broom and hoping that the stocking cap he'd given her this morning didn't blow off and expose her curls to the wind. Sarah hadn't found a hair gel or mousse yet that could withstand both curls and wind."

Dermot stood next to her but far enough away to seem professional. Jujhar stood on her other side as they all watched Ullapool creep closer. The buildings along the shore shone white in the afternoon sun as the rest of the town rose up the hills.

Sarah found herself wishing that she and Dermot could stop right there, or in any of the towns they'd been to, and start their life together. She could be happy in a town like this. Not too big, not too small, and close to the ocean. She could teach school, and he could fish or something. They could be quiet and happy. Dermot shifted away, clearing his throat. Sarah looked up and realized that she had unconsciously drifted closer to him.

He gave her a pointed look and nodded over her shoulder to where Jujhar was studiously looking in the other direction. She looked sheepish and turned back to the view of the town.

"I'll go and tell the others we're almost ready to dock. " Dermot said loud enough for Jujhar to hear. He squeezed her elbow in reassurance.

Sarah stayed at the railing. After a minute Jujhar said, "You two seem easier with each other."

She didn't hear any note of sarcasm in his voice. Jujhar wasn't prone to gossip or snark. "We've come to an understanding."

"Good."

Sarah examined him. He didn't seem bothered, but it was hard to tell what he meant. "What do you mean by that?"

He gave her a sidelong look. In the afternoon sun, his eyes looked almost black, fathomless. "Traveling as we are, we have become like a family. When there is tension, everyone feels it." He nodded over his shoulder to where Isla and Ewan were standing together, their heads bent close. "And when there is joy, we all share it."

"Was it that bad?" Sarah asked.

"Dermot is the team leader and you are his de facto second. I could feel the tension between you. Some of the others could too." He lifted a shoulder in a shrug, not taking his eyes from the shore. After several seconds though, he turned to Sarah and stepped closer lowering his voice. "But be careful. Your reconciliation might not be a welcome sight to everyone."

She stepped closer to him. "Someone on the team, or are you referring to my distinguished admirer?"

"Both." He said surprising her. Usually, Jujhar was a great listener and sounding board letting anyone who told him about their problem work their own way around to a solution. He would sometime offer a gently worded opinion, but he rarely gave advice. "You are both admired, and power can be a distraction. Sometimes the smallest pebble can alter the flow of events."

She wished he wouldn't be so cryptic, and was about to tell him so, when Isla bounced up to where they stood and threw an arm around Sarah's shoulders. "I think we're about to dock."

Sarah looked back to the shore. Workers bustled along preparing the dock for the ferry's arrival. On Shore Street, cars and shoppers hustled along. Suddenly she didn't want to land, didn't want to leave the soft quiet cocoon of sea breezes. She felt as if she was moving toward something immovable, unavoidable and she was not ready for it.

CHAPTER TWENTY-TWO

When they arrived at the hostel in Ullapool, there was a message waiting for Dermot. The young man at the desk handed it to him as the rest of the team was bringing in their bags. Sarah watched Dermot's jaw clench tighter as he read the note. His eyes sought hers.

She set aside her bag and went to him. "Audra Lennox left me a message." When she looked confused, he glanced around lowering his voice. "His assistant."

"Ah."

"I'd better call her back. Don't go too far. He'll probably want to talk to ye as well." He sounded grim.

Sarah took her bag to the room she would share with Isla and Kirstie, then stopped in the hall near the office where Dermot was on the phone. She tried to be inconspicuous as she listened to his end of the conversation.

"Well, of course she's seen it. It's at every news agent in the country." Sarah leaned against the wall waiting. Her mind's eye pictured him brows creased, one hand gripping the phone, the other hand clenched in a fist on the desktop. "No, she would never forgive either of us, if we called the rest of the trip off. We're doing great work."

She had thought about leaving. But she also thought she would be easier to recognize in a city like Edinburgh than out here in the Highlands. In the city, she would practically have to go into hiding. But then maybe that was what James wanted. He could hide her away for his own purposes. Merely thinking about it made her furious.

"Yes, she's amazing." Dermot said flatly. Sarah wondered how often over the past few months he'd been forced to listen to James gush about his supposed love for her. "Right, I'll get her."

When she heard him put the phone on the desk, she stepped into the doorway. He was standing as if about to walk around the desk. Sarah motioned for him to stay. She picked up the receiver.

"Hello, James. " Her voice had enough chill in it that she hoped he felt it on the other end.

"Sarah," He breathed. "It's so good to hear your voice."

"I might feel the same about yours if I hadn't seen our faces next to every other cash register in the Hebrides." She tried to keep her tone even in spite of her rising temper. On the other side of the desk, Dermot gave her a warning look. She answered it with a shrug and a raised eyebrow that said, 'He's not *my* boss.'

At least James sounded contrite when he said. "Darling, I'm so sorry about this. I truly tried to keep those evenings private. I don't know how someone got those pictures."

"You really don't? You're one of the... Wait. Evenings, plural? "

James drew in a hissing breath. "Have you not seen the story in the Spyglass?"

Sarah closed her eyes and lifted her face toward the ceiling praying for patience. "What story?"

James hesitated." Ah... well... More pictures have surfaced, this time from the night of the Burns Supper...we're...em...on the patio."

Sarah's looked at Dermot who was watching her with questioning eyes. "Do they show my face?"

"What?"

Sarah tried not to raise her voice despite her boiling temper. "Do these new pictures show my face?"

"Eh, not exactly, at least not in a recognizable way." Was his stilted and cryptic answer.

She took a breath, tamping down the panic. "What does that mean?" Her voice rose, and Dermot held up a hand to remind her to keep it down.

"Well, your face isn't really visible because it's blocked by mine. We're kissing."

"Oh, of course." She muttered feeling the muscles in the back of her neck bunch with tension. "Of course, the only photos they have happen to have your lips glued to mine."

James went on as if she hadn't spoken, picking up steam. "I have no idea how they got them. They must have been on the other side of the canal or on the canal. We had guards stationed at the dock to prevent anyone from coming up through the garden, so they couldn't have..."

"They could have if someone let them. Like they *could* have been strategically released to a tabloid when I'm proving resistant to someone's advances." Sarah cut him off. Her eyes blazing. "Maybe someone who is getting a bit impatient. Someone who promised me friendship, and time."

"You don't really think I did this?" He actually sounded hurt.

"I don't know what to think. Being tabloid fodder is new territory for me. And you might've forgotten, I've seen your media manipulation machine in action before." She leaned against the desk for support. In spite of her biting tone, her knees felt like jelly. "Whoever did this, it's downright masterful. Release the first round of pictures which are only suggestive and none of which show my face. Then a week later up the pressure with a second round, this time seeming to confirm a relationship while still hiding my identity. Meanwhile, I'm running around the countryside with my hair pulled back and glasses that I don't need desperately hoping that no one puts two and two together. You're used to the public eye. The only person under real pressure here is me. And I don't doubt for a second if I don't come to heel as soon as I'm back in town, then my face and name will be revealed."

"You have to know I wouldn't do that." He said urgently.

"I don't know you well enough to make that judgment." She bit out. "I do know that you're a powerful man who isn't used to hearing the words no, or not yet."

She could hear his breathing on the other end of the phone slow and deep, as if he was struggling to regain his own temper. "I will find out who is responsible for this and if it is someone in this organization, they will be dealt with."

"That's nice, but it doesn't solve my problem." She said, recognizing the note of determination. It was like the tone Granny had always used when reminding law enforcement officers where their Friday night liquor came from.

"I hate being apart while this is going on. I need to see you." James pleaded.

"Not a chance. That's what got us into this mess."

"At least let me send a helicopter for you. We can get you somewhere safe before your name gets out."

"So, I can live like a prisoner? I don't think so." Sarah snapped. "And I hope your PR department will be putting the same level of effort into keeping my name out of the papers here as they did yours in the States."

He was silent. Sarah was sure that no one in his organization challenged him like that. Maybe that would make him second guess his insistence that he was in love with her.

"Of course, we will. I will personally guarantee it."

"See that you do."

"Will I see you when you return to Edinburgh?" He sounded plaintive and uncertain.

Sarah knew she couldn't give an inch. "I doubt that. I'm not interested in a public life, and this has shown me that dating you will only become a spectacle."

"Sarah, please."

"James, I spent most of my childhood being whispered about behind people's hands. I have no interest in living that way now and definitely not on such a large scale."

"I will fix this." He said. "I hope you will give me another chance."

"I don't think so." She said softly. "Goodbye, James."

Sarah dropped the phone back in its cradle and dropped into the chair beside her. Her eyes met Dermot's across the desk. His blue eyes held hers and showed the same mix of fear, excitement and resignation that she was feeling. It was the first step in breaking away from the Stuart plans, and they both felt the weight of it.

***

Dermot stayed in the office after Sarah left. He had more phone calls to make. She had done her part in talking to

James, now he needed to do his. He picked up the phone. His fingers felt clumsy as he pressed the buttons that he now knew by heart.

"Leith House Rest Home." A cheerful voice said on the other end of the line.

He cleared his throat. "Yes, Seonag Sinclair's room please."

"One moment." He held his breath as the woman put him on hold. He always half expected someone to tell him that his mother had been moved again without his knowledge, or that he wasn't allowed to speak to her. His mother hadn't been in her right mind when she had signed over Power of Attorney to Walter Stuart, but it meant that Walter could do anything with his mother without bothering to notify Dermot. "I'll transfer to you to her room now."

"Cheers." Relief swamped him.

"Hello?"

His throat nearly closed up on him at the sound of his mother's voice. "Hi, Mum."

"Dermot?" He sighed with relief. She always had an easier time when he called her as if she couldn't recognize a grown man as her son when he was standing in front of her but could believe a voice on the phone. Her voice sounded so clear and sure. "How are ye, love."

"I'm alright. I'm doing field work collecting stories and songs." He told her.

"Ah. I remember those days." She sounded wistful. "I always loved talking legends with locals. Where are ye?"

"We're in Ullapool. We came over on the ferry from Stornoway."

"Wasn't there a butcher in Stornoway that we liked?" She said reminding him of summers they had spent on Lewis collecting folklore and researching for his mother's articles. He was always surprised by the things she remembered, even when she couldn't remember him sometimes.

"Steve? Aye, he's still there." Dermot had passed the butcher shop the other day but hadn't been able to go inside.

"He always made the best black pudding." She said with a sigh.

Dermot leaned back in the chair looking up at the ceiling. "I expect he still does."

"I suppose he does." Sadness tinged her voice. "Is yer trip going well?"

"Aye, it is. We've gotten a lot of good material and identified a lot of sources. I saw the fairy flag on Skye." He mentioned. She sometimes remembered more if she was reminded of specific things. Like a pin in a map, a particular memory could call attention to the web of knowledge around it.

She was quiet for a moment, and he feared that her period of temporary lucidity was at an end. "Those MacLeods, the fey ones, forgot the flag when they left. They should have taken it with them."

A chill went up his spine, and he sat forward resting his elbows on the desk. "What do ye mean by 'the fey ones'?"

Her voice got quiet almost reverent. "Some of the MacLeods come from the Auld Folk, but they left Skye ages ago. They joined some of their fairy kin hiding in the hills."

"Do ye know where they went?" He asked wondering if she was blending fact with legend, or worse mixing legends together in her mind.

"Och, if only! I could have set the academic world on its ear if I knew where fairies lived." She laughed. "No, they disappeared into the Highlands with naught but the Old Man of Stoer to watch them go."

"Wait. Do ye mean the Old Man of Storr or the Old Man of Stoer?" Dermot asked. "The one on Skye or the sea stack near Lochinver."

"Oh," She suddenly sounded less certain. "I...I'm not sure." Her pitch went high with worry, and he could almost picture her fidgeting as she did when she thought her memory was slipping.

"Never mind about that, mum. How are ye doing there? What are ye knitting?" He asked trying to distract her before she could get upset.

She didn't answer immediately. He hoped that was because she was calming down and not because she was getting more upset. "It's a cable pattern with baubles beside the braids."

"That sounds nice. Have ye got enough yarn? Should I send ye some?"

"Och no. I've got plenty." They continued to chat for a few more minutes. She forgot her nervousness over her moment of confusion. He let her go before she got too tired. Her memory lapses became more pronounced when she was tired, as did her inability to deal with them. They'd had a good conversation. Anytime she remembered him was good. He didn't want to ruin it by keeping her on the phone too long.

After talking with his mother, he retrieved the small address book he kept in his bag. Flipping through the pages he found the number he was looking for and dialed the phone.

"Yah." The voice on the other side barked.

"I'm calling for Desmond Thomson." Dermot said.

"Even my mother doesna call me 'Desmond Thomson'" The last was said in a comically deep and formal voice that Dermot was sure was an exaggeration of how he'd sounded. "Is that you, Sinclair?"

"How did ye know?"

"Because ye sound like a stick-up-his-arse professor, and ye're the only one of those I know." The other man said. Dez Thomson was an unlikely friend from Dermot's Army days. They'd gone through their army training together at Pirbright. Dermot had been in training for the Intelligence Corps, while Dez had shown a talent for logistics. Both of their careers had been cut short, Dermot's by injury and Dez's by misadventure. His friend had always flirted with the wrong side of the law, but after some time at the Military Corrective Training Center and being discharged in disgrace, Dez had stopped flirting and dove straight into bed with every bad element he could find. Eventually, he'd begun putting his logistical skills to work as a sort of fixer for various characters that Dermot preferred not to think about.

"Aye, well I suppose if the shoe fits." Dermot laughed along with his friend. "Listen, are ye still doing yer um…" How did a person go about asking for a new identity? "…creative endeavors?"

"Of course, I am. I'm getting better at it by the day." He could picture his old friend grinning. "Is there something I can do for ye?"

"Aye. I'm in need of a new…" He didn't know what to ask for. Identity, papers, life?

"A new image?" Dez supplied.

"Exactly."

"I can definitely help ye with that." He said as easy as if he were saying he could pick up some beer on his way to a party. "What's the occasion?"

How did he say this without saying it? "I'm planning a holiday, and I want to impress the lasses.

"Holiday? Where are ye going?" Dez asked. Dermot thought he heard a drawer slide open and then the click of a pen.

"Ah…" Somewhere international, but not where they were actually going. "…Tenerife."

"Oh yeah." Dez sounded like he was catching up with an old friend. "My cousin went there last winter. He loved it. Have ye been before?"

"Em, no. I've been to Gibraltar, but never the Canaries."

"Anyone going with ye, or are ye planning on meeting someone there?"

Dermot tried to sound cavalier. "I was hoping to meet a few someones there."

"Sly dog." Dez said. "When are ye planning this trip?"

As soon as they got back to Edinburgh. "In about 3 weeks. I'm out of town right now, but I'll be stopping back in before I go."

"Alright. Listen it's been a while. Do ye have a photo ye can send so I can get some ideas started?"

"Ah. I do, but none with me. Can that wait until I get back to town?"

Dez hemmed for a second. "I suppose I can work on some details from memory. Are ye still all warty and hideous?"

"Yeah. That's right." Dermot laughed. "So, how much does one of yer makeovers cost?"

He could almost hear Dez thinking about how much to charge him. "I'll give ye a fair deal. Ye'll want to have some cash left over for yer holiday after all. Say, thousand pounds?"

Dermot had no idea what a good price for a new identity was. He didn't think Dez would cheat him, but he had nothing to compare it to. "I reckon I can do that. Doesna leave me much though."

"Sorry, mate. Quality costs, and I'm the best around." Dez said. "Ye havena gone fat, have ye?"

"I'm still fit enough to kick yer arse." They went on for a few more minutes teasing each other before hanging up. Dermot sat for a few moments longer staring at the desk, thinking of all the things that could go wrong.

CHAPTER TWENTY-THREE

"Sarah, didn't you say that you were interested in stories about Loch Assynt?" Sarah looked up to see Isla standing next to her table. The village hall in Ullapool hummed with conversation. Sarah had recently finished talking with a man who claimed to know everything there was to know about *Sruth nam Fear Gorm*, the Blue Men of the Minch. She was making her notes on their conversation to go with the cassette.

"Yeah, I am. That's the area my Grandmother was from." Sarah said.

"I overheard the knitter Kirstie is talking to mention it." She said. "You might want to see if she has any stories." She jerked her head in the direction of the table where Kirstie was sitting with an elderly woman who held several pieces of knitting on her lap.

"Great. Thanks." Sarah grabbed her tape recorder and microphone and made her way across the room. She waited until there was a lull in the knitting conversation.

"Kirstie," Sarah said tentatively. When Kirstie looked up with only a little irritation, Sarah glanced at the elderly woman with a smile. "I understand that this lady has some stories from Assynt. Would it be possible for me to speak with her when you're done?"

Kirstie pressed her lips together and looked for a second like she was biting her tongue. "Actually, we were just finishing up." She pressed the stop button on her tape recorder, and quickly gathered her things. She turned a smile on the woman. "Thank you, Mrs. Baird."

"Thank you so much, Kirstie. I really hope I wasn't interrupting." Sarah said, but Kirstie was already turning away. Sarah smiled at the older woman. "Hello, Mrs. Baird."

"Hello, lass." She smiled at Sarah her hands resting on the knitted lace in her lap.

"I understand you have some stories from around Assynt. I'm especially interested in the area." She didn't mention her grandmother, because she wasn't sure how much she should reveal about her family history to the people of the area. If *Làrachd an Fhamhair* was still there and still secret, she didn't want to reveal it. But she did want to find out everything she could before she went looking herself.

"Aye?" The woman looked at her in speculation as if she was trying to determine why this young American would have a particular interest in Assynt. "Weel, then I've got a story to tell ye."

"I come from Elphin, near Inchnadamph and there's a story that folk tell about the land there. Ye see, there was a geologist who came through…oh, a hundred years or so ago…who said he had nightmares looking at the way the plates meet at Knockan Crag. He was scairt of getting crushed under the ground. Of course, he wanted to know the science of the thing. But my Granny kent what it was, and she told me."

"The MacLeod who brought his people here from Lewis, he was a proud man. He wanted a grand castle to secure the loch and land from Knockan Crag to Ben Mòr Assynt and Suilven. But he didna have the coin. And his men couldna build it fast enough for him. So, one night he went out in the hills, and he found a cave that went deep into the earth. He reckoned it might go all the way doon to hell. So, he shouted doon into the cave for the devil."

"Auld Clootie came up to hear what the MacLeod wanted, and the chief told him he needed help finishing his castle. He was afraid the MacKenzie's might try to take the land, and he couldna wait years to defend it."

"Now, Auld Clootie never gives a thing for free, ye ken. He told the MacLeod that he would finish the castle, but he needed something in return. And he asked the MacLeod what he had to offer."

"Well, The MacLeod tried to offer him what gold he had and years of tribute besides, but that meant nothing to the devil. 'I have no need of your money, man.' Auld Clootie said. The MacLeod tried to offer him sheep or men, but none of that interested Auld Clootie. The devil was starting to get bored with the MacLeod, so he turned to go, but then the MacLeod said, 'I have a daughter.' That got Clootie's attention."

"The MacLeod said as his daughter was still young, and he had hoped to marry her to one of the neighboring clans to form an alliance."

"Of course, Clootie's answer to that was, 'what better alliance can ye make than one with me? I will marry your daughter.' The MacLeod was horrified, but he could see the sense in it. It might even mean that he could get more help in the future. So, he agreed. But his daughter, Eimhir was young yet, and not ready to marry. So, they agreed to wait until she was old enough."

"In the meantime, Clootie saw to it that the castle was built, and quick. It stood tall and braw on a spit of land that sticks out into the loch, and the MacLeod could see almost any approach. Of course, Auld Clootie was minding his investment, and when Eimhir was old enough to marry, he came to call in his debt. The MacLeod loved his daughter, but he kent there was no way around it. He would have to give her up. Auld Clootie gave the MacLeod one more day to say goodbye to her."

"But when Eimhir learned what her father had in store for her, she was terrified. That night she decided that she wasna going to marry the devil, even for the father she loved. She jumped from a window of that very castle right into the loch. She meant to kill herself, which is poor logic because then she would hae gone to hell anyway. But instead of dying, she was turned into a mermaid. And she swam doon into the loch."

"When Auld Clootie heard what had happened, he was gey angry. He stomped his hoof into the ground so hard that the earth cracked from here to Skye and it drove one side under the other. It also made caves under the loch that trapped poor Eimhir. They say that when the water in the loch rises, it's from her crying in her prison in the caves. Ye can still see that crack in the earth today along the river in Inchnadamph." The old woman said with a definitive nod.

Sarah thought a moment. Mrs. Baird was a better storyteller than her father had been. This was more complete than what he had told Molly, tying the mermaid with other local lore. "Did your Granny ever say how Eimhir was turned into a mermaid?"

Mrs. Baird shook her head. "No, not that I recall, but it could be anything around here. There are aye mysterious things that happen. There is a cave that sings, and people have seen the green man."

"A cave that sings?" Sarah asked.

"Och, aye. It's on the Tralegill River. I dinna ken any stories about that cave. Most folk think it's the river running underground that makes the sound."

"Tralegill sounds Norse. Are there any Viking legends around there?" Sarah asked.

"I did hear that it was Norse," Mrs. Baird's looked pensive. "Something about trolls or Giants."

The hair on the back of Sarah's neck stood up at the mention of giants. "Are there any stories that you know of about giants around here?"

"Och, no. Those are fairy tales for the wee ones." She waved a wrinkled hand in dismissal. Sarah found it interesting that stories about a petulant devil stomping a fault line from there to Skye was reasonable, but tales of giants were 'fairy tales'.

"Are there any stories of fairies in the area?" Sarah asked.

The old woman thought for a minute. Sarah couldn't tell if she was trying to remember a story or debating which story to tell. "No, no I dinna think I've heard any stories of fairies. But, when I was a little girl, there were a couple of Germans who came around asking about fairy stories."

"German's?" Sarah asked remembering what her mother's journal had said about the Germans who had been looking for the village. "When was this?"

"Before the war, certainly. I was but a school girl, when one day a couple of men came to my parent's croft. I remember my mum offered them tea and bread. I was helping her in the kitchen and listening as she talked with the men. Their English was almost better than mum's, but their accents were thick. They asked her if she had heard any tales about fairies living in the hills nearby."

"Of course, this is Scotland. We've all heard stories about fairies of one kind or another, but I dinna recall hearing any in a particular location around here. If my mum had, she didna say. She waved her hand and laughed at the men saying, 'Surely they hadna come to the Highlands looking for such nonsense."

"They went about their way after that, and we never saw them again. But I always remembered it because it was so strange." She shook her head, as if she thought it was the oddest thing.

"And you're sure that was before the war?" Sarah asked. At the woman's nod, she changed topics. "Have you heard any stories about holy wells?"

"Mmm...No, I dinna think so." She answered shaking her head slowly. "You know who ye should talk to? Eilidh. Eilidh MacLeod. She would know about any wells, or fairies."

Goosebumps sprang up on Sarah's arms at the mention of her great-aunt. "Eilidh MacLeod, is she here in Ullapool?"

"Oh, no. She lives in a croft by the loch, between Inchnadamph and Lochinver." The woman said easily, as if she hadn't placed her mother's nemesis in the general geographic area of the stories from Molly's journal. The more Sarah found out about this area and their family, the more her mother's story was confirmed.

"Right. Do you think Ms. MacLeod would be willing to talk to us?" Sarah asked trying not to betray how excited and scared she was.

"Oh, I expect that she would talk to one or two of ye, but ye would have to go and see her." Mrs. Baird patted Sarah's hand. "She doesna get out much. Burned her feet in a fire some years ago, so she doesna walk so well."

"Oh, I think we can send a couple of people out to visit her." Sarah said already trying to plan when she and Dermot could get away to pay Aunt Eilidh a visit.

CHAPTER TWENTY-FOUR

She wasn't able to get Dermot alone until that evening when they returned to the hostel. She found him in the common room. Fortunately, the group had separated to find their own dinners. Isla and Ewan were going to see some musicians at a pub on Shore Street, and Kirstie and Jujhar were cooking dinner in the kitchen. Sarah could hear the murmur of their conversation punctuated by the sound of cabinet doors opening and closing as they searched for whatever they needed in the unfamiliar kitchen.

Dermot was sitting in a low chair with the day's box of tapes in his lap. The notebook that he kept as a catalog of their recordings was balanced on the arm of the chair as he recorded each tape.

Sarah sat down on the couch next to his chair. Keeping an ear out for the two in the kitchen, she said. "I talked to a woman today who knows my great-aunt. She even suggested that I should go talk to her."

He stopped writing and looked at her. "That's great. We should go see her."

"Oh, I definitely want to go see her." Sarah made a nervous huff. She hadn't told Dermot much of the story of Molly's trip to *Làrachd an Fhamhair*. At first, she'd been afraid to tell him, because she still wasn't sure how much he already knew. Then they had been at odds for months and she had been afraid to tell him, thinking he might tell James, or his people. "It's only…well, she wasn't very good to my mother."

"What do ye mean?" He put his notebook on top of the box of tapes and set the box on the floor next to his foot.

She still wasn't sure what to tell him, but if he was going to accompany her into the gorgon's den then he should know some of what he was getting into. "Well, my mother fell in love with a guy who was engaged to Eilidh's daughter. And when my mother got pregnant, Aunt Eilidh kicked her out of the village."

His eyebrows lifted in surprise. "Right. So, Aunt Eilidh might not take too kindly to ye."

"I have no idea what she'd do. She was sort of hot and cold on my mother." Sarah said.

He leaned closer over the arm of the chair and lowered his voice. "Hmm, last summer when they first sent me to North Carolina, it was on the word of someone that Walter only referred to as 'the old woman'. I have no idea if this is the same old woman as your aunt, but it seems too much of a coincidence."

Sarah thought about the talents that the three sisters were supposed to have. She and her mother and Granny could see the present, Bridget and her mother and grandmother could see the future, and Eilidh and Sheila saw the truth which Sarah supposed was a version of seeing the past and present. Dermot may not know that, and she wasn't sure she wanted him to. "Didn't you say, you were sent back to Chapel Hill after I saw Isobel MacKenzie in Cape Breton?"

"Aye, that's right." He nodded.

"Then the old woman could be Isobel." Sarah tapped her fingers thoughtfully on the arm of the sofa. "If they're talking to each other, then Eilidh might be expecting me."

He answered with a grunt that was somewhere between agreement and deep thought. After several minutes of him thinking, Sarah said. "So, when can we go see her?"

"We've got another couple of days here, and then we're moving to Lochinver, so we'll be right in the neighborhood. Might be best to wait until then. Otherwise it will look weird."

"Right. I'll try to wait patiently." Her tone implied that she doubted it would be possible.

"We might be able to get out to see her that first afternoon in Lochinver." He offered, giving her a sympathetic smile. Then he blinked and shook his head. Reaching into his backpack that was beside his chair he pulled out a newspaper. It was folded so the front page wouldn't show.

***

"I almost forgot. I found The Spyglass that James was talking about." He laid the newspaper on her knee. She stared at it. He wondered if it would have been better not to bring it to her.

Sarah looked toward the kitchen. He listened for Kirstie and Jujhar again doubting his decision to bring her the paper. He reached for it, meaning to retrieve it. "I can get rid of it."

She stopped him, with her hand on his. "No, I should know what's out there."

He watched her face as she unfolded the tabloid. Every muscle from her scalp to her neck tightened, and he feared her teeth might crack from the grinding. It wasn't too different from the reaction he'd had when he first saw it. He had run to the store for razors and toothpaste, only to be confronted with the image of the woman he loved lip-locked with James Stewart. Knowing that that very night, he'd done everything he could to drive her into James's arms added to his usual recriminations. The photo showed more of his face than hers, but he would recognize those curls anywhere. Emblazoned above the photo was the simple question, "Who IS she?".

Sarah slammed the paper closed again and lifted her face to the ceiling as she often did when she was trying to get a grip on her temper. She took a deep breath and blew it out slowly. She pressed her hand down onto the paper as if trying to keep the images from jumping off the page. "Are there more? I don't want to look."

"None that show your face." There were more images of the two of them, but Sarah's face was always in shadow or turned away from the camera. There were none that showed her whole face. Although, the article did state that the pictures were taken at the Burns Night fundraiser. Anyone who had been at the party, and recognized what Sarah was wearing, or the shawl that James had given her would know who she was.

She whispered. "You know what I told him is true, right? It was one kiss and we were outside talking for minutes before and after that. There is no way they didn't see my face. The fact that these are the only photos that made it into the press means that someone is manipulating this carefully. It has to be an inside job."

"Or a canny editor dribbling this out to build buzz before a big reveal." He said, but he knew that was wishful thinking.

"No, it might be worth that kind of delay if I was famous. But I'm nobody. What newspaper is going to get traction out of that?" She fell back against the sofa.

"I don't know. Sounds like a Cinderella story to me." He waved a hand at the paper where it still rested on her knee. "Their readers probably eat that shite up like candy."

"So, we're back to waiting for the other shoe to drop." She sighed in frustration.

"I'm not so sure. If it is someone with Alba Petroleum, after what ye said to James, he may be able to prevent any more photos from being released." He eyed her, as she stared across the room in thought. "What did he say?"

"He said he would find out who was responsible and put a stop to it." She muttered.

"I may not trust James, but I don't think he would lie to you about that." He still wanted to believe in his cousin, and one-time friend. "Sometimes I think he's being manipulated like the rest of us."

Sarah looked doubtful. "That may be, but it's hard to feel sorry for him when he's trying to do the same to me."

He sighed. "I know."

They sat there for a few more minutes, each busy with their own thoughts. Eventually, Sarah sat forward. "Well, I'm going to take a shower. I'll see you in a bit."

He watched her leave, wishing he could fix all of this for her. He felt so bloody helpless, like they were on a train with no breaks. It was similar to the feeling he'd had when the doctors first told him why his mother couldn't seem to remember where she lived or that he was an adult. Like he'd felt when he woke up in an Army hospital with a torn-up leg and bruises all over without ever seeing a day of combat. He hated it.

***

White and pink swirled around in a bright kaleidoscope. Sarah heard her mother muttering.

...They won't have you. Keep yourself...

Mama's arms gripped her tight holding her under the water. Sarah's chest tightened as she struggled to breathe.

...Not my baby...loved your father...

Mama sounded as frantic as Sarah was starting to feel. This was the bathtub dream of Sarah's childhood, from before she knew her mother's story. It was a warning.

...mama, I can't breathe...

Sarah was about to walk into the very place where Molly had been hurt, betrayed. This was what Molly had been trying to protect her from all those years ago, the Auld Folk and the Stuarts.

...won't do it to you...I'll protect...

Sarah couldn't help wondering if she was about to vindicate her mother or undo whatever Molly had thought she was doing to protect her.

Stay with me, Mama.

She heard the sickening thunk of porcelain striking her mother's head and Molly fell forward. Her face plunged into the water, her dark eyes determined.

I'm always here.

Sarah came awake with a gasp, and barely missed knocking her head on the bottom of the bunk above her. It took a moment for her to get her bearings. She looked around at the spare hostel bedroom with its bunk beds and modern furnishings. She worked to slow her breathing, listening for Isla and Kirstie. Relief swamped her when she saw that they were both still asleep.

Sarah curled up on her side. Her eyes found the small window on the other side of the room. She stared at the stars outside and wondered if her nerves and her mother would let her get any sleep over the next couple of days.

CHAPTER TWENTY-FIVE

"Oh!" Kirstie exclaimed as they came around the curve and the road dipped low to skirt the small inlet where the roofless shell of an old stone house stood. The ruins of Ardvreck Castle reached up from the spit of land in the distance. "Can we stop and look at the castle?"

Sarah had noticed the castle in the distance shortly after they had passed Inchnadamph. At first, it was a small grey speck amid the new spring green of the hills behind it. It seemed to grow as they approached, rising above the hillside that it was built on. It reminded Sarah more than a little of a scene from an old horror movie where a hand breaks through the dirt of a newly filled grave and the creature below claws its way to the surface. She had little doubt her own feelings colored the image. Judging by Kirstie's reaction it looked like a remnant from a fairy tale, a sort of Disney-fied detritus of a forgotten age.

"Sarah?" Dermot asked. She looked up to meet his eyes in the rear-view mirror.

"Sure." What else could she say? *No, I'm terrified. My mother was almost killed there. Someone was killed there and more recently than you might think.* As nervous as the place made her, she had to admit she was curious. Her parents had spent time there. If nothing else, it meant that she was getting close to finding the answers that she came to Scotland for.

Dermot pulled the car into the deserted car park. Kirstie burst out of the passenger's side. She turned to Sarah who was climbing out of the back seat. "Is this the one that Mrs. Baird was talking about?"

"Must be." Sarah answered. Kirstie hurried off to look at the marker that sat near a low stone wall that bordered the car park. Sarah could feel Dermot's eyes on her from the other side of the car. She looked over and gave him what she hoped was a reassuring smile.

Within a minute, the equipment van carrying the others had pulled in beside them. Ewan, Isla and Jujhar emerged from the van, and stretched.

"Kirstie wanted to look at the castle." Dermot called to them.

The others nodded, trailed behind Kirstie as her legs ate up the sandy ground between the car park and castle. A narrow strip of grass ran between two sandy beaches on the approach to the castle. Sarah had to hand it to the MacLeod, he had picked a spot that was hard to approach and easy to defend. She expected if the water in the loch got too high, the castle's peninsula could even be cut off from the land.

There was another low stone wall near where the land began to rise from the isthmus to the castle. Sarah stopped there and looked at the looming ruin. From what she'd read, most of the stones of the castle had been salvaged to build Calda House, the walls of which were on the other side of the carpark. What was left was only a corner of the castle it had once been, the castle that the devil had supposedly helped build. The hills beyond the castle would likely have been peppered with support buildings, like a smithy, smokehouse, maybe a tannery. Today it was peppered with sheep who went about their grazing with little regard for the visiting humans.

"Do you not want to see the castle?" Jujhar asked from beside her.

"I don't know." Sarah said. "I haven't decided yet."

He waited. As usual, in Jujhar's presence Sarah found herself relaxing. It wasn't as if he made her forget whatever she had been anxious about, his patience and calm had a way of making her believe that she could handle whatever life threw. She trusted him.

After a few minutes watching the others poke around the ruins, she said to him. "Do you remember the legend that I told you about the mermaid?"

"Yes," He said, his voice like warm honey. "This is that same castle isn't it?"

"It is. But that wasn't the first time I had heard that story." She looked at him. In the sunlight, his eyes looked the color of dark chocolate. She smiled and nodded to the castle. "My mother told it to me. She heard it from my father. They were standing in those ruins when he told it to her."

"Mmm..." Was all he said. Sarah recognized the listeners trick. Sometimes silence and patience were the best tools for getting someone to tell you something.

"A few months after that, my mother was attacked in the ruins and nearly beaten to death."

He looked at her with alarm. For the first time since they'd met, Sarah had broken through Jujhar's perpetual calm. She assured him. "Don't worry. We both survived."

Awareness dawned on him. "She was pregnant with you."

Sarah nodded. "She curled up to protect me, and because of that she left her head undefended. She was lucky a concussion was the worst that she got out of it."

"What happened to her attacker?"

"He was killed, also there in the castle." She said. "Someone shot him with an arrow. My mother lost consciousness before she ever knew who it was."

"An arrow?" Disbelief was evident in his tone.

Sarah shrugged. "That's what my mother said."

"It's like a story from another time." He said looking back at the castle.

"You don't know the half of it." Sarah said with a dark laugh.

Sarah watched the sun play across the stones. Occasionally, one or two of the team would appear outside the walls.

Jujhar held out his hand to her. "Shall we go slay a few ghosts?"

She gave him a bright smile. "You know, I came here not knowing anyone but Dermot. I'm a very private person, but somehow, I find myself telling you all my secrets. I feel like I've always known you."

Sarah took his hand and his fingers wrapped around hers. His hand was warm, as was the smile in his eyes. He tucked her hand under his arm and led her toward the castle. "I think that there are people in this world who when they meet, their souls recognize each other. My Hindu friends would say that we must have known each other in a past life. A guru would likely say that we recognize the presence of the divine in each other more easily than we might some others."

Sarah didn't subscribe to any particular religion. Most of her exposure to religion hadn't been especially positive. "Well, they can call it whatever they like. I'm just glad to know you."

He patted her hand where it rested on his arm. They stepped around the wall of the castle, and for the first time Sarah could see the inside. It was much as her mother had described it; tumbled stones covered over with dirt and grass made natural steps up to what would have been the second level. An archway below those stones was barred off lest someone try crawling through it. Looking up she saw windows and small recesses in the stone walls where the floor beams had been. And in the corner, where the ruins were the tallest was the empty tower where spiral stairs must have been, where Willie Cross had fallen after being shot.

***

Dermot watched Sarah come around the crumbled wall on Jujhar's arm. He had been wondering what was taking her so long. She'd been so excited the other night when she'd heard the story from the woman in Ullapool that he had expected her to jump at the chance to see the place in person. Instead, she lingered by the wall, eyeing the place from the leeward side as if it might be some sort of trap.

He was glad that Jujhar was with her. He could tell she was more than a little tense today. They were getting close to where her mother's people were. He wished he knew more about what they were heading into. If he hadn't driven her so far away back in January, they could have spent time researching this together. He could have read her mother's journal if Sarah would have let him.

She and Jujhar wandered through the tumbled down stones. Sarah stared up at a window hole that faced the loch. He could almost read her mind, imagining Eimhir jumping from the window to the water. She could see these things, make these connections. It was part of what made her good at what she did. He wondered how much research she had done before they left Edinburgh. He should have asked her, but she didn't like to talk about her people. Apart from the small bit she'd told him, she hadn't mentioned her mother, or father to him. He reckoned that was a mystery she wanted to solve herself. He hoped it wasn't because she didn't trust him.

Jujhar climbed the rocks that had accumulated on top of the vaulted cellars and turned to offer Sarah his hand. She took it and clambered up behind him. They explored the higher level noting where the floor joists would have been. Sarah inched her way cautiously toward the round stairwell. The wooden stairs had long since rotted away leaving a hollow space that dropped from the highest point of the stone wall to the cellars.

Sarah leaned into the space keeping one hand on the stone wall beside her. Dermot felt the muscles in his shoulders bunch, ready to leap to catch her even though he was more than thirty feet away. She leaned in further looking down the shaft. Suddenly, a wind off the loch blew at the open side of the castle and into the stairwell from the lower level. It blew Sarah's hair back. She spun around her heel landing dangerously close to the edge. Dermot's heart caught in his throat and he broke into a run. Sarah stumbled forward, her knees hitting the dirt path between the stones.

Dermot climbed the stones in a couple of strides. Jujhar got to her first, and he blocked the path. Dermot made to step around him, but Jujhar turned and held his arms out. He shook his head. The path was too narrow for Dermot to get by and he couldn't understand why the man wouldn't let him pass.

"She needs to do this." Jujhar hissed.

Dermot looked sharply at him. He didn't think he'd ever seen the man be so forceful and wasn't sure that he liked it.

Sarah whimpered and wrapped her arms around her waist. The sound cut through any politeness left in him.

"Needs to do what? She needs help, man. Let me by." Dermot growled. He was ready to shove Jujhar aside, but Sarah lifted her head and drew in a ragged breath. Her eyes focused on something behind him. He followed her gaze but saw nothing.

"I'm okay." She said, but her voice sounded reedy and weak. "It's okay, Dermot."

Jujhar moved aside and Dermot fell to his knees in front of her not noticing how hard the stones were. He brushed her hair away from her face and ran his hands over her looking for injury. "Dinna scare me like that again."

She took his hands and held them still. Her voice was still breathy but getting stronger and she gave him a rueful smile. "I probably will and worse, but it's okay for now."

"Ye nearly gave me a heart attack. What on Earth did ye think ye were doing?" He kissed her forehead, no longer caring who might see.

She looked over his shoulder at Jujhar and smiled. "Slaying ghosts."

***

If she'd ever doubted that he loved her, it was put to rest when she'd seen him on the verge of throwing Jujhar off the ruins to get to her. He was always her champion, her steward. "Let's get down from here."

"Aye." He nodded. He stood and pulled her up beside him. Jujhar was already climbing back down the stones.

Sarah stopped before where the path turned back toward the front of the castle. She turned to the spot on the top of the wall on the loch side. Of course, there was no one there. There had never been anyone there, but when she had first opened her eyes she could have sworn she'd seen the figure of a man wearing antlers and carrying a bow. No doubt it was a projection of her mother's memory of her savior from that night so many years ago.

Likewise, the overwhelming flood of images that had hit her when she looked into the stairwell was probably her own imagining of what happened between Molly and Willie Cross. She had leaned out into the cold stone shaft and seen a figure lying twisted at the bottom, an arrow sticking through his throat. He had been dark-haired, thin and dirty, like Molly had described Willie at his end. His dark eyes had been wide open and vacant staring at the sky above.

Then the wind had hit her from below and she had seen what Molly had described in her journal, but in reverse like film playing backwards. The same thin, dark-eyed man was raining blows down on her. She hadn't felt the blows but had seen him swing and like Molly had done, she had instinctively covered her belly. His eyes had looked determined, then pleading as he tried to pull her from the castle. 'Ye mun go back!' He'd said.

But then, the vision had lifted, and she had looked up to see the horned figure on the wall. He'd been behind Dermot who looked ready to claw his way through anyone who tried to come between them. Now, all she saw beyond the wall was Isla and Ewan walking with arms around each other laughing. It made Sarah think of her parents doing the same thing, in the same spot almost thirty years ago.

She turned away and picked her way down the path to the ground level, with Dermot close by ready to catch her if she stumbled again. Both feet on solid ground, she looked up at Dermot and Jujhar. They were watching her closely. "It's okay, guys. Really."

Dermot who still held her hand, turned to Jujhar and ready to read him the Riot Act. Sarah stepped between them, putting a hand on Dermot's chest. "Don't be upset. He was right. I needed to do that."

Dermot huffed and gave Jujhar a hard look before turning his eyes back to her. "Do what?"

She cleared her throat. "My mother was almost killed here, by the man she was betrothed to."

"Why didn't ye tell me?" His brows drew together in concern.

There was so much that she hadn't told him, and she had been so relieved since their reconciliation that she hadn't thought to sit him down and give him the details of her mother's fall from grace. She gave him a look that said, *I would have told you months ago, but you pushed me away.*

He cleared his throat and looked guilty. "Alright, but that was more than a memory."

She drew in a breath. "It probably won't surprise you to hear that sometimes I get visions. Do you remember finding me in the woods at Grandfather Mountain?"

"But ye were sleepwalking then?" He said.

She shook her head ever so slightly and gave him a gentle smile. It felt crazy to say that she sometimes saw her mother or even her grandmother when she was awake. The rational academic in her couldn't believe it, but after incidents like this and that vision that she'd had at Grandfather Mountain, the visions were undeniable. "No, I wasn't. I saw my mother go into the woods and I followed her. She showed me some things that I still don't quite understand, and they scared me."

"How," he stopped and cleared his throat. Sarah thought she could see the memory of that night on the mountain running through his mind. "How often does this happen?"

"Not often." She shrugged. "I don't know how to explain it. A psychologist would probably tell me that they are caused by things planted in my subconscious when I was a child combining with my imagination to make some strange, waking dream."

"Or they are actually sending you messages." Jujhar said softly. "Even if those messages were planted long ago."

Sarah thought about that. In a way it made sense. All of those stories and songs that Granny had taught her, many of them obscured by her own studies could have been a trail of psychic breadcrumbs. The big question was, what were they leading her to?

"I think before we pay Eilidh MacLeod a visit, you need to tell me more about your mother's experience here." Dermot grumbled.

"I think you're right." Sarah agreed. "But for now, let's head back to the car. I think we've seen all the castle has to offer."

The guys agreed, and they turned toward the cars. When they came around the wall of the castle, Sarah noticed Kirstie down on the strip of sand that led back to the shore. She was throwing stones into the loch. When she noticed them approaching, she stalked off toward the car park.

***

There was a picnic table on the patio beside the hostel in Lochinver. With the hills behind them and the sea loch in front of them, it was as good a place as any for the conversation that they were about to have. Dermot watched the activity in the loch as he waited for Sarah who was getting settled into her room.

She emerged from the side door carrying two steaming cups of tea. Depositing the cups on the table, she came to stand beside him at the patio's edge.

He glanced at her before looking back at the water. "If ye watch carefully, ye can see the seals peeking up out of the water. A pair of eyes and a black nose."

Sarah followed his eyes to the surface of the loch. "You can see them in the dark?"

He moved behind her and raised his arm to point to a spot in the water. "It's all in the way the light reflects. Their heads reflect rounder shapes than the ripples in the water."

Sarah leaned closer to him and looked down the length of his arm. He closed his eyes and inhaled her scent. It would be easy to let himself get distracted by her. He lowered his arm and stepped away. "I believe ye have a story to tell me."

"I do. Yes." She turned and waved him toward the table. "But first, I need you to tell me how much you know about my people. For real this time. I know you know more than you've let on in the past."

He couldn't deny that, taking a seat across from her. "I only know that they're old, older than any other clan or tribe that I've heard of. And they know something of what will happen. I don't know how."

"Do you know who they are?" Her eyes sought his.

He pressed his lips together. No matter how many times he had heard the story or how many people he knew believed it, he still found it hard to believe himself. "My mother always called them the Auld Folk. Like most people, I took that to mean fairies."

Sarah nodded. "What else did your mother tell you?"

He blew out a long breath and glanced over his shoulder. Lowering his voice, he said, "That they were kingmakers. That the Auld Folk knew of things to come and what was necessary to hold the country together and that they could steer leaders in the right direction, if the leaders would listen."

Sarah looked thoughtful as she took a tentative sip of her tea. "Your mother wrote articles about the legends of the Auld Folk and places where they were mentioned in history, but she never made mention of a role like that."

"You read her work?" He shouldn't be surprised, but in his mind, he had kept them separate.

"Of course." Sarah said. "It would be hard to study what we do and not read it."

She was right about that. Although his mother's focus had been on written history and literature, much of what was written was transmitted orally first. "Well, she told me it was secret. Like the Stuarts' ambitions are secret and have been for a long time."

"A tribe of unknown origin but vast influence still living by thousand-year-old customs? She could have made a career writing about that." Sarah arched an eyebrow at him.

"Some things are more important." He said, steel in his voice. "She always taught me that we were something special too. We had a duty to both the Stuarts and the Auld Folk to keep their secrets and wait for the day when things would change, the day when we would need your people."

"Need them for what?" Sarah asked puzzled.

He shifted in his seat. She wasn't going to like this. "The Stuarts believe they'll be needed when Scotland becomes independent. They've always thought that like The River Maiden and the king from her tale, a union with one of the Auld Folk was essential to making that happen."

"Is there anything else? About my people, I mean."

He shook his head. "Only that when I grew up, I would be expected to protect the secret like my mother was."

Sarah took another sip of her tea, processing what he'd said. She set her cup down and gave him a level look. "I guess the part that I know starts with the Nazis."

"Nazis?" He looked confused.

"Yeah. My mother's people have lived quietly and somewhat secretly in this area for a really long time; or at least, that's what my mother said in her journal. And, you know the cauldron in the story?"

"The one that never stopped giving food?" He recalled the storybook that Sarah had shown him, the one she had made as a little girl.

She nodded. "I know it sounds crazy, but Molly said she saw it. If it's true, you can see why they wanted to keep their way of life secret. So, they avoided contact with the rest of the world, and they married and, for lack of a better term, bred carefully in order to preserve their bloodlines. The cauldron to a certain extent enables them to do that."

"But somehow," Sarah went on. "The secret must have gotten out. You can imagine that the idea of ethnic purity and a sacred cauldron that never stopped feeding people would be catnip to Nazis looking to legitimize their ideas of racial entitlement. So, one day in the late 30's, a German wandered into our secret village. He was injured and sick, or at least he pretended to be. My grandmother's people fed him and gave him a place to sleep while they debated what to do to protect themselves. They thought that he would tell people about the village and that it would put them all in danger. But when they went to do something about him, he had escaped."

"That's why my grandmother left and went to Nova Scotia. After that it was decided that the three sisters should live apart for safety's sake. I'm not sure who was a part of that decision, or who chose who went where, but my grandmother settled in North Carolina, and Aunt Eilidh came home."

"The three sisters?"

She tilted her head to the side and smirked. "I know three sisters and their cauldron. I told you those witches in Macbeth came from somewhere. Three women of each generation; my grandmother, Isobel and Eilidh. For my mother's generation, it was Mama, Isobel's daughter Rona, and Eilidh's daughter Sheila."

"And now you, and Bridget, and?"

She shrugged. "I don't know. I don't know if Sheila and my father ever had a daughter. But the three sisters are seen as sacred. Their partners are carefully chosen to breed the next generation. That's why my grandmother and Isobel stayed away for so long, to protect the sisters."

He remembered what Sarah had told him about her grandmother's homesickness. "But your gran wasna happy in America."

Sarah nodded. "I think she tried to make the best of it. But something, maybe the Nazis scared her into keeping all of this a secret, even from us. So, when Mama came here in 1968 she had no idea what she was in for; like I had no idea what you and Ryan were talking about when you told me back in December." She shrugged. "I wish I knew what Granny had been thinking."

"She was probably thinking that she would tell you when the time came." He put his hand on hers where it was wrapped around the warm mug. "She couldn't have known she would die before she got the chance."

Sarah gave her head a slight shake. "At her age? I think she could have, but there's no sense in debating that now. When Mama came here, she thought she was coming for a homecoming fete. But it was a matchmaking or...mating ceremony. There was this pool, that Aunt Eilidh used to divine who the matches would be. I don't know how the men were chosen."

Sarah sighed and took a sip of tea. "Bridget's mother was matched with a young man that she liked fine. So was Sheila, in fact I got the feeling from my mother's writings that Sheila had had a crush on him for a while." She sighed. "My mother was matched with a guy who was a bit..." She hesitated searching for words. "Socially awkward and emotionally scarred. His father beat his mother to death when he was a boy, and he never got any sort of counseling on how to deal with that."

"After that ceremony, the cauldron stopped working. Thousands of years of providing food, and it just stopped. Of course, no one in the village had any idea of how to preserve food or store it. They'd never had to before. So, it fell to the stewards and my mother and Rona to teach them. A lot of the villagers blamed the newcomers for the cauldron not working, but that didn't stop them from eating the food that they stored and preserved." She said bitterly.

"While all that was going on, my mother was also falling in love, or so she thought. The trouble was that the man she fell in love with wasn't her match, he was Sheila's."

"Rab Ballantyne." Dermot filled in with the name she'd given him weeks ago.

"Yeah. She fell pretty hard and she thought he did too. Then the cauldron started working again. Which Willie couldn't quite reconcile. So, he left. Left Mama, left the village, and disappeared into the hills. Mama and Rab started sneaking around, and eventually she ended up pregnant. Of course, when Aunt Eilidh learned about that and it obviously wasn't Willie's she was furious. She humiliated my mother in front of the whole village and kicked her out."

Sarah cleared her throat and turned her hand to grip his. "Mama walked from the village to the castle, which was a few miles. At the castle, she was attacked by Willie Cross."

"Ah." Realization dawned on him. "That's what ye saw today."

She closed her eyes nodding. "I don't think he meant to hurt her, but he knocked her out. Someone shot him with an arrow. It probably saved her life, but she never saw who did it."

"What about your father? Where was he in all of this?" He wondered about the kind of man who would let the woman he loved be exiled and abused without standing up to protect her.

"He was there, hiding behind Sheila and hoping that no one would figure out that he was the father of Molly's baby. Mama was sure that he would leave Sheila and follow her. They had even set up a time and place to meet, like it was 'An Affair to Remember'. She waited, but he never came. Eventually, she made it all the way home to Granny, but she was never the same."

"And ye're going to meet Eilidh tomorrow."

She looked up at him biting her lip. "Yeah. I was surprised that the lady we met in Ullapool mentioned her. As far as I knew, Eilidh lived isolated from the outside world. You can imagine how shocked I was when she gave me directions to Eilidh's house."

"Do you think maybe Mrs. Baird was one of your people?"

She shook her head. "I don't know. She didn't seem to know any of the lore around the village of the people of *Làrachd an Fhamhair*. But then again, she could have been protecting their secrets."

"Still she steered ye in right direction."

"Hmm…" Sarah agreed.

Dermot studied her. "Maybe ye should let me do the talking tomorrow."

She gave him a half-smile. "That might not be a bad idea."

CHAPTER TWENTY-SIX

Eilidh MacLeod's house looked like almost every other croft house Sarah had seen between Edinburgh and Lochinver; whitewashed, and clean, if a little frayed about the edges. A graying barn could be seen around one corner, and a low dry-stone wall surrounded the yard. "It looks so normal."

"Ye were expecting a fairy dun?" Dermot said with a half-smile as he put the car in park and set the brake.

"Funny." She arched an eyebrow at him. "That's actually not too far off. According to Mama, the houses in *Làrachd an Fhamhair* were built into the hillsides and the roofs covered with turf. It's part of how they stayed off the map for so long. People looking down from the mountains or air surveys would never have noticed them."

"Jesus," Dermot shook his head. "Is every piece of fairy lore based on yer people?"

She laughed. "If I say yes, are you going to start calling me Tinkerbell?"

Dermot rolled his eyes and got out of the car. Dermot pulled the bag with the recording equipment from the back seat and swung the strap over his shoulder.

Sarah turned to look at the hills around, half expecting to see other houses in the style that her mother had described, turf roofs over hanging unglazed windows. But there was nothing surrounding her aunt's house but hills and sheep. She did notice an electrical line running to the roof of the croft house and as she didn't see an outhouse, she expected there was plumbing too. Sarah wondered where the village was, and why Eilidh was living like *sluagh ùr* in a modern house.

"Come on, Tink." Dermot said over the top of the car. "We've got an appointment with Queen Mab."

Sarah squared her shoulders. She wasn't sure she was ready to meet the woman her mother had described as half fairy, half gorgon or the queen Shakespeare called the 'fairy's midwife'. Before they reached the house, the door swung open and a woman hobbled out to meet them on the threshold. No fairy queen, Eilidh was far from the matriarch of *Làrachd an Fhamhair*.

Her hair had gone a dingy white with only hints of its former red. It hung thin and limp across the shoulders of her moth-eaten green cardigan. Her skin looked like thin crepe with blue veins showing through. The house coat she wore under the sweater was frayed at the hem, and Sarah thought she saw a rim of white webbed burn scars above her slouching wool socks. Her back was so bent that she had trouble lifting her head to look Dermot in the eye. For a second, Sarah doubted that this was the formidable aunt her mother had written about, the velvet steamroller whose word was obeyed without question by her people. Then the old woman shifted her cane and slippered feet on the doorstep in that distinct stump-shuffle that Molly described. Sarah felt a chill, like cold fingers on the back of her neck.

"Ms. MacLeod?" Dermot offered his hand, "I'm Dermot Sinclair, and this is…"

The old woman cut him off. "Weel, come on in then. I ken why ye're here."

Dermot started toward the house, but Sarah grabbed his arm and said in a low voice, "Hey. Don't tell her who I am yet. I'm curious what she might tell us without knowing."

"Are ye sure?" He asked. "She might not like that when she does find out."

Sarah shook her head. "Given how my mother left here, I think I'd rather test the waters first before getting into the rest."

His hand rubbed a reassuring circle low on her back. "Aye, alright."

***

"Sit ye doon, anywhere." The old woman waved at the parlor with its worn furniture that might have been new in the last century.

Dermot lowered himself into the sturdiest looking chair in the room. He wasn't sure the other furnishings were up to supporting his frame. Sarah stopped inside the door to see where Mrs. MacLeod was going.

The woman shuffled toward the kitchen, "Come and help me with the tea, lass."

Sarah set her bag down next to the ornate leg of the Victorian couch and followed the woman to the kitchen.

He listened closely while he set up the tape recorder and microphone. Half expecting an argument to break out, he was relieved when all he heard was Gaelic murmuring, clinking china and pouring water. He did note that Eilidh had started speaking Gaelic, taking it for granted that Sarah would understand.

The old woman shuffled her way back into the parlor with Sarah in tow carrying the tea tray. She set the tray down on the coffee table as Eilidh took a seat. Sarah poured tea and placed cups in front of Dermot and Eilidh. She took out her notebook and prepared to take notes. The old woman picked up her cup with fingers that looked knotted by arthritis and took a slow sip.

Dermot cleared his throat. "We are collecting stories and songs from the area. Mary Baird told us that ye might have some stories to share."

She narrowed her eyes at him and said in a low voice. "Oh, I've stories to tell."

"Wonderful," Dermot nodded. He waved a hand to the microphone propped up on the table. "D'ye mind if I record our conversation?"

The old woman made a sour face and shrugged, but didn't say no. They were accustomed to sometimes having to pull stories from subjects. After living most of her life in seclusion, he wasn't surprised that Sarah's great-aunt was a bit close-mouthed. Dermot chose to take her lack of protest as agreement. "It's May first, 1996. We're in the home of Eilidh MacLeod near Inchnadamph, Sutherland."

He nodded to Sarah, who cleared her throat and asked. "Mrs. Baird said that you might know something about holy wells in the area. Is there a holy well near here?"

Eilidh turned, watching Sarah with sharp green eyes under white brows. "That depends on what ye mean by holy. We dinna have saints' springs or clootie wells or any of that."

It was clear that Eilidh didn't think much of holy wells. Sarah amended her question. "Okay, how about wells with unique properties, or mineral springs."

Eilidh watched Sarah for a moment. When she spoke her voice was quiet, nostalgic. "Aye. We had a well like that, but it's dried up now, nae more than a puddle."

"What was it used for?" Sarah asked.

Eilidh looked down into her cup of tea as if she was looking inward at some memory. She started to speak, but the words caught in her throat. She cleared it with a tearing sound and said. "For divination. It was a mineral pool, smelled awful. I dinna ken what was in the water. But those of us who knew what to look for, could put a part of someone in the water; hair, blood, nail clippings. It would show us their future, but ye had to ken how to read it. It was a skill that only three of us had."

That fit to some extent with what Sarah had told him. It also sounded like what the locals of the last few centuries would have called witchcraft. He glanced at Sarah, but she wasn't taking her eyes off of Eilidh. She looked deep in thought. He asked. "What kind of things could you divine?"

"Och, could be anything, but mostly we used it to make matches." The old woman said, her eyes focused on Sarah.

Sarah gazed back at the old woman without wavering. Dermot continued to steer the conversation. "Is there a story about how the well came to be, or how it worked?"

Eilidh turned his way, her sharp green eyes roaming over his face and shoulders. Dermot got the impression she was deciding whether or not he was worthy of hearing the tale, or whether his shoulders were strong enough for the burden of it. "I suppose there's no harm in telling it now." When she spoke, her voice had a dreamy quality, as if pulled deep from her memory. "When our people came to be here, before the castle, before the clans this was all wilderness. There was naught but stones and forest, and not a soul for a hundred miles. In that forest, the Auld Ones found a great tree that stood near as tall as a mountain, with branches that touched the clouds and stretched so far, ye couldna see the end of them. At its roots, there was a well of murky green water. They built their village in a glen sheltered from the winds by the hills around it, hidden in the shade of the great tree.

"Three canny lasses from the village began to visit the tree. They were fascinated by the green water and would stir it and watch the colors swirl around. Soon they began to see patterns in the colors. One day, one of the lasses fell and cut herself on a sharp stone. Some of her blood dripped into the pool, and when it was stirred, the colors swirled in a pattern and her sister saw the pattern was the lass's future.

"On their next visit, the lasses all agreed to test what had happened. They each cut their hands and let the blood drip into the pool. When it was stirred, the red blood and green water swirled in patterns that told not only the story of the lasses, but of their people. They saw far into the future when the New Folk would fill the world in numbers too great to understand and the people of the footprint would be scattered and lost.

"This made the lasses greet for their people. When their tears hit the water of the pool, the green on the surface parted to show another pattern beneath. This told another story, a way for their tribe to survive. A promise that if they kept to the auld ways, and preserved their line, one day they would rule over the New Folk. That a woman of their line would lead the world back to the auld ways, who would help them all find the life of plenty that her people enjoyed.

"So, the lasses made a vow to each other over the water, at the foot of the great tree. They promised to keep to the auld ways, to preserve their lines, and to teach their children and grandchildren of the future where one of their kin would make kings. And they did for centuries, even after the tree was felled by a terrible storm, after some of their tribe left to live among the New Folk. But the people of the footprint are scattered now, many of them lost, and we canna use the pool for divination anymore. It dried up years ago." She turned to the window, her eyes going to a ridge to the east of the house.

The old woman went quiet and looked down at her cup as if she were watching the surface for patterns like the lasses watched the water in the well. Dermot looked at Sarah who still watched Eilidh's bent head. A strange mix of wonder, fear, and anger passed in waves across her face. If the story of her people was a puzzle, this was a corner piece. If they wanted to learn as much as possible from Eilidh MacLeod, Sarah needed to keep her reactions to herself. He cleared his throat and she met his eyes. Schooling her features, she quietly asked. "How did they preserve their lines?"

Eilidh lifted wary eyes to his before turning to Sarah. "Every generation, the descendants of the lasses were matched with the selected men of the tribe. The lads' hair and the lasses' blood was put into the well. When the water was stirred, it told the mothers who the right matches were. Then, they were handfast."

"What will you do now that the well has dried up?" Sarah's voice was quiet as if she was afraid of the answer.

The old woman frowned and sighed as if she had come to a decision that she wasn't entirely happy with. "We had a song that we used to sing to tell the story. We used it, so the children would remember."

***

Sarah felt goosebumps rising on her skin. She knew the song Eilidh was going to sing. She had searched and waited for almost a year to hear a Scottish version of the song she called "The River Maiden". Now that she was about to hear it, she was terrified even though she had no idea why.

Eilidh's story had tied so much together. Her three lasses sounded like the three sisters, and like the Norns of Norse mythology. The great tree that touched the clouds had to be Yggdrasil, and the pool at its feet the Well of Urd. Things she had been trying to piece together fell into place, but the resulting picture was too fantastic to be believed.

The old woman started to sing. Her voice was shaky, and low as if she too knew that this was much more than sharing a song.

> *Bha an rìgh a' siùbhlach, gu tùrsach*
> *Bha an rìgh air chall 's a cheò*
> *Shuidh e ri taobh na h-aibhne lan smaointinn*
> *Eirichidh e a-rithist*

As Eilidh went on, her voice grew stronger. Sarah's vision shrank to the old woman in front of her. In her mind she could hear another voice, singing along with Eilidh. The present blended with a memory from last summer. Sarah could almost feel the warmth of the fire and smell the sea air of Cape Breton. Isobel MacKenzie's voice joined in, the slight differences in their versions of the song overlapping each other like rounds.

Eilidh sang on. Sarah felt like a thousand ants were crawling across her skin. She was ready to leap off of the couch and run out the door never looking back. Then another voice was added to the song, one Sarah knew like her own. Granny's voice was strong and accompanied by the tang of barley mash and wood smoke. The familiarity of it calmed her better than any drug. Her limbs grew heavy.

More voices joined the song. Like a ghostly choir of generation after generation of singers faithfully repeating the same lines verse after verse.

> *Bha an rìgh air chall 's a cheò*
> *Eirichidh e a-rithist*

> *The king was lost in the mist.*
> *He will rise again.*

From the cauldron to the storm, to the king's return, the song followed the story that Sarah knew by heart. Until the last verse.

In all three versions of the song that Sarah had heard, the last verse had contained two lines of gibberish. Words that were somewhere between Gaelic and Welsh. This time she understood them.

> *Arise maiden of the river*
> *The king was lost in the mist*
> *You are the mother of the high king*

He will rise again.

Sarah's blood went cold. She was sure that her ears had heard the same sounds as every other time, but today the meaning of those words was clear. It was as if something in her own mind had been unlocked. She looked over at Dermot. He showed no surprise or new understanding. He looked like he could have heard any other song like *"Fear a' Bhàta"* or *"Blàr Inbhir Lòchaidh"*.

She must have made a sound, because his eyes shot to hers. He looked confused as she started to shake her head. His lips moved, but all Sarah heard was her own heartbeat drumming in her ears. Her nerves buzzed as if she'd touched a live wire. She had to move, had to get away. She pushed up from the couch, her notebook falling forgotten to the floor.

She spun for the door and scrabbled for the door knob with numb fingers. The damp air outside chilled her skin, and she broke into a run. Turning away from the house, Sarah ran toward the barn. Her stomach roiled. Past the barn she reached the stone wall. She began to climb over it, but the meager contents of her stomach surged in her throat and she vomited.

CHAPTER TWENTY-SEVEN

Dermot sprang up to run after her, leaving Eilidh MacLeod behind. As he reached the door he glanced back to see the old woman cackling with glee at Sarah's distress. He found Sarah leaning against the outside of the garden wall heaving.

When he caught up with her he pulled her hair back, which must have come loose in her dash from the house. She tried to push him away, but he wouldn't have it. She continued to heave until there was nothing left in her stomach. When she had exhausted herself, she wiped her mouth with her sleeve and leaned against his shoulder.

"Are ye alright then?"

"I don't think I'll ever be alright again. " She groaned.

"Well, I dinna think it's as bad as all that." He tried to sound cheerful. "It's probably something ye ate."

Sarah leaned back and looked at him. "Are you kidding? Didn't you hear her?"

"I heard an old woman sing a song, a rare song, but that's all." At the disbelieving look she gave him, he thought better. "What did ye hear?"

"You didn't hear any other voices?" She narrowed her eyes at him in disbelief.

He shook his head. "Just Eilidh."

Sarah huffed. "That woman has never in her life been *just Eilidh*. What about the last verse, what did you hear? "

He shrugged. "The same rubbish as always. Those lines are lost to time."

Sarah shook her head, tears pooling in her eyes. "No, they're not. I understood them. They're another language, or a code, or a spell... I don't know, but this time when I heard them, I knew what they meant." She pressed her lips together and breathed through her nose as if her gorge was rising again. "Arise, maiden of the river. You are the mother of the high king."

"Shite." He had worried that this meeting would change things for Sarah, the same way her meeting with Isobel MacKenzie had changed things last summer. He had almost convinced James and Walter that Sarah wasn't the girl they were looking for. Then she had met the MacKenzie woman and her granddaughter. Sarah hadn't known at the time that she was meeting family. She hadn't known that she was being tested then, like she was tested today. But for all her blindness, Isobel had seen Sarah for what she was, the daughter of the auld ways they had all been waiting for. "Are ye sure?"

She arched an eyebrow. "Believe me, I think I would rather have heard almost anything else."

"I know ye dinna want to hear this, but we knew that this day might come." He said quietly.

"Huh. Maybe you did." She pushed away from him, her tone sharp. "This is all new to me, and I don't want any of it. That stuff is myth. It's not real. It's not now. This is 1996 for heaven's sake, rational people don't go around talking about magic pools and trees and prophecies."

"I think there are a few apocalyptic religions, including Christianity that would say you're wrong about that."

She sighed, seeming to fold in on herself. "All I want is to collect songs and stories and learn and teach. And I want you."

His gut twisted at the crack in her voice. He reached for her hand where it rested on the wall. "I know, love, but ye must have known this was coming. Yer Granny left ye clues like breadcrumbs; the song, the storybook, the photo of her with Isobel. She was leading ye to this. Ye have to have known this was coming."

"Oh no." Sarah stood and faced him across the garden wall. Her face was red with fury, and her green eyes glittering like peridot. "You don't get to tell me what I've known. I have known what it's like to look up at my mother while she tried to drown me. I've known what it is to be sneered at and whispered about and looked down on by the lowest low-bottom hillbilly in the holler. And I know what it's like to get away from that and build myself a life that I can be proud of. And I am NOT going to give it up for James Stuart, or that old hag," She pointed a quivering finger at the house. "Or any of some long dead tribe of pagan zealots. This is *my* life, goddammit. I get to choose."

"I wish more than anything that was true." He kept his tone calm. "Ye have to know that all I want is for ye to be happy and safe. But no matter how much you and I want to be left to our own happiness, there are too many people pushing us in the other direction. Powerful people, and I'm not talking about the *cailleach* in the house. Ye've seen what they can do."

"This doesn't change our plans." She said leaning forward bracing her arms on the wall. "When we get back to

Edinburgh, we're getting you a new identity, and we are getting the hell out of here."

"That's not going to be as easy as we thought." When she pushed up from the wall and stepped away, he rushed to clarify. "Eilidh will be getting word to Walter as soon as she can that she's confirmed who you are. And Walter will step up his pressure on James. They're going to want to move quickly, now."

"Except that they need me to go along with it. Right?"

His shoulders sank, and he nodded.

The corner of her mouth kicked up in a smirk. "It's going to take a lot of convincing from James to get me to go along. Could take months."

He gave her a warning look. "I think ye're playing with fire there. These are master manipulators we're talking about."

"You're not giving up already?" Her brows drew together in a frown.

"No, but we need to think things through. We have to be very careful." Her shoulders relaxed slightly, but she still eyed him with suspicion. He held out his hand for her. She grudgingly placed her hand in his and moved closer. "Listen, there is nothing that I would like better than to take off and never look back. But I also don't want to be looking over our shoulders for the rest of our lives. We have to be canny about this."

She looked down at their hands where they were joined over the wall, then back up at him through her lashes. She'd had a bomb dropped on her and she needed something to hold on to. It was clear from her look that she wanted to hold on to him. It was the sort of look that could bring a man to his knees. "And you're not put off by the whole mother of the king business?"

He reached across the wall with his other hand sliding his fingers into her hair and pulling her forehead to his. "Nothing is going to change the way I feel about ye."

She smiled. "Then let's go back to the house and face the gorgon together."

***

They found Eilidh MacLeod still sitting on the sofa blithely sipping her tea as if she hadn't brought the world down on Sarah's head. Sarah took a second to marvel at the fact that the ambitions of a billionaire and potential king rested in the hands of one little old woman in a tidy little croft house in the Highlands. This woman's word could literally move mountains. Eilidh seemed to relish her position. But if Eilidh believed in the legend she had told them, then she also believed that Sarah's position was higher.

All pretense of collecting folklore was gone. Sarah decided the time for softening questions and biting tongues was over. "It's pretty clear you know who I am."

"I kent who ye were when yer car turned down the drive. I've known ye were coming for a while." Eilidh said.

"Do you see the future now too?" Sarah asked with an arch look. "I thought that was Isobel."

"Of course, I don't, not without the well." Eilidh replied bitterly.

Sarah's voice was even, but there was a sharp note beneath the polite tones. "I noticed we're not having this conversation in *Làrachd an Fhamhair*. Where are your people?"

The old woman's mouth twisted, and she lifted a hand and waved it through the air. "Scattered like the sisters said they would. They had to. There wasna food enough after the cauldron died."

"It died again?" Sarah said. "When was that?"

Eilidh turned to face them. Her eyes shot daggers at Sarah, "That'd be the day yer mother left us."

Sarah gave her a skeptical look. "Left you?"

"Aye, left us." The woman nodded. "Ran off wi' that steward o' hers. Never trusted that man. Had the stink of war on him." She eyed Dermot, and her nostrils flared. "So, do you."

"Is that what you told everyone, that Grant MacDuff was my father?" Sara cocked her head to the side. Her eyes sparking with temper. "He was in every way that counts, but I think you know exactly who my father is."

"Feh!" Eilidh made a pushing motion with her hand, as if she could push Rab Ballantyne out of her memory. "Worthless sot. I never kent what my Sheila saw in him."

Sarah moved closer and sat in the chair across from Eilidh. "Tell me what you believe is supposed to happen now."

"What I believe?" The old woman gave Sarah a hard look. "If this was about what I believe, they'd have left ye where they found ye. That ye should come here wi' yer *sluagh ùr* ways and think ye're the bloody queen when there are others worthier."

Sarah looked at Dermot. He looked surprised at Eilidh's tone. "There was another lass besides Bridget. I guess that would be yer granddaughter."

Eilidh grunted in agreement. "Aye, and there's not a finer lass to be found. Raised her with the auld ways like her mother. She kens a far sight more than you do about what's to come."

"Does she?" Sarah asked. "Maybe she can advise me then. Where did you say she is?"

The old woman narrowed her eyes and almost growled. Sarah thought she must have touched a nerve. "That's of no matter now." She waved a gnarled hand. "Ye've got what ye wanted, what yer mother wanted all along."

"I don't think you know the first thing about what my mother wanted." Sarah recalled the times that Molly had tried to talk to Eilidh about her misgivings about the matchmaking scheme, or about Willie Cross, but Eilidh hadn't listened. "I can tell you she didn't want any part of your breeding program."

"Is that so?" The old woman pointed a bony finger at Sarah. "Then why was she fornicating with Rab Ballantyne."

"Because she fell in love with him."

Eilidh scoffed. "Love. What is that when there are thousands of years of tradition to uphold, when there is the promise of a destiny like yours?"

Sarah narrowed her eyes. "But it is my destiny. My mother obviously did something right. But that still doesn't answer my question. What do you believe happens next?"

"Well, ye must marry the Stuart heir." Eilidh's eyes shifted to Dermot. Sarah thought she sounded unsure. "He's the only thing close to a king we've got."

"Why does it have to be a Scottish king?" Sarah asked. "There are other kings or men who are like kings. Why not some other high-powered man, or a prince from the middle east, or a politician? What is it about the Stuart heir?"

Eilidh was still looking at Dermot. "Have ye not told her? She doesna ken who the Stuarts are?"

Dermot squirmed. "That's a long and difficult tale to tell."

Sarah gave him a steely look. "You can tell me the long part later. Give me the quick and dirty now."

He drew in a long breath and Sarah saw the muscles in his jaw jump with tension. His next words came out in a rush. "The Stuarts are from the line of David."

She narrowed her eyes at him, not quite understanding why he was so uncomfortable telling her that. "I would hope so."

He looked confused for second, then said. "Not David Bruce." He paused. "David of Israel."

Now Sarah was confused. David of Israel was so far out of this context. "As in…King David…like from the Bible?"

At his nod, she felt the hairs stand up on her arms. She looked at Eilidh and the old woman was watching her avidly, a smug smile on her wizened face. Sarah could feel her face growing red, and every muscle in her body tensed. She turned back to Dermot and said the only possible thing that she could think of. "Of all the crazy-ass things that you have said to me over the past year, this one takes the cake. I don't know why you people are doing this or what you think you're going to achieve, but I am done."

***

"Sarah, we need to talk about this." He put his hand over hers as she reached to open the boot of the car. After declaring her opinion about the Stuart's lineage, she had picked up her things and strode from the house as if being chased by demons. Unlike her earlier flight, this time she was furious.

"What's the point?" She jerked her hand from under his and shoved him away. "You've been keeping *this* from me all this time. How can I trust anything you say?"

"It wasn't for me to tell. I was trying to protect you." His heart hammered with alarm. Once again, he was failing to balance his enforced loyalty to the Stuarts with his love for her.

"How is keeping me in the dark protecting me?" She opened the boot and threw her bag in. It bounced off the back seat and landed in a heap. "Didn't Ryan Cumberland teach you anything? I can't defend myself if I don't know why I need to."

"Ye have me to defend ye." He tried to slide his arm around her waist, but she stepped out of reach.

"When you withhold information from me?" Her voice kicked up another notch in volume. "I never know who's interests you're looking out for. Are you my lover or James's man?"

He grabbed her arm and jerked his head toward the house. "Will ye lower yer voice?" He hissed. "Ye might have doubts about me, but she is definitely on their side."

"That old bat's probably too busy laughing her head off, thinking she finally got one over on Molly MacAlpin." Sarah looked around his shoulder at the house before turning back to him. She straightened her shoulders and lifted her chin, fury in every line of her body. "Every time I think you've come clean, every time I trust that you're not hiding some other information or motive from me, you prove me wrong."

His gut twisted. "I'm only trying to protect ye."

"You're failing." Her features were like stone. Her green eyes dark like the sea in a storm. "One of these days, you're going to have to stop sitting on the fence and choose. Me or James."

He chose her. He had chosen her long ago, but that didn't change that the Stuarts were holding his mother hostage. He wanted so badly to tell her everything. He wanted to explain how he struggled every day to balance his love for the both of them. But it all got bottled up in his throat. Tears sprang to his eyes. He opened his mouth, but the words wouldn't come out.

Tears shone in Sarah's eyes too, as she shook her head. "Take me back to town."

Sitting in the car park in front of the hostel, he struggled again to think of anything to say that would make her see how difficult his situation was. But her life was more important than his problems. Hearing the old woman tell the legend had reminded him of that. And telling Sarah about the Stuarts lineage had reminded him of how much danger she was in.

"Who sent Ryan Cumberland to kill me?" She asked quietly. It was the first time that she had acknowledged that the man who tried to kill her in December may have actually been sent by someone else.

"I don't know." Sarah reached for the latch and was pushing the door open. Dermot dove across the seat and grabbed the handle pulling it closed again. "Ye wanted honesty."

She slumped back into her seat, seething.

"We think that Ryan Cumberland was sent by a group called The Circle. They're primarily American religious zealots. They're a sort of confederation of different fundamentalist groups who banded together as part of the anti-Catholic movement in the early twentieth century. Over the last few decades they have become increasingly meshed with business and political interests."

"And why do they have a problem with James?" she asked.

"A lot of reasons. Many of their business interests are energy related, Texas oil, natural gas, coal. So, they see Alba Petroleum as competition. But they also take issue with the idea that Jesus could have had children and that his descendants could be around today. James's very existence challenges some of the basic teachings of their religion. And they believe that if he were to reproduce with you, that your child would be the anti-Christ."

At first, he wasn't sure if she was laughing or crying. Within seconds she gasped for breath and he could see that her nearly silent shoulder shaking was in fact laughter. "So, they don't want to accept that James might be descended from Jesus, but they'll accept the idea that my people are somehow mystically special."

"Well, when ye put it that way." He chuckled. "Seriously, they believe that yer people are pagan devils."

"Now that sounds believable. We had a preacher in the holler who used to call us that."

"It isn't only The Circle who are dangerous. There is a Catholic brotherhood, The Invigilare, who feel it's their mission to protect the church from outside attack. The idea of Jesus having a family of his own is anathema to their notion of his purity, not to mention the inherent challenge to the church's authority if there were someone running about with divine blood in their veins."

"Of course," She said her voice tense. "Anyone else?"

"Well, there is the government. They obviously have a vested interest in preventing Scotland from becoming independent."

"But aren't they always moaning about how Scots are all on welfare and a drain on resources?" She asked.

"Aye, that's their story, but if it's true they would let us go in a heartbeat. No, they need Scotland and its resources, and I don't just mean the oil."

"Why don't they go after James? He's openly nationalist." She said.

He shook his head. "He's too famous, and a popular figure. But there is the possibility that someone in the government knows about your people. And if they know about that then they might know about James's interest in you."

Sarah blew out a long breath. "So, James Bond might be coming after me."

He was swamped with relief. If she was able to joke, then there was a chance he could reach her. "Well, James Bond is a Scot, aye? So, maybe not him."

She gave him a wan look. Maybe she wasn't ready for jokes yet. "So, there are roughly two major religions and a world power who would prefer that I not marry James Stuart."

"That sums it up."

"Well, at least we all agree." This time she was out of the car before he could stop her.

Cursing himself he followed her inside. He found her on her knees in the common room, shuffling through the pamphlets on the coffee table. They were mostly tourist information and advertisements for local guides. "What are you looking for?"

"A bus schedule." She bit out. "I'm getting out of here."

He knelt and put his hands over hers and kept his voice low. "Ye can't leave. Didn't ye hear what I said. Ye need protection."

"No," She said with determination, pulling her hands from his. She went back to searching through the pamphlets. "I heard that I need to stay away from James Stuart, and I have every intention of doing that."

"Sarah, we talked about this. We're not ready." He hissed, afraid that some of the team might overhear.

"I am." She looked up from the papers. Her green eyes pierced his. "I've been ready."

"But..." They were going together. They were getting him a new identity and they were going to go together. The look she gave him said that that plan had gone up in smoke the minute she found out about the Stuart bloodline. Because it was one more thing that he'd hidden from her. "Please, don't rush off. Ye have to think this through."

"Well. It looks like that's a moot point." She stood dropping the bus table on top of the pile. "The bus doesn't leave until tomorrow morning."

"Will ye take some time to think about this? It's dangerous." He pleaded.

"I don't need to think about it anymore. The closer I get to James, the more dangerous it is, and I'm not sure if it's James or all these others who are the most dangerous. I'm done dancing to someone else's tune. I'm leaving tomorrow."

She walked by him to the room she shared with the other ladies and shut the door. He stood there feeling as if he couldn't catch his breath. For all he'd wanted her to avoid James and this whole situation, the thought of losing her left him feeling hollowed out. Maybe it was better that she left.

Maybe she had a better chance of getting away without all the trappings that went along with James or the research team. Maybe she was better off without him.

CHAPTER TWENTY-EIGHT

"You know, you really don't have to hang with me all night." Sarah said as Jujhar slid past her to sit down at the corner table with his third cup of tea. She looked around the room half full of local musicians who they'd heard gathered informally at the Red Hart every Thursday night. After quietly packing her things that afternoon, she had considered going straight to bed but knew she would only have lain there second guessing every choice she'd made including the one to leave. Instead, she decided to go to the pub with Jujhar, Isla, and Ewan. If she was leaving in the morning, she might as well enjoy one last night with her friends.

Jujhar looked around the room at the increasing crowd, and his smile wasn't entirely put on. "This is great. Local musicians, good tea... "

"Dermot told you to keep an eye on me, didn't he?" She asked with a smile.

Jujhar looked a little embarrassed. "He did mention that you'd had a difficult day and might need some company."

She couldn't be mad at Jujhar, but it still rankled her that so many people concerned themselves with her every move. She supposed she could deal with it for one more night. "I'll bet. Did he also give me a curfew? "

Jujhar gave her a look of friendly censure. "I don't know what happened today, but he's worried about you."

"Well, I'm not his concern." She muttered and Jujhar gave her another look that said he didn't believe that for a second. She decided to change the subject. "So, tell me about your day."

"Well, we set things up in the village hall for tomorrow. I talked with a Gaelic speaker from near Drumbeg who happened to be in town. Some interesting differences between the local dialect and the Lewis Gaelic we've been hearing. Kirstie got a lead on a local potter. And Ewan and Isla made moon-eyes at each other."

Sarah giggled, as she looked over at Isla who was standing by the bar, fiddle in hand. Ewan was handing out release forms to the various musicians waiting for their drinks. Since Isla had given Ewan a chance, they had spent almost every spare minute together. "They do tend to do that."

"I fear that his documentary might focus more on traditional music than the other traditions we're collecting." Jujhar said with his usual knowing smile.

Sarah nodded agreement as she finished the last of her black and tan. "That's okay. Traditional music is the gateway drug. Let them reel 'em in with music and we'll get 'em hooked on the hard stuff like rat satires and local dialects."

That got a belly laugh from her usually placid friend. Sarah stood. "I'm going to have another. Can I get you anything?"

"No, thank you." He said, still chuckling.

Sarah was at the bar waiting for her drink when a man stumbled into her. She was glad her drink wasn't in her hand, or she might have been wearing it. Then for a second she wondered if this was it, if one of the dangers Dermot had enumerated for her this afternoon hadn't found her already, and this was a warning. Like Ryan Cumberland's strategic bump that almost landed her in the path of an oncoming bus last Halloween.

What she saw was nothing so dramatic or threatening. It was a reed-thin, scruffy looking man of middle age in a too large moth eaten Aran sweater and frayed kilt. He was simultaneously trying to balance a guitar case against the stone wall and himself against the bar. He looked down at her with green eyes that she imagined had been striking at one time but were now bleary and bloodshot. He breathed a whisky soaked, "Sorry, hen." directly into her face.

"No problem." Sarah muttered.

"American?" He grunted.

"Yeah." She agreed being polite.

"Mmm." His eyes glazed over even more, and his voice grew wistful. "I knew an American lass once."

The barman delivered Sarah's pint, which she gladly took. Leaving the money on the bar she edged her way around the drunk man, glad he didn't seem to want more conversation. Over the buzz of the small pub she heard the man slur, "Gie uz a pint, Graham."

The man clearly didn't need another pint in Sarah's opinion. It must have been the barman's opinion too, because he said. "Ye havena paid the tab from last week."

The drunk man groaned and gave an excuse that reminded Sarah of Granny's moonshine customers promising to pay her on payday if she would front them a little moonshine today. "C'mon, mate. Ruaraidh'll be back in town tomorrow and he'll take care of it."

"Then ye can have a pint tomorrow." The barman said. "Go on, Rab. Ye've had enough already."

Sarah stopped in her tracks short of her table. The drunk man's name was Rab. Could it be a coincidence? She looked up at the mirror that hung above the couch beside her table. Her mother had said that she had her father's eyes. She tried to imagine the eyes she had just seen without the capillaries and alcohol haze. It couldn't be. The drunk man slouched through the crowd and into the dining room behind the barroom. Sarah tracked him as he made his way to the door. He was tall and looked like his hair might have been blonde once though now it was gray.

Jujhar's cup was at their table, but he wasn't. Sarah put her glass down at the table and followed the man. She slipped out the door quietly, hoping she didn't look like a stalker. In the small garden behind the pub, the man was muttering to himself as he trudged across the gravel to a path that led down to the rocky beach.

He wove his way down to the shore and came to rest on a fallen tree. Sarah followed, listening to him curse greedy barkeeps, the price of pints and someone named Ruaraidh who was never around when needed. Once he sat down, he rummaged in his sporran and produced a crushed pack of cigarettes and lighter. He managed to get the right end of the cigarette into his mouth but had trouble lighting it. After a few failed attempts to spark a flame on his lighter, he then brought the flame dangerously close to his beard.

At this point, Sarah had to intervene. She stepped up beside him and took the lighter from his hand. He nearly fell off the log craning to see who had taken his lighter.

"Uh. The American." He said almost to himself.

"You looked like you could use a hand." She held the still burning and dented Zippo steady in front of him while he lit his cigarette.

"Cheers." He said before taking a long drag.

"'S e do bheatha." [You're welcome.] She said slipping into Gaelic. She knew from Molly's journal that her father spoke it.

"A bheil Gaidhlig agad?" [Do you have the Gaelic?] He leaned away and eyed her blowing a stream of smoke toward the sea.

"Fad mo bheatha." She said quietly. [All my life.]

He offered her a cigarette by lifting the pack in her direction. Instead of taking one, she put the lighter on top of the pack. He shrugged and restored it to his sporran. "Not much call for the Gaelic in America."

"There was in my house, my Granny was Scottish." She said. "Have you ever been to America?"

"Och, nah. I've been all over the UK, even played a few shows in Amsterdam once, but never been to America." His words slurred as if they all got mashed together in his mouth and dripped from his lips in a syrup of whisky and spittle.

"I made mah living as a musician once. I played the fiddle, and bodhran, and the...tin whistle...and the..." He trailed off and looked around near his feet.

"Are you looking for your guitar?"

"Aye." He said looking behind the log they were sitting on.

"I think you left it inside by the bar."

He looked up the path to the pub as if he was considering going to fetch his instrument but then waved a hand in irritation. "Eh. They'll mind it for me."

They fell silent each in their own world. Sarah wondered what else he might say while Rab smoked his cigarette. After a few minutes he sighed. "I did know a lass from America when I was young. Ye should ha seen me then. I wasna this mess ye see here. She thought I was something, and she was beautiful."

How do you end a day when you learn that you're the fulfillment of some ridiculous prophecy, your boyfriend is a liar, and your would-be boyfriend is descended from Jesus? Well, by finding out that your father is the village drunk of course. She didn't know whether to laugh or cry, but she was near to both when old Rab beside her started to drunkenly paraphrase Robert Burns. "Her dark brown hair, beyond compare, Comes trinklin down her swan-like neck. And her two eyes, like stars in skies, Would keep a sinking ship frae wreck,"

She wondered if that was how Rab saw her mother, as the one who if she hadn't gotten away could have saved his 'sinking ship frae wreck'. In the end she laughed and cried when she threw an arm over his shoulders and joined him in the refrain. "Mally's meek, Mally's sweet, Mally's modest and discreet; Mally's rare, Mally's fair, Mally's every way complete."

He sighed and leaned his head on her shoulder as if they were old friends. "Her name was Màili, my American."

"And I'm guessing she had dark hair, not yellow like Burns wrote." Sarah said, remembering her mother's dark hair beneath a crown of white windflowers.

"Aye she did. Dark as a raven's wing." He said wistfully.

"What happened to her?" Sarah asked curious how he might tell the story.

"Gone." He waved a hand at the sea as if she had flown from that very spot. "And better off wi' oot the likes o' me to be sure."

Sarah reckoned they might agree on that one.

He fell silent again, and Sarah wondered if he might have passed out on her shoulder. Then he reared back as if he'd been startled. When he stopped swaying from the waist up, he held out a hand to her. "Name's Rab Ballantyne."

She laughed and took his hand, "I know. Come on. Let's get you home."

CHAPTER TWENTY-NINE

The first thing she noticed waking up the next morning was that her neck hurt. Her nose wrinkled at the general smell of spilled beer, cigarette smoke, and stale sweat. Blinking at the sun coming through the window, she noticed a rather large person-shaped silhouette in front of her. As her vision resolved itself, the silhouette came into focus revealing an unsettlingly handsome man sitting on the coffee table in front of her.

He looked close to her in age, but his skin was weathered and slightly sunburned. His long hair was primarily red but with sun-bleached streaks. Seated as he was, she couldn't be sure, but his limbs were long and rangy in his fleece pull over and worn cargo pants. His mouth kicked up on one side in a smirk that matched his arched ginger eyebrow. Overall, he gave an impression of sunlight and self-assurance. "Ye look a bit younger than what he usually brings home."

"Brings a lot of women home, does he?" Sarah said pushing up from the couch.

"Not too many, lately. All the local lasses are on to him."

"Yeah, I expect they are." She said tilting her head from side to side stretching the sore muscles.

"Since he's upstairs and ye're down here, I can only assume that nothing happened." He said delicately.

"Oh god, no!" She rushed to assure him. "No, I only brought him home."

"So ye travel around helping hapless drunks get home?" He asked with a hint of devilment in his eyes.

"Well, I helped all the drunks in the States, so I thought Scotland would be a good place to branch out." She muttered.

His laugh was like water over smooth stones. "Ye'll do. I'm Ruaraidh."

"Sarah." She shook his hand, liking that he hadn't Anglicized his name into Rory for her American ears but stuck with the Gaelic ROO-Ree. "I believe you're expected to pay a tab down at the Red Hart."

"Eh. Wouldna be the first time, nor the last." He stood, and Sarah had to tilt her head far back to look up at him. He was tall. "Can I make ye a cup of tea?"

"Sure, thanks." Sarah unfolded herself from the couch and stretched while Ruaraidh disappeared into the kitchen. She hadn't bothered to look around last night after Jujhar had helped her haul the very drunk Rab from the beach, up the steep hillside to his cottage, and upstairs into his bed. It had been dark, and she had been exhausted after convincing Jujhar that she would be safe there.

Her friend had looked doubtful. "You can come back in the morning, you know."

"I know," She'd said. "But I've just found him after twenty-six years. I don't want to wait anymore."

"Then I'll stay with you. " He'd offered.

She smiled and took his arm, pulling him toward the door. "I appreciate you worrying, but I'll be fine. And the things I have to say to him are best done in private."

"I do NOT feel good about this." He'd said, but she noted he didn't stop when she opened the door.

He reluctantly stepped out on to the front step, before turning back. "What am I supposed to tell Dermot?"

"The truth." She said with a shrug. "That I'm with my father."

He'd shot a withering look up the stairs behind her as if to say, some *father* then reminded her to lock the door and left.

Now, with the soft morning sun filtering in through the windows, she noticed the state of the place. It was definitely the home of a bachelor, maybe two. There were dirty dishes empty bottles and food wrappers left on tables. A layer of dust covered the top of the television and mantle. The mantle also held an array of framed family photos. One showed a boy in his early teens who must have been Ruaraidh in a soccer uniform. Another showed a smiling girl of about twelve standing in front of a very good painting of Ardvreck Castle holding a blue first place ribbon. Another was a stiff looking family portrait featuring a much cleaner, younger looking version of the Rab she'd met last night as well as the two teens from the other photos, both sporting strawberry blond hair and the same striking light green eyes that Sarah saw in the mirror every day. Beside Rab with her hand resting on the girl's shoulder was a motherly looking woman with soft, bobbed auburn hair. She had beautiful bone structure, but something was off in her eyes. Despite the smile and slight tilt to her head, Sarah thought she looked miserable. This must be Sheila.

"Ugh! Those portraits are frightful." Ruaraidh said softly bumping her arm with a cup of tea.

"I don't know. I'm sure it's nice to have the memories." She took the cup from him and turned back to the photo. "We never took many photos in our house."

He gestured toward the one in front of them. "Well, mum used to make us get one every year. I think that was probably the last one we had done before they split up."

"I'm sorry." She said.

"Och, they were never really happy. I think they only stayed together as long as they did for us." He said sounding not at all bothered by his parents' divorce.

"Where is your mother now?" Sarah asked, wondering how Sheila would react to seeing Molly's daughter turning up on her doorstep.

"She moved over to Lairg, got married to a nice grocer there."

"And your sister?" He didn't seem to mind answering her questions. She supposed finding a stranger asleep on your couch led to a certain level of frankness.

"Oona, she's gone off to art school. She's actually quite..." He started to say with a fond smile before he glanced at Sarah. She met his eyes and he stopped short. He looked back at the portrait, then at Sarah again this time with a look of astonishment. His free hand found its way into his hair. "Shit."

"Actually, I think she looks pretty talented." Sarah said nodding to the photo of the girl with the prize-winning painting before hiding a wicked smile in her cup.

Ruaraidh sank into a nearby chair. "Does Da know?"

Sarah sat back down on the couch. "Not yet. I was pretty sure he wouldn't remember anything last night and I didn't want to have to tell him twice."

He looked at her with a mix of fascination and terror. "And your mother."

"Died almost twenty years ago." She said plainly.

"I'm sorry." His brows drew together. "Do ye mind my asking? Was she...was she Molly?"

She nodded. "Then you've heard of her."

He laughed, but there was little mirth in it. "Hard not to be around my da when he's drunk and not hear about the one that got away. My parents lived their whole marriage with the ghost of your mother between them like an invisible wall."

Sarah sank down onto the couch. "That may have actually been her ghost. She wore our father's betrayal like a shroud, until she killed herself when I was six."

"God!" He breathed. He raised a mischievous eyebrow at her. "My Da's been drunk every day since my mum gave up and moved out."

Sarah flashed him a smile saying. "I lived for almost twenty years among people who thought my mother was a crazy slut and my Granny was a witch. And those folks had no problems sharing their opinions with me."

"Jesus. You win." He said with a chuckle.

Sarah laughed out loud. She liked this new brother of hers. He made her feel more at ease than she had in days. "We should write laments about our troubles to sing in the pub on Thursdays."

"Ah, I'm no good at singing. Took after my mum in that."

"What are you good at, little brother?" She looked at him, suddenly very curious about the man next to her. She expected his looks around here got him plenty of female attention. She hadn't met Sheila, but Molly had described her as beautiful. Ruaraidh seemed to have combined the best features of his parents. He was built like she imagined Rab had been before years of alcoholism had done their damage; tall and straight and leanly muscled. But he had Sheila's red hair and his features were a bit sharper than Rab's. He had Rab's eyes though, Sarah's eyes, the bright clear green of glacial ice.

His mouth tilted in a half smile. "Och, I'm a wild one, and by that, I mean I'm good at living rough. I guide hill walking tours around here; Sulvein, Cnocan Craig, Bone Caves and the like. I only came back in this morning from a few nights camping. And I'm not surprised ye found da trying to beg a pint at the Red Hart. He probably ran out at home."

"Oh, he also left his guitar at the pub. He said that they would watch it." She told him.

"I'm sure they will." He was saying when someone started pounding on the door.

Ruaraidh went to answer it. The house was old and there were no peep holes or sidelights, but Sarah supposed that security wasn't as much of an issue in the village. Most people probably knew each other. Of course, that meant Ruaraidh wasn't ready when Dermot pushed his way inside as soon as he started to open it. Ruaraidh let out a surprised "Whoa!"

Dermot didn't bother to talk to him but walked into the living room looking ready to spit nails. He pinned Sarah with a look. "With yer father, aye?"

"Well, it was only my father last night when I sent Jujhar away." Sarah said calmly before smiling over his shoulder. "That was before I met Ruaraidh."

"Oh Ruaraidh, is it?" He parroted wheeling on Ruaraidh who was coming back into the living room. "And where did you come from?"

Ruaraidh raised his eyebrows but didn't rise to the bait. "I live here."

"And where were ye last night, when Sarah was hauling the old man up from the shore?" Dermot took a step toward him.

Sarah jumped up from the couch and tried to squeeze between them. "Hey, take it easy, Dermot."

"Take it easy?" He looked down at her. "After all we talked about yesterday, ye disappeared. I've been waiting outside patiently thinking ye were talking with yer father and then I hear ye laughing and flirting with this." His eyes swept down Ruaraidh's long form.

"You mean, my brother?" Sarah said flatly.

He looked back at her in confusion. "Yer, br.."

Sarah nodded turning to Ruaraidh. "Well, half-brother."

"Brother." Ruaraidh said firmly not taking his eyes off Dermot. It gave Sarah a warm feeling that she hadn't felt since the last time she'd seen Duff.

She turned to her brother. "Ruaraidh Ballantyne, this furious creature is my steward, Dermot Sinclair."

Ruaraidh rolled his shoulders to ease the tension before extending his hand to Dermot. "We were having a cup of tea while we wait for Da to wake up. Would ye like one?"

"Yeah. Cheers." Dermot said deflated.

Ruaraidh went to the kitchen to make another cup of tea.

Sarah glanced at Dermot from beneath her lashes, before teasing him. "You were jealous."

His anger hadn't dissipated quite yet. Keeping his voice low, he said. "Ye missed yer bus this morning."

"Well, then I guess you're stuck with me for another day." She said, her own mood souring at his tone.

"Ye ken well enough, that's not how I feel."

Sarah kept her voice low. "I *ken* well enough that I don't want any part of this, and I'll be taking off as soon as I'm able. Maybe my new little brother will give me a ride to Ullapool."

A noise from the hallway that sounded like a sack of potatoes falling caught their attention. They followed the sound to find a groggy cursing Rab sitting on the bottom step with one leg twisted under the other. "What's all this noise doon here then?"

CHAPTER THIRTY

"Let me give ye a hand there?" Dermot helped Rab to stand and stayed close beside him.

"Who are ye two?" Rab asked looking back and forth between them.

"I brought you home last night." Sarah said, not quite ready to drop her bombshell on him. "This is my friend, Dermot."

"Ye brought me home last night?" His eyes looked up as if he was searching his memory for anything from the night before. "Is my son here? Ruaraidh?"

"Aye, Da. Go on and sit down. I'll bring you some tea." Ruaraidh called from the kitchen.

Sarah backed into the living room watching Rab shift from wall to chair to couch for support as he made his way. She wondered if the alcohol was out of his system enough for him to remember any conversation they might have.

Ruaraidh came in with two more cups of tea as they were taking seats around the room. Sarah put herself on the couch next to Rab. Dermot went to sit in a chair near the front window. Ruaraidh said. "I see ye've met Sarah."

Rab eyed Sarah again, bewildered. "Yeah. Listen, hen, I dinna remember meeting ye last night, and I hope I didna do anything untoward."

"You were a perfect gentleman." She gave him a soft smile.

"Drink yer tea, Da. Sarah's got a thing to tell ye and ye're going to need it." Ruaraidh warned.

Rab narrowed his eyes at his son, and Sarah couldn't tell if he was battling confusion, headache or both. But he took a couple of good sips of tea. After a few minutes, the strong tea cleared some of the fog. He looked at Sarah. "What can I do for ye then?"

She wasn't sure where to begin. She had spent a good portion of the night trying to think of how she would tell him, but now that they were sitting together, there didn't seem to be a good way to say it. "Um...last night, you told me about an American girl that you used to know."

"Och. Did I go on about that? I'm sorry. I get maudlin sometimes when I'm pissed." He said.

"No, I didn't mind." She shook her head and rested a hand on his arm. "I don't mind. You see, I only have her memories to go on. And it would be good to hear yours."

"Ye what?" Rab looked at her in confusion. Maybe the fog of last night hadn't completely lifted.

Sarah shifted tactics. "Do you remember her name?"

"Màili." He sighed her mother's Gaelic name. *"Màili* MacAlpin."

"I didn't introduce myself properly before." Sarah held out her hand. *"'S mise Mòrag NicMhàili."*

Sarah watched awareness settle over him like a heavy blanket. His shoulders slumped. His back bowed slightly. His face fell, and his eyelids fluttered around unshed tears. Ruaraidh took the cup from him before it slipped from his boneless fingers. He looked down at her hand and slid his hand into it. He studied their joined hands before meeting her eyes. Sarah smiled through her own tears.

That smile released something inside him. He bent over their hands pressing his cheek to the back of hers, the tears spilled over. He collapsed in on himself under the weight of twenty-six years of regret and recrimination and wept. Sarah threw her other arm around him and let him weep. She couldn't be angry with this man, no matter how damaging his actions or inaction had been to Molly. From what Ruaraidh said and what she could see for herself, he had castigated himself enough over the years.

When he had exhausted the initial flood of emotions, he sat up wiping his eyes and nose on his sleeve. "Can ye forgive me?"

Ruaraidh found a box of tissues and offered it to Sarah, then to Rab. She took one and blotted her own cheeks. "There's nothing to forgive."

"Oh, there is, lass." Rab sighed. "There is."

"Well, that's water under the bridge now." Sarah patted his knee. "You're the only family I've got anymore."

He looked shocked." But yer mother."

"Died in a fall twenty years ago." Sarah looked pointedly at Ruaraidh. Rab didn't need to know that Molly had killed herself. It wasn't his fault anyway, but Sarah didn't want to risk him blaming himself. So, he would get the official story, the only story that anyone would find if they looked at the records. Molly MacAlpin had fallen off a cliff on their farm while walking in a fog.

Rab absorbed this information a little easier; with solemnity rather than another flood of tears. Sarah supposed there wasn't much grief left after his initial outburst. "I'm that sorry. But ye were so young then."

"Yeah, I was only six. My grandmother and Grant McDuff raised me." Sarah replied.

Rab sighed. "I remember MacDuff. He didna think much of me, and I canna say he was wrong. I'm glad to hear he stayed by your mother though. He's a good man."

"One of the best." Sarah agreed.

Rab looked down at his lap. "Did she... Did she tell ye about me?"

Sarah wiped a stray tear from her cheek. "Not while she was alive, I'm afraid. A few months ago, I found an account that she wrote of her time here. Before that, I'm afraid I didn't even know your name."

"It's just as well." He said, his shoulders sinking. "Yer mother was wronged here, wronged by all of us."

She wasn't surprised that Rab would say that given what she had read, but she did want to hear what he thought of their treatment of Molly. "Can you tell me how you remember that year?"

He pressed his lips together and blew out a long breath. "I loved yer mother the minute I clapped eyes on her. I was sure that it was yer mother I'd be matched with. It felt right. But then the pool picked me for Sheila." He nodded toward Ruaraidh. "I'm sorry, son. Lord knows I tried to be a good father to you kids, but I never loved yer mother."

Ruaraidh shook his head. "That's nothing I didna know already."

Rab turned back to Sarah. "Of course, as disappointed as I was, yer mother had the worst match. Willie Cross wasn't a bad lad, but he wasna right in the head. And when the cauldron stopped, the people in the village, the ones who hadna lived in the outside world all suspected it was yer mother's and Rona's fault because they had. It was hard for yer mum."

This all sounded very much like Molly's version of the story. Sarah decided that there was no reason to rehash that. "Now, I met Eilidh yesterday, and she said that the cauldron stopped again after my mother was driven out of the village."

He nodded grimly. "Aye, it did."

"So that wasn't the first time that it stopped?" Ruaraidh asked.

Rab turned to his son. "No, it stopped once after the matching ceremony that year. It started again a few months later. It didna stop again until yer grandmother ran Molly off."

Ruaraidh gave him a questioning look. "Ran her off? Gran said she ran away with her steward."

Sarah agreed. "Yes, that's the story she tried to tell me yesterday."

Rab shook his head. "She'd ha been better off if she had." He took Sarah's hand again giving her an earnest look. "I have never gotten over the shame of that day."

Turning to Ruaraidh he said. "Yer gran tells it that way, because it was her cruelty that broke the cauldron, her ugliness. She saw that Molly was pregnant and knew it couldna be Willie's. She shamed yer mother in front of everyone in the hall. And she demanded that the father stand up with her." He turned back to Sarah. "I was so afraid of Eilidh, of Sheila, of the anger of the whole village, that I didna stand up when I should have. I'm grateful that McDuff did. He didna say the child was his, but he told every one of those people exactly what they owed to yer mother. They had their heads in the sand when the cauldron stopped giving food. Yer mother and Rona and the stewards kept the village fed, and that was how they repaid her. They let their fear and suspicion of the *sluagh ùr* cloud everything. They lost their way, and it meant the end to their way of life."

"After yer mother left the cauldron stopped the second time, people tried to stay. They lasted for a while on the food that the young people had put by, but folk started to drift away to try their hands with the New Folk." He shrugged and shook his head. "We came back for feasts every now and then, but every feast fewer and fewer people came. The houses fell into disrepair. After Jock died, the roof of the great hall fell in and eventually folk stopped coming home."

It was sad to think of the village dying, and frustrating to think that Eilidh had been blaming Molly for its demise. She didn't believe for a second that this was Molly's fault. She still hadn't worked out an alternative explanation, but she had a theory. "So, there's something I've been trying to put together. Can you verify this sequence of events for me?"

"I can try." He said.

"The cauldron stopped working after the matching ceremony." Rab nodded. "Then it started again after Samhain when you and Molly first..." She arched an eyebrow and he caught her drift. He nodded again and cleared his throat uncomfortably. "Then it stopped again when mama left the village."

"That sounds right." Rab said.

"What if the matching ceremony was wrong?" Sarah asked.

Rab's eyebrows drew together. "I dinna always follow the auld ways, but the matching ceremony is sacred."

"Okay, but what if Eilidh misinterpreted the signs when she was divining the matches? What if you and mama really were meant to be together, and Eilidh got it wrong? If the wrong matches were made, maybe that's why the cauldron stopped." She studied Rab's face. He was trying to wrap his brain around that possibility. She went on. "I'm not one to put a lot of stock in this whole prophecy business, but the cauldron started and stopped based on the nature of your relationship with mama. I don't think it's a stretch to say that it was tied to the success of this bloodline you were preserving."

Ruaraidh sat forward in his seat. "My gran's been reading runes since she was in nappies. I can't imagine her making a mistake like that"

"But people do make mistakes." Sarah said. "And how else could you explain the sequence of the cauldron stopping and starting and stopping. I mean I guess there could have been something else going on that affected it. I only have my mother's account to go by. "

"But if that one ceremony went wrong, then what's to say that others havena gone wrong through the centuries? You're calling into question everything we've believed in for thousands of years." Ruaraidh said.

"Maybe it's about time somebody did?" Sarah shrugged looking at her new brother. "Look, I'm not trying to say that everything you believe is wrong. I'm only saying that something went wrong while my mother was here, something that broke the cauldron and changed your way of life. Wouldn't you want to know what happened?"

"I've never known Eilidh to be wrong." Rab said quietly shaking his head.

"Aye, Da." Ruaraidh said, muscles flexing in his jaw. "And she isna here to answer those questions."

"She's never been wrong, or never admitted to being wrong?" Sarah asked. The men contemplated about that one. Sarah decided to let that line of inquiry drop. "Where is the cauldron now?"

Ruaraidh glanced toward the window where Dermot sat watching the street outside. He lowered his voice. "After Jock died, Gran didna want it around. She said to put it somewhere safe, so I hid it in a cave in the hills."

Sarah absorbed this. The days of people telling tales of cauldrons of plenty were past, so she didn't think anyone would try to find it. Still, you never know. People still drank from holy wells. "There's something else I've been wondering about."

"Aye," Rab said.

"What happened to Willie Cross's body?"

Rab bristled. "What do ye know about that?"

Sarah watched him carefully. "I know that Grant MacDuff put his body in Calda House. I looked for any records or news articles of it being found, but there weren't any."

"Did MacDuff kill Willie?" Rab asked. His question seemed genuine.

"No." Sarah said. "Although, I have no doubt he would have if he'd seen him beating Molly the way he did."

"What?" Rab barked his face growing red. He didn't seem to know about the events leading up to Willie's death.

"After she left the village, Molly walked to the castle. Willie Cross found her there and tried to get her to come back to the village with him. When she refused, he beat her up. She thought he was trying to knock her out to drag her back. But someone shot him with an arrow right before Molly lost consciousness."

"Someone?" Ruaraidh asked.

Sarah looked at him. "Someone wearing antlers on his head. Do you know anything about that?"

"Am fear-uaine." Rab whispered, his face registering shock.

Sarah eyed him. "The Green Man? Seriously?"

Rab looked like he might be sick. This was a lot to take in when hung over. "There have been rumors among our people for centuries of a wild man who lives in the hills. He watches us, but they're only rumors. Stories we tell the wee-uns to keep them in line."

"I remember mum used to tell me the green man would get me if I stayed out after dark." Ruaraidh put in. "I always thought it was like the nucklavee or the boogie man."

"Aye, it was." Rab confirmed shaking his head. "Sometimes people would claim to have seen him, but no one ever took it seriously. He's like Nessie."

"Mama said she saw him at least twice." Sarah told them. "Once at the matching ceremony and then again at the castle."

"At the matching?" Rab looked alarmed that this mythical wild man had been in the same place he had.

"Over a ridge watching the proceedings." Sarah said.

Rab muttered a Gaelic oath to ward off evil.

Ruaraidh watched his father with concern. "I reckon we'll never know about that. Sounds like a legend."

"I'm a folklorist. Legends are sort of my thing." Sarah said. "And in my experience, they often start with the truth. Still, I can't imagine the same character hanging around for hundreds of years."

"Right." Ruaraidh agreed.

"We buried Willie." Rab looked almost green. "The morning after yer mother left us, we all woke up and found his body in the burn, right in the middle of the village. Arrow sticking out of his neck. Lachlan, Davie, Gavin and I all buried him over the ridge. Eilidh wouldna hear of burying him with our other dead."

"Because of the fire?" Sarah asked. Rab nodded. "How did she react when the body was found?"

"Well, I wasna exactly a master of observation that day, ye ken. I was sick with shame." He rose from the couch. Sarah and Ruaraidh rose too. Rab pushed past his son. As he stumbled out of the room he muttered. "I still am. Excuse me."

***

Dermot rose from his chair with the rest of them and checked his watch. They were well into the morning and he knew that the rest of the team would be wondering where they were. "We really need to get going."

Sarah gave him an annoyed look before turning to her brother. "He's actually right. We're working at the village hall today, collecting stories and songs from anyone who wants to share. Feel free to drop by."

Ruaraidh smiled. "Aye, that would be nice. Maybe I'll bring the old man by if I can get him cleaned up and sober enough. We could have dinner."

Sarah smiled. "I'd like that."

Dermot cleared his throat, and Sarah and Ruaraidh both gave him a look. He thought Ruaraidh was alright. He was tall and lean and had an easy way about him. He certainly won points when he had stared Dermot down earlier. He offered the man his hand. "I'm glad to see she has some family."

"And I'm glad the stewards are still protecting the sisters. I know my sister appreciates it as well." Ruaraidh said shaking his hand.

"She hasna had any trouble has she?" Dermot asked.

"Nah, not more than any other girl in a big city." He said. "I heard she gave her lad a run for his money though. Oona doesna take well to supervision."

Dermot eyed Sarah, "Must run in the family."

She gave him a sour look. Ruaraidh walked them to the door. "I'll try to come by the hall later."

Dermot went out to the car and opened the passenger door waiting for her. Sarah stopped before going out and turned to her brother. They both looked awkwardly at each other holding their arms up but keeping their elbows near their sides as if they weren't quite sure what to do. They both giggled and shared a brief hug. Under happier circumstances, he was sure he would have found it adorable.

Sarah turned away from the house looking pensive. As he was rounding the car after seating her, he noticed that Ruaraidh was still watching them from the doorway with the same thoughtful look that she wore. He nodded to the man and got into the driver's seat.

Before he had a chance to say anything, Sarah held up a hand. "Before you tell me again that I was irresponsible, I don't want to argue with you. It's been an interesting morning and I have a lot to wrap my mind around. I don't need more recriminations."

He clamped his teeth together. She knew him too well. He had been planning on castigating her for leaving the pub with

342 · MEREDITH R. STODDARD

a stranger, father or no that's what Rab Ballantyne was, and how dangerous that was. But she was right. He felt for her, finding her father only to learn that he was a drunken failure. He had no idea who his own father was. He couldn't even remember when he had stopped asking his mother about it. Still, he wasn't sure he would want to be in her shoes. She might be better off not having found him at all.

When they arrived at the hostel, he turned off the engine. Like the day before, neither of them was inclined to get out of the car. With each new revelation about her past, it felt like they were hurtling toward something. Neither of them felt ready for whatever it would be. The quiet of the car offered a safe haven. Here there would be no new-found relatives, no prophecies, no secrets, at least for the moment. He asked hopefully, "Does this mean ye're staying?"

Sarah took a breath before answering. "It means I'm not leaving today."

"And tomorrow?" He was almost afraid of her answer.

She let out a heavy sigh. "Let's get through today."

"I can cover for you at the hall, if you want to get some more sleep." He offered.

"Thanks, but I think I would like to enjoy the day working." Her next phrase was so low that he almost didn't hear it. "While I still can."

CHAPTER THIRTY-ONE

Once she had showered and downed a cup of tea, Sarah made it to the village hall as people began to show up. She greeted the team ignoring their questioning looks and settled herself in with her tape recorder for the day, determined to make the most of what might be her last day of fieldwork ever. She heard every story and song that came up as if it was the first time. She made thorough notes and helped Jujhar translate some of the more colloquial expressions that they came across. She found the Assynt dialect of Gaelic poignantly familiar. It reminded her more and more of Granny.

She had been so involved in her work that she forgot to stop for lunch. Around mid-afternoon, Isla caught her between subjects, "Let's go and grab a bite. Dermot says ye haven't eaten."

Of course, he would be watching. Sarah thought. "Sure. Let me grab my bag."

They got fish and chips from a truck near the dock and found a picnic table near the church. Eating and chatting about nothing in particular was soothing. Sarah felt like a regular woman talking with a friend. Isla knew nothing of Stuarts, or prophecies, or her newly discovered family. Sarah could pretend that everything was fine, and they were a couple of folklorists doing their work. It was easy to forget that she had been ready to leave it, abandon everything. For an hour she could pretend that things would go on as they had been.

"What did he do?" Isla asked when they were almost done with lunch.

"Who?" Sarah asked, confused by the sudden subject change.

"Father Christmas," Isla gave her an incredulous look complete with eye roll. "Dermot, of course."

"I don't know what you mean."

Isla arched an eyebrow at her. "You two have more ups and downs than a yo-yo. First, he can't take his eyes off ye. Then ye barely talk to each other. The last couple of weeks ye've been almost inseparable. And then ye stayed out all night."

"Oh, well." Clearly, they hadn't been as stealthy as they thought.

"I dinna mean to pry, but he was worried sick last night. I'm glad he found ye." Isla said.

"He really didn't need to worry. I was perfectly safe where I was." Sarah told her.

"Still, he worries." Isla folded the wax paper over the remnants of her lunch.

"No more than he does about anyone on the team." Sarah tried not to sound defensive.

Isla gave her a side-eyed look that said they both knew that wasn't true. Sarah bundled up her trash hoping that her friend would let the subject drop. Isla turned toward the row of storefronts that face the sea loch. "Do ye mind if we run to the shop? I need some shampoo."

Sarah hesitated. The little store was bound to have tabloids. She had been successful so far in avoiding places where people might recognize her. Sarah smoothed a hand over her hair, which she'd been wearing in a severe bun since they had seen the first headline in Stornoway. "I don't know."

"Come on. Yer disguise has worked so far." Isla said looking at Sarah's pulled back hair and glasses. "Besides, who would expect to see ye here?"

And it was likely the last time she would get to spend with Isla. She pushed the glasses firmly into place and said, "Okay."

They walked across the street to the store that was part grocery, part newsagent. It was the closest thing in Lochinver to a supermarket. Anyone looking for more than the basics would have to drive to Ullapool or Lairg.

She followed Isla into the store trying not to panic when her friend stopped by the front counter to ask where she could find the shampoo. Right next to the counter was a rack of tabloids with pictures of herself and James plastered across at least two of them. *Stay calm.* She told herself. *They're only profile shots and you look nothing like that in relaxed clothes with your hair pulled back and glasses on. Don't be silly. You know how to hide.* She did. She'd spent most of her childhood hiding from bullies. For the last few months of her mother's life, when Molly had been at her worst, she had learned that fine art that many kids in abusive homes learn, the art of living invisibly. If she still meant to run from all of this madness, then she would have to live that way again. She might as well start practicing today. So, with a quiet breath she steeled her nerves.

Sarah needn't have worried about the young woman behind the counter. She was oblivious to anything that wasn't printed in the romance novel she was reading. Sarah couldn't remember the last time she was that engrossed in a piece of fiction. Her life was fantastic enough. The woman didn't even look up when she pointed toward the hair care shelf in the back of the shop.

"Not much of a selection." Isla grumbled.

Sarah tried to focus on picking out shampoo instead of jumping at every little sound. "I've used this one," she said picking up a bottle. "It's pretty good."

Isla took the bottle and read the label. The bell above the door tinkled and Sarah glanced up. A man was standing by the counter talking quietly to the cashier. She couldn't hear his question, but it was hard to miss the camera hanging around his neck and the bag slung across his body. The woman behind the counter didn't seem to hear him. He repeated his question a little louder. "Where can I find the folklorists, the Scots Preservation team who are working around here?"

Sarah shifted closer to the shelves and pretended intense interest in the hair care products. Isla glanced toward the counter. "Were we expecting any journalists today?"

Sarah shook her head urgently and took Isla's arm pulling her behind the long set of shelves that ran down the center of the store. They peeked around the other side watching the two at the counter.

This time the woman at the counter looked up from her book. "Have ye tried the church? Sometimes they do that sort of thing at the church. Or maybe the village hall, or the...Oh! Hello, Ruaraidh."

The woman lit up like a candle when Sarah's brother ducked his head through the door that was tall enough for most people.

"Afternoon, Karen." Ruaraidh said casually, as if he hadn't walked into Sarah's nightmare. Sarah wondered if there was a way she could attract his attention without also alerting the photographer. "Have ye got any paracetamol?"

"Who is that ginger Adonis?" Isla breathed.

Sarah shushed her. "A friend."

"Aw, is your da the worse for it this morning?" Karen, the clerk, gave him a sympathetic look from beneath her lashes.

Ruaraidh blushed slightly before clearing his throat and saying. "Em, no, he's grand. No, I pulled something in my shoulder on my last trip up Suilven."

"Och, ye're braver than I am." Karen blathered as she turned to the shelves behind the counter to retrieve the medicine. "Ye won't catch me climbing up that mountain, or any other for that matter. Terribly afraid of heights." She turned back to Ruaraidh and gave him a doe-eyed look as she slid the box across the counter. "Course, if I had someone like you to guide me."

"Maybe you can help me, mate." The photographer cut in. He hadn't been idle while Karen had been flirting. He had pulled a tabloid from one of the racks. He slapped it down on the counter in front of Ruaraidh. "Have you seen this woman around the village?"

Sarah didn't know him well enough to read his body language, but if her brother was surprised or even angry to see her on the front page of the paper he didn't show it. His brows creased, and he bent his head toward the paper. Then he straightened shaking his head. "Can't say I have."

"What about the Scots Preservation people, the folklorists? Have you seen them?" The other man asked.

Ruaraidh tilted his head to the side with a laugh and waved at the paper on the counter. "Ye're never saying that lass is one of them. She's way too posh."

She might not be able to read his body language, but that comment convinced Sarah of one very important thing. Ruaraidh knew she was there. She felt herself relax the slightest bit. Whatever happened next, Ruaraidh had her back.

The photographer shrugged off the comment and asked again. "Have you seen the folklorists or not?"

Ruaraidh turned to the man his wide shoulders blocking the man's view of the back of the store. "Easy, mate. Yeah, I saw a couple of them in the pub last night. But I think they've moved on. They said something about going to Drumbeg today."

"Drumbeg." The man repeated, frustration obvious in his tone. "Where's that?"

"It's a way up the coast. About an hour's drive." Ruaraidh told him.

"I have maps if ye need one." Karen put in.

"I have a map." The man said, his irritation clear. "Cheers."

Ruaraidh followed him to the door and watched for a moment through the front window. When he deemed the coast clear, he dropped a few coins on the counter and took the box of pills. *"Tioraidh ma tha,* Karen. I'll be going out the back."

Karen looked back and forth between Ruaraidh and the door in confusion before saying, *"Tioraidh."*

Her brother stalked to the end of the rack that they were hiding behind and without a word plucked the bottle of shampoo from Isla's hand. He set it on the shelf and crooked his finger for them to follow. He led them to a narrow hallway at the back of the store that hid a metal door. He held up a finger telling them to wait before he opened the door and slipped out, leaving one foot inside while he checked the alley behind the store. When he deemed it clear, he motioned for them to follow.

Sarah and Isla slipped into the alley and quietly closed the door. When it was closed all the way, Ruaraidh turned to Sarah. "Where's Dermot?"

She checked her watch. "He should still be in the village hall."

"Right." He said glancing down the alley. "I know a back way. I've seen at least three more photographers around the village."

"How on earth did they find us?" Isla asked. "And who are you?"

"Oh, this is my...um...friend, Ruaraidh. Ruaraidh, this is my friend Isla Reid." Sarah made the quick introduction.

Ruaraidh nodded to Isla before motioning for them to follow him. They wound through a long alleyway that ran behind the store fronts. The alley ran out giving way to some trees. Ruaraidh stopped at the end of the row to look around.

"Is that who ye were with last night?" Isla whispered tilting her head toward Ruaraidh. "I can see why Dermot's been in such a sour mood."

"Sort of, but it's not what you think." Sarah hissed back.

Ruaraidh cast a quick look over his shoulder, and Sarah noticed the quirk of a smile at the corner of his mouth. "Come on. And if we run into anyone try to act like we're nothing more than three mates out for a walk."

They walked through the trees and emerged on the drive that ran down the side of the village hall. There was a service entrance on that side, and Ruaraidh tested the handle. He blew out a whiff of relief when it proved not to be locked. He ushered them into a storage room. Once the door was closed he turned to Sarah. "In case any of the photographers has found their way into the hall, you need to stay here. Isla, can you go and quietly tell Dermot that we're waiting."

"Got it." Isla said enthusiastically before stepping into the hallway and closing the door behind her.

"So, I'm yer friend now." He arched a russet eyebrow.

Sarah gave him a quelling look. "The people closest to me have a way of winding up in danger. Dermot almost got killed a few months ago by a guy who posed as my roommate's boyfriend. Trust me, the less people know about our relationship, the safer you are."

"You dinna need to worry about my safety. I can manage." He growled.

***

The old sailor smelled of grease and seawater. He was wrapping up his story when Dermot saw a man come through the door at the back of the hall. He had a baseball cap and a strap across his chest. The man scanned the tables they had set up around the room and the people talking, sharing stories. Dermot went forward to greet him expecting a new subject for their project. Then the man turned, and he saw the giant camera lens peeking out from behind where the strap disappeared under the man's arm.

Everything but the camera faded from his view. The hairs on the back of his neck stood straight up. No local reporter would need a lens like that. That was the lens of someone used to taking photos from a distance, like a paparazzo. This was the moment he'd been dreading. Someone had connected Sarah with the tabloid stories. They should have left when they'd had the chance. Dermot tamped down the instant rush of alarm and animosity, continuing his approach and scrambling to find some way to misdirect this photographer.

Suddenly, a hand grabbed his arm and he stopped. Isla whispered in his ear. "Sarah and someone named Ruaraidh are waiting for ye in the storage room." Dermot looked from Isla to the photographer who was still standing near the door. She said, "I'll handle him."

"You can't tell…" He started to say.

"Don't worry. I'll give him the same story Ruaraidh gave the other." She said with confidence.

"What other?" How many were there?

"You go to the store room all the way in the back. They'll explain." She turned to greet the photographer.

Shit. Shit. Shit was all he could think as he made his way past the stage and through the series of storage and dressing rooms behind it. He found them, heads together, talking softly behind the last door. "What the hell is going on?"

Ruaraidh answered. "Photographers. I've seen at least four around the village since this morning. No doubt they've figured out that it's Sarah they're looking for."

"I guess it was too much to hope that the one out front was alone. How did they figure this out?"

"Someone must have told them." Sarah seethed.

He looked at her closely. Her eyes were flashing green fire and she looked like if he offered her nails for a snack she'd have no trouble chewing them. "Ye think James did this?"

"James, Walter, I don't see much of a distinction at this point." She bit out. She put a hand on his arm. "We have to get out of here."

Was she saying what he thought she was saying? He was usually good at reading her, but at this moment he couldn't tell if her "we" meant the two of them or the whole team. Did "out of here" mean away from the cameras or out of Scotland? He thought she meant that they should run together but was afraid that might be wishful thinking.

"I think I can help." Ruaraidh's voice cut into the silence between them like a knife. He had almost forgotten that the man was there.

"What did ye have in mind?" Dermot asked.

"My car is in the car park over there." He jerked his head toward the rear of the building. "I can pull up to this back door and she can get in. You're at the place off Culag Road, right?" At their nods he went on. "There are a couple of back streets we can take to get there. We'll have minimal time on the main road. I've got a blanket ye can cover up with in the back. It's not much, but we're a bit cornered here."

He was right about that. With the ocean on one side and mountains on the other, the village was short on side streets. There weren't many ways to get from the hall to their hostel. And there were only two roads leading out of the village that offered any kind of escape. Sarah was looking at him expectantly. She certainly seemed ready to trust this man, despite having only met him this morning. Dermot wasn't so sure. "Alright, but I'm coming with ye. Give me a minute to tell the team."

***

Dermot returned to the storage room looking grim. Sarah had her ear pressed to the door that led outside. She couldn't hear much, but if Ruaraidh had any trouble getting to the car, she wanted to hear it. She let herself pull away from the door when she heard an engine rev to life in the direction her brother had taken.

"They're going to meet us back at the hostel." Dermot said nervously. "Are ye sure ye can trust this guy?"

In the dim light through the transom, he looked worried. Even at the worst moments in Chapel Hill, he had been a stable presence. Now, he looked cornered, which in all honesty they were. "Yeah. I do."

He looked at the door as if he could see through it to the street. "Ye just met him."

"I know. I'm usually paranoid about new people, but I met this guy last year who saved me from myself only hours after we met. He taught me a little about trust." She took his hand, reminding him of their misadventure on Grandfather Mountain last summer when she'd had some kind of episode in the woods, and he had found her insensible and brought her back to camp.

"Aye and look where that's gotten ye." He said bitterly.

"Don't start that." She said suddenly feeling more generous toward him. It wasn't his fault they'd been caught. "I wouldn't be alive if it weren't for you."

He ran a hand over her hair and pressed his lips to her temple. "Bet ye wish ye'd made that bus this morning."

"I wish a lot of things."

A soft knock sounded on the door behind her. Dermot poked his head out the door and looked both ways. He pulled back in and said. "There are people on the street. I'll try to block the view. You slide under the railing and into the back seat."

Sarah nodded her agreement, feeling the tension knot between her shoulder blades. Dermot slid out the door blocking the view of the stoop from the main street. Sarah followed him and gripped the iron railing. She slid under the railing and barely had to touch the ground before she climbed into the open door of Ruaraidh's car.

"There's a blanket over the back of the seat. If ye lie down and cover yerself, we shouldn't have any trouble."

Ruaraidh's "blanket" was little better than a burlap sack. There were twigs and leaves clinging to it and it smelled of dirt and smoke. Sarah crouched down in the back seat and threw it over her head. This was a new experience, running from photographers, an experience that she would happily have done without. When had this become her life? Sarah suddenly felt impossibly small. The weight of the last year with its visions of her mother, attempts on her life, spying, and intrigue pressed down on her.

Blind to her surroundings, she wasn't ready when Ruaraidh backed the car up and turned down the back street. She went tumbling into the seat in front of her. With the smell of earth all around her and twigs scratching her, it felt like falling into a hole. Her mother's words came back to her.

'It's like I fell into a hole somewhere along the way. Every time I think I've got it licked, every time I think I might find a way to climb out, I just tumble right back to the bottom.' Was this the day that Sarah tumbled into that same hole?

***

"Did they use this in the war?" Dermot groused climbing into the passenger seat of Ruaraidh's ancient Range Rover.

"It gets the job done." Ruaraidh grumbled checking his mirror before putting the car in reverse. "And it's not too much trouble to maintain."

"As long as it gets us away from the paparazzi." Dermot said. He jerked forward as Ruaraidh pointed the car toward the hostel and it lurched into gear.

Sarah lurched with the car and slammed into the back of the front seat. "Ye alright, back there?" Dermot called over his shoulder. She didn't answer immediately, he could hear her breathing, panting really. "Sarah?"

Ruaraidh looked over at him, his face registering concern. Dermot reached over the back of the seat. She was little more than a hump under the blanket. She was curled into a tight ball, trying to make herself as small as possible. He laid his hand on her back. "It's going to be alright, love. Stay with me."

"I'm going to turn back onto Culag Road to get to the hostel. As long as the photographers are still around the village hall, we should be safe." Ruaraidh said slowing the car at the end of the street.

"You hear that, Sarah? We're half way there, love. Breathe nice and slow for me." Dermot watched the road as they turned. He counted three blokes with cameras standing outside the village hall. Fortunately, their attention was still on the building where they thought their target was. He could feel Sarah's back rising and falling beneath his hand with a little more regularity.

It wasn't long before Ruaraidh was pulling the car up to the back door of the hostel. Before he could put the car in park, Dermot was out his door and looking around. He eyed every tree, picnic table, and lamp post, anything that someone could hide behind. When he was sure the coast was clear, he wrenched the door open and pulled Sarah out.

He and Ruaraidh hustled her into the back door. He said to Ruaraidh. "Make sure there's no one hanging about inside."

Turning back to Sarah, he pushed her hair away from her face. "Breathe. We made it."

Her eyes were almost frantic, and she was gulping air.

"Hey. Ye're alright. I've got ye." He pulled her into his arms whispering reassurances in her ear, like he'd done at Hogmanay.

***

Slowly, the cold that had started in her spine and spread out while she was in the car started to recede. Pressed up against Dermot, she started matching the pace of her breathing to his. His voice, his warmth, his breath pulled her back. She breathed in his scent and opened her eyes. She wasn't in the hole yet. She wasn't her mother, not today.

CHAPTER THIRTY-TWO

"They've followed us." Isla said jerking her head toward the door where the rest of the team was filing in behind her.

Dermot went to the front window. Several photographers were standing near cars parked on the street, and near the entrance to the car park beside the building. "Ballocks!"

Sarah was sitting in a chair in the corner of the common room. He could almost see her mind running through different scenarios of how to get out of this situation. Once she had calmed down after her panic attack, he had declared they would be leaving. She'd squared her shoulders and said, "I'm already packed."

According to Ruaraidh, the road the hostel was on would get them back to Ullapool, but only through an hours-long maze of single-track roads. He didn't fancy the idea of getting chased down a narrow road by a pack of rabid paparazzi. It looked like their best plan was on the A837 back through the village. "We've got to get them off the trail."

"It would be easier to fool them if we knew what they know." Jujhar took the seat next to Sarah.

"I might be able to help with that." Ruaraidh chimed in from his place on Sarah's other side. "I'm not one of your group. I can check on the pub gossip."

"That's not a bad idea." Dermot said. "Meanwhile we're all stuck here for the next few hours at least. We might as well pack our gear. We'll have to leave in the morning."

"And go where? We're not expected in Lairg for another two days." Kirstie exclaimed.

Dermot took a breath searching for patience. The last thing he needed in their current situation was for Kirstie to revert to her earlier petulance. He fixed his eyes on the girl and tried to keep an even tone. "We're not going to Lairg. There's no way we can finish the work with a gaggle of photographers following us."

"The photographers are following her." Kirstie jabbed a finger at Sarah. "Send her away, and the rest of us can get back to work."

Dermot bit down on a rude retort. "I am leading this team, Kirstie, and everyone's safety is my responsibility. I can't simply send Sarah away and wash my hands of her. Now, if things calm down once we get back to Edinburgh, then maybe we can come back to cover the rest of the places we meant to visit. But right now, we are going home."

"She's a grown woman, isn't she? I expect she can manage getting back to the city on her own." Kirstie shifted her gaze to Sarah and cocked her head sneering. "Or she can ask her boyfriend, James Stuart, for help."

The patience he'd been clinging to snapped. He was half a second away from losing any semblance of professionalism when Ruaraidh spoke.

"It was you." Sarah's brother rose from his chair eyes fixed on Kirstie. "You called the papers."

It wasn't a question. He spoke as if he was sure. Dermot looked back at Kirstie who was staring at Ruaraidh. Her face was turning red and her breath getting shorter. "Who the hell are you?"

"Is it true?" Isla demanded.

Kirstie took a step back from the group, her gaze darting from person to person before settling on Dermot. "I didn't mean for this to happen. I thought she would have to leave and the rest of us would go on with our work."

He could only stare at her. He knew that she could be jealous and petty, especially where Sarah was concerned, but he hadn't imagined that she would be this treacherous. By the silence in the room, he thought the rest of the team must be thinking the same.

Kirstie eyes darted around the group. "What are ye all looking at? Why should Sarah have everything? She's not any better at this than the rest of us? The only reason she's here is because James Stuart wants to get in her pants!"

"That's enough!" Dermot boomed.

All eyes turned to Sarah as if to see whether that last verbal blow had connected. For her part Sarah looked outwardly serene in her chair in the corner. Her eyes were focused on Kirstie, but Dermot wasn't fooled by her poise. He could tell that she was seething. "And that attitude is precisely why I told James that I didn't want to date him."

"But ye did, didn't ye?" Kirstie hissed. "Because it wasn't enough to have Dermot fawning all over ye, ye had to have a billionaire playboy too."

Sarah's voice was calm. She even smiled, soft and deadly. "You may find this hard to believe, but there are a few of us in this world who see James as something other than a bank account with legs. And yes, I went on one date with him. I did it because he is my friend, and actually a very nice person. But I also told him, that I was only interested in being friends. And your reaction right now is only one of the reasons why."

Sarah rose, and took a step toward Kirstie. Dermot stood close by in case the seething tension that Sarah was keeping in check exploded. "Kirstie, you've been working side by side with me for months now. Have I ever needed you to translate anything? Have I ever asked you how to interview a subject? How to catalog a tape? Transcribe anything?"

With each question Sarah had eased her way closer to the girl and with each step she grew more sure of herself. Meanwhile, Kirstie shrank before his eyes. She shook her head.

Sarah continued, by now looking at the top of Kirstie's bowed head. "Have I ever given you any reason to believe that I am any less capable, less effective at what I do than anyone else on this team?"

Kirstie shook her head again without meeting Sarah's eyes.

"Answer me!" Sarah barked, for the first time revealing a fraction of her controlled fury.

"No." Kirstie said.

"Good. Now, you remember that, because if I ever hear of you repeating that allegation, I will ensure that everyone in the academic world knows what you did here." Sarah turned to the rest of the team. "Can we all agree that we won't tell James Stuart or anyone else about Kirstie's mistake?"

They all looked stunned that Sarah was trying to protect Kirstie. Dermot was surprised too, although he probably shouldn't have been. She had been so patient and forgiving with Amy after her unwitting betrayal had nearly resulted in Sarah's death. Still, Amy had been a friend, Kirstie was hardly that. The team murmured their agreement.

He spoke up, "For now, Kirstie, I think ye should leave planning to the rest of us. Why don't ye go and pack yer things?"

Kirstie barely looked up as she nodded and left the room. Seconds later they heard the bedroom door slam. He squeezed Sarah's elbow. "I'm sorry."

"It was bound to happen." Her shoulder's slumped, and she blew out a long breath. She lifted her eyes to his, and he could see the sheen of tears. She whispered. "We knew it was only a matter of time."

She turned to the room, looking at the others who were looking back with pity. "It's been a privilege working with you all. I hope you'll be able to come back to continue the project."

"Surely, ye can come with us once this is cleared up." Isla said.

Sarah shook her head. "I don't think so. Kirstie won't be the only one thinking that my position on the team is a result of some relationship between James and me. I suppose I can hope that no one back in the States has seen that news. Maybe it won't affect me there."

***

It was over. Her academic career was over. She felt suddenly hollowed out, like she was a shell standing in the middle of the room. This fellowship had been a dream come true. Traveling through Scotland with the people around her had been the best weeks of her life. They were her friends, and they knew that this was her life's work. But not everyone would see it that way. She knew she'd run the risk of people thinking the way Kirstie did.

Still the temptation of the fellowship and of Dermot had been impossible to resist. She had heard more Gaelic in the last few months than any time since her Granny died, and it had done her heart good. She had heard so many stories, been accepted by the people who shared them. All her life, Granny had filled her head with dreams of Scotland. And finally, she had come home. She looked into Dermot's eyes, and knew that home was more than just a place.

He had warned her. She had thought that she could hold James Stuart at bay, that she could come to Scotland and get her answers and her man, and not get caught in the Stuart's web. She almost had, but James had been so damned thoughtful and sweet. She had grown to like him.

If she was as petty as Kirstie, she could blame Dermot. She could have resisted James if Dermot hadn't pushed her away for so long. But, no, she couldn't blame him. This was on her. She had made the decision to come here. For a few weeks it had been magical. But she had flown too close to the sun, and now it was time for the fall.

***

"We really should call James and let him know what's happening." Dermot said watching the street from between the blinds in the front window.

"Absolutely not." Sarah said from her place on the couch. The others had gone to their rooms in an attempt to get some sleep. Ruaraidh had gone to tell Rab that their dinner was off and see what he could glean from town gossip. "I don't want James within a hundred miles of this."

"He has the resources to manage the story and to get us out of here." Dermot turned back to the room and resumed pacing like a caged animal.

Sarah shook her head. "And confirm a connection between us that will have those guys out there salivating all over their cameras. Not to mention, I've seen how well his PR department manages stories. Does the name Martin Carol ring a bell?"

"He could issue a denial, say he's never even heard of ye." He suggested.

She blinked at him, with her head cocked to the side. She wondered if he was cracking under the stress.

He rolled his eyes. "Yeah, alright. He'd never do that"

"No, he's probably sitting in his office on the Mound thanking his lucky stars that they've figured it out on their own." Sarah muttered.

"What are we going to do?"

"I thought I was supposed to be asking you that." Sarah smiled at him.

"Aye, some steward I am." He slumped unto the couch beside her. He propped his elbows on his knees and rested his forehead in his hands. "I feel like I fail ye every time I turn around."

Sarah sat forward looping her arm through his. "You know I don't want you to be a steward. I want you to be a regular guy." She leaned her head on his shoulder. "I wish we could be a normal couple. We could wake up together and go about our days. Then come home and eat dinner and watch TV."

"And I'd get angry when ye spend too much on shoes." He leaned back and threw his arm over her shoulders. She snuggled into him.

"And I could get irritated when you squeeze the toothpaste from the middle of the tube or invite your friends over to watch football."

He kissed the top of her head. "But none of that will matter when ye let me hold ye, and when ye reach for me in the middle of the night."

"I keep wracking my brain trying to figure out what I did for the universe to say we can't have that; that we're not worthy of that kind of happiness."

"Ah, love." His arm tightened around her. "It's not that ye're not worthy of happiness. It's that ye're destined for something so much more."

"But I don't want anything more." She protested. "I feel like everyone else is pulling the strings, and I'm like Pinocchio. All I want is to be a real girl."

"I know," He pressed another kiss into her hair and they sat there for a while. Wrapped up in their own thoughts.

"Aye, I'll catch ye later then. Good luck wi' yer photo chasing." A voice slurred from the front door. Dermot was up like a shot, and Sarah followed after him.

They found Ruaraidh in the front hall waving out the door to someone in the car park. Dermot pulled Sarah behind him protectively. He looked ready to strangle her brother. By the looks of it, he'd taken pub duty a bit too seriously. His eyes were bright, hair was mussed, and there was a smudge of lipstick near his jaw.

But when the door closed on the street and Ruaraidh saw that they were alone, his whole demeanor changed. He was all business. "There are about a dozen of them. They'll be ready to go the minute ye leave in the morning. Some of them work in pairs with one as a spotter or driver while the other has the camera. They're mostly independent, selling pictures to the highest bidder."

"What do they know about Sarah?" Dermot got straight to the point.

"Only her name and what they see in the photos they have; profile, height, hair color. Not a lot." Ruaraidh said. "But because of the connection to James Stuart, a good photo of ye could go for tens of thousands of pounds."

"Jesus!" Sarah muttered. "You overheard all of this in the pub?"

"Actually, I ran into the one that I sent up toward Drumbeg." Ruaraidh gave an ironic smile. "He'd just come back from a couple of hours on the Drumbeg loop. I had to buy him a pint to avoid a fight. After a second pint, he didn't mind chatting about the job."

"I'll bet." Sarah said.

"How many were in the pub?" Dermot eyed the cars parked on the street through the sidelight by the door. "D'ye think we could sneak out while they're occupied?"

Ruaraidh shook his head. "Not likely. They're watching outside in shifts. When I came in, the one I was chatting with in the pub was relieving his partner." His eyebrows lifted with an idea. "Although, if they're spending their off time in the pub, early morning might be the best time to go. If ye can get out before they have a chance to fully wake up, ye might be able to get away."

"Right. Then I think we need a plan." Sarah put in, not wanting to debate any longer.

"I have some ideas on that." Dermot said.

CHAPTER THIRTY-THREE

"Here's the plan." A few hours later, Dermot stood at the head of the dining room table at the hostel, a road map spread out in front of him. Like a general he had gathered the troops around the table to lay out their strategy. All of the research team was there, even Kirstie and Ruaraidh. "You three will take the van." He said pointing to Isla, Ewan, and Kirstie. "Lairg was to be our next stop, and ye're going to head in that direction. Kirstie, ye'll ride shotgun. I want ye're hair pulled back and sunglasses on."

"I'm a decoy?" Kirstie's opinion of the role evident on her face.

"Ye're lucky we're not leaving ye here." Isla snapped.

"Ewan," Dermot said ignoring the other two. "I want ye to keep yer camera rolling and trained on them at all times. We should document what's happening. It may come in handy to explain why we had to stop the research trip. At the very least, it will make them think twice about making any dangerous driving moves while ye're on the road."

"Aye, see how they like it." Ewan agreed.

"After ye draw them away in the van, Sarah, Jujhar and I will leave in the car. We'll take a different route, once we get out of the village. We'll all meet back at the office in Edinburgh in two days. If there are photographers around the office, then I'll call ye to set up a time and place."

Everyone around the table nodded. At four o'clock in the morning, she would have expected them to be groggy. With the exception of Kirstie, the team was wired and ready to go. Kirstie's eyes were red-rimmed and puffy, and her attitude was chastened, if not agreeable. Sarah hated that it had come to this, that everyone was getting caught up in her drama.

"Alright. Let's go." Dermot folded the map.

The team filed out of the dining room to get their things. "And Kirstie," Dermot called softly.

"Yes?" She stopped in the doorway, watching him over her shoulder.

His tone was soft but deadly. "If I see or hear even a whiff of sabotage, I'll make sure ye never work in this field again."

Kirstie pressed her lips together as she nodded nervously.

**

"They seem to have taken the bait." Jujhar said from his place by the front window. "The cars that were parked out front have followed the van."

"Let's hope they don't do anything crazy while they're following them." Sarah said.

Dermot and Ruaraidh both grunted in agreement.

"We'll give it five more minutes, then we'll go." Dermot stood lifting a backpack to his shoulder. "I'll take our bags to the car, and make sure there's no one else hanging around."

Ruaraidh caught her eye and jerked his head toward the dining room. Sarah followed. He pressed a piece of paper into her hand. "This is Da's phone number. If ye need anything." He bent his head and looked directly into her eyes. "Anything.

You call. Even if I'm out in the hills, I'll get back to ye as soon as I can."

She nodded, so thankful that she had someone to turn to. "I can't thank you enough. You've helped so much already, and you don't even know me."

"I ken ye're my sister. That's enough." He said firmly.

She looked up at him through a sheen of tears. "I wish we had more time."

"We will eventually," He smiled back at her and tucked a stray curl behind her ear. "Someday. Ye'll be wondering how to get rid of yer little brother."

"Sarah," Dermot called from the other room. "It's time to go."

She threw her arms around Ruaraidh's shoulders in a fierce hug. "I'll see you again."

He whispered in her ear. "Never doubt it."

***

At that hour, the only activity in Lochinver was around the fishing boats on the dock. The village itself was silent. The water in the sea loch was calm reflecting the sky like a mirror. It looked like the sleepy fishing village that they had driven into three days ago. Inside the car however, the three of them vibrated with tension. Even Jujhar's usually calming presence had no effect on Sarah. With her hair pulled back and tucked under a knit cap, she scanned the streets from her place in the back seat looking for any stray paparazzi. It would have been nice to spend her energy committing the sights to memory, soaking it up the way she had on their other stops along their trip. Instead, her gaze darted down side streets and driveways on the lookout for anything suspicious.

Dermot kept the car within the speed limit not wanting to attract undue attention. Naturally, the slow pace made Sarah even more anxious. They cruised past the neat row of white washed loch-side houses, the village hall, and the church. Sarah looked longingly at the spot on the shore behind the pub where she'd met her father. Remembering the way the barkeep had talked to Rab, and the way everyone knew each other. It may have been Scotland and not North Carolina, but there was a Mayberry-ness about it that spoke to her. This was a place where Sarah could have made a home. If things had been different, she may very well have grown up there rather than being the whispered about pariah that she had been in Kettle Holler. If things had been different, she thought with a sigh.

"Ye alright back there?" Dermot asked from the driver's seat.

"Yeah, saying goodbye." She looked up and caught his eye in the rear-view mirror. He gave her a reassuring nod.

They were well out of the village and heading toward Loch Assynt when another car appeared behind them. Dermot looked back at the rear-view mirror and his eyebrows drew together. "Sarah, can ye stay low in yer seat, but keep an eye on that car behind us?"

Sarah crouched down in the back seat and turned so that only her eyes and forehead were peeking over. It was an unremarkable blue hatchback a few hundred feet behind them. The car maintained its distance for a couple of miles. It dropped out of view when they went around a blind curve. It emerged from the curve closer than it had been before. "It's a little closer now."

"Not too much though." Dermot glanced at his mirror. "It's probably nothing."

Sarah thought he was right but noticed that he also increased their speed. When the car came out of the next blind curve even closer than before, she began to doubt that it was a coincidence. It was as if they were accelerating into the curve, and why would they do that unless they were using it as cover to get closer without appearing to be chasing. The car was now no more than two hundred feet behind them. "They're gaining on us."

"Do you think we should pull over and let them pass?" Jujhar suggested watching the passenger side mirror.

"Nah, we'd be sitting ducks." Dermot said. "Best to keep going."

The car continued to creep up on them, even when Dermot accelerated their speed. "Sarah, ye'd better get down in case they try to overtake us."

With a groan, Sarah crouched down in the back seat. She hadn't liked this yesterday in Ruaraidh's car. It felt even worse at higher speed and knowing that someone was behind them. At least she didn't have to cover herself up this time. "Keep telling me what's happening, so I don't have another attack like yesterday."

"You drive, I'll talk." Jujhar told Dermot. "We're nearly at the place where we'll turn off. Hopefully, we'll find out that that driver is impatient or something more."

"Yeah, I'll keep my fingers crossed." She muttered.

"Brace yerself. I'm going to take this turn a little fast." Dermot warned. Sarah braced her arms against the door and the seat in front of her.

Dermot slowed down only slightly before making a hard left. Sarah tightened her muscles to prevent herself from hurtling against the door. "Keep an eye out."

Jujhar must have turned to look behind them, because when he spoke again, his voice was a little louder. "You alright, Sarah?"

"Great." She said trying not to sound as alarmed as she felt.

"Shit!" Dermot spat.

"They've turned too." Jujhar said, his voice calmer than hers and Dermot's. "They're speeding up. Maybe they're going to overtake us.

"Risky move right here. Let's hope that's all they're doing." Dermot muttered as he sped up himself.

"They're right behind us, now. I don't see a camera." Jujhar said.

"Best cover yer face, Sarah." Sarah bent one arm around her head to obscure her face.

"They're coming around us!" Jujhar's said urgently.

A second later everything jerked to the side. Dermot growled as he fought to keep the car on the road. When he'd straightened the wheel again, "Damn!"

Sarah peeked and could see the top of the other car through the window. It was coming closer fast. It hit them with more force this time, and instead of bouncing off, it must have turned into them. Both cars slid across the road. Suddenly things got very bumpy.

"Ifrinn!" Dermot hissed fighting to get the car back on the road. Tires squealed. She saw Dermot put a hand up to the roof of the car, bracing himself. "Hang on!" Suddenly, the rough ride changed to unnaturally smooth and the whole world began to twist.

CHAPTER THIRTY-FOUR

Coconuts. Why on earth was she smelling coconuts? Sarah blinked against the light coming through the window above her, several feet above her. She tried to shift, but she was on her back with her knees against her chest. She slowly pressed her legs up and away. She tried to reach up with her left hand to grab the back of the front seat for support, but from the elbow down it didn't want to follow directions. She reached up with her right arm and gripped the headrest pulling herself up into an almost sitting position.

Looking to the front seat, Jujhar was slumped against the door. Dermot was still in his seat but hanging to the side held in place only by his seatbelt. Through the bit of windshield that wasn't obscured by shattered safety glass, she could see the mountains in the distance, except that they were sideways. Everything was sideways.

They must have gone down the embankment when they ran off the road. It was a lucky thing they hadn't flipped over.

"Dermot?" She called, reaching for his shoulder with her good hand. He groaned in response.

"Jujhar?" He didn't respond but lifted one of his hands to his head.

"I'm going to try to get out." She said loudly hoping that they could hear her. "Then I'll see how we can get you guys out."

How she was going to get out of there with only one good arm was another question. Through some rather painful squirming, she managed to get her feet under her. Standing up took no small effort. Every muscle in her back hurt. But she gripped the headrest with her good hand and pulled while pushing up with her legs. She could almost stand up, though her head and shoulders butted against the door which was now the top of the car. She took a few deep breaths to prepare herself.

Opening the door one handed was like wrestling gravity. The first time she pulled the handle, the door unlatched, but re-latched before she could get her hand in position to push it up. She wound up pulling the handle and then pushing up with her head to keep the door slightly open until she could give it a solid push with her good hand. It lifted and promptly fell back into place nearly smashing into her head. On her second try, she put her hand closer toward the middle of the door, and almost got it to stay open.

For her third attempt, she pulled the handle and held it with her head. Then she placed her hand in the middle of the door. She bent her knees enough to add a little force and pushed up with both her arm and legs. The whole car rocked from the force, but the door stayed open. She breathed a sigh of relief. The other two groaned from the motion. "Sorry about the rocking, guys."

Dermot grunted in response, which she hoped was a sign that he was regaining consciousness. "I'm going to climb out."

She took a deep breath in preparation. Then she twisted her arm to grab the side of the door sill hoping that the door didn't close on her fingers. She put her left foot on the high side of the passenger seat and pushed. Finding whatever foot holds she could, she managed to get her torso out of the door. Then she grabbed the wheel well and slithered the rest of the way out. She sat up on top of the car to catch her breath.

Once outside, she realized the car wasn't exactly sideways, but it had gone down the embankment and landed at an angle that was just shy of ninety degrees from where it should be. The ground sloped steeply, and the car had stopped sliding toward the bottom of the slope about ten feet from the road. The road where a man dressed in jeans, a gray hoodie and sunglasses was walking straight toward her.

"Oh, thank goodness." She breathed before calling out to him. "My friends need help."

The man said nothing but quickened his step. Sarah was so relieved that she didn't have to pull the guys out on her own, that it was the worst kind of shock when the man raised his arm and aimed a pistol at her.

Without a second thought, Sarah rolled off the car on the side opposite the road. She landed painfully in a bush that felt like nothing but thorns and yellow flowers. Scrambling to get out of the way of a bullet and the thorns, Sarah worked her way as close to the ground as she could. The thorns snagged every inch of clothing and exposed skin on the way. She squirmed her way along the length of the car, trying to get away from it, in case it started sliding downhill again.

As she neared the passenger window, she looked up into the car to find Dermot staring at her from where he was hanging behind the steering wheel. He had definitely regained consciousness and was looking alarmed. Sarah put her finger in front of her lips and mouthed "Be still." at him. Hopefully, if the man didn't know he was conscious he wouldn't shoot him.

She squirmed past the front bumper of the car and peeked around. The man with the gun was standing near where she had rolled off. He was leaning over the top of the car, gun trained on the spot where Sarah had fallen into the bush.

He looked up toward the road suddenly. Someone must have been coming, because he tucked the gun back inside the pocket of his hoodie and took off back in the direction that he'd come from. Sarah crawled out of the bush. She almost cried with relief when Ruaraidh's geriatric Range Rover rattled into view.

***

It was the rocking motion that brought him out of his stupor. Sarah's voice shot through his bloodstream like an electric shock. "Sorry about the rocking, guys." It brought back everything that had happened before they ran off the road. The other driver had rammed them on purpose. He was sure of it. And if that was true, the driver was no doubt waiting outside to finish them off. He had to stop Sarah.

She was focused on climbing out of the car. In his head he was screaming at her to stop, but he couldn't seem to force the words out. If he made any sound, he couldn't hear it through the ringing in his ears. The car door slammed into place and with that Sarah was outside.

He had to get out of here, had to stop her. He went to unbuckle the seatbelt but stopped when he looked down. Jujhar was crumpled into the door, almost directly below him. If he undid the seatbelt he would fall on top of him. "Jujhar?"

His only response was a groan. Dermot pushed what he could of the deflated airbag behind the steering wheel trying to make room to get his legs out of the footwell. He doubted he was flexible enough to pull it off, but he had to try. That was when he heard Sarah call out to someone. "My friends need help."

He froze listening for a response. Seconds later, the car rocked again, and something fell into the bush beside it. He felt so helpless, stuck there listening. He squirmed some more trying to get his legs out. Then he heard a thunk on the car door behind him. He glanced into the side mirror and could see someone standing there with one foot propped up on the car and leaning over it. Where was Sarah? A rustling below him made him look down. He was near panic. Sarah was crawling under the car through a bloody gorse bush.

She shushed him, and silently told him to be still before crawling on past. He hoped she would at least have the sense to stay hidden. He listened hard for any sound that might let him know where she was and watched the man in the mirror. The man looked up sharply, before disappearing. Bloody hell, he must be after her. Dermot held his breath waiting, sure that the next thing he heard would be a gunshot.

Instead he heard an engine, after a few more seconds he heard Sarah say. "Am I ever glad to see you."

A car door opened, and Ruaraidh Ballantyne's voice said, "What happened?"

"Somebody ran us off the road." She told him, the adrenaline of the last few minutes must be leaving her. Her voice was starting to shake. "And he came back with a gun."

"Right." Ruaraidh said. His voice devoid of his usual bonhomie. "Let's get ye in the truck. I'll come back for the guys."

"I'd rather help with that." She said, his brave girl.

"Alright. We need some blankets."

"Dermot?" Jujhar said groggily.

He sighed in relief. "Glad ye're awake. How are ye feeling?"

"Like I've had my bell rung, but I don't think anything is seriously wrong."

"Feeling in all yer extremities then?"

Jujhar responded with a grunt that he thought was affirmative and tried to push himself away from the door.

"Hang on, mate. Help is coming." He told him, hoping that they would be able to get out without further injury.

A minute or so later, Ruaraidh and Sarah came into view through the hole in the shattered windshield, arms full of blankets and sleeping bags. They set about covering the bush in thick layers. Once they had done that, Ruaraidh climbed over the few feet of blanket. His face appearing in the hole in the windshield. "How are ye faring, lads?"

"Ready to get out." Dermot said.

"On your own power?" Ruaraidh asked.

"I think I'll move fine, once I get my legs out of here." He nodded at his legs in the foot well.

"Same here. Everything feels sore, but fine." Jujhar added.

"That's grand. It's uneven and thorny out here, but I think we can manage it well enough." Ruaraidh said. "I would try the door, but I'm afraid the extra weight and jostling might dislodge ye and send ye even further down the hill. I think our best plan is to kick through the windshield down your way, Jujhar. Then ye can both slide out."

Dermot looked at Jujhar for agreement. "Sounds like a good plan."

"Can ye cover yer face, in case any glass flies?" Ruaraidh asked looking at Jujhar.

Jujhar shifted to shield his face with his arms. Ruaraidh disappeared behind a kaleidoscope of shattered glass. Seconds later he delivered a solid kick to the windshield in front of Jujhar. After a couple more good kicks, the windshield began to bow inward. Ruaraidh pressed his foot slowly, and steadily to the windshield until it pushed through. Then he shifted to pulling the torn safety glass out with his gloved hands. Ruaraidh squatted down to the opening and helped Jujhar crawl out. "Mind where ye put yer hands. It's not all solid under these blankets and the thorns are fierce."

Dermot braced an arm against the side of the passenger's seat and finally unbuckled his seat belt. He carefully slid one leg at a time out of the foot well and braced them against the frame of the passenger door. It took some twisting to get his torso down to the hole that Ruaraidh had made, but he managed it. Even with the blankets the gorse thorns picked at his clothes and hands as he crawled over to solid ground.

Sarah was there fussing over Jujhar who had a small cut over his left eyebrow and was moving stiffly. He looked around for the man who had been there before Ruaraidh arrived. "We need to find cover in case he comes back."

"Everyone get in my car." Ruaraidh called over his shoulder as he hurried to collect his blankets from the bush.

They hobbled up the embankment to the Land Rover. As Sarah was climbing into the back, another car pulled into the layby about a hundred feet away. Two men got out and began taking pictures of their retreating car before turning to the wreckage. Sarah ducked below window level. Ruaraidh threw the blankets into the back seat and took off before Dermot could get his seatbelt buckled.

"They're not even checking to see if anyone needs help." Ruaraidh scowled at the paparazzi in his rear-view mirror.

"I guess they figured out our decoy." Dermot muttered.

"Aye. In a second, they'll be following us." Ruaraidh said.

"What can we do?" Jujhar asked.

"I've got an idea." Ruaraidh punched the accelerator.

"We need to get to a hospital. Both of you guys were knocked out." Sarah put in.

"I'm fine." He bit out. He was happy to hear Jujhar say the same, albeit in a nicer tone.

"Hang on. Sharp right." Ruaraidh jerked the steering wheel to the right. Dermot braced an arm on the dash board and one on the roof. They crossed the other lane and skidded onto an overgrown gravel drive between two ridges. Within seconds they were out of sight of the road. Ruaraidh checked the rear-view mirror as they barreled along a rough path. "I think we lost them."

Everyone in the car breathed a sigh of relief. Ruaraidh slowed down to a safer speed.

"Where are we going?" Dermot asked.

"Somewhere we can lay low for a bit." Ruaraidh answered.

"Sarah, you're bleeding." Jujhar said from the back seat.

Dermot whirled around. For the first time since he'd come to; he had a chance to take a good look at her. Blood was seeping from scratches all over her face and arms, and there were twigs sticking out of her hair.

She brushed her fingers across her cheek smearing a trail of blood. "Yeah, I fell into that bush getting away from the guy with the gun."

"That's why ye fell off the car." Dermot said.

"So, whoever ran us off the road came back to make sure the job was done?" There was a hint of alarm in Jujhar's tone.

"Do you think it's the same people who sent Ryan Cumberland?" Sarah's tone mirrored Jujhar's.

"Who?" Ruaraidh asked.

"He was sent to kill Sarah. He wormed his way into her roommate's heart and waited for an opportunity." Dermot explained.

"Are ye serious?" Ruaraidh's grip tightened on the steering wheel and he looked for his sister's eyes in the mirror.

She finished the story. "The police killed him."

"So, ye think this is another person trying to kill her." Ruaraidh fumed.

"And he's using the crowd of photographers as cover. Cumberland said he wanted to make it look like an accident. Maybe this one wants that too. It's a lot easier to fly under the radar that way."

"Bloody hell." Ruaraidh hissed.

CHAPTER THIRTY-FIVE

Through a creek and around a series of ridges, they wound their way along the drive. Sarah alternated her attention between Dermot and Jujhar. They'd both been unconscious, and she was afraid they had concussions. If they were more than superficially injured, they hid it pretty well. Jujhar was developing a knot over his left eyebrow that worried her.

Eventually, a low stone wall came into view, then Sarah recognized the barn inside the wall. Her already sore muscles stiffened. Eilidh MacLeod was the last person she wanted to see in her current state. "This is your big idea? Your grandmother's house?"

"D'ye have somewhere better?" Ruaraidh bristled.

"I don't know. Anywhere?" Sarah groaned.

"You all need medical attention. I've worked Mountain Rescue. I'm no doctor, but I can do in a pinch. But we need a place with clean water and a warm fire. Cup of tea wouldna go amiss either." Ruaraidh told them. "She may be difficult, but her house is the closest. It's the best option we've got."

"Fine." Sarah huffed. "But I'm not responsible for what I say if she goads me like she did the other day."

"You've been here before?" Jujhar said.

"Mmhmm. Day before yesterday." Sarah said. "Someone told me she knew stories about holy wells in the area."

"Ha." Ruaraidh cut in. "A holy well. That's one thing to call it."

Sarah let that comment pass as they pulled to a stop near the kitchen door. They got out and Ruaraidh retrieved a sizable hard-sided first aid kit from under one of the bench seats in the back of the Land Rover. He didn't bother knocking before opening the door. "Mum?"

Sarah looked around his shoulder. Standing in the kitchen holding the tea kettle was a middle-aged woman whose shoulder length red hair was shot through with strands of white. Age had thickened her form, but Sarah immediately recognized the ethereal beauty that her mother had described. This was Sheila MacLeod.

Her eyes were red-rimmed as if she'd been crying. She brushed her cheek with her free hand and sniffed. "Hello, love." She looked past Ruaraidh. "Ye've brought friends?"

Her brother's eyebrows drew together in concern as he bent to kiss his mother's cheek. "Aye, and family too. There's been an accident."

Sarah, Jujhar and Dermot followed him into the kitchen. Dermot closed the door behind them. Sheila looked at each of them, her eyes eventually settling on Sarah. "Good heavens! Don't you all look a fright? Sit ye down then. I'll put the kettle on and Ruaraidh will see to ye."

Sarah didn't know what to think. She was frozen. The guys moved around her pulling out chairs and taking off jackets and making introductions. Ruaraidh set the first aid kit on the table with a solid thunk. Sarah stood there, watching the woman who had been so cruel to her mother bustling around the kitchen. Twenty odd years' worth of bitterness bubbled up from her chest, but she couldn't seem to turn it into words.

This was the woman who had relished telling her mother that Rab had forsaken her. Sarah wanted to hate and expected to be hated in return. She was the child whose very existence had come between Sheila and her husband. She was the living evidence of Rab's perfidy. But here she was bustling around the kitchen, fetching mugs and hand towels, resting a hand on Ruaraidh's shoulder as she passed by. This woman was a mother, a normal one. She fussed and fed and loved her children; all the things that Molly hadn't been around to do.

The bitterness that Molly's story had planted in her turned into a bone-deep longing for the kind of mother she had lost. Sheila stopped in front of Sarah. Her eyes held nothing but kindness. Sarah felt her own eyes fill with tears.

"Och. A nighean," Sheila breathed, putting an arm around her. Sarah turned into the woman's arms letting loose a flood of tears. "I know, lass."

Sheila wrapped her arms around Sarah, murmuring comforting words in Gaelic and stroking her hair. Through her weeping, Sarah didn't catch much of it. Of what she did hear, the most important, and surprising was *'Tha mi dulich. Tha mi uabhasabh dulich'* [I'm sorry. I'm ever so sorry.] It was enough.

Sheila pulled back keeping an arm around Sarah. "Let's go in the other room and get ye cleaned up. Aye?"

Sarah could only nod. Sheila reached for some gauze pads, a pair of tweezers, and alcohol that Ruaraidh held out to her. Dermot stood as if he would follow, but Sheila stopped him. "She'll be alright. I'll not hurt her."

Dermot looked as if he might insist, but something in Sheila's eyes made him relent.

Sheila ushered Sarah past the living room where Eilidh sat face turned to the window. They went into a bedroom and closed the door.

***

Sheila deposited her supplies on the night table and nodded toward the bed. "Have a seat there, love." Sarah sat down on the edge of the bed. Sheila handed her a tissue and waited patiently while Sarah blew her nose and composed herself.

When Sarah had collected herself, Sheila straightened her shoulders and said kindly, "I can tell ye know who I am, and I ken well enough who you are. I reckon ye'll have a few things to say to me, and I've got my piece to say to you. But ye're in no state to hear it bleeding all over with thorns in yer clothes. So, let's take care of that first. Then we'll go and have a chat with my mum. Aye?" Sarah nodded. Sheila's eyes brightened. "D'ye smell coconuts?"

The question surprised Sarah out of her emotional fog. "Yes! How did you know?"

Sheila reached up to pluck a cluster of bright yellow flowers from Sarah's hair and held them in front of her nose. "Ye've got gorse flowers in yer hair."

Sarah sniffed the flowers and they did indeed smell like coconuts. She sighed in relief. "Thank goodness! I thought I was having a stroke."

Sheila laughed. "They don't usually smell that strong unless ye crush them."

"Oh, they got crushed. Our car landed in the bush. Then I fell off the car right into it." Sarah told her.

Sheila gave her a pitying look. "That explains it. Ye're covered in thorns and scratches. I'm afraid this might take a while. Ye dinna want to leave any in there to get infected. Let me help ye out of that shirt. I think Oona left some clothes here ye can use. Ye look about her size."

She turned to the dresser on the other side of the room and rummaged through the drawers. Still unable to really control her left arm from the elbow down, Sarah tried to pull her shirt off one-handed. The thorns that were in it scraped against her good arm and her ribs.

"That smell always reminds me of my honeymoon with my second husband. He took me to Jamaica. He was a bit more worldly than I was." Sheila said from across the room. She laughed nervously. "I'd never seen a coconut. At the bar he ordered me something called a Painkiller. When I got a whiff of it, I whispered to him. 'My drink smells like gorse.' He had a right chuckle over that."

Sarah was still struggling with her shirt when Sheila came back. "Let me help with that." Sheila held the shirt away from Sarah's body as she pulled her injured arm through. "Thanks, I did something to my arm in the crash. I don't think it's broken, but it doesn't want to do right."

Sheila smiled and made a soft noise in her throat. "That accent. Ye sound just like yer mother."

Sarah blushed not sure if Sheila meant that as a compliment. Sheila shook her head. "But that talk's for later. Let's get this clean shirt on ye, and we'll have Ruaraidh look at that arm."

Sheila helped her into a T-Shirt and left to fetch Ruaraidh. Of all the surreal things that had happened to her, being fussed over by her mother's former nemesis was near the top of the list. Sheila was not at all what Sarah had expected.

***

"Are ye sure that's wise?" Dermot turned back to Ruaraidh after Sarah and his mother walked out of the room.

"Mum has experience treating gorse thorns. She treated plenty of mine." Ruaraidh told him bending to examine the growing lump on Jujhar's forehead.

Dermot wasn't so sure. He only knew the little that Sarah had told him from her mother's journal. "Wasn't there bad blood between yer mother and hers?"

"Ye could say that. But the fault there was mostly my da's. Sarah and I are only a few months apart in age. Mum was bitter about it for a while, but eventually she realized that hanging on to bitterness like that will only make yer life miserable." He turned back to Jujhar. "I'll get ye some ice for the swelling. Ye're lucky. Better to have swelling outside the skull than in."

"I'll remind myself of that next time I look in the mirror." Jujhar muttered.

Ruaraidh fetched a bag of frozen peas from the freezer and passed it to Jujhar. "Hold this on it and tell me right away if ye feel sick or dizzy at all."

"Right."

"Now then, let's have a look at ye." Ruaraidh said turning to Dermot and nodding toward a chair.

Despite Ruaraidh's assurances, Dermot was standing near the doorway head cocked as if he was listening for trouble down the hall. "I'm fine."

"Sarah said ye were unconscious." Ruaraidh said patiently. "Ye canna protect her if ye have a head injury."

"I said, I'm fine." Dermot snarled before turning his attention back to the hallway.

Ruaraidh let out a heavy sigh and rolled his eyes. He picked up a chair from the table and set it down behind Dermot where he stood. Then he firmly pressed down on Dermot's bruised shoulder.

"Ow!" Dermot twisted his shoulder out from under Ruaraidh's hand and lowered himself into the chair.

"Sorry." Ruaraidh's face said he was anything but sorry. He bent down to peer into Dermot's eyes before waving a penlight from his first aid kit back and forth in front of them. "Does the light bother ye at all?"

"No more than usual." Dermot said, irritated.

"What day of the week is it?" Ruaraidh asked as soon as Dermot was done with the previous answer.

"Thursday." Dermot looked up into those green eyes that were so much like Sarah's.

"What's the date?" Ruaraidh fired at him.

"Twenty-ninth of April 1996." Dermot answered without hesitation.

"Who's the prime minister?"

"John Major."

"Who won the last World Cup?"

"Brazil on penalties."

"Right then." Ruaraidh straightened and turned back toward the table. The penlight slipped from his hand and landed between them.

"Can ye pick that up for me?" Ruaraidh asked over his shoulder.

It was far enough out of Dermot's reach that he had to leave his chair. He bent, lunging toward the light and scooped it up from the floor. It was only in standing that his illusion of fitness cracked. When he straightened, his head spun, and he found himself leaning back on his heels to compensate. When the dizziness settled, Ruaraidh was leaning against the table, arms folded, and one eyebrow raised.

He would be damned if he let Sarah's instant brother get the better of him. He'd been protecting her a lot longer than this lad. Dermot leaned toward the younger man until their noses nearly touched. It took more strength than he expected to not to wobble. "I'll. Be. Fine."

"Ruaraidh, love." Sheila called from the doorway. "Sarah's arm could use some tending."

"I'll be right there." Ruaraidh said pushing away from the table and into Dermot's personal space.

Dermot barely managed not to sway when he moved out of Ruaraidh's way.

***

"Mum says yer arm is hurt." Ruaraidh came into the bedroom. Sarah lifted her arm as far as she could; the lower half hung useless from her elbow. She winced. It did hurt if she let it dangle without support. "Yeah. It won't do what I tell it to."

"Does it hurt?"

"It didn't at first, but it does now. I guess I was distracted from the pain before."

"Ye should've said something. I would've seen to ye first." He came into the room and knelt in front of her. Taking her elbow in one hand he felt down the length of her arm with the other. "Did it get pulled in the accident?"

Sarah tried to remember. "I really don't know. I was ducked down in the back seat, when he started ramming the car. I did have a grip on the armrest on the door to steady myself. It could have gotten pulled when we went off the road."

He nodded, but focused on feeling the bones in her arm. "Doesna feel broken, but ye should probably see a doctor to make sure nothing's fractured." He shifted his attention to her elbow. He pressed on one particularly knobby bone on the outside of the joint. Sarah winced as pain shot up and down her arm. "Hurts, aye?"

"Yeah." She breathed.

"That's because it doesn't belong there. Ye've dislocated yer elbow. We see it a lot in Mountain Rescue, climbers catching themselves or breaking a fall. I'll pop it back in for ye, and ye'll be right as rain."

He smiled at her. He cupped her elbow placing his thumb over the part that was sticking out. "This might hurt, but it should be better in a minute."

He took her hand in his other hand and guided her forearm across her body until her elbow was near a ninety-degree angle. Then he guided her hand into an arc up and away from her body. With the thumb of his other hand, he pressed the bone back into place. Sarah felt the tension and pain in the muscles around her elbow increase until the bone popped back in. Suddenly, it felt much better.

"There we go. Give it a wave. Make sure it's working again." He said watching her arm. Sarah lifted it and waved it back and forth wiggling her fingers.

"Nice job, little brother."

"It'll be sore for a bit, and ye should still have a doctor look at it. At least ye can move it now." He said.

"How are the other two patients?" She asked.

"They seem fine. But we'll have to keep an eye on them for a few hours. Beyond that, it's only bruises and scrapes." He shrugged as if their injuries were nothing. His expression shifted to a look of apology. "I didna know my mum was going to be here. I hope ye're okay with that."

Surprisingly, she was. "It's fine. I mean it. She's being really nice to me."

"Good. She's changed a lot since she left my father. I think finding someone else to love has given her some perspective." He pushed up from his knees and gave her a mischievous grin. "Since ye seem to be getting along, I'll let her help ye with the thorns. Ye know, in case ye have any stuck someplace a brother doesna need to see."

CHAPTER THIRTY-SIX

The process of plucking all of the thorns from Sarah's skin and clothes took forever. Sheila tried her best to make it go faster by chatting. She was curious about Sarah's work, her life in Edinburgh and back in Chapel Hill. She stayed away from any questions about Sarah's childhood, or her mother. Sheila told her about Ruaraidh's sister, Oona, and her life in Lairg with her new husband, Liam Cameron. They spent an amiable hour or so. Sheila picked thorns out of Sarah's hands, arms, and hair before cleaning the wounds with alcohol. Sarah meanwhile used her free hand to pick them out of her sweatshirt.

"Ye have Rab's hair." Sheila commented while brushing out the thorns. Her voice held a wistful note. It was the first time she had come near the subject of what had happened between Sheila, Rab, and Molly. "It's thinned out now, but when he was a lad it was like this, thick and golden like honey in sunlight."

"Does that bother you?" Sarah asked.

"Och, no! It's lovely hair." She laid a hand on Sarah's shoulder. "No, love. I've had enough of moaning about the past. I was angry for a long time. But that doesna make for a happy life. And I've found that ye canna make someone love ye from sheer will, especially when they've known love with someone else. People who've been in love, really in love, are better at recognizing its absence. And they don't like to settle for less. Yer mother and Rab, they were really in love. I see that now."

It was like a punch to the gut. Not many people would willingly admit to that kind of mistake. But the smallest, meanest part of her also raged that Sheila's wisdom and candor came too late for Molly. "Your mother doesn't seem to see it that way."

Sheila sat down on the bed next to her. "Sometimes, ye can tell a story so many times and for so long that ye convince yourself it's the truth, especially when the actual truth doesn't show ye in the best light. In her mind, she saved me from the pain of being tied to Willie Cross. If she were to accept a different story, then she would have to accept that a lot of what has happened since then; the cauldron dying, the village dying, our people scattered...is her fault. I love my mother, but I dinna think that's a thing she's likely to admit."

Sarah wasn't so sure that was the reason for Eilidh's lie all those years ago, but she could see how the old woman might convince herself that it was, or how Sheila might believe it. Sarah thought about James convincing himself that he was in love with her, or Dermot convincing himself that they were a lost cause, or Molly convincing herself that there was no hope. They might be wrong in her perspective, but they felt those things to be true. Truth isn't always absolute. It means different things to different people. "I guess I can see that."

Sheila gave her knee a pat. "I think that's all the thorns in yer hair. How about yer legs? Any thorns get through yer trousers?"

"I don't think so." Sarah looked down at her legs. "These jeans are pretty tough. Although there do seem to be some thorns stuck to the fabric."

"Here's a pair of Oona's trousers." Sheila nodded at the pants on the bed. "Ye can wear those while I run these through the wash."

Sarah changed out of her jeans and handed them to Sheila. She put on the pair of her half-sister's paint-stained cargo pants wondering if Oona would be as accepting of her as Ruaraidh had been.

**

An hour, that's what the clock said. It was an hour since Ruaraidh had returned to the kitchen after fixing Sarah's arm, the arm he hadn't even noticed was injured. Dermot had been kicking himself since hearing about it. He'd tried to go back with Sheila when she had returned, but the woman had shooed him away before he could even see Sarah. "Sit ye down in the kitchen. I'll mind her." Ruaraidh's mother had told him. He'd almost protested, but Ruaraidh had given him a look that said his mother's word was law.

He felt pinned down and anxious. And his head bloody hurt. The situation made even worse by the occasional hissing sound of an in-drawn breath. She was in the other room with a woman whose husband had cheated with Sarah's mother, and he was stuck out there sipping tea and waiting. Was that laughter he heard coming from the other room?

"Are ye sure it was just her elbow?" He asked Ruaraidh for the dozenth time.

"I told ye." He groaned, obviously losing patience. "She should still have an X-ray, but I think it's fixed."

"As far as ye know?" Dermot's lack of confidence in the other man's skills as a medic obvious.

"Mate," Ruaraidh bit out. "If ye doubt my skills, yer welcome to try yer chances walking to the nearest clinic."

"Aye, ye'd..." He bit off his retort as Eilidh MacLeod appeared in the doorway leaning on her cane. The old woman shuffled her way to the tea kettle and began to pour herself some water. Dermot and Ruaraidh watched her, holding their tongues.

The old woman took her time adding milk and blowing across the top of her tea to cool it. She took a sip. When she spoke, her voice was low and gravelly. "Did that girl get hurt?"

Ruaraidh watched his grandmother closely, "Nothing serious, Gran."

She grunted. "Good. Then she can leave when yer ma's done with her."

"She'll leave when it's safe." Dermot fought the urge to slam his fist on the table. He'd be damned if this old woman was going to treat Sarah the way she had the other day.

"This is my house, steward." Eilidh rounded on him moving faster than he would have thought her capable of. "And I'll not have that *slua*..."

"Not another word." Dermot rose to tower over the old woman. He was not about to allow her to fling insults at Sarah after the morning they'd had.

Ruaraidh stepped between them. Blue eyes met green in a fierce but silent battle of wills.

"Everyone snarling like dogs over a bone isn't going to protect Sarah." Jujhar said still holding the bag of peas to his forehead.

Dermot turned his gaze to the quiet man who had been through the worst of the day with them, without complaint or question. "And what would you know about it?"

"I know she needs to be kept safe." Jujhar said.

Dermot tried to remember his reactions during the car chase and aftermath. He and Sarah and Ruaraidh had talked freely without thinking about things that should have shocked someone who didn't know about her people. The talk of Ryan Cumberland had shocked Ruaraidh, but Jujhar hadn't said a word. "Now that I think about it. You didna seem surprised by anything that happened today. I thought ye were keeping yer cool through the chase, but you weren't shocked when Sarah mentioned the man with the gun, or the man who tried to kill her last year."

Jujhar lifted his head. His almost black eyes found Dermot's from under the cover of his makeshift ice pack. "That's because I wasn't surprised at all."

***

Sarah tied her hair back and examined the worst of the scratches on her face in the mirror while Sheila cleaned up the mess from the minor surgery of getting all the thorns out of her. Suddenly, a crash and a loud thump sounded from the kitchen. Sarah went for the door, Sheila hard behind her. As maddening as the day had been, it couldn't have prepared her for what she saw in the kitchen.

Dermot had Jujhar pressed to the wall one forearm pressed under the smaller man's chin. The other arm was holding a knife. He snarled in Jujhar's face. "Ye've got five seconds to explain before I gut ye!"

By the color of his face, Sarah guessed Jujhar couldn't breathe much less talk. She knew Dermot had a temper, but she couldn't imagine what their mild-mannered friend could have said to set him off like this.

"Whoa." Sarah said trying to make her voice as soothing as possible. Stepping up to where they were standing, she laid a hand on the hand that held the knife and gently pushed it away from Jujhar's torso. "Let's slow down and talk about whatever it is."

"Oh, he'll talk." Dermot fumed never taking his eyes from Jujhar's.

The look Dermot was giving him would have struck terror in most people, but Jujhar looked calm in spite of turning red under the pressure of Dermot's arm.

"Well, I don't think he can breathe, much less talk." Sarah said in her best taming-an-angry-bear voice.

"He knows something." Dermot said through his teeth not letting up the pressure on Jujhar's throat.

The breath went out of Sarah, and she could hear her heart pounding in her ears. Had she been fooled into letting someone get so close to her only to find out he had ulterior motives? Worse, was Jujhar the new Cumberland? She looked again at the man she'd thought was her friend, who turned his eyes to her pleading.

"Okay," Sarah said. "But he can't explain if you won't let him. There's only one way to find out what he knows."

Dermot straightened, relaxing the pressure on Jujhar's throat slowly before letting his arm fall to his side. Sarah slipped the knife from his fingers and handed it to Ruaraidh who had moved beside them. Flanked by Dermot and Ruaraidh, Sarah waited for Jujhar to explain himself.

Without Dermot's arm pressing on him, Jujhar slumped forward taking several ragged breaths. When he was able to speak, he straightened and looked at Sarah. "I've been studying the Nine for years. You are part of the Nine, are you not?"

"Who sent you?" Dermot snapped before she could answer. His fury barely contained.

Jujhar glanced around the room at all of them. "No one sent me. I'm chasing a legend, a theory."

Sarah arched an eyebrow at him, waiting for him to elaborate.

"I swear to you, no one sent me." Jujhar took a step toward her but stopped short when Dermot and Ruaraidh stepped in front of her. He backed up.

Sarah slid her hands between the shoulders of the men in front of her and pushed them apart so that she could see him. "Then why?"

Jujhar pressed his lips together and appeared to consider his next words. "A few years ago, I went to India to study languages. Part of the work I did was in translating rare documents and I came across one that caught my attention. Have you ever heard of the Nava Durga?"

Sarah shook her head. Her education in non-Western religions was only cursory.

Jujhar nodded and went on. "They are the nine manifestations of Durga, the Mother Goddess. They each have their own characteristics and are often depicted as separate beings. Many people view these separate depictions as allegorical, different aspects of one goddess. But in art they are sometimes depicted together as nine women.

"Being educated in the West, this sounded familiar to me, so I began a comparative study of the Nine. Across cultures from India, to ancient China, Egypt, Greece, all the way to medieval Europe there are groups of nine beings embodying some form of wisdom or power."

"And you think that's what we are?" Sarah asked incredulously.

"We are." Eilidh croaked from her position near the stove. "And ye ken it, well enough."

All eyes turned to the old woman as she stump-shuffled into the center of the room. "We've been preserving our auld ways for countless generations, long before we settled here. Ye ken yer power. I've got mine. Sheila has hers. Even yer mother had her own, much good it did her."

"To what end though?" Sarah asked the old woman, "To help the Stuart's? All this effort and special skills for something as petty as political power?"

"Dinna underestimate what that power can do, lass." Eilidh scolded. "It'll be wasted on the likes of you."

Sarah narrowed her eyes at the crone before turning back to Jujhar. He continued. "The final incarnation of Durga, Siddhidatri, gives wisdom and supernatural power. The Egyptian Pesedjet, the Muses, nine universal elements in Hinduism, the nine mothers of Heimdallr, nine maidens of Avalon. These legends don't cross that many cultures, that many millennia, without some element of truth. The Nine are the guardians of the world."

"What makes you think the Nine exists now, that it's not some relic of the past?" Dermot asked.

Jujhar looked at him, "How else would it have persisted for so long?"

Sarah looked over at Eilidh, who leaned on her cane, her jaw jutting out mouth twisted by bitterness. She shifted her gaze to Sheila, motherly and kind. "And you think we're the guardians of the world?"

"I think you are part of them." Jujhar gave her a pointed look. "Do you not have a supernatural power?"

All of her interactions with him raced through her mind as Sarah tried to figure out when she might have given him any indication that she had any special ability. Any attempts she had made to use her gift had been private. "What makes you think that?"

He shrugged, looking a little disappointed. "It's a guess. In every culture I've researched, the Nine have had either supernatural powers or some form of insight that most people lack."

"And all of this is nothing more than academic curiosity?" Dermot asked.

Jujhar smirked. "Well, I had originally hoped to write a book, but I have come to believe that this knowledge is better kept secret."

"He's telling the truth." Sheila said.

Sarah turned to study her, remembering what she had told Molly all those years ago. *I see the truth.* Sheila had been so kind to her today, that she wanted to trust her. Given Molly's experience, trust was hard to give among her people. She turned to look at Ruaraidh. He had outed Kirstie the night before. Did he have the same gift that his mother did?

The question in her eyes was obvious to him. "Not half as strongly as Mum, but yeah. I think he's telling the truth."

"He is." Eilidh barked sounding annoyed with the whole conversation.

"Well, you speaking up for him doesn't give me much confidence." Sarah muttered.

"Why do you think the Nine should be kept secret?" Ruaraidh asked turning back to Jujhar.

He shrugged. "Because they have been for so long. Because if people knew about their gifts, or their role in the world, they would be exploited. Because those who don't want to exploit those gifts will be terrified of them. I want the Nine to be able to continue doing what they have done for thousands of years."

"What makes you think we are the Nine?" Sarah asked.

"The most recent cultural references to the Nine come in Arthurian legends. I traced Arthur and Merlin to Scotland. I believe the parts of their legends that relates to the Nine come from the Gaels. That's why I came to Scotland." A blush rose in Jujhar's cheeks and his eyes met Sarah's. "Also, I saw your research notes. You left your notebook on your desk in the office."

"Dearmadach!" [Careless] Eilidh spat out.

Sarah ignored her. "Except that we're not nine anymore. Three of us are dead."

"We dinna need nine anymore. Only one." Eilidh said her eyes focused on Sarah. "It's time for the Nine to become one."

This again. Sarah thought. She didn't have the heart to argue. She shook her head and stepped away.

CHAPTER THIRTY-SEVEN

They were still reeling from Jujhar's explanation when Rab came through the back door. He stood straighter and taller than he had the last time Sarah had seen him. Now, his hair was combed, and his clothes were on straight. He smelled of mist and sea breeze rather than whisky and cigarettes. His eyes went directly to Sarah. He walked past Jujhar and Dermot to stand in front of her. Sarah looked into the green eyes that were so much like her own. In them, she saw the same mix of recriminations and apologies as she had the day before. But with the alcoholic fog cleared, there was a new determination in his gaze. After a moment of wordless communication, he kissed her forehead and wrapped an arm around her.

"De tha e a deanmh an seo?" [What's he doing here?] Sarah heard Eilidh mutter.

"I called him." Ruaraidh answered her. "We needed someone to scout the roads out of here."

"And ye couldna think of *anyone* else?" The old woman snapped.

"Mum!" Sheila tried to forestall an argument.

"No." Rab stopped her. "I deserve that. I've been a terrible husband and a terrible father. But I havena had a drink since ye told me who ye are. I canna promise that I'll never drink again, but I'm here to help."

"Thanks, Da." Ruaraidh said. "What did ye find?"

"There aren't as many photographers as there were before. Maybe some of them took the bait. But there are a couple parked on the layby near the wreck, and another couple waiting near Inchnadamph. I think I saw one left in the village as well."

"Well, that's grand." Ruaraidh slammed the lid on his first aid kit closed in frustration. "Every road out of here covered."

"And who knows which one the assassin is on." Dermot added.

"Assassin?" Sheila gasped.

Sarah told her. "There was a man with a gun at the crash site. Ruaraidh scared him off when he pulled up."

"Apparently, it's not the first time someone has tried to kill her." Ruaraidh added.

"Because she's the mother of the king!" Eilidh shouted.

Everyone's eyes turned to the old woman in the middle of the room. Everyone except Sarah, who lifted hers to the ceiling struggling for patience.

"Ye can try to deny it all ye want, lass. By the cauldron I wish it werna true." The old woman went on stumping her way over to where Sarah stood, still wrapped in her father's arms. "I saw yer face when I sang ye the song. Ye heard the call."

Sarah pulled away from Rab and eyed the crone. "How can that be true? If your magical gene matching pool is never wrong, and my parents weren't matched to each other how can I be the one you think I am?"

"Could be that I read the runes wrong. I don't know." The old woman said through gritted teeth.

"Yes, ye do." Sheila cut in, a note of resignation in her voice. All eyes turned to her, but her attention was on her mother. "Ye didna read it wrong. Ye lied." Sheila shifted her gaze to Rab. Her own guilt written all over her face. "We both lied."

Sarah and her father both went still, their muscles rigid. He hissed. "What?"

"Seeing the truth, doesna mean we always tell the truth." Tears pooled in Sheila's eyes as she stepped closer to Rab. "I loved ye from the time I was a wee girl. I couldna bear the thought of being paired wi' Willie Cross, and Mum knew it. So, when the pool made the matches, she lied about what we saw. I kent it was wrong, but I wanted ye so much, I let her." Tears spilled down her cheeks. "Can ye forgive me?"

Muscles flexed in Rab's jaw as he looked into the eyes of his ex-wife. Sarah imagined there were twenty years' worth of things to say between them, but he couldn't seem to form any of those feelings into words. Tears tracked silently down his cheeks.

After a short silence, Sheila turned, her eyes red with tears to Sarah's. "I ken what happened to yer mother. I saw the truth of it when ye walked in the door. Nothing I can say will make up for my part in it. I can't ask ye to forgive me, but I hope ye'll let me be a friend to ye."

What could she say to that? Sheila had been cruel, and selfish when she was younger. She had driven Molly into a deep depression, but Molly had made her own choices. Sheila might blame herself in part for Molly's death, but Sarah couldn't. "It wasn't you." She whispered. "It was me. She didn't want to see this very thing happen to me, but she thought she couldn't stop it."

Sheila stifled a sob before pulling Sarah into her arms. "I'm so sorry."

"Gòraiche!" [Foolishness!] Eilidh muttered turning away from them to shuffle toward the other room. "Thousands of years of faithful breeding led to ye and ye dinna even want it."

Realization dawned on Sarah and she stepped around Sheila to block Eilidh's path. "But you did, didn't you?"

The old woman grunted not meeting her eyes.

"Yeah, I've got your number now." Sarah went on. "You didn't lie out of kindness to Sheila because she didn't want Willie. You lied out of ambition."

Eilidh shifted to go around Sarah, but she wouldn't relent. "You knew. You knew that Rab's child was going to be the one, and you wanted Sheila to be the mother. That way you could hold on to control."

"Bah!" Eilidh waved a dismissive hand at Sarah turning back to the room.

"Mum?" Sheila looked at her mother in confusion.

"Didn't you ever wonder why the cauldron started working again after that Samhain?" Sarah asked not taking her eyes off of the old woman. "Tell them, Rab. Tell them what happened that night."

"I married Molly." Rab's voice came from behind her soft but strong. "We met at the pool and let our blood into the water. I made her the bride of my heart."

"And the cauldron went back to giving food. You knew it then and you know it now. That cauldron lost its magic when you lied about what you saw in the pool. That's why it stopped again when you drove my mother out of the village."

"She broke faith!" Eilidh shouted pounding her cane on the floor.

"No, you did!" Something else dawned on her. "And it was you who kept my grandmother from coming back after the war. Wasn't it? You argued for her to go to the States so that you could consolidate control of the village. With the other sisters gone, that left you to rule as queen bee. And what could be more *sluagh ùr* than that?"

"And why shouldn't I rule?" Eilidh jabbed a bony thumb at her own chest. "It's our gift that matters most. Ours that'll be needed when the time comes. What good is your gift compared to seeing the truth?"

"What gift?" Dermot asked.

"I see the present, like remote viewing." Sarah glanced over her shoulder at him before turning her attention back to Eilidh. Sarah pulled her shoulders back and stood tall like her dancer mother had taught her. "Your gift looks backward. Mine sees the world as it is now. While you're so worried about how we got here, I'm the one who can set us on the right path forward. Tell me again how yours is more useful."

***

She's bloody magnificent. Dermot thought watching Sarah pull herself up to her full height. Although he wasn't sure what she meant by remote viewing. If he'd ever doubted that Sarah was a fit match for James, all those doubts were erased. Whether she liked it or not, she was a queen.

"Ye dinna even want it!" The hag shouted at her.

"Who would?" Sarah shouted back. She had reached the end of her tether. "Go ask your granddaughter if she's willing to leave art school. Ask her if she'll give up everything she has to marry a stranger."

"And be sure to mention the part about always being in danger. In the last 9 months, I've been stalked, pushed in front of a bus, had my brakes tampered with, had guns pointed at me multiple times, and I've just been run off the road into a bloody gorse bush!" Sarah was standing in front of the old woman ticking each item off on her fingers. And with each one his stomach twisted. He had brought that to her door. All of it.

"And I'm the lucky one." Sarah continued quietly, her energy drained. "It got Bridget killed."

"Did any of you ever meet Bridget MacKenzie?" She looked around the room at her new-found extended family. His heart lurched at the crack in her voice. "I did. And she was smart, and funny, and beautiful. She had her whole life ahead of her. But instead, she was washed up on a beach half eaten by fish, all for some ridiculous destiny that you tried to pervert for your own gain."

She rounded on the old woman standing still defiant in the middle of the room. Sarah leaned down to meet the old woman's eyes. "You can keep your cauldron, and your gifts, and your prophecy. You're right. I don't want them...any more than my mother did."

She turned to him, and he almost stepped back. He'd been the Stuarts' vanguard. Everything she'd listed and more felt like stones hung around his neck. He'd never felt less worthy. But it was still him that she trusted, him that she turned to for comfort, for strength. It was him that she turned to and said, with pleading tears in her eyes. "Get me out of here."

His arms felt like lead, but somehow, he managed to wrap them around her. She hid her face in his chest and wound her arms about his waist. He slid one hand in her hair letting his fingers tangle in her curls. The other arm pulled her close, enveloping her with all the strength he had left. He didn't care that her father and brother were watching, nor the *cailleach*, nor Sheila. Any opinion other than hers was a petty thing, beneath his notice. All that mattered was that he loved her and needed to keep her safe.

CHAPTER THIRTY-EIGHT

"I might be able to help with that." Ruaraidh's voice broke through the tense silence that followed Sarah's outburst. Dermot pulled back and looked down at her. His blue eyes searching. Sarah tried to look more confident than she felt. In truth she was shaky, and not only from the accident. For all she'd told them she didn't want this supposed destiny, she wasn't at all sure it was something she could avoid. It felt like the entire world was conspiring against her.

She wiped her cheeks dry and took a deep breath before turning to face her brother. "What do you suggest?"

Ruaraidh's eyes went from Dermot's to hers. "We walk out."

"Walk." Sarah tried to think of a nice way to tell her brother that his idea was crazy.

Ruaraidh reached into his backpack and pulled out a folded map and began to clear the table. "I know it sounds mad but hear me out."

He spread the topographical map on the table covered with orange lines indicating elevation and pointed to all of the major roads leading away from Eilidh's house. "There are only two roads out of here. The A837 goes back to Lochinver or in the other direction to Inchnadamph." His finger traced the red line of the road in both directions. "We might be able to get out by way of the A894, but there are paparazzi lying in wait at the crash site and it's not that far from where we would turn onto the road. I dinna see how we can get out by car without being followed."

"So, you think we should hike out?" Sarah was incredulous.

"If we cross over where the ridge breaks here, at Loch nan Cuaran, we can make it over to the road near Corriekinloch by tomorrow afternoon." His finger showed a path between two ridges to another glen where a small road led back to a larger one. "Someone can meet us with a car there and drive back to the city. Ye can bypass the paparazzi and hopefully…"

"Avoid the man with the gun." Sarah finished for him. She looked hard at the map for any other options. Ruaraidh was right. None of the other roads would let them get past the photographers waiting for them.

"We might need to help with that one." Ruaraidh said. "Maybe ye could look and see where he is."

Sarah supposed that keeping her gift a secret had been too much to ask. Still, it was one thing to say she had a gift, another to demonstrate it in front of people who would likely think she was crazy. "I guess, but who's going to meet us on the other side?"

"I can, if I can get hold of a car." Jujhar spoke up for the first time since confessing his goal to find the Nine. Sarah cut him a look that said she wasn't quite ready to trust him. "I have no interest in exposing any of you. Give me a chance to prove myself. Please."

Ruaraidh studied him before turning to Sarah. "I think he's telling the truth, but it's up to you."

Sarah eyed Jujhar trying to puzzle out his motives. She could understand being fascinated with the Nine, she had been herself. Still, he had lied to them for months. His belief that they were some sort of mythical guardians made her more than a little uncomfortable. But Ruaraidh and Sheila believed him, and she believed them. "Where can we get a car? I don't think ours is going to be drivable once it's hauled back up onto the road."

"Actually, we have an extra one in the barn." Sheila spoke up. "It's Oona's. She's not going to need it anytime soon."

"It's been sitting for a while." Rab added. "We might need to check the battery."

Ruaraidh turned to her. "Is this the plan then?"

"Wait." Dermot cut in before she could answer. He turned her to face him and gripped her arms. "We can wait them out. By tomorrow, they'll be on to a different story and we can drive out of here cool as ye please."

"Except for the assassin that ran us off the road." Sarah leaned closer focusing his attention on her. "Is he going to move on to the next job?"

"No, but one man will be easier to avoid."

"Assuming there's only one." She arched an eyebrow at him.

Dermot jerked his head toward the map on the table. "That's quite a hike. Those might look flat on the paper, but they're mountains between here and there. Are ye sure ye're up for it?"

"Are you forgetting that I'm from the mountains?" Sarah cocked her head to the side and gave him a half smile. "Besides, I can't spend a night under the same roof as Eilidh MacLeod."

"See about the car." He looked over her shoulder.

"Right," Sarah heard Rab answer. "Come on then."

When Sarah turned around, Rab, Ruaraidh and Jujhar had gone out the back door. She was left in the kitchen with Dermot and Sheila. Eilidh thankfully was stump-shuffling her way out of the room grumbling in Gaelic. Sarah had no doubt it was some grievance about the *sluagh ùr* in her kitchen.

"I'll go gather up some supplies." Sheila went down the hallway.

Sarah watched her go before turning back to Dermot. "I'm pretty sure the pantry is in the other direction."

"I'm pretty sure, she's giving us a minute alone." Dermot said softly slipping his arm around her waist.

Because it was the most natural thing in the world, she stepped closer letting her head rest on his chest. She breathed in his scent, a bit earthier than usual after their adventure, but still familiar. He kissed the top of her head before using a knuckle under her chin to tilt her head up. He pierced her with those eyes of his, as blue as the water in the loch. "When were ye going to tell me about yer gift?"

"I don't know. Maybe never. The more people know about it, the more I'll be expected to use it. It'll be one more thing that the Stuarts or anyone else might try to control. The more people know, the less it will feel like a gift."

"Well, I think Ruaraidh's right. It will help us avoid running into any unsavory characters."

"Did you say my brother is right about something?" Sarah teased.

"Well, ye know what they say about broken clocks." He shot back. In spite of everything, a small laugh bubbled up. "Was that how ye knew about Martin Carol and the reporter back in Chapel Hill? Ye saw them?"

She nodded. "I wanted to know where the leak was, so I thought about that reporter who was harassing me. When I saw her, she was with Carol at his hotel. It was kind of a shock. I had expected the leak to be a cop."

"That was a shock to us all."

Sarah was almost afraid to ask, but she had been wondering for months. "What happened to Martin Carol?"

"He was removed from his position. I doubt he'll be able to find work in public relations again." He said.

Sarah heaved a sigh of relief. "That reporter thought he'd been killed. She was terrified."

"No doubt that was the idea." He led her to a chair. "Now, about this gift of yours. I expect ye prefer not to have an audience when ye use it."

"I'm still getting used to it, but I have to be relaxed to do it." She took the seat that he'd indicated.

"Alright." He squatted down to her level. "I'm going to help the lads with the car. Ye, do whatever ye do, and we'll make a plan when ye're done. Aye?"

He leaned in brushing her lips softly with his before going out. Sarah settled herself into the chair, back straight and laid her hands palms up on her lap. She drew in a deep breath and focused on relaxing her muscles. When she had relaxed her body, she focused her mind on the crash site.

Rab had been right. There were two cars in the layby near where the car had crashed. One man was lounging against the side of one of the cars, his camera resting on the hood. She cast out further, toward Lochinver. There was a car waiting at the car park for a walking trail between them and the village. And two more near the old kirk in Inchnadamph. However, none of the people she saw were the man she had seen at the

wreck. Sarah tried to picture the man's face in her mind. She
didn't remember much about his car apart from it being blue.
With another deep breath she tried to focus on the blue car
hoping that if she found that, she could find the man.

On the exhale, she saw a bird's eye view of the A894, and
Dermot's wrecked car. She saw the hidden turn off nearby
where Ruaraidh had left the road to get to Eilidh's. Further up
the road, around the next bend, a blue car was parked on the
narrow shoulder. Sarah couldn't see the face of the man who
was slouched down in the driver's seat, but she recognized the
gray sweatshirt. Even if they were able to get out of the
driveway unnoticed by the photographers near the wreck, they
wouldn't have gotten past him. Ruaraidh was right. Walking
out appeared to be their best option.

***

"Here ye go." Ruaraidh handed her a handful of protein
bars that he had retrieved from a locker under the bench in the
Land Rover. She shoved them into a pocket on her borrowed
cargo pants while he fixed a sleeping bag to her backpack.

"Thanks. Where are we planning to sleep again?" She
asked.

"I've got a nice dry spot in mind." He looked out the
window at the afternoon light. "But we'd better get going soon
if we're going to make it before dark."

Dermot joined them, hefting his backpack onto a shoulder.
"Right then. Shall we?"

Ruaraidh handed Sarah a bottle of water which she added
to her bag. He lifted his own bag and swung it over one

shoulder before turning to Sheila. "I'll stop by yer house on my way back from the city."

She straightened the collar of the flannel shirt he wore. "Call me when ye get to Edinburgh."

"I will." He kissed her cheeks and went to talk with Rab.

Sheila approached Sarah. Her eyes brimming with a wealth of emotions as she reached to embrace her. "I'm so glad to have met ye, Sarah. I hope ye'll come to see us as your family here."

Sarah returned the hug. She was still surprised by the kindness and warmth Sheila had shown her. "Thanks. I'm short on family these days."

"I canna tell ye how sorry I am for my part in what happened to yer mother." Sheila's hand shook as it gripped Sarah's.

Sarah smiled. "Like you said, that's enough of moaning about the past. We learn and move on. I've filled in a few blanks in her story here. Hopefully, I can put all of that behind me now."

Sheila smoothed a stray curl behind Sarah's ear. "I'm sure Molly would be proud of ye."

Tears stung Sarah's eyes, and she found she couldn't speak, only nod.

"Och, none of that, lass." Rab said coming to put his arm around her. Sheila smiled weakly and left the two of them alone. Rab's eye followed his ex-wife as she went to say something to Ruaraidh.

"Don't be upset with her." Sarah told him. "She told the truth today."

"Aye, but she didna tell it in time to prevent what happened." He said still watching Sheila.

"No, that's true." She blinked back the tears.

He turned to face her. Clearing his throat, he pinned her with a look. "Yer mother didna die in an accident, did she?"

"No," Rab was a lot more perceptive when he was sober. She had wanted to spare him that knowledge. Sarah looked off to the hills beyond the stone wall unable to look at him. She didn't want to see her own pain reflected in his eyes. "But that's what every written record says, so that's where we should leave it."

"Did ye…" He pressed a hand to his chest as if he was trying to keep the pain from spilling out. "Did ye have someone? Someone to take care of ye?"

"Oh, yeah." She reassured him. "I had my grandmother and Duff."

"Grant MacDuff? Were he and yer ma?" He trailed off making a back and forth hand gesture.

Sarah shook her head. "No, not really. I don't think she ever saw him that way."

"But he?"

"He was as close to a father as I had." She took a deep breath. "He loved us, and he taught me a lot."

Rab looked away, taking a minute to absorb the hurt of knowing that another man had raised his child. "He was a steady lad, was Duff."

Sarah thought of Duff, the man who had devoted his life to Molly without getting much in return. "That's a good word for him, steady."

"Canna really say the same for me. I was a coward." Rab shrugged and kicked a stone across the driveway. "Well, ye saw me the other night. I'm sorry to say that's been most nights over the last twenty years. I would straighten myself out for a while. Then I'd hear a song that made me think of her or see a wee girl who looked like I imagined ye would look, and I'd need a drink to level me out. Only it never did."

"Do I look like you imagined?" She asked trying to stop him from sliding into melancholy.

He laughed. "I always thought ye'd look like yer mother. It never occurred to me that ye would have my hair or my eyes. Doesna matter." His voice cracked on the next words. "Ye're so beautiful."

Sarah leaned into his shoulder. Sheila laughed at something Ruaraidh said, their red hair catching the sun. "You know. You've raised a very fine son there. I hear your daughter is a talented artist."

"Och, that's all down to their mother." He looked at her, his mouth pressed into a firm line. "I'm a shite father."

Sarah watched her brother. "It doesn't have to be that way. It's never too late to straighten things out. Sheila has found a way to let the past stay in the past. Maybe you can too, but you need help."

He was quiet for a minute. "Aye. I think today might be a start. Ye've given me a great gift today. Knowing the truth means something. Maybe it'll help."

"I hope so." Her eyes sought his. "But don't try to stop on your own. You need to talk to other people who have the same problem. There should be meetings around here with people who can help."

"Aye." He looked down. "I've tried them before. Maybe this time will be different."

"We'd better get going." Dermot said from a discreet distance.

Sarah sniffed back tears and turned to hug her father. "Take care of yourself."

"I should say the same to you." He said kissing the top of her head.

"I'll see you again." Sarah stepped back and walked toward where Dermot and Ruaraidh were waiting.

"Sarah?" Jujhar stepped into her path. His brown eyes begging her to talk to him, to return to the friendship they'd shared. "Can we talk?"

She wasn't ready to deal with him yet. She still didn't know what to make of his role in the last few months. She wasn't sure she could trust him. "I need to go. Be there tomorrow. That'll be a start."

He looked like he wanted to say more but thought better of it. He pressed his lips together with a guilty nod before stepping aside.

CHAPTER THIRTY-NINE

They'd been walking for at least three hours by the time they reached the glen. The land was deceptive. What looked close from the loch or the house, was miles away on foot. The terrain was mixed; rocky one minute and boggy the next. It made for difficult walking. According to Ruaraidh, there were established trails, but none that covered the route they were taking.

They crossed between some ridges and were suddenly in their own tiny glen. The rest of the world disappeared. They couldn't see the loch, or roads, or houses. They were surrounded by hills. A few trees grew where there was enough water and soil to support roots, but the ground was covered with grass and heather.

Sarah was the first to spot the ruins of a stone house. On a ledge, overlooking a creek that twisted through the center of the glen. Gray stones tumbled away from what must have been the corner where two walls met. A smaller rectangle of blackened stones stood where the hearth must have been. She knelt down in front of them trying to imagine someone cooking there or spending an evening by the firelight. It felt so lonely, tucked away from the rest of the world.

"Everything alright?" She looked over her shoulder to see Dermot standing between two piles of stones, a doorway maybe.

"Yeah, I was imagining how lonely it must have been here." She stood up and brushed the dirt from her knees.

"Not so lonely." He looked down into the glen before raising a hand to point to more ruins. "Looks like it wasna the only house here."

Sarah followed where he was pointing. Sure enough, there were other spots on the sides of the hills where there were piles of gray stone in regular shapes. Some were obscured by plants growing over them, but the corners at the front of each were easy enough to spot. One even had the remnants of a door lying nearby partially covered in moss. "This must be it."

Sarah pushed past Dermot and caught up with Ruaraidh further down the hillside. "Hey! Is this?"

She didn't have to finish her question. He grinned. "It is."

Sarah slowed down and he stopped a few feet ahead of her. "No wonder I couldn't find it with my gift. There's nothing left."

He braced his hands on his hips and surveyed the area. "Yeah. There's been no one living here for at least ten years. For a while we came back for feast days, but after Uncle Jock died there was no one else to care for it."

"Of course, I couldn't find him either." Sarah muttered to herself, thinking of her frustrated attempt to find Jock with her gift.

"Come on." Ruaraidh held out a hand for her. "I'll show ye the hall or what's left of it."

She took his hand and he helped her down the narrow rocky trail that led to the bottom. There beside the burn on the largest flat space was an oblong patch of green moss that rose up on the sides like a bowl.

"The roof caved in about a year after Jock died. Ye can see where some of the walls still stand under all the moss and rotting thatch. Careful as ye go. There are holes and patches where the ground isn't supported by much beyond a rotting piece of furniture. The center aisle should be safe." He said walking to the center of the bowl.

Sarah followed him more slowly. "Do you remember coming here?"

"Oh, aye." He turned back to face her. "Like I said, we kept the feast days even after everyone left. We would gather here, carrying in our food. They were grand parties, out here with music and dancing under the stars. Kids at school would ask what we'd done on weekends and we'd tell them we'd 'gone away with the fairies'. When the feast was over, and Gran had said her piece about keeping the auld ways, we'd all go back to whatever towns we lived in and back to the *sluagh ùr* life."

He went on casting his eyes around what was left of the hall. "All except for Jock. He never left. He stayed in the village and cared for the houses and the cauldron. I don't think he ever gave up hope that it would come back, that we would be able to return to the old way of living."

Sarah looked up at the rest of the glen at the ruined houses around the village. Most of them grown over depressions like smaller versions of the one she was standing in. "What happened to him?"

Ruaraidh sighed. "Da and I found him when we came to bring him some supplies. I don't know what killed him, old age probably. He'd been dead for a while."

"That sounds so lonely." She said. "My mother described him as the heart of the village."

"Aye, that he was." Ruaraidh walked further down the center of the hall.

Sarah tried to imagine the place with a roof and rows of tables, as her mother had described. Something over Ruaraidh's shoulder caught her eye. "Is that the smokehouse they built?"

He turned to see what she was looking at. "Aye. Da said they couldna have built that without yer mum."

Sarah walked out of the hall and went to examine what was left of the smokehouse. The small square roof had caved in, but the walls were clearly visible, and unlike the rest of the walls in the village these were almost intact. It looked very much like the one that Granny had kept in the holler.

"My parents say they would have starved that year without the food yer mother put by. Once Gran sent yer mother away, and the cauldron stopped, the weather turned. It was freezing and snowed for days. She did save them."

"For all the thanks she got." Sarah muttered.

He made a grunt of agreement.

"Where did you say the cauldron is now?" She looked back toward the hall, as if she might see the shape of it through the carpet of moss.

Ruaraidh gave her a sideways smile. "It's safe. A trusted friend is keeping an eye on it for us."

Dermot called to them as he came around the bowl of the old hall. "I can't tell if it's getting late in the afternoon, or we're too low in the glen to see the sun."

Ruaraidh chuckled, "Yeah, the hills can have that effect. We should probably get going."

"Can I have a minute?" Sarah asked.

The lads looked at each other and shrugged before walking back toward the hall. Sarah closed her eyes and took a deep breath. When she opened them, she imagined the glen as Molly had seen it. A village full of residents, living in their stone houses cut into the hillside with sod on the roofs to hide them. They were like fairies living in their duns. And they'd be living there still if it hadn't been for Eilidh's thirst for power. Instead it was in ruins. After what was supposedly thousands of years, it was being reclaimed by the earth in only a few.

Looking up at the ridge they had just skirted around, something caught Sarah's eye. It looked like stag horns peeking over the top of a stone. They had seen some grazing earlier on a meadow above the loch. It struck her how closely the wildlife lived with the livestock here. Sheep with their vaccinations, dips, and sprayed on markings roamed the hills unmolested as easily as the red deer. Much like her people, the people of *Làrachd an Fhamhair* now moved through society keeping the old ways while New Folk went about unknowing.

She jogged to catch up with the guys and tapped Ruaraidh on the arm. "Hey, do we have time to go to the pool?"

He hesitated. "Are ye sure? It's almost dried up. Mum says it's nothing like what it used to be."

"Still, I'd like to see it." Sarah insisted.

Ruaraidh gave her an understanding nod. "It's not far out of the way."

***

"It's not more than a puddle." Dermot looked down at the black water surrounded by a ring of mud. His nose wrinkled at the earthy smell of rot that rose from it.

Sarah stood on the tree stump that her mother had said was used for the ceremony. It was no longer at the edge of the pool. Now, several feet of silt stretched between the stump and the water. Ruaraidh was right. It had almost completely dried up. "Do you remember when there was water?"

Ruaraidh nodded. "We never needed it to divine anything, what with the matches already made. But Oona and I rambled all over the hills near the village when we were small."

"How long did it take for it to get like this?" She asked her brother.

"It's been steadily shrinking for as long as I can remember." Ruaraidh said. "Some said it started to dry up when the cauldron failed, or when yer mother came, or when she left."

"Or when your grandmother lied about what it showed her." Dermot added.

"Or that." Ruaraidh conceded with a nod of his head.

Sarah stared into the murky puddle wondering exactly what generations of her family could have seen that made them decide who should mate with whom. "It seems utterly ludicrous to think that generations of genetic engineering was managed by swirling blood and burnt hair together in this soup. I don't see how it's even possible."

"Maybe there are chemicals in the water that react to the compounds in the blood and hair. Plenty of holy wells are actually mineral springs." Sarah looked up at Ruaraidh. "Are there any mineral springs around here?"

Her brother chuckled and shook his head. "Now that's the modern lass talking. Always looking for a scientific explanation. It couldna be a matter of faith, could it?"

"Don't you go all Eilidh MacLeod on me." Sarah warned him.

He held up his hands in surrender. "Calm down. I'm not going to bash the New Folk. They're my bread and butter. But there has to be something left of the auld faith in ye. Did yer Granny not teach ye these things?"

"Of course, she did, but she never told me about a matchmaking well or a seer breeding program." Sarah hopped off of the stump and took a couple of steps back toward the trail. "She never even told me that life in her village was different from anywhere else in the Highlands. Most of what I know about this place comes from what my mother wrote. I wish I knew why Granny kept all this a secret."

"My da said that Molly had no idea what she'd come here for. I can imagine that was a tough pill to swallow." Ruaraidh said.

Sarah's green eyes met his. "It was. Then to be matched up with Willie Cross on top of it. Well, you can see why she tried to run away."

"And why she found comfort with my da." He came to stand beside her.

She looked over at Dermot who bent to pick up a smooth stone from the pool's edge. "Here I am twenty-six years later, running around Assynt hating the match that everyone seems to have made for me."

"And in love with the wrong man?" Ruaraidh said softly so Dermot couldn't hear.

She looked at him sharply before shrugging. "Of course, you would figure that out."

"I am fairly perceptive, and I've a little of the sight." He threw an arm around her shoulders. "He's in love with ye too. I can tell, but I think ye know that. Ye probably dinna want to be showing it around the Stuart though."

Sarah sighed. "Yeah. Although sometimes, I think he's so wrapped up in his own ambition that he can't see anything else."

Ruaraidh looked at the puddle and Dermot who stood across from them. "Of course, there could be another option."

"I'm open to any option that lets me choose my own future."

"Well, there is the idea that we instinctively pick the best genetic partners for ourselves. Natural selection and all. So, it could be that ye're attracted to him, because he's the best match." Ruaraidh explained.

"Listen to you with yer scientific, *sluagh ùr* theories." Sarah gave him a soft elbow to the ribs.

"Easy now," He gave a mock warning. "Think about it. The pool knew the right match for our parents, and so did they. Even though they were matched to other people, that was overwhelmed by their natural attraction to each other. Why should ye be any different?" She gave him a skeptical look, but he continued. "Maybe you and your steward over there are actually meant for each other."

"Well, you're preaching to the choir here, little brother. But since he's neither one of the Auld Folk nor a Stuart heir, it's hard to convince anyone else. Some days I have a hard time convincing him." She nodded toward Dermot who suddenly stood up straighter his eyes fixed somewhere behind them.

"What's that?" He asked rounding the muddy puddle and running up the side of the basin.

Sarah turned to watch him. "What?"

Dermot reached the top and looked around. He was clearly not seeing something that he expected to see.

Ruaraidh followed him at a slower pace. "What is it?"

Dermot slowed down but was still looking all around. "I could have sworn I saw someone running by. A head and shoulders hunched over like they were trying not to be seen."

Ruaraidh reached the spot where Dermot was standing and joined him in looking around. "I dinna see anything."

"Yeah," Dermot ran a hand through his hair in frustration. "If anyone was there, he's good at hiding."

Ruaraidh smirked, green eyes sparkling with humor. "Probably the Green Man melting back into the moss and grasses."

***

Two hours, three ridges and a wide meadow later they were within sight of Loch nan Cuaran when Ruaraidh looked back with a grin. "We're nearly there."

"None too soon." Dermot grumbled as he watched Sarah climb up to the ledge where her brother stood. "It'll be dark before long."

She turned to look back to the mountains they'd crossed as she caught her breath from the climb. There wasn't a manmade thing in sight that they hadn't brought with them. They could be a thousand miles from anywhere. The events of the morning felt like a lifetime ago, and she was near exhaustion. "Come on then. I'll be happy to get off my f…"

She was cut off when something hit the rock face beside her sending shards of stone back at her face. Before she knew what was happening Dermot tackled her covering her with his body.

"Are ye hit?" He barked.

"I don't think so. You?"

"Nah." He said, and Sarah felt the breath come back into her lungs.

She looked ahead of them on the trail. Her brother was flat on the ground in front of them. His face was turned away from them. "Ruaraidh?"

No answer. Sarah's heart lurched as seconds ticked by. Dermot barked "Ruaraidh!"

"Yah." Finally, he turned his head. "I canna see where it came from?"

"We'll get to that. Are ye hit?" Dermot eyed him.

"No, I'm fine." He jerked his head in the direction to their left. "Has to be somewhere over there."

"Aye. There's a lot to hide behind, and there's an echo." Dermot rolled to the side taking his weight off Sarah, while still shielding her from any potential shots. "He's got to be close though. I didn't hear the shot before it hit the rock. Within a hundred meters maybe."

Ruaraidh grunted his agreement. He twisted his head around scanning the terrain before looking back at them. He kept his voice low. "If we can get around this ridge, we should be out of sight at least until he moves."

"Right." Dermot said. The ledge turned around the rock face about fifteen feet in from where they were pinned down.

"We'll have to be quick. Sarah, can ye get ready to move without looking too obvious?"

"I can try." She pulled her arms up and flattened her palms on the ground while shifting her feet to get better purchase. Her injured elbow twinged, and she expected it would hurt a lot more when she pushed up, but she would have to ignore that.

Dermot pulled a knee up and braced a foot against the ground near her hip. Ruaraidh readied himself to spring into action as well. Dermot said. "Once we're moving no one stops until we're around that rock there."

Sarah eyed the space between them and safety. It wasn't that far, but she knew that as soon as they started moving it would stretch out for what would feel like miles.

"It's seven steps, eight at the most. He willna even be able to get off a shot." Dermot whispered to her. She was always amazed at his seeming ability to read her mind.

Sarah nodded. Seven steps. She could make seven steps.

"On three." Dermot said loud enough for Ruaraidh to hear. Sarah felt him winding the tail of her shirt around his hand at the small of her back. "One, two, three."

Sarah pushed up at the same time that Dermot did. With his hand at her back, he kept her close in a position that was exactly on the safe side of his larger body. And he kept her moving faster than she thought she could. Seven steps he'd said, but she didn't have time to count them. Somewhere around step three another shot hit the rock face. Ruaraidh who was ahead of them had rounded the corner already.

Once they were on the leeward side of the ridge, Dermot released her shirt and Sarah sank to her knees gasping for breath. Ruaraidh hissed sharply, and Dermot and Sarah turned back. Her brother fell against the rock next to them gripping his upper arm.

Sarah and Dermot turned to him in alarm. Ruaraidh waved them off. He tore at the sleeve of his jacket and poked his fingers inside feeling around and grimacing. "Relax. It's a graze."

"That better be the truth." Sarah watched as her brother wiped bloody fingers on his pants.

He held up his hands. "I promise. I'm fine."

"Good. Now what?" Dermot asked looking around for a more secure place to hide.

Ruaraidh nodded ahead of them. "See that ridge over there?" At their nods, "That's where I meant for us to bed down. There are caves there that make good shelter."

Dermot grunted. "Caves are good, but we've got to get rid of whoever is shooting at us."

"It's got to be the one that ran ye off the road." Ruaraidh said.

"Probably." Dermot glanced back in the direction they'd come from. "He's followed us a long way. I'm surprised he hasn't taken a shot before now."

"He was probably waiting for us to get far enough away from civilization that he won't be seen or heard. Ye could dispose of a body or three around here and no one would find it for years if ever."

"Aye. And these ridges around here offer better cover than he's had before." Dermot said eying the ridges that surrounded the small loch. "Either way he's going to keep following us if we dinna find him first. It's only a matter of minutes before he changes position and we're in his sights again."

"Sarah, could ye?" Ruaraidh waggled his head as if that explained his meaning.

Sarah narrowed her eyes at him. "What, use my gift?"

They both looked at her expectantly.

"It doesn't work like that. I have to be relaxed." She waved back in the direction that the shots had come from. "This isn't exactly conducive to meditation."

"If we could make it to the cave, d'ye think ye could?" Dermot asked her.

"Maybe?"

Dermot turned to Ruaraidh. "Ye're back in the lead. Get us to the nearest cave, fast."

With a quick nod, Ruaraidh struck out down the ridge that they were on, and across a ravine. Sticking to the low ground for as long as they could they made their way around the rise between the loch and the caves. Then they started to climb. Sarah scrambled up a hill behind her brother. She half expected their pursuer to start taking shots at them at any second. Ruaraidh looked back at her. "The cave entrance is behind this boulder here. If ye lose sight of me, keep going. Ye won't miss it."

He reached the top of the rise but stayed hunched down. Sarah followed his lead and hustled her way around the boulder and ducked into the narrow opening careful not to snag her backpack. By the time her eyes had adjusted to the change in light, Dermot was coming in after them.

"Is this safe enough for ye to do whatever ye do?" he asked.

"Yeah. This should do." She sat down with her back to a rock wall and prepared herself to cast out. She took a deep breath and closed her eyes, but still couldn't relax. She could feel Dermot watching her. She cracked her eyes open and raised an eyebrow at him. He shrugged and turned to look out the opening of the cave.

Sarah closed her eyes feeling the cold stone at her back and the damp air of the cave around her. She took in a deep breath and let it out. With each breath her body relaxed and got heavier, but her awareness heightened. Each breath freed her mind from her body until she was floating. She could see herself in the cave, see Dermot and Ruaraidh quietly standing guard and looking the other way. Further out she saw the ridges they'd crossed and the loch beyond them. She sought out the direction they thought the shots had come from. It wasn't long before she saw him.

"He's coming." She gasped after jolting back to herself.

Dermot spun around and knelt in front of her. "Coming here?"

"I don't know exactly, but he came around the ridge where we were when he shot at us." She wished she could have seen his intent. "He's got a rifle, and probably the same pistol he had at the car."

"So, it is the same bloke?" He asked.

She nodded. "He's definitely looking for us."

"That might not be bad." Dermot said looking thoughtful. "We know where he's headed, but he can't see us. That gives us an advantage. I wish I could get you out of here."

"We can." Ruaraidh said from the cave opening. "This cave runs into another. If we go deeper, we can get to the cave I meant to spend the night in without ever going above ground.

Dermot thought about it for a few heartbeats. "That's perfect. Ye take Sarah there through the caves. I'll deal with him and catch up."

"Right. Take this." Ruaraidh handed him a survival knife from the sheath on his belt. "When ye're done, head for the back of the cave and take the first left, then the second left after that. Ye won't miss us."

"Spare torch?" Dermot asked.

"No!" Sarah burst out. "Are you crazy?"

"I'm yer steward." He said calmly looking in her eyes as Ruaraidh shoved a flashlight into his pocket.

She shook her head. "I'm not leaving you."

"Yes, ye are."

Sarah still shook her head. "No. You don't have to do this alone. We can help."

He gave her a look of patience. "I'm trained for this. Ye're not. Ye'll be more distraction than help."

Sarah felt Ruaraidh's hands at her shoulders ready to pull her away. She reached out and grabbed a fistful of Dermot's shirt, refusing to let go. He cupped the back of her head and pulled her into a fierce and too short kiss. His other hand pried her fingers open. "You are what's important. Go with yer brother. I'll be there in a tic."

With a nod to Ruaraidh who slipped an arm around her waist and pulled her toward the back of the cave, Dermot stepped out into the fading daylight.

CHAPTER FORTY

Dermot stood on the ledge in front of the cave and looked in the direction Sarah had indicated. He didn't really understand her so-called 'gift', but he had faith in her. He looked around for a place to hide. Surprise would be his only advantage. The other man would be well armed and all he had was Ruaraidh's knife. He tested the edge with his thumb. At least Sarah's brother kept his knife sharp.

There was an outcropping right above and to the side of the cave entrance. He should be able to hide behind it until the assassin was within striking distance. He climbed up and hid behind the outcrop. From there he could see the approach to the cave, but not the ledge itself. He took a deep breath and began to prepare.

Some steward he'd been. For months he'd felt useless at protecting Sarah. First, he'd been keeping her at arm's length, watching other stewards look to her safety. Then he hadn't been able to protect her from James, or the menace of the press, or even a jealous girl. But this he could do. He was trained to fight, to kill even. There weren't enough research papers, or field notes, or tweed jackets in the world to take that out of him.

There he was. A man came into view making his way along the top of the rise on the other side. He had a rifle slung over his shoulder, a knife strapped to one thigh and a pistol strapped to the other. Dermot felt the muscles in his shoulders shift and flex ready for action. The other man's eyes were trained on the bottom of the ravine, hoping to get ahead of them no doubt.

Dermot saw when the man spotted the entrance to the cave. He headed for the cave, scanning the ravine for signs of his quarry. When the assassin decided that was where they had gone, he started the climb. Dermot had to admire his cunning. If they were still hiding in the cave the man wouldn't want to alert them to his approach. Dermot hoped like hell that Ruaraidh had gotten Sarah far enough away by now that she wouldn't hear anything that was about to happen.

He kept an eye on the man until he got too close to see from Dermot's hiding place. Then he had to listen. There was the slight shuffle of rubber soles on the rock ledge. Dermot counted one second, two, giving the man enough time to get into the cave. Then Dermot swung himself over the outcrop and dropped softly onto the ledge. The man, rifle at the ready was facing into the cave. He froze. Rather than turn around the man swung back with the butt of the rifle aiming for Dermot's face. Dermot dodged left and threaded his arm under the man's to grab the stock of the gun. Hooking his foot behind the man's ankle he shoved the assassin to the ground breaking the man's hold on the rifle. Dermot brought the rifle to his shoulder and aimed it at the assassin on the ground.

Undeterred, the assassin moved to grab the pistol at his hip. In a blink Dermot shifted his aim and fired a shot into the man's shoulder. "Next one's in yer head, mate."

The man froze there on the ground looking up at Dermot. Panting from the shock and the pain in his shoulder, his dark eyes were full of pure hate.

"Who sent ye?" Dermot asked, his voice soft and deadly calm.

The man grimaced with pain and said through gritted teeth. "You know I will not tell you."

His English was good, but Dermot heard something Latin in his continental vowels and sharp consonants. "What are ye, Italian? Spanish?"

The man coughed and raised an eyebrow at him.

"Invigilare?" Dermot asked, keeping the rifle pointed between the man's eyes.

"You're going to kill me anyway. Why would I tell you?" The man huffed.

"What have ye got to lose?" Dermot asked.

The man smirked through the pain, "Salvation."

A sound came from inside the cave. All he could think of was Sarah coming back. For half a second, no more, he took his eyes off the man. That was all the assassin needed. The man grabbed the barrel of the rifle with his good arm and yanked sending the gun skittering off into the dark of the cave. Dermot pitched forward but managed to stay on his feet. The assassin grabbed the knife that was strapped to his thigh and went for Dermot's legs. He must have been aiming for the Achilles tendon, but Dermot shifted in time and the knife sliced a trail of fire up his calf. Reaching for Ruaraidh's knife that he had tucked into his belt, Dermot whirled to face his attacker.

Half sitting on the ground, the other man kicked at the leg he'd just sliced. Dermot roared in pain and fell onto the man grabbing the assassin's knife hand as he went down. He brought his own knife to the man's throat. The assassin managed to use his injured arm to grab Dermot, but there was no strength left in the shoulder. Try as he might he couldn't stop Dermot from dragging the knife across his throat.

The man's eyes went wide, his lips moving as if he was trying to speak, but Dermot was deaf to all but the sound of the blood roaring in his ears. He rested a forearm on the man's chest unable to hold himself up anymore. After a few seconds, the fog cleared. Dermot heard the gurgling of blood and air coming from the throat he'd slit. He pushed himself up and scrambled away from the still dying man. Back against the wall of the cave, he sat there watching what was left of the man's life ebb away.

He had trained for that, known it could happen someday, but nothing prepares a man for the intimacy of looking someone in the eye as you kill him. That was someone's son, someone's brother, maybe someone's lover. And he had killed him to save the woman he'd pledge his life for. As the life drained away from his opponent, awareness rose up in Dermot. His knee and calf were throbbing. His shoulders ached. The adrenalin that had kept him going ran out, and the stone wall behind him felt like ice making him shiver.

He needed to close his eyes for a minute. Only a minute, and then he would be all right. A minute of quiet, and he would go find Sarah.

***

They had already taken the first turn down the dark passages of the cave with only Ruaraidh's flashlight to guide them when Sarah heard the shot echo off the cave walls. Panic surged through her. She whirled around heart in her throat, ready to run back to Dermot's side. Ruaraidh was only a step or two behind her and she smashed right into him. He'd been ready for it and his arms gripped her tight.

"I have to go back."

"That is the last thing ye have to do." His voice was patient, but firm.

"He needs me!" She pushed at Ruaraidh's arms desperate to get to Dermot.

"Think, Sarah!" Ruaraidh gave her a good shake. "If he fired the shot, then he's got the situation in hand. If he's hit, then the other man has the upper hand and ye'll be in even more danger. I canna let ye go."

She watched her brother in the dim fringe of the flashlight beam for several heartbeats, listening for any further sound from the cave behind them. There was nothing more. It was silent as a grave. Sarah closed her eyes and drew in a long breath trying to calm her racing heart, to think rationally when all she wanted to do was take off running into the pitch black of the cave.

When she exhaled, Ruaraidh's hold gentled. "He sent us away for a reason. Aye? He's trained for combat. I'm sure that he'll catch up to us. Ye have to have faith in the man."

"I can't do this without him." She breathed.

"I know it feels that way. I think ye're stronger than ye know." Her brother smoothed a hand over her hair. "Now we're almost to the next passage, and the place where I meant to spend the night. We can wait for him there. He'll come."

"What if he doesn't?" She asked, her voice small.

"Then we'll figure it out. What kind of brother would I be, if I left ye unprotected?"

After another minute of listening to the silence, Sarah allowed Ruaraidh to guide her to the next turn in the passage.

The ceiling got lower and lower until even Sarah had to slouch to avoid hitting her head. The floor of the cave soon tilted up in an incline which became slippery.

"There are footholds." Ruaraidh shined the flashlight beam over her shoulder, aiming it at the places in the cave floor where there were small, evenly spaced hollows in the stone big enough for part of an adult foot.

"Did you carve these?" Sarah asked putting her toes into the first foothold.

"Nah, they've been here as long as I remember." He started climbing behind her.

Less than a dozen steps up the incline, the cave floor leveled out, and the ceiling was high enough that she could stand upright.

"Do you think Dermot will be able to find this if he's injured?" She looked back at the makeshift stairs behind them.

"I think if Dermot has breath left in him, some slippery rocks and darkness aren't going to keep him away from you." He gave her a gentle nudge forward, and she followed the beam of his flashlight. "If ye can wait until we get to where we're going, ye can use yer gift to find him."

Sarah wasn't sure if she wanted to use her gift. She was afraid she might look for him and see him dead on the hillside. She tamped down her panic and kept walking. A few minutes later, Sarah's nose wrinkled. "Is that peat smoke I smell?"

Ruaraidh sniffed behind her. "I wasna expecting anyone else to be here."

"Should we stop?" Sarah's pulse kicked up. Were they walking into an ambush?

"No. I know who it probably is. He'll no be a problem. In fact, he might be able to help us." Ruaraidh said, sounding only a little less than certain.

"Right." Sarah followed the flashlight beam until the cave narrowed in front of them before taking a turn around a wall. If she hadn't had Ruaraidh to guide her, Sarah might have thought they had reached a dead end. But the narrow passage took a sharp right. A faint glow outlined another sharp turn back to the left. Ruaraidh stopped Sarah before she could follow it.

"Let me go first, in case it isna who I expect." Ruaraidh whispered passing her. He turned off his flashlight and leaned around the corner.

He must not have seen what he was looking for. He leaned back to Sarah and whispered. "Stay here." In a way that brooked no argument.

Sarah stayed rooted to the spot as Ruaraidh silently stepped around the corner. She held her breath half-expecting to hear a scuffle on the other side of the opening.

After several breathless seconds she heard her brother heave a gusty sigh, saying, *"Sin thu, a charaid."* [There you are, friend.]

Another voice answered in Gaelic, "Who else would it be, lad?"

"I didn't know you would be here." Ruaraidh continued in their native language.

"I am never far from where she is." The other man said. Then he addressed Sarah. "You can come in, Princess. You are welcome here."

Sarah felt a cold finger run down her spine. She would never get used to being called princess, but it didn't seem to strike the same level of terror that it had before. She stepped around the corner into a large chamber.

It was practically furnished with a rustic wooden table and a couple of chairs. Near the cave opening where she could see that the sun had set, in the simple hearth was the orange glow of a peat fire, with a kettle hanging over it on an iron frame. There was even a rustic bed set heaped with furs and plain woolen blankets. At first glance it looked like the hovel of a hermit.

The man standing next to the table was entirely at ease, as if this were his home. Sarah stayed close to her brother, unsure of this new stranger. The man's hair was long and pulled back into a ponytail that was clubbed in the way that men used to centuries ago. His beard was neatly trimmed and showed more salt than pepper. He looked to be in his late fifties or early sixties by the crow's feet that appeared when he gave her a warm smile.

"My name is Lailoken Green. I have waited a long time to meet you." His voice was both confident and kind when he walked toward her and offered his hand.

Sarah fought the urge to hide behind her brother. For all his grandfatherly warmth, there was something about this man that made her uneasy. For one thing, he knew much more about her than she did about him. She shook his hand and he enveloped hers in both of his. His grip was firm. It left no doubt that he was glad to meet her.

Ruaraidh put his arm around her shoulders and gave her a reassuring squeeze. "Lailoken is *An Draoidh-Uaine.*"

Sarah looked sharply from Ruaraidh back to the man in front of them, The Green Druid. *"An Draidh-Uaine?"*

The man's smile grew. "I go by many names, that is but one of them."

"I'll bet you do." Sarah said. "You look very familiar."

Green's cheeks pinkened and he looked a touch embarrassed. "You have seen me before."

With that he straightened his shoulders and turned to the side. His whole demeanor changed reminding her of an annoyed professor. Holding his hands up like a book, he gave her a sidelong look and raised a superior eyebrow. Instantly, Sarah was taken back to the library at the university. He'd been there on the day when she'd found the book of Burns poems on her bag. When he saw the recognition in her face, he shifted again. This time, his shoulder's slumped and his eyes went glassy. He looked past her. She didn't need a worn-out coat or a rusted can to remember the homeless man she'd given the money to on the street in Edinburgh.

"You've been following me." She accused, taking a half step back only to bump into Ruaraidh.

"I have, princess, though it's not what you think." He drew her to the table and invited her to sit down. Sarah looked back at Ruaraidh who was retrieving a water bottle from his bag.

"I'm going to keep watch over here." With a guilty shrug, he jerked his head toward the passage back into the cave.

CHAPTER FORTY-ONE

"There is no need to be afraid." Green said kindly as Sarah took a seat at the table. "Your brother will not leave us. Can I offer you a cup of tea?"

"I don't know." She didn't take her eyes off of him as he bustled around between the table and the kettle above the fire. "Am I going to end up stuck in this cave forever if I drink it."

His laugh was low and friendly as he pulled a box of commercial tea bags out of his pack. "It will only warm you on a cold night, and perhaps help you relax a bit."

"I'll relax when my steward gets here." She told him.

Green looked up from the kettle where he'd been pouring water for tea. His eyes met hers, and they held nothing but certainty. "And he will. Never doubt it."

"I wish I had your confidence." She muttered.

He patted her hand setting a sturdy looking cup in front of her. "You have had many disappointments, my dear, and will probably endure many more but Dermot Sinclair will not be one of them."

"You seem to know a lot about me." Her suspicion roused again. She eyed the cup in front of her still unsure if she should drink.

He picked up the cup and drank from it himself without any hint of reproach. He set it back in front of her and took a seat across the table. "It is my calling to observe and assist your people."

"Are you from *Làrachd an Fhamhair*?" She didn't remember her mother mentioning him.

"No, I am something else." He said without expanding on what kind of something else he was. "But I have been watching your progress from the time that I met your mother in Inverness."

Sarah gasped with recognition. "Mr. Green! You helped my mother get back to America."

He bowed his head in acknowledgment. "As I said, my calling is to observe and assist when needed."

"What exactly does that entail?" She took a sip of the perfectly normal tasting tea.

He shrugged. "It can be anything that is needed, such as paying for a plane ticket as I did for your mother and her steward. Sometimes I gently guide events in the necessary direction. Sometimes I care for an important treasure."

He shifted his eyes to a corner near the hearth. She hadn't noticed it before in the dim glow from the fire, but there stood a large black cauldron on an iron stand.

"Is that?" Sarah asked trying to remember what Ruaraidh had said about the cauldron's location.

"It is." Green nodded. "Your brother brought it to me after Jock MacKenzie died. I think Jock always hoped that it would start working again. He had never known a different life, and never wanted to."

"And now?" A small part of her hoped that Ruaraidh's theory about the cauldron was right. Maybe now that she was here, along with Dermot, the cauldron would start again. It would be something she could hold up as proof that she and Dermot were meant to be together. "Does it?"

"It holds rainwater. Nothing more." His eyes filled with pity as if he had read the hope in hers. "I believe the cauldron's time has passed. It was a tool for preserving your people. Now, the only thing left to preserve is you."

"I still can't understand that." Sarah shook her head. "I'm different from other folks sure, but I'm not some kind of lost princess."

"Well, not lost." He smiled. "I always knew where you were."

"And yet, I've been abused, robbed of opportunities, endured heartbreak, and survived numerous attempts on my life."

He sighed and gave her a fatherly look. "What sort of leader would you grow into, if someone was always fixing things for you? I aid your people when needed."

"Like when mama broke down."

He nodded. "And when you lost hope in your research."

She thought she understood. "And you observe us."

He nodded.

Sarah raised an eyebrow in suspicion. "Did you observe Eilidh MacKenzie lie about the matches made that summer?"

"I did. And if your parents had not found each other on their own, I would have done something to draw them together. I did offer young Willie Cross a place to stay after he left the village."

"He stayed here?"

He leaned back in his chair taking a sip of tea. "The poor lad was so lost and confused. I hoped that teaching him some of what I know about your people could ease some of the stress on his mind." He set his cup back on the table. "I fear I was too late to help him. When he learned of Eilidh's perfidy, I'm afraid he became unhinged."

"That was when he set her cottage on fire." Sarah remembered her mother's story about seeing Willie Cross scampering about the hills and shouting about Eilidh's lies after setting the fire.

"Yes, and why he was so determined that your mother should return to the village." Green looked down at the table top as if he were seeing the memory of that awful day when Willie Cross had beaten her pregnant mother.

She also remembered how the assault ended. Willie had been shot with an arrow by a mysterious figure with antlers. "Was it you who shot him?"

He nodded, not meeting her eyes. "I wish I hadn't been forced to. He was a sad figure."

"You saved us."

"I had to." His gaze met hers. "You had to be born."

"Because of whatever this prophecy is." She let her shoulders slump as she leaned back in her chair. Her tone was full of skepticism.

"You doubt it." He cocked his head to the side.

"Yes. I do." She wasn't going to apologize for wanting to make her own choices. "I may have grown up in the old ways, but I'm from the modern world. *Sluagh ùr*, if you want to call me that. People expect to make their own choices, run their own lives. I have a career, a life of my own that I don't want to abandon."

Green leaned forward bracing his elbows on the table. "Have you considered that your choice of career, the life that you have built is what led you to this destiny? Perhaps your upbringing, the difficulties you've had, your course of study, were all in preparation for what comes next?"

"What does come next?"

He gave a soft laugh. "I'm afraid I'm not the one with the gift of seeing the future. You will have to take it as it comes."

Sarah sighed. "You know so much about us. Can you tell me why my grandmother kept all of this a secret for so long?"

His eyebrows lifted, and he pressed his lips together. He seemed to be considering what to tell her. After a moment's thought he rose. "I think perhaps it is best if I show you. Did your grandmother ever teach you to scry?"

"I saw her do it on occasion, but she never taught me." She told him as he moved to the corner near the cauldron. "I thought that was for looking into the future."

He smiled at her over his shoulder as he pulled something from a shelf. "It can be, but it can be used to see anything that isn't easily viewed on your own."

He returned to the table with a wide shallow bowl filled with rainwater. The inside was glazed black with a shine that reflected any hint of light. "You merely have to concentrate on the question you want answered."

"It can't be that simple." She watched as he went to his pack.

He retrieved a small canvas bag the size of a man's shaving kit from deep inside his backpack. "I have a few tools to help you on your way."

He returned to the table and opened the bag. He pulled out a bundle of herbs and a short, wide candle that looked like beeswax. Lighting the candle, he set it near the bowl. Then with the ease of long practice, he lit the bundle of herbs, letting it burn for a moment before blowing it out. He walked around her waving the still smoldering herbs. When the cave was nice and fragrant, Green took a clay pipe out of his bag and began packing something dried into the bowl of it.

"Tell me about the mountains where you grew up, in the height of summer." He sat in the chair across from her keeping his eyes on his task.

Sarah wondered at the seeming change in subject but followed his lead. "Well, that's usually August. It's hot there, and it bakes everything. The days are pretty quiet, but at night when it cools down, everything seems to come out; bugs, animals, people, more bugs."

"What does it smell like?" He lit the pipe and began to smoke.

Sarah thought about summer nights in the holler. She closed her eyes remembering. "In the hot sun all day, everything smells stronger. There's grass and barley that's still growing. Cucumbers, tomatoes, and watermelon are ripe then, and peaches. They all smell so sweet."

She could almost see it, almost taste the fruits of summer. Her stomach rumbled, and she glanced up at Green with a shy smile. Before she had time to turn away, he blew a long stream of smoke directly into her face. Sarah recoiled coughing and closed her eyes against the sting. But it didn't smell like tobacco smoke, or smoke at all. It smelled like a summer night in the holler; like sliced tomatoes and bacon grease, cucumbers in vinegar and watermelon with salt.

A gentle hand on her head turned her face down toward the bowl on the table. Green's low voice sounded far away when he said, "Open your eyes."

***

Sarah lifted her eyelids, to find her home in the holler, though not quite the home of her memory. The kitchen was different. The old wood stove that Sarah had finally convinced Granny to give up was back in its place, and the refrigerator was gone. It was hot, even at night, and she could hear the night bugs singing through the open window.

There was food left on the table, and dishes soaking in the sink. Granny had never been one to let a mess sit, and Sarah wondered why the kitchen was left half-cleaned. That was when Granny walked in, a much younger and heavily pregnant version of the grandmother who had raised her. She was lovely with her dark hair put up loosely. Thin tendrils escaped drifting around her neck. It was strange to see her young and pretty wearing a flowered housecoat. This was before life had put the lines on her face and worn away her smile.

Sarah took a step back wondering if Granny would see her, but her grandmother showed no sign that she was anything but alone. With a fatigued sigh, she set about covering the bowls of food with clean towels to keep the bugs out. Then she went to the sink to start on the dishes. Wanting to help out of reflex, Sarah tried to pick up a fork that had been left on the table, but her hand went right through it. So, she was forced to watch Granny wash the dishes arms stretched out and belly resting against the side of the sink.

Her grandmother had never been overly emotional, but Sarah could tell by the set of her shoulders and the tilt of her head that something beyond the baby weighed on her. One faraway look out the kitchen window, told Sarah what it was. How many times had she seen her grandmother look out the window in just that way when she was growing up? As if Granny was looking out at the yard and forest but seeing something else. She had always thought of that as Granny's lonely look.

Granny was finishing the dishes when a pair of headlights came up the drive. A truck came swerving up the driveway and parked at an odd angle. The light was low enough outside, that Sarah couldn't see the features of the man who got out. But she heard his shout. "Maggie!"

Sarah looked back to Granny who stood by the sink. Her shoulders were tense, and muscles jumped in her jaw as if she was gritting her teeth. Turning from the sink, Granny waddled over to the pantry and pulled something out from behind the door. She came back with the broom, and began sweeping the floor, determined not to be put off her task by whoever the man was.

"Maggie!" The man shouted, from the porch this time. His footsteps heavy on the boards.

Granny braced herself there in the middle of the kitchen.

"I know you're in there." The man slurred in a down east accent that reminded Sarah a little of Duff's. The screen door swung back into the frame with a crack that made Sarah jump. "Maggie!"

Sarah watched Granny's face lose that weary, lonely look. Every muscle in her tightened, ready to spring into action.

"There you are." The man sneered as he staggered into the kitchen. He stopped and braced an elbow against the door frame in a pose that Sarah thought was meant to look casual but betrayed how unsteady on his feet he was.

"And where else would I be?" Granny said flatly.

"Oh, you could be out in the woods doing whatever it is your people do." His voice was dripping with derision. He shoved away from the door frame and stumbled his way into the room. Mimicking her grandmother's accent, he added, "Ye Auld Folk."

He must have smelled because Granny reared back blinking when he stopped in front of her. "I didna know they were serving whisky at the tent revival."

"Good corn whisky. None of that barley water you been working on." He sneered turning toward the cabinet where Granny kept the bottle that she maintained for medicinal purposes. He poured some of it into a jelly glass. "They served up a lot a things at that revival meeting."

Sarah recognized the danger underlying his tone. Granny did too, from the way she watched him, her knuckles going white from her grip on the broom handle. "Why don't ye take the rest of that bottle up to your room?"

He slammed the jelly glass on the small counter, but he didn't turn back to face her "Oh you'd like that wouldn't you."

Turning back to face her he sauntered closer, imitating her accent again. "Here's yer whishky, laddie. Go on to yer room and leave me alone." He flipped a hand at the collar of her housecoat making her flinch. "Dinna mind me, making my potions and casting my spells."

"What are ye going on about?" Granny said taking a step back from him.

"What am I going on about? What am I going on about?" He mocked. "Well, Maggie, I'm going on about the devil's work. You think I don't know what you people are."

"What?"

"But I know." He tapped a finger to his temple. "You see I was sitting there at that revival watching Bertie Jennings twirl that pretty yella hair of hers when I finally heard what the preacher was saying."

Maggie took another step back.

"He was talking about the forces of the devil trying to trick us into sin." He leaned into Granny's face.

If Sarah hadn't known her better, she would have said that Granny looked annoyed with the man. But the way Granny gripped the broom with one hand and wrapped the other around her belly, Sarah knew she was terrified. "No one is tricking ye."

He laughed. "My family tricked me. Told me I had some sacred mission to watch you and keep you safe. Because that's what we've always done. Because some ancestor of mine swore an oath to a king that's been dead for hundreds of years. They didn't tell me I was going to be living out my days in the ass-end of nowhere watching over another man's leavings with no hope of happiness myself."

"No one is keeping ye here, Asa Durant. Ye ken well enough where the door is." Maggie tried to shove past him, but he sidestepped in front of her.

"And you, pretty Maggie," He stepped closer, his body brushing her belly. "You're the biggest trick of them all. Everyone's supposed to feel bad for the poor deserted Maggie having her baby all alone. Don't everybody feel bad for her so far away from home? But they don't know you like I do, do they?"

He knocked the broom from her hand and grabbed her arms walking her backwards until they reached the table. All the while he sneered into her face. "They don't know you're a witch, but I do. I see you gathering your plants and roots. I know what you do with 'em. I know you go out cavorting in the woods at night. I see you giving thanks for when I bring home a deer, and I know it ain't the God of Israel you're thankin'."

Granny's eyes shot fury at him, but he was beyond caring. He went on, "They don't know that's the devil's spawn you're carrying."

Granny's hand fumbled behind her looking for anything to use to defend herself. Her fingers closed around the fork that Sarah had tried to pick up.

"But I know." He spat. "I know I ought to cut it out of you."

He braced a hand on the table trapping Granny in place while he pulled a short knife from his pocket.

Granny sprang into action raising the fork she'd grabbed and bringing it down with all the force she could muster into the hand near her hip. He roared grabbing his injured hand. Granny ran past him and made for the parlor. She nearly tripped catching her shoulder on the door jamb but managing to protect the baby she carried. Regaining her balance, she sprinted for the mantle where an old hunting rifle hung above the fireplace. Well, it had been old when Sarah was a girl.

Maggie braced a hand on the mantle and grasped the rifle by the stock. She broke it open running to the shelf where she kept the ammunition. With shaking fingers, she loaded two shells into it. She was snapping the breech closed when Asa stumbled into the parlor. His eyes burned with a toxic mix of pain and drunken resentment. Granny lifted the gun to her shoulder ready to fire.

Asa pulled up short ten feet away from her, but he was either too drunk or too angry to be afraid. "You gonna shoot me, Maggie?"

"Not if ye walk out that door and never come back." Granny looked down the sight, making a show of taking aim.

Asa Durant had the nerve to laugh at that. "You don't have the stones for it."

"My people came from stone." Granny bit out. "Ye want to try me?"

"You put the gun down now, Maggie." He took a step closer to her. Granny's finger tightened on the trigger. Sarah held her breath.

Asa was about to take another step toward her when another car skidded into the drive stopping in front of the steps. In the space of a heartbeat. Granny glanced out the front door at the newcomer. Asa lunged for the gun, and she pulled the trigger. The sound exploded Sarah's ears, and she ducked as if she could avoid it. When she looked up again, Asa Durant was on the floor face down. Blood and brains were sprayed all over the front wall of the parlor, and a sheriff's deputy stood dumbstruck on the other side of the screen door.

Granny lowered herself into a slat back chair that stood by the fireplace and let the gun slip from her fingers to the floor. She fought to catch her breath never taking her eyes off the man she'd killed.

The deputy came through the screen door, stepping around the body. He didn't need to check for a pulse, half the man's head was gone.

He knelt in front of Granny. "Maggie? Are you alright? Did he hurt you?"

"I had to, Cal. I had to do it." Granny muttered between gasps.

"I know, honey. I saw him go for you." He tentatively put a hand on her knee trying to draw her attention. "Are you alright? Did he hurt you?"

Granny wrapped an arm around her belly. "He said he was going to cut out my baby."

The deputy cursed under his breath. "Let's get you out of this room."

He stood and helped her up with an arm around her waist. He kept his arm around her as they made their way past the body and down the hall to the kitchen. He helped her into a chair and checked her over for injuries before asking. "Is the baby alright? I mean, did anything happen that I need to fetch the doctor for?"

Granny ran her hands over her belly, her eyebrows drawn together. She cupped a hand over a particularly round part on her right side and pressed three fingers down a few inches to the left. She must have felt an answering push back because she sighed in relief. "I think she's fine."

He went to the sink and filled a glass with water bringing it back to her at the table. Granny's hand shook as she took a sip. The deputy pulled up a chair and sat down facing her. "I wish I had gotten here sooner. I was supervising the traffic coming out of the revival and I heard some boys talking about how Asa had left drunk and raving about you being a witch."

"What am I going to do, Cal?" Granny looked at him pleading. "I canna go to prison. I canna have my name in the paper, or the court records."

"It was self-defense, Maggie. I saw it. You've got nothing to worry about." He assured her.

"No, ye dinna understand." Maggie gulped down what was left of the water he'd brought her. "There are people looking for me. People who would do me harm. Asa was supposed to be here to protect me."

"Who would want to hurt you?" He asked.

Granny let her shoulders slump and her hand came up to cover her mouth as if she could stop the story from coming out of her mouth. Sarah knew the story, the fable that Granny told people about why she was there in the mountains alone, so far from her people. "My family." Her voice cracked. "They wanted me to marry someone I hated. He was cruel to everyone, but he was wealthy, and they saw it as an opportunity for the family. I couldna do it. So, I ran away."

Cal laid a hand on top of hers in sympathy.

"He chased me. He had the money to. That's why I left Scotland." Her voice cracked again. "I know he's still looking for me. Ye ken how telling some people no makes them want a thing all the more?"

He nodded.

"If my name is in the news, if there's a record of me being here, I'm afraid he'll find me." She looked up at the deputy with tears in her eyes.

"Is he?" He cleared his throat, looking at her intensely. "Is he the baby's father?"

Maggie shook her head looking down at her belly. A blush crept up her cheeks. "No. I met a man in Boone, a scoundrel. I should ha' known better, but I was so lonely."

The deputy watched her deep in thought. Eventually, he came to a decision. He took Granny's hand in both of his. "I don't want you to worry about this. I'm going to take care of it. And if anyone else comes up here to bother you, you tell me. I'll do what I can for you, Maggie."

That was when Sarah recognized him. She'd heard him say very similar words to her grandmother some twenty-five years later after her mother's body had been found at the bottom of a cliff. Cal was none other than Sheriff Calvin Vance. The same sheriff who turned a blind eye to Granny's still for decades. The sheriff who had made sure that every written record of Molly's death said it had been from a fall in spite of her slashed wrists.

Cal stood up from the table. He rested a hand on Granny's shoulder and kissed the top of her head. Then he straightened his shoulders and walked back to the parlor to take care of the mess.

***

She smelled damp rock and herbs. It took a few seconds for her eyes to adjust to the change in light. When she could see better, Lailoken Green was sitting across from her with a gentle smile on his face.

No wonder Granny hadn't told them about their people. They had sent her away without protection to live with people who were suspicious of anyone different. Tent revivals weren't as common in the area when Sarah was growing up, but back in the late forties Granny had been one vicious sermon away from pitchforks and torches.

The exhaustion of the day swept back over Sarah. Her body wanted nothing but to curl up and sleep for weeks. But her mind was full of anger and questions. "Who was Asa Durant?"

"Your grandmother's steward, and a very poor one." Green said, the pipe still held between his teeth.

"And Calvin Vance, was he a steward too?"

"Yes and no." He shrugged.

"What's that supposed to mean?" Her tone was impatient.

"He did the job of a steward, but out of love. He was not a Sinclair, merely a good man who cared for your grandmother." He brushed a bit of ash off the knee of his trousers.

Sarah pushed the bowl aside and rested her elbows on the table, pinning the old man with a look. "If your job is to facilitate, then why was she so alone?"

He arched a bushy eyebrow at her. Sarah got the impression that Mr. Green wasn't used to being questioned so directly. "I'm afraid that I cannot be everywhere at all times. I have your people and the Stuarts to watch out for. I have some magic, but I am not a god." He clapped his hands together and stood up. "Now, I think it's time we had some dinner."

CHAPTER FORTY-TWO

He smelled smoke. Dermot stumbled forward eager to find the source. It was the first sign of life since he'd awakened in the cave to find the body of the assassin cooling in front of him outlined in silver moonlight. Thank heaven there hadn't been more than one.

He'd quickly found Ruaraidh's knife where he'd dropped it near his hip, but the torch Ruaraidh had tucked into his pocket must have fallen out in the struggle. He'd searched for it along the cave floor but found nothing and got his hands once again covered in blood. He'd gagged and almost lost what little he'd eaten that day when he checked the dead man's pockets for identification. Nothing. Not a single sign of who he was or who'd sent him.

Dermot pocketed the pistol and took the rifle, not wanting to leave them to be found by some unsuspecting hill walker. Sliding his pack onto his back, he cast one more look around the moonlit cave. He or Ruaraidh would have to come back for the body. He was in no fit state to dispose of it now.

His first full step toward where Sarah and her brother had gone had him wincing in pain. His limbs felt full of lead. His blasted knee throbbed where he'd landed on it. Worse though, was the burning pain in his calf. A quick inspection told him there was a slice down the back of it. He remembered the man going for his Achilles tendon. It didn't feel like the muscle was too damaged, but he reckoned some of the blood soaking the back of his trousers must be his own.

He'd tried to remember Ruaraidh's instructions on where to go. The only word that stood out in his mind was left. So, with his left hand trailing the wall and using the rifle for support he'd set off into the blackness of the cave.

He'd stopped counting the number of times he'd hit his head on the lowering ceiling or slipped down the steep incline to get to the higher passage. The climbing must have reopened the cut in his leg. He could feel his trousers below the wound clinging, hot and wet.

The smoke though, that meant people. He prayed they were his people. He needed to see Sarah, to know that she was alive, that he hadn't killed that man only to lose her some other way. Grateful that the ceiling was high enough now for him to stand upright, he hobbled faster through the dark. He expected to see the orange glow of a peat fire any moment.

That was when he stumbled right into the wall. He grunted and dropped the rifle. Feeling with both hands he tried to find where the cave turned next. But there was rock on three sides of him, and the only way to go was to be back the way he'd come. "Ballocks! Bloody dead end."

"Ah, mate. I hoped it was you." Another voice in the dark said.

Dermot started reaching for the gun in his pocket. He stopped short when a torch clicked on showing Ruaraidh from the shoulders up seeming to come out of the cave wall. Ruaraidh turned the light on him and he was nearly blinded.

"Jesus! Is that your blood!?" He heard the man gasp. Dermot grunted, still blinded by the sudden change in light. Ruaraidh's arm slipped under his and around his waist. He let himself be led forward. They reached the break in the cave wall by the time his eyes adjusted.

Around the wall the light was soft and orange. He didn't have time to look around before Sarah slid under his other arm and helped him to a chair. Turning to her, he buried his nose in her curls and inhaled. Someone slid the pack from his shoulders.

"Is this your blood?" She leaned down to look him in the eye once he was seated. Her eyes full of concern.

The nearness of her swamped him with such relief that he didn't want to speak. He didn't want to worry about practical things like injuries or getting out of there. He wanted to wrap himself around her and sleep, shutting the rest of the world away for another time. In the end he shook his head. "Not all of it. My leg. Probably needs stitches."

"I'll get my things." Ruaraidh rose and went to his pack.

Somehow a cup of tea appeared in Sarah's hand and she held it out to him. "Can you hold it?"

He lifted his hand, but when he flexed his fingers to take the cup he felt the cracking of the blood caked there. "My hands."

Sarah looked down at his hands. He noticed her eyes widen slightly at the blood on them. Her jaw firmed, and she set the cup on the table. "Mr. Green, can you get me some of that water."

A bowl was set near his feet, and a figure behind Sarah draped a hand towel over her shoulder. She knelt in front of him and dipped the towel in the bowl before wrapping it around his hands. She asked, "Do we have another towel?"

"Here." Ruaraidh returned bearing a smaller first aid kit than the one he'd had earlier and handed her a small cloth.

Sarah set that cloth in the bowl and set about untying his shoelaces. She pulled off his shoes careful of his injured leg. He could see lips pressing together to suppress her disgust at his blood-soaked trainers. She handed the shoes to the man behind her. He knew he should be concerned about the stranger, but he was so bloody glad to see Sarah he couldn't take his eyes off her.

Ruaraidh knelt beside him and peeled back the fabric around his calf, pulling it away from the gash. Sarah wrapped her hands around the cloth that covered his and gave him a reassuring squeeze before beginning to wipe the blood away. Meanwhile, Ruaraidh dipped another cloth in the bowl of water and swabbed the blood around the wound.

When she had cleaned his hands enough, Sarah stood tugging his shirt up. "Do we have another shirt?"

"I have one in my bag." He pulled the rest of it over his head.

Without another thought, she threw the blood-soaked shirt onto the fire. She handed him the cup of tea before taking the bowl to the front of the cave and tossing the bloody water out. She went to a dark corner. When she returned the bowl was filled with clean water. Placing the water where Ruaraidh could also reach it, she stepped between his knees and began cleaning his face.

When she spoke, her voice was soft but determined. "That's the last time I'm running away when you're in danger."

"S' my job." He mumbled. Her body was so close. Only a few inches and he could lean his head on her breast. He wanted nothing more than to forget the two other people in the cave with him and take his rest in her arms. She was his home. And what he'd done, had been for her, for this. He'd be damned if he was going to give that up.

"I don't think you get paid enough for this." She said softly, tilting his head up to rub at a smear of blood along his jawline.

He let out a short huff of a laugh and squeezed the back of her thigh with his free hand. "I do alright."

"Sarah," Ruaraidh said, still down by Dermot's leg. "You should see this."

She shifted to look at the wound on his calf. Dermot leaned over to see what was so interesting. He could see the cut on the back of his leg. It really didn't look as bad as he'd expected, but he reckoned that was thanks to Ruaraidh's cleaning.

"Watch." Ruaraidh dipped the cloth he'd been using into the water bowl and dabbed it onto the wound. The water ran over the cut. It only stung a little. As they watched, the ends of the cut appeared to be knitting back together. "I noticed it when I turned away to get the butterfly closures. When I looked back the wound was smaller."

"Mr. Green?" Sarah called to the other man in the cave. The man came over and Dermot looked at him for the first time. He looked older, maybe around sixty, and somewhat familiar.

"Do it again." Sarah nudged Ruaraidh.

He wet the cloth again and pressed it above the wound. Water ran over it, and again the wound became smaller. The difference was slight but noticeable.

"Do you feel it?" Sarah asked.

Dermot shook his head. "It doesna hurt as much, but I don't feel anything when it's happening."

Sarah looked at Green, and they both looked into the darkened corner where she had gotten the water. Now that his eyes had adjusted, he could see the dark outline of a giant pot. "Is that?"

"Looks like the old pot still has some juice left." She looked over her shoulder at the older man. "Has it done this before?"

His face full of speculation. "Not since it was brought to me for safe keeping."

Sarah's eyes sparkled as she looked at each of them before settling her eyes on his. "Something must be going right."

Dermot could feel the other men's eyes on them, but he didn't care. He was lost in her eyes, green like new spring leaves and full of hope.

"I think the water in the kettle is hot enough now. Let's have some soup." The old man said.

"Great." Sarah said. "I'm starving."

The man Sarah called Mr. Green straightened. He went to a pack that rested against one leg of the table and retrieved a jar of dried soup. Collecting the cups, he set about making instant soup.

"Can you eat?" She asked him.

If she had asked him the same question five minutes before the answer would have been a resounding no. Suddenly, he was ravenous. "Aye. I can eat. Let me get some fresh trousers."

Ruaraidh helped him hobble away from the fire. His calf already felt better than it had. He wondered if the water could do anything for his knee. With a glance over his shoulder at Sarah who was busying herself cleaning up, he slid his blood-crusted trousers down and stepped out of them.

"Is that going to be a problem tomorrow?" Ruaraidh nodded at the dark bruise blooming on his knee before handing him his clean clothes.

"I willna let it be." Dermot grunted as he tested his weight on his bad knee. "I wonder if yer magic water would help it."

Ruaraidh's mouth kicked up at one corner. "Worth a try."

"Maybe after we've eaten."

It wasn't much, but the hot soup warmed him more than sitting by the fire. He hadn't realized how cold he was until he'd felt the hot broth trickle down his throat. The three young people drank the soup with enthusiasm. Green took his time, watching them. Dermot tried to place where he'd seen the man before. It was when Green held his cup between his hands and braced his forearms on the table that it struck him. He'd seen this man do that same thing before in a very different context.

"I know you." He pinned the older man with a look suddenly not sure if he was friend or foe. "You're on the board of Alba Petroleum."

Sarah's eyes widened as she turned to Green who straightened in his seat. "Is that true? Do you work for James?"

Green's eyes shifted between the two of them, but his look was guileless. "I am on the board of Alba Petroleum, but I do not work for the Stuarts. I watch them. Just as I watch your people."

Dermot and Sarah stared at him in silence. She asked. "Who exactly are you?"

"I go by many names. People in the Edinburgh business community know me as Lyall Green." He nodded to Sarah.

"Lailoken is the name that my mother gave me. Most people think it's terribly old fashioned."

"I'll bet." Dermot muttered. His tone frigid. "And what connects you to the Auld Folk and the Stuarts?"

Green smiled unperturbed by Dermot's tone. "As I told the princess, I am a facilitator, the latest in a long line. I do my best to make sure that things happen as they are supposed to."

"And who decides how things are supposed to happen?" Dermot could feel the tension creeping back into his shoulders.

"The Auld Folk foretold Miss MacAlpin's fate ages ago. I am merely here to observe and help where I can."

Sarah put a hand on his arm and turned to him. "Mr. Green saved my mother's life, and mine."

Dermot rested his hand on top of hers without taking his eyes off of Green's. "You're him aren't ye?"

Green's dark eyes danced with some mischief, and he chuckled smugly. "And who would that be?"

"Say it." Dermot hissed.

Sarah's hand tightened on his arm and they watched Green. The old man, and he did mean old, sobered. "There is so much useless baggage attached to that name. We cannot use it anymore. We've not used it for a thousand years."

Sarah looked between the two of them, her brows creased in confusion. "What are you talking about?"

Dermot arched an impatient eyebrow at Green. The old man drew in a long breath before saying. "Once, long ago, the New Folk called us Merlin."

All of them went still. The name alone conjured a thousand years of legends, fiction, and theater to appear right there in the cave with them. Merlin was lately the stuff of pop culture.

Cartoon wizards and over the top Hollywood productions made him into anything from bumbling to god-like.

But Dermot knew better. His mother had made a study of the legends of the old man of the forest, or the madman as some said. He knew different legends, that placed Merlin in Scotland fighting to keep the Auld Ways alive in spite of the encroaching church. His mission had been to protect the knowledge of the Auld Folk. It made sense that he would be here, with the cauldron, following Sarah. The question was, what did they do with him now?

Beside him, Sarah began quietly laughing and shaking her head. All the men turned to her. Under her breath she said. "Why not?" She looked up at him, her green eyes so bleak belying her shaking shoulders. She threw up her hands before pushing away from the table. Rising, she backed away gesturing at the cave around them. "I mean ancient prophecies, magic cauldron, people descended from Jesus…why not throw Merlin into the mix?"

"Sarah," he rose reaching for her.

She warded him off with a sharp shake of her head. "I told you before, that I always wondered when I would crack like mama. This might be it."

She made for the mouth of the cave. Dermot took a step to follow her, but his bad knee buckled, and pain shot up his thigh.

Ruaraidh jumped up to follow her as Sarah disappeared into the dark.

***

Sarah drew in a deep breath of the cold night air and blew it out slowly trying to fight her rising panic. She hadn't gone far, couldn't in the dark. She pressed her back against the solid stone behind her, the coolness seeping through her jacket. She took another breath. There was no sense in letting herself spiral into a hundred different scenarios that were popping into her brain; how could she have avoided this, what had she done to put herself in this situation, what the hell was she going to do now. The way out of all of this could well be right in front of her, but she wasn't going to see it if she let herself freak out.

"It's not safe to be out here alone." Ruaraidh's soft voice came to her through the night. She couldn't see him but could feel a difference in the air to her left, like he was blocking the breeze. At least she wasn't hearing voices, yet.

"What, assassins around every corner?" She joked.

He shifted and leaned against the rock beside her, his shoulder bumping hers. "I think that's been taken care of for now. I'm more concerned about ye falling off a ledge."

She leaned her head back on the rock. "I feel like I've already done that."

"I know."

"Or down the rabbit hole." She added. "And I've just met the Cheshire Cat."

Ruaraidh laughed softly. "He does have a disconcerting smile."

"Did you know he would be here?" She had trusted her brand-new little brother since the moment they met. Suddenly, she wasn't sure that had been wise.

"No. I didn't." It sounded like the truth. "I probably should have. Between the accident and the assassin, I really didn't give him a thought."

"Should I be afraid of him?"

"No." That was definite, unequivocal. "He is here to help us, help you."

"What if my interests aren't in line with *our* interests? Because I didn't sign up for any of this." She waved a hand at the dark in front of her.

"I'm not sure it can be avoided. You said yerself that our father and yer mother still found their way to each other in spite of all the obstacles. Maybe this will always find you, like gravity."

"Thanks." She sounded far from grateful. "That didn't exactly turn out well for them."

He nudged her elbow with his. "It gave us you. Maybe that's enough."

"Not for me." She shook her head, imagining a lifetime with James Stuart, without her career, without Dermot spooling out in front of her. "Are we seriously debating free will? Is this what it's come to?"

"Aren't we always debating free will to one extent or another?" She felt his shoulder lift in a shrug. "It could be the God of the New Folk, the stars above us or runes appearing in the water or tumbled onto a table. We're always trying to divine what's next. Hoping that it'll be good news."

She looked above them at the stars. They were much brighter, and she could see so many more away from the glow of nearby cities. There was nothing here to compete with the expanse of the night sky. Her eyes traced along what looked like a river of stars that ran across to the north of them, wishing it could lead her anywhere else. "Except that my future doesn't look too hopeful at the moment."

"Maybe not, but there are always surprises along the way." She felt him lean toward her. "I mean ye didna know ye had a brother until yesterday."

"Jesus, was that only yesterday?" So much had happened in the last forty-eight hours. She pressed a hand to her forehead. "I'm so tired."

"I know." He stood and reached down for her. "Let's get ye inside. Ye can sleep for a while. We've a long walk in the morning."

By the low light of the fire, she could see Dermot waiting at the table, a look of concern on his face. He sat up straighter at the sight of the two of them.

"Where's Green?" She asked.

Dermot jerked his head toward the cot that she had noticed earlier. Mr. Green was curled up facing the wall of the cave. "He said he was tired after treating my knee."

"Is it better?" She nodded at the knee in question.

"We'll see in the morning." He shrugged before gesturing to the opposite side of the cave from Green's cot. "I laid our sleeping bags out over there."

Ruaraidh went to the packs they had left against the back wall and retrieved his roll. "I'll take the spot near the mouth of the cave."

Dermot labored to his feet. However tired Sarah felt, she had no doubt that he was exhausted. She went to him and slid under his arm. He let her take some of his weight as she helped him hobble to their sleeping bags. He had combined them into one pallet, obviously not caring to hide that they were together from the others.

She helped him down onto the pallet and slid in with him. He turned her to face the fire her back to his chest and curled his arm around her. Sarah settled herself against him, loving his warm strength. His breath tickled her ear. Her muscles began to relax. Whatever had happened that day, this was the perfect end; wrapped in his arms.

As Sarah was drifting off to sleep, she heard his voice in her ear. He spoke low enough that the others wouldn't be able to hear. "I'm taking ye away from this. I won't let them get you. Dinna tell anyone, not even yer brother. We'll have Jujhar drop us off in the city, and we'll find a cheap place to stay. I'll get whatever papers I need, and we'll be gone before they can find us again. I'll keep you safe."

He went on making plans, as Sarah drifted off to sleep. His voice blending with her mother's cooing in her ear.

I won't let them have you...not my baby...

CHAPTER FORTY-THREE

A soft shuffling sound pulled Sarah from sleep. Hours on a cave floor should have made her sore, but Dermot's warmth had kept her relaxed. She peeked through the screen of her lashes to catch a glimpse of a hunched, blanket-wrapped figure making his slow, pained way to the mouth of the cave. He looked ancient, as if the work of holding him up was too much for old bones. He shuffled past the sleeping Ruaraidh and disappeared into the thick morning mist.

Sarah sat up, curious. Dermot's arm slid down to rest in her lap. She glanced over to the cot where Lailoken Green had slept. It was empty. It had to have been Green who had left the cave. Although he had looked like a man in his fifties when she'd met him last night, he hadn't been hunched or had trouble walking. She watched the gray fog where the figure had disappeared wondering if she should follow, partly because she was afraid he might need help and partly out of pure curiosity.

She slipped out of their pallet careful not to wake Dermot. Stretching in the chilly morning air, she didn't take her eyes off of the cave's entrance. The mist was so thick that she couldn't see anything past where Ruaraidh slept. Last night, she had looked from the ledge beyond at the vastness of the Highland sky, but this morning it was as if the opening was blocked by a wall of gray.

After a few minutes, Mr. Green appeared through the fog, walking upright and fluidly, tendrils of mist clinging around his limbs like phantom fingers. This was the man she had seen last night; poised, confident, a little past middle age. The difference between the figure who had hobbled out of the cave and the one who returned was so stark that Sarah had trouble believing he was the same man. He noticed her watching him and smiled as he returned the blanket he'd worn around his shoulders to the cot. "Can I make you a cup of tea, princess?"

"Can you call me anything besides princess?" She joined him near what was left of the fire. "The first person who called me that was trying to kill me. It sort of ruined it."

He gave her a sympathetic look as he stirred the coals in the fire before adding another brick of peat. "I do wish that hadn't been the first you heard of it. I had not thought that they would find you before the Stuarts did."

Sarah helped him make the tea. "Do you know who *they* are?"

"Not exactly, though I have my suspicions."

"Dermot mentioned something called The Circle." Sarah offered.

"If the man they sent was American, then it very likely was The Circle." Green hung the kettle over the fire. "It could also have been a business rival who knew of the Stuart's interest in you. I believe the lass that he killed was a geologist who had been offered a job with Alba Petroleum."

"She was." Sarah said remembering Bridget MacKenzie, her cousin who had been oddly relieved when she met Sarah. They had talked about Scotland and stones. A sinking feeling pulled at her as she realized something. "She knew what was coming. Her mother and grandmother saw the future. She must have too. She even equivocated when I asked her about her career plans."

Green bowed his head. "Sometimes your gifts can be curses. You must be careful who you allow to know what you can do."

She had already shown more people than she intended when she'd used it to avoid the assassin. "Do the Stuarts know?"

"They know that you have knowledge that they can use. They don't know what any of the sisters can do."

"Let's hope they don't find out." Sarah muttered. "I don't even want to imagine what Walter Stuart would do if he knew about my gift."

He gave her a penetrating look. "Walter Stuart is one you should keep an eye on. His own ambition sometimes overrides what is best for the rest of us."

That sounded right given what Dermot had told her about James's Uncle Walter. "He sounds like my Aunt Eilidh."

Green cut his eyes over to where Ruaraidh still slept his chest rising and falling evenly. "Yes, it is a pity that Eilidh lost her focus. It took some work to repair the damage that her deception caused."

Sarah cocked her head in question. "Work?"

"Nothing obvious; a nudge in the right direction, distractions created for Sheila and Willie to allow your mother and Rab to be together. I tried to teach Willie Cross, but I'm afraid his mind was never quite right after his parents died."

"Teach him? About the cauldron?"

"Mmhmm." He rose to retrieve the water that had started to boil. "I have not always been what I am. We green men are long-lived thanks to the cauldron, but not immortal. I am one hundred forty-seven years old. That is older than a man should live to be, but I must continue in my role until I can find someone to replace me. I had hoped to pass the mantle to Willie Cross. His faith was strong, sometimes too strong. When he was presented with a challenge to what he believed, he cracked. Some people face that kind of challenge with good sense and flexibility, others push back with fundamentalism as Willie did. He would have made a bad green man."

Sarah couldn't disagree with that. Her mother had made a similar observation about Willie, and Sarah had seen plenty of people in the holler faced challenges of faith by holding on to what they believed with white-knuckled grips. "And when you find a replacement for you?"

He smiled softly. "I will teach them the old ways, so that I can retire."

"Retire?" The idea of a legendary wizard retiring seemed strange.

"This is a lonely existence." For a second, so short she almost missed it, he looked bone tired.

"And do you have someone now, an apprentice?" She asked.

Green looked past her shoulder to where Ruaraidh snored away. "I think I do, a much better candidate."

Sarah followed his look and felt a chill course up her spine. No, she couldn't imagine her fierce, funny brother living like this man. Moving easily from cave to boardroom to street corner. Ruaraidh was so full of life. He couldn't be sentenced to this man's 'lonely existence'.

She couldn't imagine that her brother would want that either. "How's that working out?"

Green laughed softly, "His mind is much more facile than Willie Cross's, but your brother presents his own set of challenges. His curiosity tends toward the more scientific aspects of what we do, and less toward the spiritual and political. And he is a man of action. I am not sure he will be content to live on the fringes of events."

Sarah considered her brother. No, she couldn't see him practicing magic and manipulating pawns on a chess board. He was more straightforward than that. Green needed a dark horse, someone content to move quietly, but perceptive enough to see things as they were. "I think I know someone who might be better suited to the job."

Green's gray eyes turned to her questioning.

"He's been researching the Nine for years. He found us on his own. He says he's not connected with any group. His interest in us is academic and spiritual. Ruaraidh and Sheila heard him say it and vouched that it was the truth."

Green's eyebrows went up with what she hoped was curiosity. "Who is this person?"

"His name is Jujhar Gurudat. He's a linguist, but his research has led him into history and spirituality." She thought about the calming affect that being near Jujhar had on her. "He might have exactly the right temperament."

***

The closer they got to their appointed meeting place, the more nervous Dermot got. It had been a leap of faith trusting Jujhar to pick them up. It had felt more acceptable standing in Eilidh MacLeod's kitchen surrounded by Sarah's people, but their rendezvous point was a secluded road on the north end of Loch Shin. There would be no one around to protect them if Jujhar double-crossed them calling in reinforcements or the press.

After yesterday's unwanted guest and the appearance of Lailoken Green, Dermot was coming to expect all manner of surprises good and ill. One good surprise had been the state of his injured knee when he woke up that morning. It had felt almost new, like his injury from his army days hadn't happened. Even after a second day of hill walking, his knee felt like it could go on for miles longer. Whether it was the water from the cauldron or some magic that Green had applied with the water, he'd never know, but he had little doubt that he would be limping his way to the rendezvous without it.

All he wanted to do was get Sarah out of there. He'd meant every word that he'd told her the night before. He needed the documents and would like to see his mother one last time. But after that, they would be in the wind. They were halfway there now. He could count on his fingers the number of people who knew where Sarah was. He trusted that neither Ruaraidh nor his parents would tell anyone. That left only the old witch and Jujhar as variables.

As they came around a line of trees and into view of the road, one of those variables came into view leaning against Oona Ballantyne's car. He'd parked in the layby on the road to Corriekinloch. They made quick work of crossing the stream that fed the loch. As they approached the car, Dermot and Ruaraidh closed ranks around Sarah, with Dermot taking the lead. Jujhar pushed away from the car and waited for them to come closer. Dermot didn't see any signals furtive or overt that would suggest Jujhar wasn't alone. He appeared to have kept his word.

This was further confirmed when Ruaraidh said sotto voce, "If there's danger it's not his doing."

Dermot grunted and scanned the area for anyone who might have followed Jujhar. It looked clear. As they got closer, Jujhar walked to the rear of the car and moved to open the trunk.

Awareness shot through Dermot like electricity. Quick as lightning the pistol he'd taken from the assassin was in his hand. Keeping the gun pointed at the ground, Dermot spoke loud enough to reach him. "Stop."

Jujhar froze, lifting his hands to shoulder level, keys dangling from one finger. Dermot approached the car leaving Ruaraidh to step in front of his sister. Dermot patted Jujhar down, "What am I going to find in the trunk?"

"Perhaps a spare tire? I thought you would want to put your packs in there." Jujhar said fighting to keep his voice calm.

"That's all?" Dermot asked sharply.

"I don't know what was in there before, but I haven't put anything else in there." Jujhar sputtered.

"He's telling the truth, mate." Ruaraidh said from behind Dermot.

Dermot wasn't sure he trusted Ruaraidh's instincts as much as Sarah did, but he tucked the gun back into his waistband. "Sorry, Jujhar. We canna be too careful."

"I understand." Jujhar said struggling to regain his usual calm.

Dermot opened the trunk and looked inside. It was empty except for a canvas drop cloth smudged with a rainbow of colors and an assortment of empty drink bottles, and food sacks. Ruaraidh stepped up beside him and dropped his pack into the trunk. "My sister is an artist. She's not the neatest person, but I still would have thought she'd have cleaned the car out before leaving it in the barn."

Dermot made sure there was nothing in or under the drop cloth before putting his pack into the car and reaching for Sarah's.

"What's that smell? It's heavenly." Sarah asked.

Jujhar smiled at her. "Ruaraidh's mother sent some hot food for you all."

"Fantastic!" Ruaraidh clapped his hands together. "I'm starved."

They loaded into the car, Dermot and Sarah in the back seat. Ruaraidh rode in the passenger seat to eat while Jujhar drove. They pulled onto the road and set out for the long drive.

"So," Dermot said taking a couple of hot foil wrapped packages of food that Ruaraidh had retrieved from the sack. "What news can ye tell us?"

Jujhar's eyes met his in the rearview mirror and Dermot could tell that he wouldn't like what he was about to say. "I'm afraid it's all over the news that we're missing from the crash site. The rest of the team made it to Inverness, and have been interviewed, well, everyone but Kirstie. Isla made clear the role the paparazzi played in our flight from Lochinver and suggested that we were run off the road by them. Ewan got plenty of footage from their drive as the decoy. Some of it is pretty harrowing and supports that story."

"They weren't hurt, were they?" Sarah asked.

"It doesn't look like it." Jujhar said. "But James Stuart has issued a terse statement to the press about their pursuit of you."

Sarah rolled her eyes. "Does he suggest that we're a couple?"

"No, he only talked about the aggression of the paparazzi and how it may have resulted in terrorizing an innocent woman."

"Well, thank goodness for that." She muttered.

Dermot put a comforting hand on hers. "He knows ye're not ready for all of that."

"I'm not ready for any of it." She turned her hand up and laced her fingers with his.

"Let's not borrow trouble. I'm sure if ye lay low for a few days they'll all forget about ye and move on to the next big story." Ruaraidh offered.

"I hope you're right." Sarah looked down at the food that she held and set it aside.

Dermot picked it up and put it back in her lap. "Ye need to eat."

She made a petulant face but unwrapped the food in her lap. A hot sandwich with homemade roast beef. The aroma had his mouth watering.

He unwrapped his own sandwich and settled in for the long drive back to Edinburgh.

CHAPTER FORTY-FOUR

"Stop here." Dermot leaned forward to tap Ruaraidh on the shoulder. Sarah sat up from where she had been snoozing against his chest. They were in the city, but Sarah didn't recognize the neighborhood.

"What?" Ruaraidh asked puzzled. "I thought ye said to go to the University."

"There's something I need to do first." Dermot turned to Jujhar. "We'll catch up with ye at the office."

"Are you sure it's a good idea." Jujhar's brows drew together in concern.

Dermot leveled him with a significant look. "Aye, I'm sure."

Ruaraidh pulled the car into a parking space on the busy street. Dermot turned to her and pulled a stocking cap over her head and tucked a few stray strands under it. His eyes met hers and he smiled. *This is it.* She thought. *Don't give it away.*

"We'll see you guys at the office in a couple of hours." She told them.

Dermot nodded to her and got out of the car. Sarah followed him out. She had expected to hop out and watch Ruaraidh drive away, but her brother put the car in park and walked to the back to open the trunk. He retrieved their packs and tucked something from his into Sarah's. When he'd handed the backpack to her, he pulled her into a bear hug. "I don't know what yer man has planned, but I get the feeling it'll be a while before I see ye again. Be careful, and ye ken where we are if ye ever need us."

Sarah fought back the tears that pooled in her eyes. She squeezed him tighter. "I've got nothing to compare with, but I have a feeling you're the best brother a girl could ask for."

Ruaraidh pulled back and she was surprised to see tears in his own green eyes. This man who she'd only known for a couple of days, had taken her to his heart. "I always knew ye were out there. I didna know I'd like ye so much."

"Tell Rab that he's forgiven. I have a feeling he needs to hear it." Her voice caught in her throat.

"He does. And I will." Ruaraidh pressed a kiss to her forehead before stepping back. He looked over to Dermot. "Take care of her."

Dermot looked solemn when he said, "Always."

Sarah stepped close to Dermot, as Ruaraidh made his way back around the car. He gave her one last look before lowering himself into the driver's seat. Sarah sighed as she watched Ruaraidh and Jujhar pull into traffic thinking that she would probably never see them again.

Dermot gave her hand a squeeze. "They'll be alright."

She worried her bottom lip with her teeth. "I know. It's so unfair to find them only to leave them. I didn't really say goodbye to Jujhar."

"We shouldn't say goodbye. We can't give them any reason to think we've disappeared on purpose or put them in a position of being questioned by the Stuarts. At least with Ruaraidh, Jujhar knows that he's going home soon. That goodbye wouldna raise suspicion."

"You're right, but that doesn't make me feel any less guilty." She turned to him. "Where are we going?"

"We're going to a hotel where ye're going to wait for me while I get what I need." He sounded very sure of this plan.

"You think you're going to leave me to wait?" She cocked her head at him.

"I think that all of the city has seen yer face on the news and I don't want ye running around. Ye'll be safe. And I'll be faster if I dinna have to fret over ye."

She made a sound in her throat that conveyed something like; *We'll see about that.* Without saying the words.

"But first, I have to see someone." He said pulling her down the street.

***

"Who are we going to see?" She asked when they rounded the corner.

"My mother." Dermot tried to ignore the lump already forming in his throat.

Sarah stopped and pulled on his hand. "Wait. If it's dangerous for Jujhar to know where we're going, won't it be dangerous for her too."

He gave her hand a reassuring squeeze. "It'll be fine. Ye'll see why."

She let him pull her down the block and into the entrance of a modern looking building. When she saw Leith House Care Home on the door, Sarah went quiet. She followed him through reception, up the elevator, and down the hall without saying a word.

He stopped at the corner in his mother's hall and looked around. A nurse was pushing a cart in the opposite direction.

He waited until she had rounded a corner further down the hall before pulling Sarah into his mother's room.

His mother was sitting in her chair in front of the window, knitting by lamplight and humming to herself. She looked so much older than she was in her nightgown with her knitting across her lap. When Dermot went to step around the bed to go to her, Sarah let go of his hand. He looked back at her and she gave him a tentative smile. She nodded in the direction of his mother and made a shooing motion, telling him to go on.

He knelt beside his mother's chair. "Hello, mum."

Seonag stopped her knitting and turned to him. "Oh, hello there, lad. I didna hear ye come in."

"I was very quiet." His throat ached with unshed tears. This was one of those days when she wouldn't recognize him. "How are you today?"

"Och, fine." She patted his hand where it rested on the arm of the chair. "The weather seems to be warming up. I've heard the spring flowers are starting to bloom. It would be ever so nice if I could see them."

He cleared his throat. "Maybe we can make some arrangements to have you taken to the park for an afternoon."

"That would be lovely." Her smile was a ray of sunshine, like a bolt right to his heart.

"I've brought someone I'd like you to meet." He told her, motioning for Sarah to step forward.

Sarah came around the bed to stand next to him. She rested a comforting hand on his shoulder. Seonag lifted her eyes to look at the newcomer, and her smile widened further.

"A bhana phrionnsa." His mother said with awe in her voice. Sarah and Dermot looked at each other in shock. His

mother hadn't even recognized him, but somehow knew Sarah.

"You recognize me?" Sarah asked as Dermot hurried to bring her the other chair that was in the room. He slid the chair behind her and she sat down without taking her eyes off of his mother.

The color rose in Seonag's cheeks and she leaned toward Sarah. "Only from a dream that I have."

"I hope it's a good dream." Sarah laid a hand on Seonag's.

"Och, it's a dream only a mother could have." She looked shyly at the younger woman. "I dream that ye love my Dermot. I know it's silly to think of, but ye couldna find a better lad."

Sarah glanced up at Dermot smiling. "I think you're right about that. He's definitely a catch."

Seonag followed Sarah's gaze to look at Dermot. "Have ye seen my Dermot? He hasna been to visit me in some time."

Sarah's eyebrows drew together in confusion. She studied Seonag before looking back at him. Dermot read the realization in her eyes. She could see that his mother didn't recognize him. Tears pricked the backs of his eyes, and he cleared his throat before answering Seonag. "I... mmph ...I think he's been working. His research team has been in the Highlands."

"Ah, I remember, now. He called a while ago." Seonag said leaning back in her chair. She turned her head again to Sarah. "Ye should meet my lad. He's so sweet and very good to me, though he canna always visit as often as I'd like. I know it's difficult for him."

He couldn't listen to his mother talk about how hard her illness had been on him. His part in this was nothing, minimal compared to what she went through. He didn't even care for her day-to-day anymore. The pain and guilt of her illness, of his inability to keep her safe outside the care home, of him leaving her bubbled up in his chest like a boiling stew. He pushed away from the wall and went to the bathroom closing the door softly. Turning on the faucet, he braced his hands on either side of the sink and let go of the tears he'd been holding back since they'd walked in the door.

It shouldn't hurt this much. He'd had years to get used to the idea of losing his mother, years of watching the brilliant woman that she had been slipping away. He'd been visiting her every week for months and had only seen brief moments of lucidity. But knowing this was the last time he would see her made his chest feel hot and hollow. He looked down between his arms, because it was easier than looking at himself in the mirror. His tears rinsing the dust off the toes of his shoes and dotting the dull institutional tiles on the floor.

He could still hear the lilting sound of their conversation through the door. Sarah listened to Seonag talk about him as if he weren't there and like him, she never let on that there was anything wrong with Seonag's memory. He had stopped pointing out her mental lapses ages ago. It only caused her stress and made the whole thing that much harder.

A small part of him was relieved that she didn't know who he was. It would make what he was about to do so much harder if she knew he was saying goodbye. He splashed some cold water on his face and dried it with a paper towel. Standing straight he sniffed and squared his shoulders. He opened the door to find the two people he loved most in the world, heads bent together talking about whatever his mother was knitting. Seonag laughed at something Sarah said, and he almost had to leave the room again.

If they were a normal couple, this would be a good day. Even in her diminished state, his mother liked Sarah, and Sarah was handling the situation with all the grace and goodness that he knew her capable of. In any other family, she would be able to join him on his weekly visits. He could have talked to Sarah about his mother's decline, about the challenges of taking care of her, about the heartbreak of having your mother forget who you are. She could have shared his burden.

But they weren't a normal family.

He returned to stand near them and bask in the simple interaction of Sarah helping Seonag pick up a stitch she had dropped in her knitting. Sarah handed the needles back to Seonag and pointed to a part of the fabric that had already been done. "I like this moss stitch section here."

Dermot looked at his mother's knitting for the first time. It was a hodgepodge of different stitches and patterns as if she had started one pattern, then forgotten what she had planned and switched to another. He listened to them talk, enjoying their easy conversation. When they had exhausted the subject of knitting, Dermot knelt in front of Seonag again. "I think that we'd better be on our way."

Sarah stood and leaned down to kiss Seonag's cheek. "It's been so nice meeting you."

"Lovely meeting you as well. I'm honored ye would come to see me." Seonag gushed giving Sarah's hand one last squeeze before walking toward the door.

Dermot looked up into his mother's eyes hoping that she wouldn't see that his heart was breaking. "I'll tell Dermot that ye were thinking of him."

Seonag's gaze grew sharper on his face. "I willna see ye again, will I?"

His breath caught in his throat and he couldn't speak. He shook his head.

Seonag hooked a hand behind his head and pulled him closer. She kissed his forehead and whispered to him. "Take care of her. She's more important than I am."

He choked back a sob and brought her other hand to his lips. "I love ye, mum."

"I know, lad."

***

Sarah stepped into the hallway blinking back the tears that had been threatening since she had realized why they were there. It reminded her so much of her mother when she was at her worst, after the bathtub incident. Molly had been there, but remote like a ghost still inhabiting her own skin. Taking up space, but unreachable. Molly's vacant ghost state had been occasionally broken by violent outbursts, directed at her own daughter. Sarah was willing to bet that Seonag Sinclair wasn't prone to murderous rages directed at Dermot. Still, this seemed harder. Seonag's apparent sweetness made her remoteness even more painful.

Dermot came out closing the door behind him. He continued to watch his mother through the narrow window beside the door. Even in profile, his face was enough to show her that his heart was breaking. She wished she could offer some wisdom about losing a parent, some kind thing to say. She had only been six years old when she had lost her mother. How could her childhood perspective help him now? What did she know?

Sarah slipped her hand into his where it hung limp at his side. His fingers threaded through hers. His grip was tight.

"Walter Stuart moved her here while I was doing fieldwork on Lewis last spring. I had no idea until I went to visit her at the previous home where she'd been." He didn't take his eyes off of his mother on the other side of the glass. She had gone back to her knitting and rocking. "They told me where she'd been moved to. No doubt Walter paid them not to tell me when it happened."

He gave a wet sniff. "When I came here, they wouldna let me see her. All they did was hand me a card with Walter Stuart's phone number on it. When I called him, he told me I was going to play along, or I'd never see her again."

The tears overflowed, and Sarah felt one slide down her cheek.

Dermot went on, his voice barely above a whisper. "At first, I was supposed to make contact with you. To see if ye were really who we thought ye were." His grip on her hand tightened. "After last summer, after I kissed ye, I tried to tell them ye weren't the one. But then ye went to Nova Scotia and Isabel MacKenzie called them after she met ye. She knew, ye see, knew as soon as she met ye."

She would, Sarah thought remembering the way Isobel had appeared to know she was coming. At the time she hadn't known that Isobel and her granddaughter were her kin, that Isobel was her grandmother's cousin or that like Granny she had a gift. Isobel's gift was seeing the future. She had even tried to warn Sarah of trouble to come. "That's why you came back."

He nodded, turning from the window to look at her tears sparkling in his own eyes. "Ye have to know that I wouldna have done this to ye were it not for her. She's all I had."

She lifted her other hand to his cheek in a caress. "Is it Alzheimer's?"

"Aye. Early onset." His jaw flexed as he worked to get a grip on his emotions. "It started when she was in her forties. She would forget little things more often than before. But now, ye can see she doesna even know me. I'm still a teenager in her mind."

"I wish you had told me. I've said such awful things to you in frustration. If I had known..." Sarah hugged their joined hands to her chest.

He gave her a watery smile. "Ye'd have what? Tried to let me go? Gone easy on me?"

"I might have, yes. I definitely would have been more understanding." She stepped closer to him as he turned toward her. "You shouldn't have had to go through the last few months alone."

He lifted his other hand to wrap around where theirs were joined. "I didna bring ye here to make ye feel guilty."

He was silent for a moment. She watched as his throat worked, as if he was preparing his next words, changing his mind, and preparing more, choosing carefully. "Ye see what Walter Stuart is. He'll do anything to get whatever serves his ambition. I dinna think James knows about this. He's not as bad as Walter, at least not yet. But they know ye now, and they'll not let ye go easy."

"I never thought they would." She said her eyes searching his. "You don't have to do this."

"Aye. I do. I love ye so much. God! Sometimes I think I'll starve for all I can't swallow past those words in my throat. I want to shout them. I love ye, Sarah. I can't give ye up any more than Grant MacDuff could have given up your mother. We're stewards, aye? Champions. And there is nothing more important to us than the women we're charged with protecting."

"I'm not going to propose to ye now, because that should be a moment of joy, and I dinna want it tainted. But I will promise ye this." Sarah's heart raced as Dermot sank to his knees. *"S'mise Tormoid Mac na Ceardadh.* For as long as my body is able I will serve you. My hands and my heart are yours, *Mòrag NicMhàili.* I pledge my life to the protection of yours and the lives of your children."

Her hand shook as she lifted it and rested it on the top of his bowed head. Tears streamed down her cheeks, and a sob caught in her throat. Dermot kissed her other hand that he held in his own. Sarah struggled to think of something anything to say after such a declaration.

A bang of the stairwell doors down the hall announced that someone was coming. Dermot stood up, his eyes on the hallway behind her.

"I'm sorry, mate. Visiting hours are over." A man's voice said.

Dermot nodded and tried to act nonchalant as if the man hadn't interrupted something important. "Cheers. We're leaving."

To Sarah, he whispered. "Keep yer head down. Act like ye're upset."

Shouldn't be a problem she thought. Upset didn't quite describe the way she was feeling, but she was definitely emotional.

Dermot drew her down the hall toward the elevators. They had to pass the man who turned out to be a security guard on their way. Sarah kept her head down, as Dermot had warned her to. She couldn't risk being recognized by the security guard at the nursing home where his mother was staying. Then the Stuarts would know they were together.

CHAPTER FORTY-FIVE

Sarah paced back and forth as much as their shoebox of a hotel room would allow. Dermot had been gone for three hours and seventeen minutes and she had counted every one. They had talked about their plan over takeaway at the tiny table, and it had sounded so easy.

"I have a mate from the army. I called him when we were in Ullapool about getting some documents. He should have everything, but the pictures taken care of. I dinna think I'll be gone long, a couple of hours."

"How are you going to pay this guy?" She had asked.

"I've got some cash stashed away. I had to get a storage locker for my mum's things when she went into the home. I keep some extra there in case of emergency." He said as if everybody kept a stash of cash hidden away from home or a bank.

Sarah had looked at him puzzled. "What kind of emergency were you preparing for?"

He shrugged. "I started keeping a separate cache of money and clothes after I was attacked in the army. I thought that if Walter could get to me in the middle of a war, then I needed to be prepared. To be honest, I'm angry with myself for not making another identity part of that plan before now. I really should have thought of it sooner."

"I have some money too." She had told him nodding to where her backpack leaned against the night table. "It's in the lining of my bag."

He shot her a look of surprise. "That's thinking ahead or were ye planning to run before now."

She shook her head. "I didn't know what was going to happen if I found my family, or if James got too aggressive. I had to be prepared."

He laughed. "We are two seriously paranoid people."

She had pointed her fork at him. "Not paranoid, prepared."

Once they had documents for Dermot and his contribution to the runaway fund, they were going to take the train south all the way to France. From there they would be able to decide their next step without worrying about Sarah's face being all over the television. The toughest part would be getting out of Edinburgh.

He made it sound so easy, and she wanted to think as positively as he was. Life had kicked her in the teeth a few too many times to allow that kind of optimism.

"I don't understand why I can't go with you." She had said before he had left to meet his army buddy.

He cocked his head at her and arched an eyebrow. "I think ye do. Yer picture has been in every tabloid and on the news. Ye could be recognized."

"I know, but the thought of waiting here makes me feel like a sitting duck." She countered.

He rubbed his hands up and down her arms in what was meant to be a comforting gesture. "The only person who kens ye're here is me, and I'm not telling anyone."

"I'm going to worry myself sick."

One corner of his smile kicked up in that way that she loved. "Hopefully, I'll be back before then."

She gripped his shirt and pulled him in for a thorough kiss. "Make sure you come back."

He cupped her face in his hands and kissed her again. "In a tic."

Three hours and twenty-eight minutes. She should be exhausted after the last couple of days, but there was no way she would fall asleep before Dermot got back.

She needed a distraction, something to keep her imagination from conjuring the worst-case scenario. She turned on the television and decided to make herself a cup of tea in the hopes that something mundane would help get her nerves under control. She focused her attention on filling the electric kettle with water and turning it on. She unwrapped a tea bag and placed it in one of the paper cups the hotel provided. The television beside her switched over to the news.

The main story was about the new reorganization of local governments in Scotland, and the establishment of local council areas in the islands. Sarah snickered as the newscaster stumbled over *Na h-Eileannan Siar*, the new official name for the Western Isles. No matter how many Gaelic speakers there were or how official they made the language in certain areas, there would always be English speakers making Gaelic speakers feel foreign in their own country.

Sarah was still shaking her head and pouring the water into the paper cup when she heard James Stuart's voice coming from the television. She set the kettle down and stepped in front of the TV to see him.

He stood in front of his house surrounded by reporters holding out microphones and mini cassette recorders. At his elbow was Felicia Banks. Sarah tried to view her as an Alba Petroleum employee rather than the woman Dermot had been dating before their research trip. Camera flashes flared around them as he read a statement from a piece of paper. Sarah took a step back and sat down on the foot of the bed to watch.

"The aggressive behavior of the photographers in pursuit of a woman that I have been rumored to be dating..." To Sarah's surprise he stressed the word rumored. She would have thought he wouldn't miss a chance to publicly claim a relationship cementing her as his in the public eye. "...has resulted in a car accident and disappearance of three people. These people are not politicians, or celebrities or public figures in any way. They are private citizens, academics who were only trying to do their jobs. Dermot Sinclair is a distant cousin of mine and a lifelong friend. Jujhar Gurudat is a gifted linguist and dedicated student. And Sarah Mac..."

His voice cracked on her name. He cleared his throat and bowed his head while he tried to marshal his emotions. When he looked up again, his eyes were full of fury. "Sarah MacAlpin is an incredible person and a valued friend who has inadvertently been caught up in this..." He pressed his lips together to gain control. "...meat grinder of sudden fame. My friends have been assaulted and are missing. We do not know if they have been kidnapped or are in hiding for fear of being pursued again. The authorities in the Highlands are doing everything they can to find them."

At this he paused, his brows drawing together in apparent anger. "The paparazzi and the editors who buy photos from them, need to take a long hard look in the mirror and examine whether their own personal gain is worth the danger that their actions pose to innocent people. This sort of behavior has to stop. I will be throwing all of my considerable resources into promoting laws to prevent actions like those that occurred in Lochinver from happening again."

Another pause. James let his hand that was holding the statement fall to his side and looked at the reporters around him. "In the meantime, I am offering a reward of ten thousand pounds to anyone who helps us find my friends and another ten thousand to anyone who can identify the driver of the car that caused the accident." He lifted his red-rimmed blue eyes to look directly into the camera. "Dermot, Sarah, Jujhar, if you are in hiding, please, please contact me to let me know you are safe. I can help you."

* * *

"There." Dermot adjusted his position in front of the light gray background, glancing up at the lights that Desmond had clipped to shelves and hanging from the metal rafters around his photo booth. Dez waved a hand from behind the camera. "Eyes straight into the camera."

Dermot looked straight ahead, trying not to look as nervous as he truly was. Dez pressed a button and, the click of the shutter echoed through the warehouse space from which Dez ran his enterprise. They were in an office area on a raised platform at the back of the building. The platform was filled with desks, filing cabinets, and worktables with various machines; a copy machine, laminator, several typewriters of various brands, all tools used for forging documents.

"One more for good measure." Dez said before Dermot had a chance to move. The shutter clicked again.

"How long did ye say it would take?" He asked trying not to sound too impatient.

Dez lifted the camera off the tripod and sauntered closer winding the film. "I'll have it to ye by morning."

Dermot ground his teeth at the thought of another delay. "Ye can't finish it tonight?"

Dez arched an eyebrow at him. "I will finish it tonight, but I have to develop the photos and affix them to the documents, laminating. Good work takes time, mate, and I have an appointment."

"Where do ye get the photos developed?" He asked. The fewer people saw his new passport photo the better.

"I do it right over there." He jerked his head toward a door at the foot of the stairs. "I made a darkroom out of the ladies' room."

Dermot silently reminded himself that Dez was already rushing the job that he should have had weeks more to accomplish. "Sorry. I'm anxious to get moving."

"And ye will. Relax." Dez pulled the roll of film out of the camera and placed it into a small plastic container and set it in a tray on the corner of a desk. "In the meantime, I am meeting an associate. Care to join me? We can grab a pint on the way back. Talk about the army days, the old Double D back on the town."

Dermot rolled his eyes, he had never liked the nickname they had been given in the army. "No, I need to go. What time can I meet ye tomorrow?"

"Ye wouldna be rushing back to that lovely lass I saw on the tele, would ye?" Dez asked.

Dermot's blood went cold. "What lass?"

Dez smirked. "The one whose picture they're flashing next to yours and some other lad's. The one they say is dating James Stuart. Word is ye went missing after a car accident up in the Highlands."

"And that was on the tele?" Dermot's pulse jumped, and the breath seized in his lungs.

"Mmm. On the news since this morning." Dez said giving him a sidelong look as he put his camera away. "There's even a reward for information about yer whereabouts and information on whoever ran ye off the road, ten thousand pounds."

Dermot pinned Dez with a glare and stepped closer until they were nose to nose. "Do I need to be concerned about you?"

Dez leaned back as if affronted. "Not me. We're mates. Just make sure that my hard work doesna fall into the wrong hands."

Dermot made a skeptical noise in his throat and pulled an envelope out of his jacket pocket. He opened the envelope and slid half the cash out. He handed the envelope to Dez. "The other half when ye deliver. Where can I meet ye in the morning?"

"I'm wounded." Dez feigned a hurt look. "I'll deliver the goods in the morning. Where are ye staying?"

Dermot gave him a flat look. He said nothing more but Dez got the message.

"Fine. That wee café down on Cockburn street, near the train station. The one with the red door. Eight o'clock."

"Come alone. I don't want anyone else to see." Dermot said.

"I have done this before, ye know." Dez gave him a withering look.

Dermot sighed. "Cheers, mate.

"It's good to see ye again, Dermot." Dez gave him a genuine smile.

Dermot pulled the hood of his jacket forward around his face and made his way through the warehouse space to the door. He tucked his hands in his pocket and bowed his head against the rain. He walked back to the bus stop and tried not to look at his watch counting the minutes until he saw Sarah again.

When he made it back to their hotel, after changing buses a few times and walking through the rain until he was sure he hadn't been followed, Sarah burst from the bathroom and threw her arms around him in a fierce hug. "Were ye hiding in the toilet?"

She leaned back and unzipped his jacket looking a little sheepish. "I wasn't sure it was you."

Alarm surged through him and he grabbed her arm. "Has anyone else tried to get in?"

"No, no." She waved away the idea, talking fast as she pulled the wet jacket from his shoulders. "But our faces are all over the news and James offered a reward. Who knows who saw us come in here, or what the hotel staff might think. I might be getting a little paranoid now."

So that was what Dez had been talking about, a reward. He needed information, but first he needed to ease her worries. He tossed his jacket on the chair and brought his hands up to smooth her curls and pull her in for a kiss. Her lips were warm and welcoming, while his were still cold from being outside. He took his time, taking small sips of her like a too hot cup of tea. When he felt the tension leave the muscles in her neck, he deepened the kiss, drinking her in.

When she felt pliant in his arms, he pulled back. "What exactly did James say?"

Her eyes lifted to his. They were less frantic than they had been a few minutes ago. "He made a personal plea. He said we were his friends, even Jujhar, that you were family to him, and that he needed to know that we were safe. He offered ten thousand pounds to anyone who could help him find us, and ten thousand more to anyone with information leading to the capture of whoever ran us off the road."

"I wouldna worry about it." He tried to reassure her. "Most people are expecting us to be in the Highlands still. That's where they'll be looking."

"But what if someone recognizes us?" Her eyebrows drew together in worry.

He couldn't resist brushing his thumb over the crease between them. "I wouldna worry about that. People see what they expect to see, and dinna tend to look past the surface. Keep yer hair pulled back and those glasses ye've been wearing on. No one will recognize ye."

"What about you?" She asked.

"I'll wear a hat or hood or both. It'll be fine, *a' ghràidh*." This time he pressed a kiss between her eyebrows willing away her worries, in spite of his own.

"Did you get what you need?" She asked.

"Not quite." He said with a sigh. "He has to develop the photos, so it'll be ready tomorrow. I'm going to meet him near the train station."

"Do you trust him?" The worried look came back.

"I've been asking myself the same thing since I first called him. My instinct says, yes. But I'm still going to be careful." He stepped closer to her, boxing her in between his body and the bed. "And you will not be with me when I meet him."

"Where will I be?"

"I'll have to think about that. Somewhere safe, but near the station so ye can get away if I'm nicked." He came closer, looming over her.

She looked behind her as her legs bumped into the mattress. "What are you doing?"

He slid his fingers into her hair and tilted her head up to meet his gaze. "I'm going to make love to ye in a proper bed for the first time ever. Not a futon, or a van, or a storage closet. A bed. Then I'm going to get some much-needed sleep with you in my arms. All. Bloody. Night."

She smiled up at him, but he could see the tears pooling in her eyes. He shook his head. "No tears. We're done with tears. Aye? We've been together in desperation, in anger, in a hurry. This time is in joy." He kissed her quickly. "And love." Another kiss. "And I mean to take my time with it."

Sarah stretched up to him for the next kiss, pulling his head down to meet hers. Her tongue teased his and her teeth nipped his bottom lip. "You can take your time later. I need you inside me right now."

"Yes, ma'am." He said in an exaggerated American accent.

Sarah giggled. God, when was the last time he'd heard that sound? He grabbed the hem of her shirt and pulled it over her head. She fell back onto the bed, laughing when he tossed it over his shoulder. Yanking his own shirt off, he then started on his trousers. Sarah undid hers, and he pulled them off. "Take off that bra."

She arched a mischievous eyebrow at him and pointed to her chest. "This bra?"

He growled, and she laughed again as she reached behind her to undo the clasp. She pulled it down her arms and swung it in a circle before throwing it over his shoulder. He laughed along with her as he slid the last of their clothes off and lowered himself to the bed.

***

She didn't know what time it was, around three in the morning maybe. The hotel was eerily quiet. A distant door banged closed, but she heard nothing else apart from the general hum of a large building and Dermot's heartbeat under her ear. Their limbs tangled together, and her head rested on his chest, rising and falling with each breath like a boat on the tide. She didn't think she would ever tire of listening to that strong thump of his heart, of being this close to him.

A footstep shuffled by in the hall right outside their door. Startled, Sarah pushed herself up to a sitting position and stared at the door willing whoever it was to go away. Her own heart thumping so hard she was afraid she might not be able to hear anything else. Had they been found? Maybe someone had seen Dermot and followed him back to the hotel. Someone out in the hall muttered something. She picked up a few slurred words. "Bloody key...pocket...gonna boak." Followed by a groan and shuffling footsteps moving away from them.

Sarah closed her eyes and breathed a sigh of relief. Dermot stirred beside her. He ran his hand down her back and mumbled sleepily, *"De tha e?"* [What is it?]

"Chan eil heat. Cadail." She told him settling back down beside him. [It's nothing. Sleep.] He shifted his shoulders as if he was settling himself further into the mattress. His arm still around her. Sarah looped her arm under his and propped her head up on her hand. She watched him as he descended into sleep again.

A few days' worth of stubble dusted his jaw. He hadn't shaved since Lochinver, and he probably wouldn't again until they were well away from Scotland. Sarah decided that she liked this scruffier version of him. It made for a good disguise, and it was like his face was their own shared secret. A small secret, a harmless one, among so many dangerous ones.

Now, all their secrets were in the open. He knew about her family, and she finally knew about his mother. She had known that there was something hanging over him, something that held him back beyond family allegiance. Now she knew. For almost the entire time she'd known him, he had been quietly aching with fear and guilt at having to choose between her and his mother, between being his own man or Walter Stuart's reluctant agent.

He'd been sent to North Carolina to guard her, to bring her home like Lancelot rescuing Guinevere from Meleagant. Dermot was sent by his king to bring home his wife, only to fall in love with her himself. He had chosen her over his king. He was willing to abandon everything to be with her, her knight without armor.

ACKNOWLEDGMENTS

I couldn't create this world or produce these books without my supportive tribe starting with the Kettle Holler Literary Society. This go around my beta readers did yeoman's/yoewoman's work; Stacy for fixing my spelling and missing words, Cheryl for helping me find zero in on plot holes, McKenzie and my mother for policing punctuation, and also Diane, Tanya and Wendy for their valuable feedback. I couldn't do this without you all.

It is often said that you should write the book that you want to read. Fortunately, there are a lot of people who want to read the same kind of books that I do. I often find a home where those readers are gathered. For that I have to thank my fellow Outlander, All Souls, and Lymond fans for showing me that there is a place for complicated stories about smart ladies.

Last but far from least my husband and kids for tolerating the many hours that I've spent working on this. Also, my extended family for their lifelong support.

ONCE & FUTURE SERIES

The River Maiden

Sarah MacAlpin has always felt like an outsider. Raised by her Scottish grandmother deep in the Blue Ridge Mountains, Sarah grew up with one foot in the old world and one foot in the new world. Her childhood friends were the stuff of ancient Celtic legends. But Sarah's seemingly idyllic past hides a horrifying secret. As a little girl she watched her mother's inexorable slide into madness. But she hasn't let her past stop her from reaching for her dreams. She has managed to put together a pretty good life for herself. She has great friends, a boyfriend, and her career as a folklorist is all planned out. That is until she meets Dermot Sinclair. The handsome Scot seems to be dogging her every step. At best he's a fellow folklorist who can help her research. At worst, he could be there to steal her work. All she has to do is find one song that proves her thesis and her dissertation will be done. Unfortunately, unlocking that song may also mean unlocking some buried memories and a dangerous destiny set in motion generations ago.

Cauldron

The traumatic events of The River Maiden have left Sarah MacAlpin's life in shambles. Her best friend won't talk to her. The man she loves says they can't be together. She's just discovered something that destroys the main thesis of her dissertation. To top it off, she's learned that her dream fellowship in Scotland was given to her with ulterior motives by her billionaire benefactor. Sarah has to choose whether to accept the fellowship anyway or try to find a different path.

Meanwhile, she's battles her own personal demons and questions about her family. She hopes to find some answers in her mother's memoir. What she finds are some upsetting parallels to her own life. Like Sarah, Molly left Kettle Holler on the verge of making her dreams come true, but her ambitions were derailed by a family secret that took her across an ocean and left her a broken shade of her former self.

Once & Future Short Stories

Unfit (ebook short)

When she left Kettle Hollow, Molly MacAlpin hoped never to see her remote mountain home again. She returned eighteen months later angry, pregnant and abandoned by the man she loved. So, she threw all her energy into making sure her daughter had the best life possible.

With the help and sometimes interference of her mother, she is raising a bright, sweet child she they hopes will have every possible opportunity. Until one spring day a brief conversation with her little girl brings her world crashing down around her.

Buddy (ebook short)

As the youngest of the contentious Corbett clan, Buddy has spent most of his life trying to get away from the remote mountain hollow where they all grew up. Now at the end of a long day, he can't avoid talking to them. When one of his brothers mentions their old neighbor, Maggie MacAlpin, he can't help thinking about Old Maggie's granddaughter, Sarah. She was as tough and wild as she was beautiful. And she was the first girl that Buddy ever loved.

One summer when they were barely old enough for kissing, Buddy learned just how much that love could cost them.

ABOUT THE AUTHOR

Meredith R. Stoddard writes folklore-inspired fiction from her attic hideaway in Central Virginia. She studied literature and folklore at the University of North Carolina at Chapel Hill before working as a corporate trainer and instructional designer. Her love of storytelling is inspired by years spent listening to stories at her grandmother's kitchen table. She also advocates for the preservation of traditional fiber arts and the Scottish Gaelic language.

You can also follow @M_R_Stoddard on Twitter.

www.ingramcontent.com/pod-product-compliance
Lightning Source LLC
Chambersburg PA
CBHW030844030726
47495CB00005B/1366